EXODUS

NEW BEGINNINGS

By: LAUREN VICTORIA

Books & Things Publishing, LLC
4410 Brookfield Corporate Dr. #220149
Chantilly, VA 20153

Exodus: New Beginnings
Text copyright © 2025 Lauren Victoria
Cover design by Butter Bird Books
Design and format by Books & Things Publishing, LLC
First Edition: June 2025
ISBN 978-1-962140-26-3
Library of Congress Control Number: 2025905343

This book is a work of fiction. All rights reserved, including the right of reproduction in whole or in part in any form. Thank you for purchasing an authorized edition of this book and for complying with copyright laws by not reproducing, scanning, or reproducing any part without permission. Names, characters, places and incidents are either a product of the author's imagination or are used fictitiously. Any resemblance to actual persons, living or dead, business establishments, companies, events or locales is entirely coincidental. Please note that no part of this book may be used for the purpose of training artificial intelligence technologies or systems.

Books & Things Publishing supports copyright and its protection of diverse authors who create inclusive books.

To schedule author events and order in bulk, visit
www.booksandthingspublishing.com.

Help support the author by leaving a review.

For all the Black & Brown girls who need to see themselves in all stories. If you have a dream, work towards it no matter what. You'll want to give up and that's okay, but continue to push through. It's worth it in the end. And if no one gets it - so what! Do what makes you happy and the people that get it will get it.

For Mom, Dad, Trey & Diesel

EXODUS
NEW BEGINNINGS

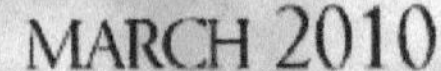

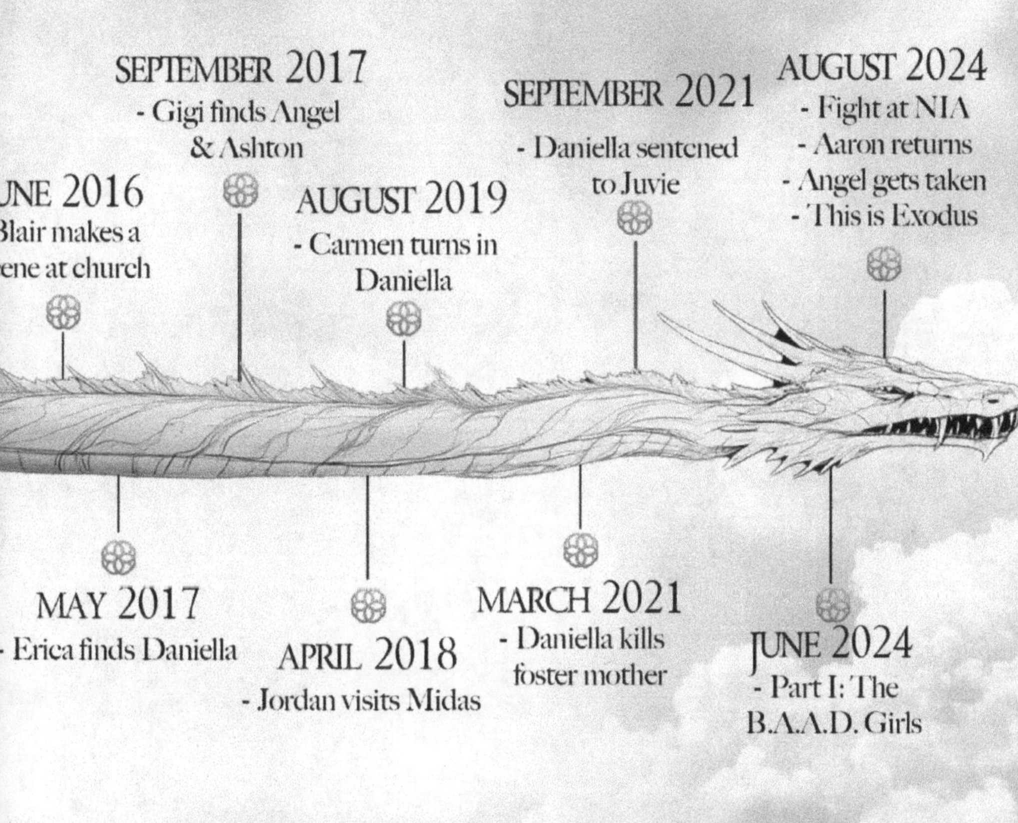

SEPTEMBER 2017
- Gigi finds Angel
& Ashton
JUNE 2016
- Blair makes a
scene at church
AUGUST 2019
- Carmen turns in
Daniella
SEPTEMBER 2021
- Daniella sentened
to Juvie
AUGUST 2024
- Fight at NIA
- Aaron returns
- Angel gets taken
- This is Exodus
MAY 2017
- Erica finds Daniella
APRIL 2018
- Jordan visits Midas
MARCH 2021
- Daniella kills
foster mother
JUNE 2024
- Part I: The
B.A.A.D. Girls

Contents

PART I – The B.A.A.D Girls

Chapter 1

Angel stares blankly out the passenger window of a 1969 smoke grey Camaro. Strong winds blow through her long, black, coarse hair and along her browned caramel skin. She promised herself she would never be in this situation again, but here she is waiting for the next mark. She studies the melting pot of average, everyday people moving about the busy streets of New York City. They don't know how good they have it – being able to rush to work, attend school, meet friends for lunch – unconsciously taking these necessities and moments for granted.

"Ang?" She's in deep thought, unable to hear her sister in the driver's seat crunching on fries. "Angel?!"

"Huh? What?" She breaks from thought.

"I said, are you going to finish your shake?" Ashton asks with a mouth full of food.

"Uh…no, here." Angel and Ashton are fraternal twins. As much as they are similar, they are different. Both 18, they have always been athletically built with milk chocolatey eyes that are hard to resist.

"So, are you going to tell me what you're thinking about over there?" Ashton waits for an answer as she takes a big gulp of her sister's shake.

"Nothing," Angel says.

"If it was nothing then you wouldn't be fidgeting with that ring on your finger," Ashton says.

"That doesn't mean anything. I do this all the time." Angel looks down at her right index finger as she spins a golden ring with an ouroboros wrapped around the middle, unaware that she's doing it.

"No. You only do it when you're over thinking or you're nervous. That's why our mother gave it to you. So, which is it?"

Angel takes a moment to respond. She knows Ashton hates the topic she's about to bring up once more. "I just –"

"You just what?"

Angel searches for the right words, unable to stop fidgeting with her ring. "Have you considered what it would be like if we were…normal?"

Ashton lets out at small chuckle and shakes her head in disbelief. "Angel, we've lived on our own for most of our lives. Our parents are dead and to add a little razzle dazzle, we have psychic powers. We will never be normal, so can we please stop bringing it up for once? We're fine just the way we are."

Angel wishes Ashton would understand but, she's Ashton and it's hard to change her mind.

"And what would we be doing besides this anyways? College?" Ashton chuckles.

"Yes. You do know there's still time to go. I mean we would have to get our GED first but I'm sure we can do it." Angel said.

Ashton busts out into laughter. "What are we going to study? Criminology? We are the criminals."

"And that's the problem," Angel said under her breath.

Angel doesn't speak on the topic for now. She checks her watch for the tenth time since being parked across the street from Atlantis Bank. "Are you ready to go?"

"As ready as I'll ever be," Ashton finishes the rest of her stakeout food. They exit Ashton's car. It's used, but she's fixed it up well enough to look brand new. It's her in car form.

They walk across the street to Atlantis Bank. "Have you talked to Gigi?" Angel asks.

"No, I figured we'd surprise her," Ashton says, excited to see the woman that raised them.

"She hates surprises."

"We haven't seen her in months. It won't be that bad."

Angels rolls her eyes at her sister's carelessness. They enter the local bank filled with ordinary clients and bank tellers. They instantly begin to study the room, moving around in a way that's not suspicious but so that their faces aren't shown in what could possibly be hidden cameras. There are more than a dozen clients, a lazy security guard and six tellers: three working the counter assisting with funds and three at private cubicles helping with the approval of loans.

Angel discreetly surveys several surveillance cameras pointed at the obvious two exits -- the front and side doors – but she knows there are more. They move about the bank as if they're like any other client. Angel scribbles on a deposit slip at a desk and Ashton reads a 'Reasons to Open a Savings Account' pamphlet.

"Is your contact legit?" Ashton speaks in a hushed tone.

"Of course. Faye always gives us valid information on the next hit."

"Oh. Right. Faye." Ashton lets out a heavy sigh and dismisses the mention of their connect.

"I don't understand why you have an issue with her. She's good at her job and she hasn't failed us."

"Yet. Look, it's not that I think she doesn't do a decent job, it's more so I don't trust her. She came out of nowhere wanting to work with us. We were doing fine without her."

"We didn't meet her out of nowhere; we met her through Kendrick. You remember him, right? Love of your life, eyes sparkling every time he entered a room," Angel gives her a teasing smile which is the quickest way to get Ashton to stop complaining.

"I thought we agreed to never speak of that double-crossing backstabber again," Ashton snaps back as they walk to the back of the teller line.

"You started it," Angel smirks.

"All I'm saying is that if she's willing to double cross the people she works for by helping us, who's to say she won't do the same to us down the line?" Before Angel responds, she places her hand on her forehead trying to ease a headache she's had for a few weeks.

"Are they getting better?" Ashton asks, concerned.

"Not lately, but it's nothing I can't handle."

As she turns to face the line, Ashton notices a young girl, no more than ten years old, staring at her. The young girl stands ahead of them in line with her mom. Ashton follows the young girl's gaze to the tactical knife sticking out of her leather jacket. Sliding the knife back in, Ashton gives a devilish smile and puts her finger over her pursed lips.

Casually waiting in line, Angel and Ashton check the time on their watches. It's 1:35 p.m.; they're right on schedule. New clients have entered the bank – three men – and they immediately begin to observe the people around them. One man is of average height with a stocky build. He wears a hat and sunglasses to cover his face, but his thick ginger beard sticks out like a sore thumb. One would say he looks like a compact lumberjack. The other is tall and lanky. He has a mask to cover his face, but his crystal-clear blue eyes stand out like the ocean. Both men wear long-sleeved black shirts and a heavy armored vest with heavy cargo pants and boots. They are led by a man with brown skin. He has a high build with muscles stretching out his black armored jacket and cornrows on his head, a cross embedded in the middle. Only a pair of sunglasses hide his face.

He nods to his men to proceed moving throughout the bank. Angel notices them instantly, watching through the convex mirror placed in the nearby corner of the ceiling. She's careful with not staring too long.

As Angel and Ashton approach the teller counter, Angel signals Ashton by running her right hand through her hair. Ashton sees the signal through her peripheral. Just as Angel gives the signal, the lead robber nods to his men, giving them the 'all clear'.

In sync, they swing their guns toward the bank clients. "Everybody down on the floor now!" Muscles grabs a teller nearby, snatching her up from the floor as she screams for mercy. "You. Take me to your vault now." He points a gun at her head as she nods, tears blurring her vision.

"I-I-It's back there," she points to a secluded hallway behind the teller counter.

"Don't you touch it! All of you, over here!" Blue Eyes aims his automatic gun at a teller attempting to discreetly press a panic button beneath the counter.

Before leaving the room, Muscles directs his men on their next steps. "Take one and cut surveillance." Compact Lumberjack grabs another teller, taking them to a back room to disable and destroy all security footage.

"We don't want any problems. Everybody does what they're told, and everybody makes it out alive," Muscles says, shoving the teller towards the hallway. Some hostages hide under tables and others cover their heads, face to the floor.

"Lower the blinds and lock the door," Blue Eyes commands the lazy security guard equipped with only a flashlight and strong pepper spray.

"I can't believe out of all the banks in New York City, they choose this one," Ashton whispers.

"I can't believe they're this stupid," Angel whispers. "And how can you be eating right now?" Angel watches as Ashton opens a piece of candy she took from the teller's desk before dropping to the floor.

"I eat when I'm nervous."

"You eat with all of your emotions."

In the vault room, Muscles aims his gun at the teller as her hands tremble uncontrollably trying to type in the code and turn the key. "Hurry up!" he shouts at her, becoming increasingly agitated.

"Th-There! It's open." She opens the vault to reveal close to ten million dollars, documents, and other assets. He tosses seven duffle bags to her.

"Fill 'em up. Go!" he orders. The teller begins filling the bags with as much money as she can fit. She has close to five million in all the duffle bags. She carries four duffle bags, two in each hand, out of the room. Muscles carries the other three in one hand while still pressing his gun on the teller's back.

The robbers come together. Compact Lumberjack now holds the security officer at gunpoint while watching the other hostages lined up along the wall. "Footage destroyed and driver's out back," he says.

"Go. I'll stay here to make sure no one calls the cops," Muscles says. "And take her." He shoves the teller holding the four duffle bags towards his men. "The boss will want to use her as collateral. Take some of them, too." He points his gun towards the hostages along the wall. Taking a pleading teller and security guard, the two robbers push through the side door and into an oversized truck to meet their driver. Now only Muscles, Angel and Ashton, and a few hostages remain. There's a silence as he walks around. He walks with his gun waiting for someone to give him a reason to shoot.

Suddenly, Angel feels and hears a vibration coming from the mother near her and Ashton. The mother frantically reaches into her purse to shut off her phone but it's far too late. Muscles moves past Angel and Ashton then abruptly stops.

"Get up! Now!" He grabs the mother lying on the floor near them. Her daughter, the young girl Ashton noticed earlier, screams through it all.

"Please! No!" the mother yells.

"Were you trying to call the cops?!"

"No! I wasn't!"

"Liar!" He takes her arm, squeezing tightly. "Let's go. You're coming with me!" He struggles to leave with her as she tries to stay with her daughter, who cries underneath a table. "If anyone knows what's good for them, you won't move until we're long gone." Before exiting, he gives one final warning to the terrified clients not able to look at him from the floor. He moves towards the side door and leaves with the mother.

Atlantis Bank remains silent. The only sounds heard are those coming from the cars and pedestrians outside. Everyone is afraid to move. "You ready?" Ashton asks Angel.

"Always," Angel and Ashton stand, proceeding with their plan. "I never understood the point of them yelling demands. The whole point is to not get caught."

"What do you expect from mindless men?" Ashton dusts off her clothes. The clients and tellers watch as Angel and Ashton move about the bank nonchalantly, as though they didn't have guns pointed at them.

"Hey! We should not move before the authorities have arrived." A bank manger peers over the counter watching Angel and Ashton.

"Sir, it's okay," Angel replies, then turns to her sister. "You take the roads and I'll catch them up high." Angel is the eldest of the twins by five minutes and the leader of the two because Ashton could not care less about a lot of people and things.

"Got it. See you in five," Ashton says. Angel leaves out the side door. Once she's out of view from prying eyes, she removes her own slick 9mm pistols from her back holster and checks the clips. Then she swiftly catches up to the robbers.

"All right, people! Everything is going to be fine," Ashton says. "You can get up from the floor now. They won't be back."

"How do you know?!" a client shouts.

"You have no idea what they're capable of!" a teller shouts.

"They took four people!" from another.

Clients begin shouting at Ashton like a wild pack of hyenas and she's getting agitated by the second, rolling her eyes and removing her knife from her jacket. "Everyone, please! I think we all know what they're capable of – hence the kidnapping and guns being pointed at your faces. So if you would, please shut up or we might have a worse situation on our hands." Ashton points her knife at the nearest client. Ashton can be very irreverent at times, even most of the time. She goes behind the teller counter and motions the bank manager to follow her to a nearby phone.

"I want you to call the cops in exactly ten minutes. No more, no less. Understood?" The manager nods in agreement, taking point near the phone.

As Ashton proceeds to exit the bank, the young girl runs up to her with a tear-stained face, tugging on Ashton's black leather jacket. "Are you going to use that to get my mom back?" She points to Ashton's knife.

Ashton kneels in front of her. "What's your name?"

"Taylor," she says softly, wiping away tears.

"Okay, Taylor. I'm going to do everything I can to get your mom back, I promise. But can you do me a favor?" Taylor nods. "Can you watch out for the adults in here?" Ashton cups her hand to Taylor's ear, whispering, "I don't think they're as brave as you are." Ashton smiles and gives Taylor a fist bump. Ashton leaves through the front door of the bank and gets into her car. She ties her large curly hair into a ponytail and drives away.

"Ang, where are they going?" she asks Angel through an earpiece.

"Looks like they're headed for an abandoned apartment building ten blocks ahead," Angel hastily jogs across rooftops.

"On my way." Ashton speeds through New York City traffic to beat the robbers to their destination. Angel and Ashton have been chasing after robbers for four years now; it's a job that stumbled upon them. "So, how's the air up there?" Ashton snickers.

"Just peachy. I needed a run today. You should have joined me."

"Nah. I get enough exercise," Ashton retorted.

"Of course you do. Running to taco trucks every afternoon is a real workout."

"I know, right? Nothing feels better than a three-mile run and chicken tacos." Ashton smiles as she reminisces about the savory food near her Boston home. Angel laughs as she continues to jog across buildings. Moments later, Ashton parks her car across from the abandoned apartment building. The robbers haven't arrived yet. Leaning against her car, she waits for them to arrive. "Made it," Ashton says over her earpiece.

"I'll be in position soon and try not to cause too much damage, please." Angel leaps over worn-down rooftop ventilation and runs from one building to the next, not breaking a sweat.

"These guys are pretty bold." Ashton licks on a lollipop. "Like, who robs a local, popular bank, drives away in a truck the size of a tank, and then drives to a very visible building?"

"You should be glad they're this easy this time. Less work we have to do," Angel jokes.

"Touché," Ashton laughs.

The robbers have arrived at the abandoned apartment. The building is enclosed with no outlet and a fire escape attached to each of the three connected apartment buildings surrounding it. The driver has backed the truck deeper into the enclosed alley, away from the busy street, in front of a vacant garage and dumpster. The alley is dark, even with the sun shining over them.

"They're here. We've got exactly 15 minutes before the cops come," Ashton smiles down at her watch, ready for a fight.

Angel continues across the rooftops but slows down and begins to wrestle with the pain of her headaches. She kneels, trying to steady herself and regain her strength. Using the ledge of the building to brace herself, her surroundings begin to disappear. She's losing focus and everything becomes an instant blur. She's immobile but feels her soul drifting to another place. Her pupils become enlarged, and she sees flashes of a beautiful woman. Unable to make out her facial features, Angel can tell by her smooth mahogany skin and her presence that this woman is something out of a fairy tale. She jumps back into reality, gasping like coming up for air and her strength is fully restored. She exhales, getting her bearings, and proceeds to complete her job even though she doesn't have the mental strength to do so. Ashton needs her, but these jobs are taking a toll on her mentally.

Down below, Ashton prepares to confront the robbers. She walks across the street with the swag of knowing they can't handle her and what she's about to bring their way. In the alley, the three robbers from the bank are met by two more men from their team. They unload their truck. They hide duffle bag after duffle bag in the nearby garage. "Umm…Ang? I don't think these are some small-time petty criminals," Ashton says.

"What do you mean?" Angel asks.

"I'm seeing a lot more duffle bags than what our guys took out the bank." Ashton peers around the corner of the wall, watching as the robbers swiftly remove far more than seven duffle bags – more like 20 – from the truck.

Angel peeks over the ledge to see multiple duffle bags, which means a lot more money and a greedy Ashton. "That's fine. Our plan doesn't change. We get our portion and then we're gone. So, stay focused."

"Don't I always," Ashton grins mischievously.

"No. Not at all," Angel says, not convinced.

"Well, it's too late to change now." Ashton sneaks her way around the truck and peers through the window to see the teller, security guard, a bank client and Taylor's mom tied up and blindfolded. Casually as if she's a random pedestrian, she walks from around the truck and approaches the robbers. "Excuse me. I'm sort of new around here and I'm trying to find this museum. Think one of you could help me?" Ashton holds up a New York city tourist map. The robbers stop unloading their truck.

"Who is this kid?" A hefty robber asks throwing the last of the duffle bags in the garage.

"Kid, you got to get out of here!" Blue Eyes says.

Ashton dismisses his need for her to leave. "I'm sorry, but…" Ashton gasps dramatically. "Wait, are you the guys?! The ones that robbed that bank on 15th Street?" She eases her way closer to them, keeping their focus on her Oscar-worthy performance. "You guys are going to be legends! It's all over the news!" Ashton turns up the façade as if she didn't just witness three of them take hostages from the same bank moments ago. Luckily for her, they're too focused on getting their job done to notice the mockery. Angel sits on the ledge of the apartment rooftop, feet dangling and laughing at the exchange between Ashton and the robbers.

"Either shoot her or get her out here! We need to move!" The driver shouts, throwing duffle bags in the garage.

"You don't have to do that!" Ashton raises her voice high enough to show fear but even she doesn't believe it.

"Let's go! Move!" Muscles begins to shove her out.

"W-wait! I've got to tell you something!" she shouts, continuing to be pushed out of the alley. He ignores her. He would rather threaten her than kill her because that would involve bloodshed at the very spot they want clean.

Ashton spins around to face him and tacks on the best nervous expression she can muster up, eyeing him and his fellow men.

"You need to give me that money." Ashton instantly changes her tone from a scared young woman to a young woman who has nothing to lose.

Muscles gives a small chuckle that rises into a loud laugh that dismisses her command. With a swift move he removes his gun from his thigh holster and aims it straight between Ashton's eyes, ready to pull the trigger. "Leave now! I won't say it again."

"You just did." Ashton stands firm, refusing to move.

His face grows red with anger, infuriated anger. He lifts the butt of his gun and whips it across Ashton's face. She falls to the ground, scraping her hand on the pavement, her vision a blur. Most would think Angel would be worried about her sister, but it's the robbers who have her sympathy.

"Ash?" Angel calls for her sister nervously over her earpiece. "Ashton?!"

"What?!" Ashton responds under her breath. She sits on the ground attempting to restore her vision and her balance. Rage grows inside of her and when she gets like this there is no telling what damage she can cause.

"Calm down, we came here for one thing. We can't draw any more attention." Angel knows Ashton's temper and that temper has gotten them in trouble before.

Ashton slowly stands, keeping her eyes trained on the man in front of her. As she stares deeply into him as if she's ripping his soul apart, the corner of her left eye is leaking with blood. "Too late."

"Was that not enough for you!?" Before Muscles can pull the trigger on Ashton, she throws out her hand towards him, letting him fly back deep into the apartment building's brick wall like a gush of wind. He's unable to move any part of his body, stuck on the wall like a human magnet. His eyes are widening with terror and sweat pours from his body. Ashton sprints towards him, leaping over crates, old apartment junk and the remaining robbers, who are in disbelief in what they witnessed.

"Is this enough for you?" Knife in hand, Ashton presses it firmly against his throat. "Move an inch and I swear you'll be taking his head in one of those duffle bags." Ashton keeps her rage-filled eyes focused on Muscles as she dishes out promises to his fellow men.

The robbers stop, frozen with uncertainty, and conflicted between running away or fighting their way through Ashton. The Driver and Blue Eyes run and lunge for Ashton, guns in hand. Ashton doesn't bother looking behind her because Angel isn't too far away.

In an instant, Angel jumps down from the apartment fire escape above, landing perfectly on the ground like a panther. She kicks the driver with enough power that he falls to the ground, unconscious. Blue Eyes attempts to land a punch to Angel's face, but she swiftly dodges and kicks him in a not-so-appropriate place. Compact Lumberjack comes from behind her and wraps his arms around her neck. Angel uses the side of the truck as leverage and braces herself to push off and slam him into the dumpster.

The last remaining robber, a quirky stout young man, kneels with his hands up, dropping his weapon and calling for a truce. "I'm on your side. Faye told me to help."

Angel steps back from him, lowering her fist that was in mid-air. She glances over to Ashton and Muscles and says, "I think you need to do what she says."

"Let's try this again, shall we?" Ashton says to the robber still pressed on the wall, now with a leaking eye due to Ashton's punching during the quick scuffle Angel had with his men. He is terrified, suffocating from the outside in. Ashton presses the knife on his throat harder and deeper, and he starts to bleed.

"Alright, alright! Take the money! There's more in the truck!" Ashton steps away from him. He falls to the ground, coughing and gasping for air.

"A pleasure doing business with you," Ashton smiles down at him, enjoying the pain he feels.

"You just…made…the worst…mistake…of your life." He attempts to catch his breath, but he wants to get the last word.

"We aren't the only ones," Angel reminds him of his recent deeds.

"Did you forget the hostages in your truck and all this money you stole? From the government?!" Ashton mocks them.

He ignores Ashton and turns to face his betrayer. "Jimmy, you're dead!"

"I had to do what's best for me."

"We'll see about that once Boss finds out."

"Oh! Boo hoo! Jimmy, get the bags," Ashton demands.

Angel uses zip ties to tie up Muscles, who is still attempting to regain his bearings. She's only able to tie up one arm before Ashton pulls her to the side. Speaking in hushed tones, she asks, "Did you know about him?!"

"No, but I'm sure Faye has her reasons for using him. And I'm glad she did."

Angel and Ashton continue to bicker about Jimmy's role in their plan. They are unaware Muscles has maneuvered towards his leg and grabbed the pistol strapped in a holster.

"Watch it!" Jimmy shouts, rushing out of the garage as he sees Muscles take the opportunity with him in the garage and Angel's and Ashton's backs turned. Muscles fires a shot at Ashton and misses by a hair. Angel tackles Ashton to the ground. Before Muscles fires another shot, Ashton flings her arm out and twists her hand swiftly. She snaps his wrist like a twig.

"AHHHHH! My wrist!" He tries to cradle his broken wrist but his restrained hand is making matters difficult.

"I should break more than that," Ashton lunges for him but feels arms wrapped around her, holding her back.

"Focus." Angel takes Ashton's chin between her thumb and index finger, looking her straight in the eye.

"You're dead! I swear when I get out -- "

Tired of his complaining and shouting, because who knows what attention he has drawn with that shot, Angel quiets him with a forceful kick to his face. He goes limp on the ground, unconscious.

"We need to remember why we're here," she reminds Ashton. "Take a breath. Get it together and let's get out of here. The police will be here any minute!" Angel helps Jimmy gather the duffle bags and they make their way to Ashton's car. "Jimmy, can you call Faye and see if she can buy us some time?"

"On it," Jimmy says.

Ashton hastily makes her way to the robbers' truck to untie the hostages. Opening the door, the hostages quiver as they see nothing but the dim light of the sun and hear each other's cries. Ashton removes the blindfolds and rushes them out of the truck.

"The cops will be here soon. You saw and heard nothing," Ashton pressures them, slightly revealing the bloody knife within her jacket. Hysterically crying, they open their arms wide to embrace her, hugging her tightly and thanking her profusely. Ashton cringes, trying desperately to remove them. "O-okay, you're welcome. It's safe for you to go now."

The hostages quickly make their exit, but one stops to look back at Ashton. "You were at the bank."

Ashton doesn't respond, face emotionless.

"Di-Did you see my daughter, Taylor? Is she safe? Please, I need to know."

Ashton removes her guard and relaxes her stone face. "Taylor is fine. She was a lot stronger than most of the adults in there." Ashton gives a faint smile. "You should be proud."

The mother smiles and steps towards Ashton to embrace her once more but hesitates to realize that Ashton doesn't like that sort of thing. She hurries away, leaving Ashton to wish she would have embraced her as only a mother would. Ashton takes a moment to watch the mother as she rushes to see her daughter. She longs for the moments she had someone to rush and rescue her. Ashton quickly shakes off the feeling and makes her way to her car, where Angel and Jimmy stand near the side of Ashton's trunk.

"Are we good to go?" Ashton stops abruptly when she sees the bullet hole the size of a quarter on the back driver's side of the car. "What the hell?! Are you kidding me?!"

"Calm down. You can fix it later."

"Can't you use your superpower thing to fix it?" Jimmy asks, giving his unsolicited advice.

Ashton holds her head in her hand attempting to calm herself. "Let's just go," Ashton opens her driver door.

"You guys are an interesting pair," Jimmy says, waiting for Ashton to move her front seat so he can get in the backseat.

"Yeah, tell us something we don't know," Angel mumbles to herself, getting into the passenger seat.

"Faye is not going to believe the day we had," Jimmy jokes.

Ashton pauses as the words replay in her head.

"Umm...you going to let me in or what?" Jimmy asks as Ashton contemplates her next moves.

"Ash?! Quit playing and let him in!"

Ashton looks up from her door to face him and realizes he's a liability. "Sorry, Jimmy. No room," Ashton flings her arm, letting out a gush of wind that sends Jimmy flying back towards the apartment buildings along with his counterparts.

Angel rushes out of the car towards a sprinting Ashton. "What are you doing?!"

Once back in the alley, Ashton uses her telekinetic abilities to move the robbers' unconscious bodies in such a way it looks as though Jimmy turned against them, which is somewhat true. "I'm not working with some small-time crook and I'm damn sure not splitting half a million dollars four ways."

"This was not the plan! We could have dealt with this a better way," Angel says.

"How many people know about us? How many people know about our powers!?" Angel doesn't respond as Ashton rounds on her. "I will do anything and everything to keep us safe and protected and if I have to hurt some people along the way...so be it." Ashton returns to maneuvering her crime scene. "We're not normal, so get over it."

Those seven words hit Angel like a gut punch. "You know what? Do what you want like you always do. I always have to come back and clean up whatever damage you caused anyways."

Ashton continues to move the men around the alley, seeming to ignore Angel's comments. Angel leaves Ashton to do whatever she wants to do and waits for her in the car.

Ashton takes Muscles' gun and places it in his unconscious hands. "It's nothing personal," Ashton says to him, dusting off her hands. Quickly, she makes her way to her car, knowing the police could be there at any moment.

"We're all good," she says to a drained Angel.

"I'm really getting tired of all of this," Angel mumbles, but loud enough for Ashton to hear.

"Yeah, like I haven't heard that one before." Ashton speeds away from the scene. Looking in her rearview mirror, she sees the police approaching the apartment alley with their guns drawn on the robbers, waking them up with brute force and putting them in cuffs. The officers begin examining the scene. A tall, polished, young woman watches from the crime scene as Ashton leaves exhaust smoke in her wake around the corner.

"Officer Brown?" she asks.

"Yes, Detective?"

"Did you happen to see the car that just left?"

"No, ma'am."

The detective stares off into the distance, her expression serious. "Have Brinks run a trace on all the cars in and out of this block within the last hour."

"Yes, Detective Spiller." Officer Brown swiftly walks away to make that call to his department's intelligence division.

Detective Spiller walks until she is alone and discreetly moves away from the busy scene. "Hey, I think we got them."

"Can you bring them in?" asks a deep, husky and distorted voice that would make anyone's skin crawl.

"Not yet. But trust me, they'll slip up. Once we have them, I'll let you know." Detective Spiller hangs up her phone and returns to the scene.

Chapter 2

Bleak, grim and grungy is the all-girls Rochester Juvenile Detention Center. The girls here aren't the friendliest people. Murder, assault, theft, drug distribution are all on the list of crimes these girls have committed. Girls as young as 13 are completing sentences here at the center. Once they turn 18, it will be time for them to be processed out and complete the rest of their time at a prison facility.

It's lunchtime and they've crowded into the cafeteria, where the floors have torn through the plywood. Tables and chairs are made of cold metal. Some girls are laughing and joking with one another, others are arguing and shouting, but suddenly everything and everyone comes to a halt. Two correctional officers come walking in with a young girl. Her arms, wrist and ankles are chained tightly, and a forest green suit covers her butterscotch skin. She has a scar on the right side of her forehead; it looks as though she's had it for some time, but her dark brown hair covers most of it.

Daniella may be a threat to the other girls, but they respect her. It's not an awkward silence. They just know who's in the room.

"Don't try nothing," the officer says, unchaining her.

She rubs her left wrist revealing a tattoo of stars. This is only one of three tattoos Daniella has. The other is behind her right ear with the date 10/15/2010 in roman numerals (X. XV. MMX), and another, on the inside of her right forearm reveals a wolf.

The correctional officers keep their eyes on her as she walks through the cafeteria. Most of the others keep their faces in their trays, trying not to make eye contact as she walks by. Some whisper behind her back about how she ended up at the center.

"I heard she stabbed everyone in her foster home while they were asleep," one girl says.

"I heard she stole her last warden's gun and then shot him," another girl whispers.

She hears the whispers as she walks to the cafeteria line, ignoring them along the way. Daniella is quiet, some would even say introverted. She's silent but deadly. The cafeteria worker slaps what looks like food on her tray. She goes to find a seat and runs straight into a much taller and wider juvenile girl three times her size, more like the size of a linebacker, and spills her food on herself and the floor.

"Watch where you're going, crack baby!" Jones shouts.

"Keep it moving, Jones," the C.O. shouts at the solidly built juvenile girl.

The room becomes silent. Everyone looks worried about what will happen next. Jones walks away, believing she got the best of Daniella. With her back turned, Daniella grabs her tray from the floor and slams it against Jones' head. She falls on the floor, her head beginning to swell and her ear leaking with blood. She slowly stands and tackles Daniella to the floor. The entire cafeteria is in an uproar. Everyone cheers the fight on. Girls stand on tables, shouting for either of them to take the other down. Daniella and Jones go blow for blow on the floor as the cafeteria watches with excitement. Daniella sits on top of her, punching her repeatedly until she breaks skin.

Before the fight goes any further, the C.O.s rush in to separate them. Daniella refuses to stop, not letting it go. One correctional officer pulls her away and grabs her by her shoulders, squeezing tightly. "I told you, the next time you want to fight, you're taking it to the ring!"

Daniella's hazel eyes have turned red with rage. No one is going to make a fool of her. The two correctional officers put the chains on tightly and shove her down the hall to a creaking elevator that makes its way to the lowest level of the detention center.

The basement is dark and cold and the concrete walls are thick and soundproof. No one can hear a scream. Walking further into the basement, the correctional officers lead Daniella and Jones to a homemade rundown boxing ring surrounded by excited and scheming correctional officers ready for a show. Daniella is brought to one side of the ring and Jones to the other.

"I have a lot of money riding on this, so you better knock her out," C.O. O'Neal demands. He takes off her chains to allow her to change into her boxing attire: a white prison sports bra, old torn shorts and worn shoes. He places her gloves on her and rushes her into the ring. Daniella, still enraged, refuses to touch the gloves of her opponent, who now realizes this isn't what she wanted when she picked the fight with Daniella.

The bell sounds and Daniella gets into her boxing stance. Jones wastes no time and lunges for Daniella, throwing punches one after another, knocking her against the ropes. Daniella puts her hands up to protect her head, but the punches are coming too fast. Jones tries her hardest to knock Daniella down. Some of her punches land and Daniella's eyebrow begins to swell. They separate from the ropes and Daniella lands punches to her opponent's body. She throws a right hook to her face, breaking her nose, and with all her strength lands a right uppercut to her opponent's chin. She sends her down to the mat, unconscious.

C.O. O'Neal runs into the ring and raises Daniella's hand in the air, showing that the girl he betted on just made him a semi-wealthy man. The losing officers drag Jones out of the ring and take her to the infirmary, slapping stacks of cash into C.O. O'Neal's hand as he rubs his gunslinger mustache. He grins from ear to ear; it's pretty cringey.

As C.O. O'Neal counts his earnings, Daniella waits for her cut. "Is some of that mine?" she asks.

He laughs off her request. "You should be glad I didn't lock you in solitary for that stunt you pulled." O'Neal places her arms behind her back and tightens the chains. "Don't worry. There'll be more opportunities. Perry has us set up for the next few months." He smiles sinisterly and takes her back to her cell.

Moments later, he shoves her in her cell, which is secluded from the rest of the juvenile girls, and locks it. "Rest up, you got a big day tomorrow," he taunts as he walks away.

Daniella's adrenaline consumes her and she punches a hole in the wall in her small and confined room. It has only a bed and tiny window, just big enough for an arm to fit through. She hates it here. She's struggled her entire life. She wonders if she'll ever feel at peace, but right now she just wants to be left alone.

Hours pass and Daniella continues to sit in her cell, enraged she's even there. Jones should be in solitary, not her. But instead, she's stuck in between four walls with nowhere to go, she thought. She screams and starts to hit the walls. She would throw something but there's nothing in here except for a steel bed. There used to be a small stack of her favorite books but the warden took those because Daniella keeps leaving her cell. She stops. "It's okay, it's okay," she says, trying to calm herself. She inhales and exhales, regaining her composure. She has to get out of here.

Daniella walks to her cell door and kneels to open the slot to see if there are any guards nearby, but they're gone for the night. She steps back from the cell door and stretches her arm out; the door lets out a loud crack. The lock on the door bursts and she walks out of her cell. Again. She discreetly moves through the hallway trying to avoid guards until she turns the corner.

"Hey, what are -- " Daniella slams into a guard, but with the flick of her wrist, she freezes the guard mid-sentence. She didn't freeze him as if he turned into ice; she stopped time, leaving the guard frozen and still reaching for his taser. Daniella quickly moves behind him, wrapping her arms around his waist, and drags him into a secluded corner of the hallway. She leans him up against the wall. Luckily, he will have no recollection of the events prior to being frozen.

Daniella makes her way through the detention hall. So far, no more guards. Just as she is about to turn the corner, she overhears a voice.

"She's doing well. We've been keeping a close eye on her," the voice speaks in a hushed tone.

Daniella leans out of cover from the wall to see Warden Perry talking on his cell phone. He has his back to her, looking around to make sure no one is nearby. Warden Perry is an ordinary man, dressed in a white polo shirt buttoned up to his neck and tucked into his black slacks with worn-out black dress shoes. This job has aged him, and it shows with the heavy bags and dark circles surrounding his tired eyes.

"That wasn't the deal. You said if we transfer her to you then you'll pay. I --" Daniella quickly hides behind the wall just as Warden Perry turns in her direction. "Hold on." He peaks down the hallway, believing he heard someone approach. "Hello?" Once he realizes he could be paranoid, he turns and makes his way toward his office. "Yes. I'm here." Daniella carefully leans out of cover. Warden Perry moves down the hall, phone tightly pressed to his ear. She thinks nothing of the conversation she overheard, only that the warden is being as corrupt as usual. She waits a moment for the hallway to be clear and makes her way to the cafeteria. She hasn't eaten all day due to her scuffle earlier.

Entering the empty cafeteria, she makes her way to the kitchen and prepares some of the good food the guards always hide for themselves. Searching through the pristine kitchen and its cabinets she finds snacks galore: cookies, cakes, chips, ramen noodles, pop, you name it. She takes what she can carry – a tray of hot ramen noodles and a pop, along with some snacks – to an empty table in the middle of the cafeteria. It is empty and the quiet is troubling. She continues to enjoy the best meal she's had in a year until she looks up from her tray and sees Sergeant Erica Campbell standing in the doorway.

"Vega?!" Erica shouts. "We talked about this." Sergeant Erica Campbell is of average size, slim, her skin a tawny beige. Sergeant Campbell knows this isn't the first time Daniella has used her powers to get out of her cell without permission.

Daniella knows she's there but doesn't care. She continues to finish her meal. "I didn't get to eat."

"I know the girl is in the clinic now. She's beat up pretty badly," the sergeant says, sitting across from Daniella.

"Why are you here?"

"Warden Perry called and said you caused a disturbance earlier in the cafeteria. He knows to call me because I'm the only one that can talk some sense into that stubborn head of yours."

"Then you should also know it wasn't my fault and Perry is only out for himself."

"Don't I know," Campbell says rolling her eyes, knowing all about Warden Perry's shady deals. "But it would be a lot easier for the both of us if you wouldn't give him any more ammunition."

"That's easier said than done if you knew what he and his officers have me and the other girls do to each other."

"I don't know anything because you never tell me what's going on."

"Why should I? There's nothing you can do about it." Daniella brushes her off like she does to most.

"That's not true and you know it," Erica says, searching for an answer from Daniella. But she's silent, continuing to eat her snacks. "Daniella, I can't help you if you don't meet me halfway."

Sergeant Erica Campbell has known Daniella since she was seven years old. Daniella was taken away from her father and mother and put into foster care. She'll never admit it, but Erica Campbell is the only person who's looked out for her after all these years.

May 10th, 2017

Blue, red, and white police lights brightened up the dark neighborhood. Police cars, ambulances and fire trucks surrounded an old, rundown, brown apartment building with broken municipal sidewalks left and right. The night was cold and gloomy as some tenants stood outside the building waiting for the police to give the order for them to go back inside. A young Erica Campbell, with her NYPD 60th precinct jacket and badge on her hip, walked under the bright yellow crime scene tape leading into the grime-filled apartment. She showed her badge to the officer guarding the front door.

"What do we have?" Officer Campbell asked her partner, Officer Connor.

"Possible suicide. 30-year-old Hispanic male. Gunshot wound to the head," the officer said as they stood over the large, crimson stained floor. Paramedics walked past them with a lifeless body on a gurney.

"Hold on," Officer Campbell stopped the paramedics. She lifted the crisp white sheet from the cold and stiff man's face. She leaned down and looked at her partner through the hole on the side of the body's forehead. "You sure this was an apparent suicide?"

"We took a statement from the wife," Officer Connor said.

Officer Campbell and Officer Connor saw a woman sitting on the couch shaking with fear as she barely listened to another female officer badger her with questions about tonight's events. Her disheveled clothes were covered in dark crimson stains. Officer Campbell motioned the paramedics to remove the woman's husband and they stepped out to discuss the scene further.

"Were we able to ID the victim?" Officer Campbell asked.

Officer Connor takes out a pad, "Jason Pérez."

"THE Jason Pérez? We've been trying to get to this guy for months!" Officer Campbell exclaimed. "He sold drugs throughout the city, ran a whole organization."

"Well, this case just got a lot more interesting."

"And the wife, is she talking?" Officer Campbell asked, watching her from the hallway.

"Carmen Vega? Barely."

"I'll see what else I can find out," Officer Campbell said as she re-entered the home. One would almost be afraid to enter this home; the grime was visible. Walking into the kitchen where dishes that hadn't been touched in days. Officer Campbell opened the slightly hollow refrigerator only filled with a half-gallon of milk, beer, eggs and deli meat. She also saw a large box of baking soda in the back; it stuck out like a sore thumb. She opened it and found a large number of $100 bills. She contemplated taking it as evidence but based on the living conditions, Carmen would need it more.

Officer Campbell then proceeded to the crowded bedrooms. She passed by a small room with a twin-size bed. At first, she wasn't sure whose room this could have been, but then saw a small stuffed animal laid on the floor. It was raggedy, but homemade with a small button for an eye. Walking further into the room, she picked up books. The pages were worn out with some of the ink fading away. She began to exit then heard movement near the closet. Her gun ready in one hand, she aimed at the door, opening it with her other hand. A shriek arose from an old broken hamper. A small child stood up in the hamper with her hands up. Officer Campbell quickly put her gun away. She realized this room belonged to this young girl.

"Hey, hey, it's okay. I'm not going shoot you, you just startled me," she stretched out her hand to the girl. It took her a moment to accept it. "Really, it's okay. I'll help you."

She finally emerged from the dark closet and Officer Campbell was taken aback with what she saw. Crimson dots were scattered across the side of the young girl's face, her smooth-as-chocolate hair tied in a ponytail and her clothes two sizes too small. She continued to examine her and noticed scars on multiple parts of her body. A long scar across her left wrist, a fresh scar on the right side of her forehead, a bruise on her shoulder and some scratches on her forearm.

"Can you tell me what happened tonight?" Officer Campbell kneeled in front of her. She didn't speak. "It's okay. Can you tell me your name?" The young girl still didn't speak. "All right, well let's go find your mom." Officer Campbell walked with her out of the room and a commotion erupted from the living room.

"NO! NO! YOU CAN'T DO THIS! WHERE'S MY DAUGHTER?!" Carmen Vega yells.

Officer Campbell witnessed as Carmen struggled to get away from the officers taking her away. She glanced down at the young girl trembling with fear. "Can you wait right here for me?" The young girl nodded.

"What's going on?" Office Campbell asked Officer Connor.

"She hasn't just been using the husband's product," Officer Connor said.

"NO! YOU CAN'T DO THIS!" the woman shouted.

"We got to take the kid, too," Officer Connor continued.

Officer Campbell glanced over her shoulder and saw a troubled young girl with no idea of what was going on. She won't let the system get to her. "Okay, but let me take her to the station, she can sleep there…just…let her say goodbye to her mother."

The young girl slowly approached her mom. "C-Come here, mija," Carmen said, gently grabbing her daughter's face. "E-Esta bien, estarás bien. ¿Me oyes? No foe tu intención hacerlo." She hugged her daughter tightly and the officers separated them, hand cuffing the woman and pushing her through the gloomy apartment building hallway.

Moments later, Officer Campbell walked hand in hand with the young girl to her police car. They sat in the car for a moment, silent, then she spoke. "Daniella."

Officer Campbell was surprised she spoke, "I'm sorry?"

"My name is Daniella."

"All right, Daniella. Well, whatever you need I'm here to help. I got your back," Officer Campbell said. Unfortunately, Daniella said nothing more the rest of the night.

"Why do you care so much? I never asked you to do anything for me! We both know I would've been fine on my own!" Daniella cried.

"No, you wouldn't! Daniella, you're facing murder charges!"

"Well, that's what happens when the system doesn't care less about where they put you. That woman had it coming. She beat us almost every night!" Daniella says, remembering the night she refused to take any more abuse from anyone. Not her father, her mother and certainly not some random foster parent.

"I know… and I'm sorry I let that happen to you. But I am in your corner," Sergeant Campbell said.

Daniella can never allow herself to show how happy she is that Sergeant Campbell is in her life, so she sits there emotionless.

"I want to show you something," Sergeant Campbell takes out a brochure that reads: *Clarks University: A School for the Gifted. Located in Wales, United Kingdom.* Pictures of young people happily working in classrooms, laboratories and actively involved in sports light up the pages.

"What is this?" Daniella looks at the brochure. It's quite scary.

"The president of this school came to me looking for… special students and now you can be around others like you, learning new skills every day." Sergeant Campbell shows Daniella she can start a new life, have a second chance.

Daniella picks up the pamphlet and studies it, flipping it back and forth. "I don't think so," she says, and she means it.

"You have the opportunity, right now, to get out of here. They're willing to take time off your sentence so just take it!" She's frustrated by Daniella.

"You told me a long time ago that I'm in here for my protection. Is that still true?" Daniella asks when she already knows the answer.

"Of course."

"Well, how do you know these aren't the same people who have been looking for me?!" During her time awaiting her sentence, three men approached Daniella. They attempted to kidnap her, and they attacked because they knew of her powers. She fought them off and made her way to Sergeant Campbell, who told Daniella that for her safety it was best to take the plea deal; her sentence being 10 years. Daniella reluctantly agreed.

"I spoke to her myself and she's legit," she tries to reassure her. This conversation is not important to Daniella and Sergeant Campbell can see it, but she needs to tell Daniella the next set of news; she braces herself.

"You'll be turning 18 in a few months." Daniella knows where this is going. "And when you do, they will take you to a correctional facility, to prison. The prosecutor is motioning to modify your sentence. You could be given a few more years or life. The room is intense now. "The moment you walk out of those doors I can't protect you anymore. You'll be on your own with real-life criminals who don't care who you are." Sergeant Campbell explains sternly.

Daniella doesn't quite understand why this is a topic of discussion. She knows she's strong. No one will mess with her. "Like I said, it was an accident. It's her word against mine. They can't give me life for that, and I can obviously handle myself."

"Anything can happen. You're a young girl that committed murder and yes, you and I both know you can handle yourself, but what do you think is going to happen to you when someone sees you freeze another inmate or explode the hinges of a door because you can't control your anger?" Daniella is quiet once again, knowing Sergeant Campbell is partially correct. Sometimes her anger gets out of control, and she can't control her abilities. "When you came to me, I told you I would find a way to help you and I did. I don't ask you to do a lot, just follow the rules and life will be easier for the both of us."

How can life be easier? She's the one in the handcuffs every day, Daniella thought to herself.

"The president will be here tomorrow, and a guard will come to your cell. You can either stay or leave. It's up to you." She leaves Daniella to ponder her decision. "I hope you make the right choice."

Daniella looks through the brochure, possibly considering meeting with the president tomorrow. If she does consider attending the meeting, what type of stuck-up lifestyle will she be living? Daniella has never gone outside of her own neighborhood in New York and now Sergeant Campbell wants her to go outside the country. That's a huge decision to make.

"And can you please unfreeze these people and get back to your cell?" Sergeant Campbell leaves the mess hall and Daniella begins to unfreeze the workers that have no recollection of being frozen. She takes the brochure back to her cell, tired of everyone and everything.

Chapter 3

B reathe, Blair." Michelle Hahn stands small and thin behind her daughter, Blair Hahn. They practice the art of tai chi in their cozy basement. It is a standard basement with a laundry room, bins of holiday decorations on shelves and a furnace room. Except for the room that is set up in the back of the basement housing all of Blair's personal items, including her bed. This is her room away from the public.

Michelle guides Blair's arms in a fluid motion – guiding them as they flow through the air like waves in the ocean. "You need to relax; don't be so tense. Take control of the fear you are feeling. You're stronger than you think," her mother said.

Blair is of average height with long, jet-black hair and hazel eyes. She inhales and exhales as she and her mother, who looks like an older version of Blair, stand barefooted on a large yoga mat.

"Your movement is all about grace and staying calm." As Michelle walks around Blair adjusting her posture, Blair has her eyes closed, moving her body smoothly and pushing her arms in and out. "The sooner you learn to stay calm, the sooner you can take control of your abilities."

The Hahn family lives a semi-normal life in the sunshine state of Florida. The father is a software engineer, the mother works as a nurse, the eldest sibling attends an ivy league college, the youngest is at the top of his class and the middle child, well, Blair, is the outcast.

"Follow my movements," Michelle says. She faces Blair head on and blocks her hits quickly. It's a dance between them as Blair tries to punch her on her right and Michelle blocks it, hitting her where she's left herself open. "Loosen up!" Michelle demands.

"I'm trying!" Blair becomes restless and Michelle knocks her down on the mat.

They both breathe heavily sitting on the mat. "You can do this, Bibi, you just need to keep your focus."

"You say that like it's easy. Did you forget who you're married to?"

"Your father is only hard on you because he loves you and wants to protect you," Michelle says. Blair stands, turning her head away as she rolls her eyes. Her mother is so oblivious.

"Michelle, I need to speak with you," Blair's father calls from atop the stairs.

"We'll practice some more tomorrow." Michelle gently grabs Blair's chin and kisses her forehead. She makes her way upstairs to talk to her husband.

Blair is used to being on her own. She's always thought maybe these powers are cursed. Maybe they aren't meant for her, but they make her Blair. She wishes people would accept her, but that may be too much to ask.

Moments pass and she hears a lot of commotion coming from upstairs. Blair turns down her music and hears her parents, Samuel and Michelle, arguing over her...again.

"I'm sending her to this school," Samuel shouts, holding up a packet. "It's in South Korea and she'll get all the help she'll need!"

"She's still our daughter!" Michelle shouts.

"She is an abomination to this household!" Samuel snaps back, condemning his daughter. Samuel Hahn stands tall over his wife and his jet-black hair stands on his head due to him raking his hands through it. He has always not only wanted to get rid of his daughter's abilities the moment they became apparent, but he's wanted to change her entirely, including her feelings and her wants. He's known since Blair was very young that she would bring trouble, but he hoped maybe it was just a phase. She was four years old, and chaos erupted.

"They will treat her and then she'll be normal," Samuel pleads.

"How can you say that, Sam?! The school is on another continent!" Michelle loves her daughter no matter who she is and what powers she possesses, but because her husband is the man of the household and a man of God, she must follow her husband's lead.

"No daughter of mine will leave this house with such sorcery!" He believes if anything is not of God, it's a sin. Michelle hates to side with her husband regarding Blair, but she has no choice on the matter.

"I guess you've made your decision."

Blair sits on the steps, listening to her parents argue about getting rid of her. Are they that embarrassed by her? Do they hate her so much they're willing to completely change who she is? Blair questions. She walks away from the basement steps and sits on the sofa, her knees to her chest, and she begins to cry. Suddenly, sprinkles of snow begin to fall on the top of her head and a white streak begins to form in her hair. A normal occurrence that she's used to when she feels melancholy.

Blair's father has locked her in this basement. She's only allowed to go to school and church, which she hates, mainly due to her father.

She wipes away her tears and walks to her desk in the corner. It's covered with maps and brochures from different cities across the United States. Lifting a poster of the Amazon rainforest on the wall, she reveals a large map with red marks slashed across states and post-it notes attached. Blair has had this hidden for some time now, a time when it was meant for her to take back control of her own life. Blair looks for the nearest bus stations in Hunter's Creek, Florida. She doesn't know exactly where she's going, but wherever it is, it must be better than living here. She packs a bag and waits for her family to leave for the night.

Later that night, Blair grabs her book bag and zips up her dark hoodie. She had to pack as little as possible as there isn't much time to leave. She walks upstairs, the first time in her own home in three weeks. During this time of night, her family should be out of the house doing their own activities. The house is quiet as she walks to the front door to leave.

"What are you doing?!" Blair is startled by her father and mother sitting quietly in the family room.

"What?"

"Where are you going?! You know you aren't allowed to leave this house without permission," Samuel says, sternly pushing up his square-rimmed glasses, asserting his authority.

Blair is stuck for a moment. She knew if her father found out the real reason she was leaving, she could kiss the outside world goodbye forever. "I thought I'd go to the health center, I heard you and Mom talking about them needing help this morning," Blair creates a story on the spot.

"It's fine sweetie, but we need to talk to you," Michelle says. "Come sit down." Blair instantly knows from their conversation they had this afternoon that this talk won't be all sunshine and rainbows.

"These…capabilities that you have, they have put this family through many troubling situations, and I can't have anything or anyone in this house not lifting up the glory of God," her father says. Agitation and frustration come over her every time he speaks. It's the same story every day: 'my daughter is an abomination, and she needs help.' Sometimes she hopes her mom would say something for once – the smallest comment to let her know her mom is still the only person who cares. "But you are still my daughter," Samuel lays the packet on the coffee table in front of her. A strange-looking man is on the cover. He looks like a monk, but scarier and not so sacred. The title reads: *Eliminating the Power Within.*

Blair skims through the booklet. There are pictures of people bowing down to these monks like they're God. She continues to flip through the offensive booklet.

"This monastery will take away those powers and…feelings you have, and you don't have to worry about school because they will provide that too. All you have do is sign the paperwork and you can leave next week." Samuel dominates the conversation as usual. Her father has really crossed the line this time.

Blair throws the packet down on the coffee table. "I don't think it's fair you are making decisions about my life without giving a second thought about how I'll feel about it."

"We're only –" Michelle finally begins to speak until she is interrupted, once again.

"Don't you dare explain yourself to this child!" Samuel demands. "You will sign these papers because as long as you are living in my home, you will do as I say!"

"Well, what if I don't want to get rid of my powers? What if I actually like being the way I am?" Blair tests her father. Samuel stands up from his seat and looks down on Blair, intimidating her.

"You either sign the papers or I promise, you will never see the light of day again."

This is it. Blair has taken all she can with her father. She's eighteen now and she can finally stand up to his dominating, verbally and mentally abusive ways.

"You know what? You walk around here with your head held high, quoting the bible, verse for verse, book after book, but it wasn't until this morning I realized you only quote what suits you at the moment. You cherry-pick." Blair stands up and faces her father. "Has it ever occurred to you that maybe you're the hypocrite? Maybe you're the devil in disguise?!"

All the emotions she's felt towards her father in the past have led to this moment. Samuel is fuming, his olive skin turning red as fire. He can't believe she would talk to him this way. Something comes over him and he raises his hand and backslaps Blair across her face.

"Samuel!" Michelle shouts, astonished.

"Honor your father and your mother, so that you may live long in the land the LORD your God is giving you," he sharply quotes the scripture to Blair.

Blair holds her face and looks at her father, disappointed, and she runs out of the house before she does something she can't control.

"Blair!" Michelle calls out, trying to catch up to her before she leaves her home, possibly forever.

Blair walks down the quiet streets of Hunter's Creek, Florida, using the sleeves of her hoodie to wipe the tears falling onto the bright red mark on her face. She tries to hide from the people walking past her because if anyone recognized her, they would call her parents. Blair's powers are becoming more visible as she walks. Every step she takes, she leaves a footprint of snow right behind her. This dramatic situation with her father is taking a toll on her and she must calm herself down.

Blair enters a quiet pub with a jukebox playing in the background and sits at a table all the way in the back. Taking a menu from the display on the table, she reads it, hiding her face at the same time. She can slightly see some of the old customers, the only three in the entire place, looking at her and whispering, but she's use to it.

A waitress comes over to take her order. "How can I help you, honey?" The bright red-headed waitress says, comforting her with her bright smile.

"A hot chocolate, please," Blair says, not wanting to draw any more attention.

"Coming right up."

Blair thinks she has everything under control now until she looks underneath the table. Her hands start to shake and tremble with ice crystals forming on the palms of her hands, sort of like a Snow Queen thing, except she can't turn the entire town into ice. Closing her hands tightly, Blair quickly glances up to see if anyone saw her. Fortunately, no one is paying attention. She reaches into her book bag and grabs her gloves to suppress her powers.

The waitress comes over to bring Blair her drink. "Will there be anything else?" the waitress asks, startling Blair.

"Uh, no, thank you."

Everything is going smoothly with Blair, her abilities have calmed, she's relaxed, and she's somewhat dealt with her father's actions. Unfortunately, nothing ever goes smoothly for too long.

As she drinks her hot chocolate, a woman comes and sits with her at the table. Blair stops drinking, completely puzzled, and thrown off guard that this beautiful woman, whose skin is as smooth as mahogany and whose long, natural, black hair flows down her back, sits in front of her.

"You know, I never know what to order here. I mean do I get onion rings or loaded cheese fries? Everything is just so good," the woman says as she looks over the menu.

Blair stares at the woman, unable to resist her milk chocolate eyes, realizing she must be up to something.

"Umm…Who are you and what do you want?" Blair asks suspiciously of the woman sitting there in her expensive business suit.

"Who I am isn't important. It's who you are, Blair."

Blair is taken aback by how she knows her name. "Tell me who you are, or I swear I'm calling the cops." Blair is not playing any games, so this lady better start talking and fast.

The woman places her hair behind her ears and gives Blair a conniving smile. "My name is Lieutenant Jordan Knox, and I represent an elite, and private, organization. My people are looking to recruit young people with gifted minds such as yourself to serve under our direction," Jordan gives this speech. She's clearly practiced and waits for Blair to comment.

They're both quiet for a moment until Blair bursts out in laughter. "A secret organization?! Really?!" Blair continues to laugh, something she needed. "I'm 18 and currently maintain a 2.7 GPA. I don't know what gifted mind you see, but it's not mine." She goes back to her hot chocolate and Jordan watches as she drinks with her gloves on.

"I don't think that's true. You see, you have abilities that could be of great use to us." As Jordan speaks on Blair's abilities, it makes her nervous and terrified as to who Jordan is and how she knows about her powers.

"I-I don't have any abilities."

"Really? So, you just like wearing gloves in 70-degree weather?" Jordan points out how ridiculous Blair looks wearing winter gloves in the middle of Florida heat.

Blair, for a split second, forgot she had them on. "How did you know?" Blair gives up. Clearly this lady knows more than she's letting on.

Jordan leans forward, closer to Blair. "You'll come to realize, I know a lot," Jordan whispers, "and people usually don't order hot chocolate during this time of the year." Jordan mentions Blair's now cold, hot chocolate. Good, now she can stop pretending to enjoy this drink.

Blair pushes it away and takes off her winter gloves. "Since you know so much, do you know why I'm drinking hot chocolate and wearing winter gloves like it's a blizzard outside?"

"You're an environmentalist. You manipulate the weather based on your emotions and right now you seem awfully depressed. Care to explain?" Jordan spins the questions right back to Blair, knowing the answer already.

"No, I don't." Blair is quickly losing the little bit of patience she has with Jordan.

"Okay, so if it's all right with you I would rather keep the unnecessary questions to a minimum," Jordan says.

"Okay then, what is that you want from me?"

"I want you to stop running. I want to give you the opportunity to use your gifts freely without the judgment and disapproval of your family and the lonely people of this town. You can't tell me there hasn't been a day where you haven't felt like you can do better for yourself." Jordan wants Blair to trust her and understand there's more to life than what she knows.

Blair, on the other hand, just can't take this woman seriously. There are a lot of crazy people in this world, and who knows – this lady could be one of them. But if Ms. Knox wants to get real, let's get real.

"You're right. I have felt like that, every day of my life, but nothing's going to change. And you…what you're telling me seems too good to be true. Yeah, you might be working for some 'secret' organization, and I don't know why anyone would just say that freely, but, you have yet to prove it to me." Blair stands from her seat. She's lost all the patience she had for this conversation. "And for all I know, you could be someone trying to lock me up in the crazy house, so I'm going to get out of here before you do." Blair begins to leave.

Jordan knew something like this would happen. It would have been too easy if Blair joined her right away. Jordan stands to stop Blair.

"You know, I get it, and I completely understand if you don't trust me, but if you change your mind." Jordan reaches into her jacket pocket and takes out a black business card. "I'm always available and I'm always around," she says. Blair takes the card and Jordan leaves.

"I bet you are," Blair says to herself, annoyed by Jordan and her secrets. She stands there confused, anxious and irritated. She begins flipping the card back and forth and sees that it's blank. "Oh, now I know she's crazy." Blair puts the card in her pocket and walks to the bus station.

She waits for the next bus to come. Deep down she has a feeling Jordan could be telling the truth, but who knows, with her luck these days. The bus pulls up and Blair gets ready to get on, until a man covered up by his hoodie bumps her and she drops her phone.

"Excuse you!" Blair shouts at him. He continues to walk down the street as if he never saw or pushed her. She picks up her phone and gets on the bus headed to Georgia. Blair sits at the front, trying to grasp everything that has happened tonight, from the argument with her father to Lieutenant Knox knowing about her powers. It's been a lot to handle. She can't get it out of her head how much Jordan knew. Blair tries to focus her attention on something else and takes out her phone. She sees a voicemail from her mom, opens it up and listens.

"Honey! Please come home. Your father never meant for any of that to happen. Despite what you may believe, your father is a good man and we both love you very much. This family wouldn't know what to do if something were to-. J-Just come home or at least call us to let us know you're safe," Michelle cried out on the phone.

Blair hangs up her phone. Even though the rest of her family may not be too fond of her, her mother has always been there for her, in her own way. It's the intimidation of her father that can sometimes sway her mother to side with him. Blair loves her mother so she would hate herself if she just left her without at least saying goodbye. Blair pulls the cord to stop the bus and gets off to head back home.

Chapter 4

Blair hesitates before entering her house, keys dangling in her hand. She doesn't want to be here but leaving without she and her father understanding and respecting one another is not the way she wants to move on. Blair exhales the deep breath she's been holding since getting off the bus and enters her house.

"Blair! Oh sweetie!" Michelle says with open arms, embracing her daughter and holding her tight.

It takes a second for Blair to reciprocate. Then she wraps her mother in a tight hug and allows herself to let go. They release, and Michelle places her hands on Blair's cheeks. She doesn't speak and they don't stop staring at one another.

Slowly coming down the stairs, watching the exchange between Blair and Michelle, is Samuel. He stands with authority and no remorse; he waits for an apology. Blair steps away from her mother and stands face-to-face with her father. "I'm…sorry."

"For what?" He stands firm, head held high.

It's taking everything in Blair not to lash out again. "I'm sorry…for disrespecting you."

Samuel nods his head and takes a set of keys out of his pocket. Blair instantly knows what those unlock. She looks at her mother one more time before following her father to the basement door. She walks with confidence, mostly to avoid activating her powers and causing any more issues this evening.

"I think you've earned some time…alone." He gestures for her to go down the steps, but before she goes, he takes out the packet, *Eliminating the Power Within.* "I suggest you look this over. We'll discuss it in the morning."

Blair takes the packet, her eyes glistening with tears and hurries down to the basement. Snow begins to cover the basement floor as she tosses the packet across the room, and she flops on her bed sobbing.

Samuel locks the door, and Michelle looks at him with disgust, leaving him with his thoughts.

As the hours pass, Blair practices maintaining her powers on her own, thinking that if she can show she can control them, maybe her father will give her old room back or at least treat her like a decent human being. Luckily, the basement is her space. She has some freedom. She sits at her cluttered desk, intensely focusing on a bag of popcorn, trying to make it pop with her hands placed around the bag. She's concentrating hard, so hard she doesn't have the most pleasant look on her face. Smoke creeps from the bag and moves slightly. Blair gets excited but that is short-lived and she ends up freezing the bag instead.

"Are you kidding me?!" Blair throws the rock-solid bag across the room, and it chips some paint off the wall. She gives up controlling her powers for the time being and makes her way to her private workout area with a heavy-duty boxing stand. She puts on her boxing gloves and gives the bag a couple of hard-hitting combination punches she learned from her mother. She releases all her aggression out on to the bag, hitting it harder and harder, repeatedly, until her hands begin to release steam from her anger. She stops suddenly when she hears laughter coming from upstairs.

"Blair, can you come upstairs, please?" her father calls from the steps.

Why is he suddenly in a good mood, she wonders. Blair takes a moment before going upstairs, believing it must be a setup for her father to be so cheery. Blair enters the dining area and hears the laughter growing louder. She walks in and is stunned at who she sees sitting at the table surrounded by her family. Jordan laughs and talks with them as if she's known them their entire lives.

"Hey. What's going on?" Blair cautiously enters the room, still on guard.

Jordan glances at her over Michelle's shoulder. She smiles at Blair as if they didn't just meet hours ago.

"BiBi!" Michelle shouts, happy to see her like the last few hours didn't happen. "Come sit down and eat something."

"I'm fine, I already ate," Blair says, keeping her focus on Jordan.

"Blair, this is President Knox. She runs the top gifted academy for girls in Wales and she wants you to attend," Samuel introduces the two.

Jordan stands to shake Blair's hand. "Nice to meet you, Blair," she says. Jordan has the biggest and brightest smile, giving her a firm handshake.

Blair looks at her, slightly agitated but more amazed at how she knew where she lived and at this facade she's putting on in front of her parents and brother.

"Benji, go upstairs and finish your homework. We want to talk to your sister in private," Samuel instructs his son, one of the two ambitious children he's most proud of.

"Good luck," Benji whispers to Blair before leaving.

Michelle pours tea. Blair and Jordan take a quick glimpse of each other. Jordan taunts her, and Blair tries to figure out Jordan's true motives.

"Mrs. Knox, tell us more about your program," Samuel asserts his authority once again.

Jordan despises this type of demeanor. She chuckles at the command – a tactic to keep her calm. "Well, first and foremost it's Ms. Knox," Jordan chuckles, "and as you know, our school offers many advanced programs from math and sciences, fine arts, engineering and medical." Jordan takes out the brochure for the gifted academy from her purse and gives it to Michelle and Samuel.

"You have a very elite program, Ms. Knox, but I'm curious, do you normally make visits this time of night… and from across the country?" Michelle asks curiously as she and Samuel study the brochure. Blair waits to see how Jordan will get out of this one.

"Unfortunately, I don't, but when I heard of the…gifted talents and mind Blair has, I just had to come see for myself," Jordan said. "When I want something, I make every effort to get it."

"And you'll be able to…fix Blair's situation?" Samuel glances at Blair, still committed to making Blair his version of normal.

Blair continues to sit in her seat, not saying a word. She wishes she was surprised her father still wanted to get rid of her powers after everything that took place, but it's typical Samuel Hahn. She is surprised her parents are falling for this act Jordan is putting on.

While speaking to Samuel, Jordan understands why Blair would want to run away: her father is really over-bearing. He occasionally tries to dominate the conversation, but he's met his match with Jordan. "I think the word you're looking for, sir, is 'maintain' and yes, but we like to focus on the academic side." Jordan matches Samuel's dominance.

"You are absolutely right, Ms. Knox. We just want to make sure Bibi, I mean Blair…will be getting the best education possible," Michelle says.

Jordan glances at Blair, who is distanced from this conversation, especially since no one has asked her opinion about this – 'new journey.'

"Well, Blair, how do you feel about our program?" Jordan asks.

"What…oh…umm…," Blair fidgets with her fingers, not paying attention, not sure what to say with her parents in the room.

"Blair, Ms. Knox asked you a question," Samuel says. There's a moment of silence in the room.

"Umm…you know what? Can I speak to Ms. Knox alone?" Blair asks her parents.

There's a hesitance in Samuel's body. He doesn't want to leave because who knows what Blair could say to jeopardize this great opportunity, but he has a reputation to uphold. "Okay, but your mother and I will just be in the living room if you need us." Blair's parents exit the dining room, sliding the double doors closed behind them to give Blair and Jordan their privacy.

Blair gives the fakest smile as she watches them leave.

"So, Blair, what is it that you want to talk about?" Jordan asks, sitting confidently and calmly.

"Oh, give it up! They're gone," Blair whispers, but loud enough for Jordan to hear.

"All right, all right," Jordan stops the façade, lifting her hands in surrender.

"How did you know where I lived?!"

"I told you; I know things. Perks of the job," Jordan smirks. Jordan leans in closer to Blair. "Look, I'm not here to take you to the crazy house or take you to some privileged, preppy boarding school in Wales."

"Then why are you here?"

"Earlier, you were right. My team and I don't go around telling civilians about our line of work and so far, I've told you twice."

"So…" Blair says wanting more.

"You're not normal."

"Oh, thanks," Blair says sarcastically, rolling her eyes.

"I mean in a good way, a special way," Jordan sits next to Blair trying her best to establish trust, "and once you realize it, you'll have the potential to do incredible things."

"Then, what do I do?" Blair can sense Jordan's genuineness, and she just might take her up on her offer – or maybe she's just that desperate to leave her life.

"Well, I don't know. That's up to you," Jordan said. I can't make you do anything you don't want to do. But what I do know is if you continue to live in this town with everyone judging your every move, you won't make it. You're going to do something that will be unforgivable."

Blair ponders Jordan's words. She does hate this town, especially since that incident at church.

St. Augustine's Church, where the Hahn family has attended for generations. The church holds a couple hundred people, with pews on the main floor and in the balcony. The stained-glass windows surround the building with different images depicting main stories within the bible. The antique, wooden décor of the church shows that it's been here for years. The Hahn family's reputation precedes them. They attended every church service and every charity event together, putting on the best show.

One Sunday, the pastor preached about the people needing to give their all to God, and when it's judgment day those who have followed the ways of our Lord and Savior, he himself will say, 'Well done, my good and faithful servant.' The congregation was in awe of the pastor's insightful words, except for Blair, who would rather be at home watching cartoons.

It was almost the end of service. The pastor extended an invitation to anyone in the congregation to come down to the altar and give their life over to Christ. A few members had slowly made their way down to the altar and the pastor and his associate ministers began to pray over them. Samuel glanced down at Blair, nudging her to join those at the altar. Blair was only ten years old and very timid. She didn't want to go up there in front of everyone, but the look on her father's face said he meant business. She slowly walked towards the altar, not moving as fast as Samuel would like her to. He began walking alongside her.

"Praises be to him! Samuel Hahn has come with his daughter, Blair Hahn, to support her as she gives her life over to Christ." The pastor wrapped his arms around her, as her father smiled proudly.

"Blair, do you believe in Jesus Christ?"

"Y-y-yes," Blair said, terrified.

"Do you believe He died on the cross for your sins?"

Blair nodded.

"Let Him hear you, Blair," Samuel said, giving a rehearsed smile. Blair wanted to run out of the church, but her father would never have it.

"Y-yes."

"Now we will cleanse the soul." The pastor, his associate ministers and Samuel crowded around Blair.

She was scared and she began to panic. Her father laid his hands on her shoulder and allowed the pastor and his ministers to lay their hands on her head. They began to pray over her. This wasn't the first time her father had allowed this, but he had never done it with a crowd of people watching.

As the pastor began to pray harder, the once-bright sun that glared through the church's large stained-glass windows was literally covered by a dark cloud. Blair continued to panic and then suddenly, BOOM! Lightning struck from the roof of the church to the floor next to the circle praying over Blair. Samuel, the pastor and his associates jumped apart as Blair ducked down in the middle of the floor, covering her ears with her hands. The congregation came to a halt, not knowing what happened; maybe it was a sign from God. The only people who understood what happened that day were the Hahn family, and at that moment Samuel knew he had to take matters into his own hands when it came to his daughter's abnormalities.

Blair sits at the dining table with Jordan, contemplating whether she should join her agency.

"Who else knows about me?" Blair takes the black card Jordan gave her from out of her pocket.

"Just my small team, equipped with only people I trust, and I trust very few."

"So, if I join you, I'll have to leave my entire life?"

"For a while, yes. You'll work for my agency under my supervision," Jordan says, slowly persuading her.

"When would I start?" Blair hesitates. Is she really going to trust this woman? She seems genuine and heartfelt, and anything would be better than living here, right?

"Actually, that's not up to me." Now Blair is truly confused, it's always a puzzle to solve with this woman. "This card I gave you has the location of my agency. It will only reveal the location when you're ready," Jordan points to the black card.

"But I am. I literally just said I was ready," Blair exclaims.

"No, you're ready to run away like always. When you're confident enough in yourself to take matters into your own hands and do something more with your life, I'll be there."

Blair still has her doubts about Jordan, but she knows Jordan is right about a few things. She needs to stop running and face her demons, her father. "I get it…and thanks, I'll think about it."

"I think I'll be seeing you very soon," Jordan says proudly. They smile. They have each other's trust. "Now how about we tell your parents the good news. That should keep them off your back for a little while," Jordan jokes.

"You are a saint." They both laugh, lighting up the room. "The Academy for Gifted Girls, here I come." They stand up from their seats to go talk to Blair's parents about her joining the "gifted" academy.

Chapter 5

After a day of "crime fighting" and unbearable arguments, Angel and Ashton drive to one of the most expensive hotels in Manhattan. A golden stallion fountain sits in the center of the grand lobby. Ashton parks her own car in a nearby parking garage, refusing to give her keys over to the valet. Duffle bags in hand and backpacks on their backs, they walk through the extravagant building with art deco floors and walls. Prestigious businessmen and businesswomen walk throughout the lobby.

They approach the front desk as if they stay here often. The desk clerk eyes them both, her eyes moving up and down their rugged attire.

"How may I help you?" she asks.

"We would like to book a suite for the night, please," Angel politely requests.

"Our suites run $5500 a night," the desk clerk tells them condescendingly, not believing two young women that look like them could buy a room so luxurious.

"Wow! Really?! We had no idea. WE can only afford to stay at the raggedy motel down the street but we decided, 'Hey, why the heck not, let's go to the most expensive hotel in New York and see if they'll give us a room for free'," Ashton mocks the desk clerk and Angel shakes her head, pressing two fingers onto the bridge of her nose.

Angel stretches her arm out in front of Ashton, attempting to de-escalate yet another unnecessary situation. "Yes, we are well aware of the price and are more than able to pay for the room." Angel reaches into her brown leather jacket and places a stack of cash onto the desk. She smiles, leaning closer to the clerk. "There's enough there for your tip as well."

The desk clerk takes the stack of cash, discreetly taking her cut. "Enjoy your stay here at The Swan Hotel." She hands Angel an activated room key with a chipper smile on her face.

They leave the lobby and approach the exclusive elevator for suites.

"Did you really have to give her a tip?" Ashton asks, leaning nonchalantly against the elevator wall.

Angel pays her no mind. "You want them off our backs, right? Give them a little cash and you can get them to do anything."

They ride the elevator the rest of the way in silence.

Moments later, they enter their luxury suite. Angel is exhausted from the day, throwing her duffle bags on a nearby dining table. Ashton runs around the room like a kid in a candy store.

"This was worth every shattered spine," Ashton rushes around the suite opening the kitchen fridge, bedroom drawers and cabinets.

"Sure it was," Angel is uninterested as she grabs a glass of water.

Ashton is excited about their new place for the time being and enjoyed the trouble she made to get here. Angel stands in the kitchen in silence as she stares down the pill bottle she took out of her jacket. She hates taking these pills but they're the only thing that helps with the headaches.

Ashton goes into one of the bedrooms within the suite, jumps on the king-sized bed and lays down, content with the world. "I feel like I'm lying on a fluffy cloud! You need to come feel this."

"No, I'm okay," Angel separates bricks of cash.

"Ang, you really need to relax, come on, lay with me!" Ashton continues pressuring Angel.

"I said, I'm fine, Ash."

"I'm telling you, you're really-"

"Ash! Stop it! I said I'm fine, so drop it!" Angel stops her, slamming a stack of cash on the table. Silence takes over the room. Angel instantly regrets her outburst, exhaling her frustrations.

Ashton leaves the bedroom, worried about her sister. It's normal for Angel to be annoyed with her but this is different. She's different.

"You want to tell me what that was about?" Ashton asks walking into the living room.

"Forget it."

"No. We're talking about this now."

"Leave it alone."

"What is your problem?!" Ashton snaps. "You haven't said two words to me while driving all the way up here and you can't even look at me now. I thought you'd be a little happier after how well that job went. It's like you don't even care things are finally looking up for us."

"Because I don't care!" Angel, agitated, stops fidgeting with the money in the duffle bag, finally making eye contact with Ashton the first time since arriving at their hotel. "I don't care that we stole over $500,000 dollars. I don't care that we're staying in the best hotel in Manhattan, and I couldn't care less about a bed with unnecessarily expensive sheets," she continues. This lifestyle was only supposed to last them until they had enough to make a better life for themselves, then they would live a semi-normal life.

"What are you talking about?" Ashton asks worried her sister might be serious this time about quitting their work and leaving her alone.

"This. All of this!" Angel takes a stack of money from the table and slams it down. "It's not a better life. None of this is!"

"You don't think this is better?! Okay, well how about living in a broom closet in your school because you have no place to live or sneaking into people's houses and stealing their leftovers because you haven't eaten in days? That's a great way to live, right?" Ashton reminds her of the hard times they experienced after their parents died. They've been on their own since the age of nine. "Angel, please tell me what's better, so I can find it."

Angel shakes her head at her sister, knowing she will never understand. "Why do I even try explaining anything to you? You'll never understand." Angel fights the tears ready to stream down her face. "Leave me alone."

"Will do." Ashton says in her signature sarcastic tone. She plops down on the suite's living room couch and begins pushing the remote buttons aggressively. At that same moment, loud pounding is heard at the suite's double doors.

"If that's housekeeping, can you tell them we need more pillows. I want to sleep like a baby tonight," Ashton says lounging comfortably. Then she mumbles, "At least one of us should relax tonight."

"It's not housekeeping. It's Faye," Angel replies, taking her time letting Faye in.

"Here we go," Ashton says, not moving an inch out of her comfortable position, feet propped up on the couch.

Angel opens the double doors as a fair-skinned woman with hair as black as night storms her way in, heading straight for Ashton. "You want to tell me what the hell made you turn on my guy?!"

"Faye, lovely night, isn't it? How may we help you?" Ashton says to Faye as she keeps her eyes focused on the TV screen.

"Cut the sarcastic bull, Ashton! You know exactly why I'm here!"

Angel leaves them, not wanting to deal with any more drama tonight. Ashton seems to have everything handled, right?

"Unfortunately, I don't. You see I'm pretty busy these days. You know, with fighting crimes and all for dirty cops," Ashton says, "so why don't you do us both a favor and get to the point."

Faye moves to stand in front of the TV, forcing Ashton to pay attention. "You turning on Jimmy. I brought him on to help you, but instead I get a call that him along with five others were arrested by the FBI, and they took the $1.5 million dollars."

"And yet I still don't see the problem here."

Faye sits on the edge of the coffee table to face Ashton.

"Then let me remind you. The little stunt you pulled put us all at risk. There is video evidence of your car leaving the scene seconds before the cops pulled up," Faye said.

Angel, watching the exchange from within her bedroom door frame, glances at Ashton, who returns the same worried stare. They've never been caught – at least not since taking on these higher paying jobs. Ashton sits up to make direct eye contact with Faye. Faye's words have her attention now.

"As long as we're clear on what our roles are in all of this, we should be okay, right? I mean you have all the connections with being with the Central Intelligence Agency and all." Ashton pretends to brush something off Faye's shoulders.

Faye smacks Ashton's hand away. "What are you trying to say?"

"I'm just saying if that video were to ever get out you could make it disappear. You're the expert intelligence specialist." Ashton leans back on the couch with her arms folded, knowing her threats are hitting a nerve in Faye. "Or if it were to get out and they found out it was us then…Well, you're smart. You know what would happen." Ashton gives Faye a conniving smirk.

Faye simply stands hovering over Ashton. She runs her hand through her hair and with a swift motion pulls out her pistol, barrel aiming down at Ashton. Ashton's smirk quickly erased. "Now what happens if I pull the trigger?"

Ashton stands, calling her bluff. She stands with pride, touching her forehead to the gun.

"So, you're going to shoot me now," Ashton raises her voice a few notches. "Then tell me Faye, what would happen?"

"I could kill you right here. Tell everyone from the NYPD, the CPD and the FBI that I caught wanted criminals. And I'm sure Mateo would love to hear how I handled the girls who have been stealing his money; he may even give me a promotion." Faye smiles, tightening her grip on the gun. "No one would be the wiser."

Ashton keeps her eyes trained on Faye as Angel discreetly eases her way out of the bedroom and towards the bar counter where Ashton's knives sit.

"You won't do it. You need us because you're so far deep in your own problems that you need a backup plan in case Mateo realizes you're no use to him."

"You think I need you?! I never needed you! I only took you on because of your little boyfriend and now he's gone. You were just another helpless child I could use to benefit me."

With Angel near the bar and Faye occupied, Ashton, enraged, takes the opportunity to take matters in her own hands. Ashton grabs Faye's wrist and twists as she holds the gun. Ashton then grabs Faye's neck and kicks her straight back into Angel, all in one fluid motion.

Angel holds Faye tightly against her, knife pressed to her throat.

"You don't know anything about us. We are not what you think we are, and we are not to be played with," Angel threatens.

Faye begins to turn a bright red as she holds her hands up in surrender, struggling to release from Angel's hold.

"Okay," Faye strains her voice, barely able to speak.

"Take your money and go." Angel pushes her away, releasing her.

"We don't look so helpless now, do we?" Ashton says.

Faye walks to the dining table to retrieve her portion of the stolen money. Looking back towards Angel and Ashton, she knows she's outnumbered and outpowered. She won't take the risk of fighting her way through them.

"We'll see each other soon," Faye says, leaving.

"Faye? After this warehouse job, we're done. You'll get your cut; we'll get ours and then we'll part ways," Angel says.

Faye exits the suite without another word.

There's an awkward silence between the sisters.

"You think what she said was true?" Ashton asks.

Angel exhales the deep breath she's been holding in since the exchange with Faye. "I don't know, but we have no choice but to believe her."

"I told you we couldn't trust her." Ashton flops down on the couch shaking her head.

"Really, Ash!? You want to do this now?!"

"I'm just saying that if you listened to me, we would have gotten rid of Faye a long time ago."

Angel gets ready to argue but stops herself before she says something she'll regret. She runs her hands down her face and makes her way to the other bedroom with her back turned to Ashton. "Just get the money ready so we can take it to GiGi tomorrow," she says.

Angel slams the door behind her, leaving an infuriated Ashton by herself to reflect on the day. She's so upset she pulls a knife out of her jacket and aims for a picture on the wall. "I swear, if she wasn't my sister…" Ashton is just as overprotective of Angel as Angel is over her. She would never intentionally hurt Angel, but right now, at this moment, she has the sudden urge to punch her in the face.

Just as Ashton is about to launch her knife through the irreplaceable portrait on the wall, Angel shouts from the other room, "And drop the knife!"

Ashton puts the knife down, pouting and continues working on splitting the money.

Reeling from all the stress from the day, Angel gets ready for bed. She takes off her jacket and throws it on a chair nearby. She's exhausted, not from the events of today, but of every day of her life. Angel had dreams when she was younger, but she never thought this would be the life she would now live. She gets up from the bed and goes to the bedside chair, grabbing a picture out of the side pocket of her book bag. She opens the folded picture. It's a picture of her, Ashton, their dad and their mom. She reaches down into her shirt and pulls out a black steel army dog tag, her name engraved on it. Ashton has the same one; they mean a lot to them. She holds her dog tag tightly in hand and sits in the chair, staring at the picture. She closes her eyes and reminisces about the good times she had with her family. Times when they would all sit at the kitchen table before school to have breakfast.

As Angel finally relaxes, remembering the good times in her life, she hears something shatter in the next room.

"I can fix it!" Ashton shouts, taking her knife out of the wall above the broken vase.

Chapter 6

The next morning, Angel and Ashton drive to a Victorian style home in Massachusetts. Taking their overnight bags and duffle bags of money out of the trunk, they make their way to the white picket front gate of 'Gigi's Place - Bed & Breakfast Inn', as stated on the oval-shaped hanging sign swaying high in the air above the gate. The home is blue and white with classic, white-topped turrets. Purple and yellow Angelonia and magnolias surround the front, blooming through the whitewashed porch banister, bringing a sense of a family home to its guests upon entry. Before entering, Angel stops on the porch steps.

"Can we at least act like we tolerate each other in front of Gigi? You know how she is," Angel tries to be the bigger person.

"Whatever," rolling her eyes, Ashton opens the front door.

They enter Gigi's Place, with its Creole cottage inspired interior design and polished wooden walls and staircase.

"Hi, Marie!" Angel eagerly greets the front desk attendant stationed in the middle of the foyer connecting the crowded dining room on the right and the common room on the left.

"Angel. Ashton. It's so great to see you! How have you been?! How's school?" Marie asked warmly.

Angel and Ashton glance at one another. They forget sometimes not everyone knows about their…extracurricular activities when they're not staying here at Gigi's.

"You know, same old, same old. Professors nagging you about turning in papers on time," Ashton says.

"And you know this one is always giving the professors a headache," Angel plays along, jokingly pointing at Ashton.

Marie laughs along with her, pushing up her oval glasses. Ashton keeps quiet, knowing Angel was secretly taking a jab at her.

"Well, you two have to go say 'hi' to the rest of the crew. They're in the dining room."

"Thanks, Marie. I'll come see you later," Angel says.

Angel and Ashton take their bags and enter the dining room filled with guests. They are immediately greeted with warm welcomes by many, especially Benny, the cook, who eagerly comes out from looking through the serving hatch.

"Angie! Ash! How are my two favorite girls?" Angel and Ashton hug everyone.

Over the years, they've developed a strong bond with everyone who works here at the B&B. They've only been here for seven years, and it seems like they've known them their whole lives.

"Hey Benny!" Angel greets.

"Benny!" Ashton says, excited to see one of the very, very few people she considers family.

"Ash! Your hair! Has it gotten bigger!?" an employee asks.

"Every time we see you it's like it's grown out a couple of inches," Benny tries to touch Ashton's large kinky hair.

"Yeah, I know, just don't touch it. It takes a lot of work to get this to perfection. Who am I kidding – I wake up like this!" Ashton says as they all laugh and joke like any family that hasn't seen each other in a while.

"Say that to my cramped hands. I greased that dry scalp twice a day." Suddenly, a 60-year-old southern woman who looks as young as any 30-year-old with skin as smooth as chestnut, stands in the archway of the bed and breakfast's kitchen.

"Gigi!" Angel and Ashton shout, excited to see her. They quickly turn into the little girls she will always see them as. They run to Gigi, and she hugs them both tightly. It's been a while since she last saw them – five whole months.

"We missed you!" Angel can't contain her excitement.

"Well, we have a lot to catch up on, don't we?" Gigi says.

Guests of the B&B watch in admiration as Angel and Ashton express their love for Gigi just as if she were their mother. A B&B regular, dressed in a casual business suit, watches the exchange at a nearby table.

"Hey Georgia, are these your daughters?" he asks.

"You can say that. I've raised these girls since they were 11 years old. These are my babies." Gigi lovingly wraps her arms around Angel and Ashton.

"Well, they must be well-behaved young ladies if they were raised by you," the man says and smiles as he crosses his legs and finishes his coffee, reading a financial magazine with business tycoon William Calloway on the cover.

Gigi walks Angel and Ashton inside the kitchen away from guests. Ashton looks over her shoulder, trying to figure out what this accountant-looking guy is all about. Sometimes not trusting others can make her paranoid and that's exactly how she's feeling now. "Gigi, you know him?"

"Paul? Of course! He comes here every time he has business up in New York. He works for that famous businessman, Mr. Calloway."

"There's something off about him." Ashton watches him through the kitchen serving hatch.

"You think something is off with everyone," Angel says, rolling her eyes at Ashton's accusations.

"Including you," Ashton gives Angel a sarcastic smile. Gigi notices the awkward exchange between them.

"Okay, okay, now I know it took y'all a long drive to get here and you argued the entire way. So, I want you to go downstairs and unpack and get ready for dinner," Gigi instructs them as if they'd never left.

Still reeling from their fight last night, Ashton needs some space. "I'm going to stay up here with Benny, see what he can cook for me," Ashton says.

Angel walks away, frustrated that Ashton is acting like a brat, and heads towards the door in the back of the kitchen. Gigi can sense the tension with her girls, but she doesn't speak on it, following Angel to the basement.

Angel and Gigi walk down to a cozy and modern basement, clearly made up for Angel and Ashton, like their own little apartment with wood-paneled walls and soft carpeted floors. There's a sitting area with a 75" TV on the wall and two beds on the other side of the room; it's obvious whose side is whose. Ashton's side has a rack where she keeps her knives and a variety of snacks in a mini fridge on her nightstand. Angel's side is neatly cleaned, with a desk where she cleans her guns and a picture of her parents by the side of her bed.

Angel sets one of the duffle bags on the coffee table. "The money is all there," she says nonchalantly. "It should be enough to build that greenhouse you've been talking about."

"Thank you, it will be a great addition to the gardens out back. The guests can't get enough of the indoor pool we just added. Again, thanks to you and Ash," Gigi says.

Angel goes to her desk and lays out her guns, removing the clips, blocking out Gigi as she speaks. It's clear she has a lot on her mind and Gigi knows it.

"You know, you girls are becoming more and more beautiful each time I see you," Gigi slowly tries to get Angel to speak. She always knows when something is wrong with them, and she must approach them differently. "Y'all must have had a lot of jobs to do because we haven't seen you in months. Some of the staff think you're loving college too much to come see me," Gigi jokes, hoping Angel will respond, but she's deep in cleaning her weapons. Angel isn't ignoring her purposely, but she's been through a lot the last couple of weeks. "Angie, what's wrong?" Gigi moves closer to her, attempting to get a good read on how Angel is feeling. "You and Ash are usually running off at the mouth or bickering at each other the moment you walk through those doors and today you came in with the fakest smiles I have ever seen." Gigi sits on Angel's bed waiting for a response.

Angel lets out a strong sigh and stops cleaning her gun to sit next to Gigi. "Have you ever dreamed of doing something more with your life? Like, was the B&B always the dream?" Angel asks, truly wanting advice on what to do with her future.

"No, but it was eventually. I guess you can say it fell in my lap." She moves closer to Angel. "I was born in the south, sweetie. My dream was to survive and make it out. You see, we weren't allowed in hotels, so we'd find someone, like us, that would take us in, and they would give us a nice meal before we left. That's when I knew I wanted to help people. The B&B started out in my home down in Chicago, helping people here and there." She pauses briefly staring at Angel, being careful with her next words. "But because of certain…circumstances, I moved my business here. I remember the very first person I was able to help. It was a young man living in his car, hadn't eaten in weeks. So, I gave him a place to stay, something to eat and he never left."

Angel listens to the story and quickly knows of the man Gigi is speaking of – Benny. Angel gives a soft smile; Gigi always knew how to make that happen.

"He was the first and then more came and next thing I knew I had an established business and I've been open for over 20 years." Gigi takes her loving advice a step further. "Honey, a dream is lovely, it's pretty and its magical, but it only lasts for a short time. It doesn't come true just because you dream and fantasize it."

"So, what are you saying? I can't dream of a better life for myself?" Angel asks.

"No. I'm saying it's what you do to make your dream a reality that's important. You work hard and you stay strong. Us women have no choice."

"It's not that easy," Angel says quietly.

"This isn't the first time you mentioned wanting a better life, and I can't understand how you could let those words fall out of your mouth when you have me raising you, but I can't tell you how to feel, so what is going on with you?" Gig asks.

Angel hasn't been able to look Gigi in her eyes most of their conversation. "I appreciate everything you've done for us; I don't think we would be alive if it weren't for you randomly showing up at that drug store and rescuing us from that store owner."

"But..." Gigi can feel there's more Angel wants to say as she struggles with her next words.

"I-I don't...I can't..." Angel can barely look at Gigi and she just sits there, quiet for a moment, and Gigi now knows what's bothering her so much.

"You don't want to rob anymore? Is that it?" Finally, Angel holds her head up with tears streaming down her face, pouring down onto her tank top.

"I can't do it anymore!" Angel cries out, finally releasing. "It was one thing when we were doing it to make it through, but now…it's like we're just being greedy, taking money we don't even need, and my headaches are getting worse. I can barely focus. I'm scared. I'm scared that I'm going to get us killed!" she exclaims.

"You can stop any time," Gigi symphonizes with her.

"No. I can't! Ashton tells me every day she finally found something she's good at and if I just quit on her, I-I don't know what she'll do," Angel exclaimed, standing from her bed. "And I can't lose her…I can't lose anyone else."

"You listen to me, there is nothing wrong with wanting more for your life and you don't ever have to feel bad about that. Ashton is going to have to get over it. She'll be fine. She'll be mad at you for a while, but she'll get over it. She loves you too much," Gigi comforts her.

"And that's what I'm afraid of." Angel and Ashton have never been apart once in their life and Angel, for the first time, wanting to do more with her life, is afraid to lose the only person who's always been by her side. "What if I get out there and I can't find what I'm good at it?"

Gigi stops the conversation before Angel loses all the faith she has in herself. "Let me show you something. Grab that bag."

Angel grabs the duffle bag and follows Gigi to a back room in the basement. It's a small room with a storage locker and a large safe. Angel sets the duffle bag on the nearby table and watches as Gigi unlocks the safe. When it opens, there are stacks of cash, around $800,000.

"Gigi, this is literally all the money we've given to you over the last few years," Angel is confused yet surprised.

"No, I've spent some. Where do you think that new stove and fancy sign came from?"

"Then why are you saving it?" Angel asked.

"The day I found out you and Ash robbed robbers, I wanted to kill you myself, but then you told me why you did it, so I let it go. It still didn't make sense to me because you had a roof over your head and I was feeding you. It took some time, but I understood, eventually." Gigi takes out the money from the duffle bag and puts it in the safe. "Some people would probably look at me and wonder why I let you all do the things you do, and you know what I'd say?"

"What?"

"I know my girls and they can handle anything that comes their way. They're strong, powerful, and they take care of the ones they love," Gigi continues to speak highly of her girls. "And they are so hardheaded they'd give you a headache."

"Yeah, no one could tell us nothing. Still can't, actually," Angel says jokingly.

"I've been waiting for the day that both of you, or at least one of you, would come to me and say you didn't want to risk your lives anymore. I held onto some of the money y'all gave me for a time like this, so if you want to go to school or start a business or travel the world you can do it." Gigi gives Angel the key to the safe.

"Thank you," Angel wraps her arms tightly around Gigi, embracing her for a long moment. Then she releases. "But I'm going to need some time to think about it."

"You have another job coming up, don't you?"

"It's one of the biggest hits we've done...and it just might be my last," Angel says, afraid of what Ashton might do when she finds out the truth.

"No matter what you choose, I'm always here for the both of you," Gigi says, wrapping her arm around Angel's shoulder as they walk out the room.

As they're coming out, Ashton rushes down the stairs with a plate of food in her hands.

"Are you guys coming to eat or not?" Ashton asks with her mouth full.

"Let's go upstairs before your sister eats me out of a house and business," Gigi says to Angel, laughing as they follow Ashton upstairs.

Chapter 7

Bullets ricochet off the walls and through windows of an abandoned warehouse hidden in the dark city of New York. A group of heavily built men fire their weapons at two pillars from inside the warehouse. Behind the concrete pillars are Angel and Ashton firing their weapons, going in and out of cover. They never expected to land themselves in this situation.

"So, you couldn't have seen this?!" Ashton shouts in her usual irreverent way over the loud bullets firing at them.

"Now is not the time," Angel says, trying to figure out how they'll get out here alive and in one piece. "Just give me a minute." Angel takes a second to gather her thoughts. She looks on the ground and in front of her lie bullet casings from the guns of the men. Angel picks up a casing from the floor and grips it in her hands tightly. She relaxes her body and closes her eyes. Angel's future body, also known as her astral body, now stands in front of her present form, motionless. This is Angel's world, where everything moves slow, slow enough so she can see what will happen next. Astral Angel walks around the pillar to study where each man is taking cover and their next moves. Astral Angel walks to her present form, and she's back. The men are still firing and Ashton, well…

"Ang! Angel!" she's calling for Angel's help, franticly trying to keep behind the chipped-away pillar. "I think now is the time to have a plan!" Ashton yells, getting agitated from the men firing their weapons at them.

"Follow my lead." Angel takes out another gun from the holster inside her leather jacket and quickly reloads her clips, ready to kill. Angel spins from out of cover behind the pillars with dual weapons and starts firing, shooting the men up top on the balcony, and they fall over. She's like a young assassin where her only mission is to shoot first and ask questions later. All the men have their eyes on her, which is exactly what she wants.

Ashton is on the other side of the warehouse, moving in and out behind pillars and tables with her favorite knives in hand. As Angel shoots, Ashton sneaks up behind the remaining men in cover and stabs them repeatedly, literally in the back. As Angel shoots her last man, she feels something pressing hard against the back of her head.

"Drop your weapons and kick them." She hears a deep voice, a Northern English accent, and realizes there's a gun pressed up against her head.

Angel does what she's told and slowly lays her gun on the floor.

"You are very well-known; did you know that?" the man says with a snide tone. He is a tall man with the face of a European model. He has scars across his cheek that have been there for some time. His presence would give anyone the sense that he is a boss or leader of some sorts, and that would be correct. His name is Mateo Cavanagh. He was the leader of this entire operation Angel and Ashton interrupted. They'd never met him in person. They only heard of him through Faye. Angel stands there as bold as she can be, not answering him.

"I'm partly to blame for all…this. My men tried to warn me that some girls were stealing my money, interrupting my jobs, but I thought they were out of their minds. And now I see I was wrong." He patronizes Angel. "Sully!" He calls out into the warehouse as a muscular man limps his way out from a room in the back of the warehouse to stand next him, his arm in a sling. "Is this her?" Sully limps around to come face to face with Angel.

"Yeah boss, that's her. Her and her partner attacked me and my guys after the job last week and took your money. Jimmy's working with them." He limps back to stand next to Mateo.

Ashton crouches behind a van nearby watching the exchange between the two, figuring out her next move. She immediately recognizes Muscles standing next to him. She could never forget that bruise her knife left on his neck. Ashton knows she needs to rescue Angel quickly.

"It's quite smart how you do it. Steal the money, then leave some for the police to find so they don't suspect you. It's untraceable. It's just sad we won't be able to work together. Officially that is. We could have really done some damage, you and I." He tightens his trigger finger. "Now I must turn you over. There are some powerful men who are willing to give me ten times more than what you've stolen."

Angel at this point is hoping Ashton has a plan to get her out of this.

"Where is your partner in crime?" he asks.

Angel refuses to answer. He will never get a word out of her, and she will die before she'll tell him anything about her sister.

"Answer me?!" He becomes flustered, Angel still refusing to answer. "Where is she!" he yells, enraged. He presses the gun harder to her head and moves closer to her ear. Not paying attention, he doesn't notice that his flunky is being stabbed in the chest by a knife Ashton lifted from his back pocket. She sneaks up behind Sully, covering his mouth so he doesn't reveal her position and plunges the knife deep.

"You have five seconds to tell me, or I blow your head of-" Mateo stops and begins to turn bright red, veins popping out of the side of his fully tatted neck. He's trying to gasp for air. Angel realizes what's happening, but she remains facing forward. Behind him is Ashton.

"Back away slowly," Ashton says, giving him an intense stare. Ashton is choking him using her telekinetic abilities. He does as she says and turns to face her, shocked as he sees her standing near the lifeless body of his man. He wants to speak but can't. His face begins to turn bright red as the veins in his forehead protrude out of his face. "Now give me the gun," Ashton commands. She walks towards him, and he places the gun in her hands. "You know what, you talk too much," Ashton mocks him and then frees him, but not before she snaps his arm.

"AHHHHH!" he screams in agony, falling to the ground and cradling his arm.

Angel turns around to see the damage. "It's times like this where I'm glad you don't listen to me." Angel is relieved she made it out alive. They smile at one another.

"W-What are you?!" Mateo cries out.

"Someone you shouldn't underestimate," Angel says.

"What do you want to do with him?" Ashton asks, raising her knife ready to fling it right into Mateo's chest.

"Leave him. It'll cause us more problems," Angel says.

"Unless you want to get arrested with that noodle of an arm, I suggest you get out of here," Ashton says to Mateo.

He gives her a sinister smile that sends chills down her body, but she's strong enough to not let him see her sweat. He walks away knowing Angel and Ashton won this round but it's far from over. Angel and Ashton look around the room to see their next move.

"How much time do we have?" Angel asks.

"Cops will be here in five," Ashton says, looking at her smart watch.

"You know what to do?"

"Yep," Ashton says confidently.

"All right then, let's make this quick." Angel takes leather gloves out of her jacket pocket and puts them on. She goes over to the tables lined up in the middle of the room with stacks of cash in plastic bags sitting on top. Angel is in awe of all the money she's touching, but she also continues to struggle with the thoughts of this being her last job. She shakes off the mixed feelings and focuses on what is important: the right here and now.

Ashton stands in the middle of the room, studying the dead men, and then she lifts her leather-gloved hand until one man is levitating. Ashton meticulously moves the very much dead men around the room to make it seem as though there was an argument that went terribly wrong with the group.

"Are we finished?" Angel walks over to Ashton with four duffle bags in hand.

"Just about," Ashton says, as she walks towards a deceased Sully and lays a cord beside him, along with the knife that stabbed him. "Now I am." Ashton grabs two of the duffle bags from Angel and they leave the warehouse. Ashton has an SUV parked in the back of the warehouse and they put their bags in the trunk.

"We got to move," Angel says, looking at her phone. They get into the truck and of course Ashton is driving. "Did you get the cars?" Angel asks.

"I'm sorry, have we met?" Ashton answers her sarcastically. If there's one thing Ashton is good at, it's being able to drive any vehicle.

"Okay, okay. I need to trust you more," Angel smiles.

"Yeah, you do," Ashton smiles back.

Watching as they proudly load duffle bags into an SUV is Detective Spiller, sitting beneath a dark viaduct in an all-black 2024 BMW i5. They leave the warehouse and drive to their next destination. Spiller quickly calls an unknown number. "They're on the way," she says to the person on the other end of the line.

Ashton drives through the busy streets of New York City. "I can't believe we pulled this off." This was their biggest and most dangerous job yet and Ashton knows she can do anything now; she can do no wrong. Angel, on her phone, looks at how happy her sister is, which makes it that much harder to have this conversation with her once this is all over. "The place should just be up here," Ashton points to a large parking garage. Entering the garage, Ashton drives up through the floors and parks in a space facing the city. When they get out of the car, Angel sees a parking sign: *Reserved for William Calloway.*

"You did not!" Angel says, shocked Ashton was able to even steal the SUV unnoticed. Ashton pushes the wires underneath the steering wheel back into place.

"You really didn't expect me to drive *my* car and risk it being shot up, did you? I just got it detailed!" Ashton says as they both get out of the SUV and make their way to the trunk. "I heard his building was nearby, so it was easy and the guy at Gigi's helped in his own way." Ashton smirks and grabs the bags.

"Why am I not surprised?" They close the trunk and leave to go in their separate cars.

"I'll meet you at the safe house in an hour?" Ashton asks.

"Right. No stops, be careful…please."

"Always am."

They do their unique sibling headshake and go their separate ways. As they're about to split, three men in suits approach them with guns, but they don't look like cops —more like henchmen from an early James Bond film.

"Drop the bags and put your hands in the air!" one of the men shouts.

They place the bags slowly on the ground with their hands up. Angel is suspicious of the three men because there is no way someone could have found them; they did everything right. Could Mateo have sent them?

"Ang?" Ashton whispers.

"Yeah?"

"What do we do?"

"We do what Dad would do."

Their Dad was in the military, black ops, and he taught them how to defend themselves.

"Give me your weapons, we know you got them," one of the men said, moving closer to them and revealing a silencer on the gun pointed at them.

Ashton quickly studies the men to see which one she should take out first. Her hands are up, but the moment he walks towards her, she uses her powers and sends him flying back across the garage, slamming him into a car. The remaining start to fire their weapons, but they come up short. Angel kicks the guns out of their hands. Angel and Ashton fight the men, throwing blow for blow in sync. It's beautiful – like a well-coordinated dance. These men are no match for them. They give the men one last strong punch and they're on the ground unconscious.

"Nice job," Angel says, breathing heavily.

"Thanks," Ashton replies, breathing the same.

They walk over to pick up their bags and just when they pick them up, they fall to the ground. They've been shocked with some type of device that looks like a taser, but so much more advanced. The pain hurts like nothing they've ever experienced. Ashton is on the ground unconscious. Angel tries to regain some of her strength, but when she looks up, everything is a blur. Trying to focus, she sees a slender woman, similar to the woman in her vision, alongside a man in a suit – not like the suits the three men were wearing, but much more expensive. He has a smooth, caramel-skinned complexion with a boyish, curly fade cut. He stands tall over her as his chiseled and taut muscles stick out of his white button downed shirt. Angel's vision slowly becomes clear.

"Donovan, grab the bags," Jordan says.

"What should we do with them?" Donovan asks, looking at the three men Angel and Ashton attacked.

"Nothing. Call David. He'll know what to do." Bending down in front of Angel, Jordan taunts her, "Only 18 and overpowered one of the most notorious criminals…impressive."

"We're all good," Donovan says.

Jordan stands, leaving Angel still in a great amount of pain and Ashton very much unconscious. She walks away with Donovan.

"You think that was the right move?" Donovan asks.

"Of course, it was," Jordan says. They walk up to their luxury SUV and their driver gets out and opens the door for them. "Just wait, Donovan, just wait." They leave the garage with Angel's and Ashton's money.

Angel rolls over to check on Ashton.

"A-Ash. Ash," Angel winces. Angel shakes her, trying to wake her. "Ash!" Angel shouts, giving Ashton one last push.

Ashton suddenly jumps up, breathing heavily like she had drowned and someone gave her mouth-to-mouth resuscitation.

"What the hell happened?" Ashton asks as the pain quickly consumes her.

"This woman came and tased us with something. I think it was a set-up. She knew we were here," Angel said.

"Could have been Faye."

Both struggling to stand, they help one another. "Are you okay?" Angel asks.

"I've been better." Ashton looks around the floor anxiously. "Wait…where's the money?"

Angel is dreading telling her the truth. "She took it," Angel says cautiously. Angel looks at Ashton for a reaction and there's nothing for a second until Ashton regains some of her power and flips a car over.

"Ash…" Angel wants her to calm down, still reeling from the pain.

"No, don't 'Ash' me. You're going to use your little future thing and you're going to tell me where she is and then we're going to kill her and then we're going to pay Faye a visit and then kill her like we should have done at the hotel," Ashton exclaims.

"I'm not killing anyone, and neither are you."

"And I'm not losing $750,000!" Ashton yells.

"I get it, but we're going to have to play this smart." Ashton has no patience whatsoever, but Angel's the boss, so what she says goes; that was the deal. "Let's get out of here," Angel says, limping away.

"Yeah, a hospital sounds pretty good right now," Ashton winces as they walk to her car.

Chapter 8

Daniella sits on the edge of her bed, reflecting on her life and the decisions she's made that have gotten her into this predicament. She thinks about the conversation she had with Sergeant Campbell; is she right about everything? Will she really be able to handle herself in a real prison? All these questions replay in her head.

"Vega!" Her cell doors open and there stand three guards to take her to her meeting.

If she walks out the door, she's agreeing to go to a school with some preppy, privileged kids, but if she stays in her cell, she's looking at a life full of constant surviving. She walks towards one of the guards. He cautiously handcuffs her and they leave.

The guards take her to the visitation room. It's empty except for a woman sitting at a round table in the middle of the room. It's Jordan. Daniella puts on her strongest face. She doesn't get along with or accept people with ease. It'll take a lot of convincing from Jordan to get Daniella on her side.

"We're watching you." The guard pushes Daniella towards Jordan.

She looks back at them, ready to burst out of the cuffs and punch them in their throats and make her own escape. It would be quite simple to do, but she made a promise. She makes her way towards Jordan and gets ready to sit.

"One second," Jordan holds up her index finger and stops Daniella from sitting down. "Guys, really, lose the cuffs," Jordan commands.

"Ma'am, it's for your safety that we leave those on."

"I can handle myself. Take off the cuffs."

The guard eyes Daniella while he takes off the handcuffs, making sure she knows not to try anything. He walks away and Daniella sits down in front of Jordan. Just as Jordan speaks, she sees the guards hovering in the doorway.

"Guys!" Jordan shoos them away and they exit the room, giving her and Daniella their privacy. "Those guards are pretty uptight. I would hate to be you in here." She laughs trying to make light of the situation, but Daniella sits there quietly with no expression. It's an uncomfortable silence.

"Oh, my apologies. I'm Jordan Knox. And don't worry, Sergeant Campbell told me all about you." Jordan stretches her hand out for Daniella to shake it, but Daniella only looks at it. "So, Daniella, what bought you here?" Jordan returns her hand to the other, placed on her crossed legs. Daniella is confused but mostly agitated that Jordan would ask such a question. Daniella knew the moment she walked in here this wasn't some president of a school. She looks like she's up to something, like you can't tell what's she about, but you know she has an agenda.

"I guess I'll tell you why I'm here," Jordan said. "I'm president of the top gifted academy in Wales and I would love for you to attend." Jordan can see this will be harder than she thought, she needs to switch up her approach. "Okay Daniella, I see you're not interested in anything I have to say," the tone in Jordan's voice quickly changed from a cheery school president to a boss that is all about her business, "so I'm going to be honest with you. I run an elite secret organization that could use your strength and abilities."

Now Daniella is paying attention. How did Jordan know about her powers? Is she working with the people trying to find her and take her away? Daniella wonders. She continues to stay silent, trying to figure her out.

"I know Sergeant Campbell gave you a choice to be here with me, and you sitting in front of me right now says you want better for yourself. I understand trust does not come easy, but I hope you choose to work with me because this isn't a place for someone like you. The only thing this place can teach you is how to survive. Working for me will give you stability, a stable place to live."

There's the trigger. Daniella gives a small chuckle that eventually grows into full-blown laughter. Jordan talks a big game, but she knows nothing about Daniella's life.

"May 9, 2010, I watched my father take his fist to my mother's face again and again until I could barely recognize her. October 15, 2012, I caught my mother using for the first time, she had the needle right there in her arm. She must have been doing it all day because she was passed out on the couch until the next morning. I learned how to cook for myself that day. Then there was August 16, 2019, that was…an unforgettable day. My mother turned me into the authorities for killing my father when I was nine. Guess she didn't want to take the fall for my screw-up."

Jordan sits uncomfortably in her seat as Daniella reveals the tragedies from her life. Jordan was awkwardly trying not to make eye contact with Daniella because she would just put her foot in her mouth. She can't help but feel heartache for this young woman. No one should have to go through what Daniella has been through. She's only 17 and has gone through more than most adults do in a lifetime. Daniella leans closer to Jordan, intertwining her hands together on top of the round steel table. The room is silent as Daniella looks down at her hands.

"You know kids don't ask to be here…in this world…and we damn sure don't get to choose our parents, but somehow life deals us the bad hand." Daniella looks up and faces Jordan. "A mother or father can decide to give up a child without having a single thought about how that kid is going to feel when they get older. Questions appearing in their mind like a revolving door: 'Why didn't they want me?' 'Why wasn't I good enough?' 'Is anyone ever going to love me?' 'What did I ever do that was so wrong?' All the while, they're pushing restart on their life, moving on like you didn't exist."

Jordan sits uneasily, releasing the dominant posture she had before this conversation took a turn. She takes a breath before expressing her next words to Daniella.

"This is why I want…I need…you to come join me. I'm giving you the opportunity to leave your past right there in that jail cell. You may have more privileges than all the girls in here, but you're not free. I know you don't want to be here. If you did, you wouldn't have made the effort to come see me," Jordan said. Daniella stares at her, searching her eyes for any sign of deceit, but finds none. Still, Daniella doesn't trust her enough to take the risk.

"Here," Jordan reaches into her blazer pocket and takes out a black business card to give to Daniella.

"What is this?"

"This is the location of my agency."

"It's blank."

"When you're ready to take me up on my offer and move on from this life that is holding you back, I'll be here." Jordan points to the card, hoping this sparks something in Daniella to want to join.

Daniella studies the card, flipping it back and forth in her hand. "I appreciate you coming here to talk to me. Really, I do. I don't get many visitors. Coming here to offer me a job says to me you might not be that bad of a person, but I'd rather take my chances in this prison." Daniella stands from the table and begins walking away to exit the visitation room. "At least I know what to expect with them," she says, indicating the guards who are watching her closely.

Jordan resumes her dominant posture, leaning back in her chair with one leg crossed over the other. She lets Daniella walk away and as the guards enter back into the room to take her, Jordan decides she won't leave without having Daniella at least think about her and her offer. "Not even if I can guarantee your record wiped cleaned and your freedom?"

Daniella immediately stops at the door. Could Jordan really make all her problems go away? Does she have that much power? Daniella wondered. She looks back at Jordan, beginning to contemplate her offer. She even steps back into the visitation room but shakes off her feelings and walks to the guards to be cuffed. Daniella has learned her lesson, more than she would like. She can't afford to be disappointed again.

Jordan watches as the guards remove Daniella from the room and guide her back to her cell. She keeps her boss-like demeanor intact until everyone has exited the room and are no longer in view of her.

"Damn it," Jordan curses under breath. She can't understand how she let this one get away. She stands, bracing herself by placing both hands on the table. Daniella's words ring through her head, '*A mother can decide to give up a child without having a single thought about how that kid is going to feel when they get older.*' No words have ever been more accurate. She stands, brushes off her blazer and exits the building, moving on to her next objective.

Angel and Ashton watch from a distance as Jordan leaves from the Rochester Juvenile Detention center and gets into her luxury SUV parked in front of the facility.

"You sure that's her?" Ashton says, eating a sub sandwich in the front seat of her car.

"Yep, the tire marks led me right to them," Angel says. "I can't believe you made time to make a sandwich." Angel watches her sister shove a turkey club sandwich into her mouth.

"Actually, Benny made it for me," Ashton says with her mouth full. "He knows stakeouts make me hungry."

"Everything makes you hungry," Angel jokes. "Okay, they're leaving. Let's go."

Ashton quickly wraps up the last of her sandwich, tosses it in her backseat and quickly tails them. "Who do you think she is?" Ashton asks.

"I don't know, but she either works for some powerful people or she is the powerful people." Little does Angel know that Jordan is both.

"Well, at this point I don't care who she is or what she does," Ashton says. "All I know is she's the woman who stole my money and I'll stop her or anyone who gets in my way."

Angel doesn't comment on Ashton's threat. She's used to it, but that's the problem. She wants to fight for a purpose, not for revenge.

Jordan and Donovan James sit in the back of their SUV.

"How did it go?" Donovan asks.

"Not the way I hoped, but let's hope the others are on board," Jordan says, doing business on her phone, keeping her focus on something other than her failures.

"Lieutenant, I know I shouldn't ask." Donovan has had a lot on his mind since taking on this task with Jordan.

"Then don't." Jordan is a very busy and secretive woman; the less people know the better. Even the people who work side by side with her every day, like Donovan, don't know all her plans.

"Why are you going through all of this trouble for these girls?" he asks. "What is so special about them?"

Looking up from her phone, Jordan says, "You know I can't discuss this with you. I'll tell you when it's time, trust me."

Donovan sighs loudly, fixes his suit jacket and faces the window. He hates being kept in the dark, especially when it comes to his job, but he trusts Jordan. She's done a lot for him and if keeping this information from him is for his own good, he'll trust her. "I trust you, Lieutenant."

Jordan smiles at him. She has always considered Donovan a male version of herself. His work ethic is superb and his combat skills are the best she's ever seen. She returns to working on her phone.

"Lieutenant, are we heading back to the agency?" the driver asks.

"Yes, we are, Charlie. Make a right."

"Our flight doesn't leave for another two hours." Donovan looks at his Rolex watch.

"Yeah, I know." Jordan smiles and turns her phone around to show Donovan a map of the city they're in. It shows two dotted markers: one blue and one yellow. "We're being followed," she says.

"Who is that?" Donovan asks.

"Remember our young criminal masterminds?"

"The girls at the parking garage? You put a tracker on their car," Donovan smiles. She never ceases to amaze him.

"No, that beautiful job was done by Detective Spiller. I knew they weren't going to let three-quarters of a million dollars go that easily," Jordan says.

Donovan turns around to get a good look at their car. "They had to have done a good number of jobs to be riding around in that."

"They're smart kids," Jordan says, closing out her phone. "Charlie, speed up a little and head towards the jet. The team should be waiting for us," she continues.

"What's the plan when they get there?" Donovan pulls out his gun and changes clips.

"We'll wait," Jordan lowers Donovan's gun.

Ashton and Angel slowly follow behind Jordan from afar, just enough to see where they're going.

"I wonder who she was visiting," Angel says.

"You couldn't see?" Ashton asks, referring to Angel's visions while eating a lollipop.

"No, I could only see the location she was going to. Anything inside wasn't visible." Angel sometimes becomes frustrated with her visions; sometimes they make sense and other times she has not a clue as to what they mean. Unfortunately, if she doesn't see her visions through, she becomes very sick. Medicine prescribed to her helps.

"She was probably bailing out her partner, leader of a drug cartel," Ashton predicts.

"Okay, now you're overdoing it," Angel laughs. Ashton follows Jordan's truck behind the airport.

"Now where could she be running off to?" Ashton asks.

"I don't know, but stay out of sight," Angel answers. Ashton drives away from them and parks on the side of the building.

In the airport's private tarmac, Charlie lets Jordan out of the truck and Donovan comes around to meet her. They've parked in front of a private jet.

"Where are they?" Donovan asks.

"They'll be here soon," Jordan says arrogantly.

On the side of the airport tarmac, Ashton and Angel are standing in front of their car, weapons laid out on the hood, getting ready for a possible fight. Angel reloads her gun and Ashton sharpens her knives.

"No gun?" Angel asks, loading hers.

"I want her and whoever else is with her to regret they ever stole from us." Ashton continues to sharpen her knives.

"Let's be smart," Angel says.

"I don't know any other way," Ashton says in her own irreverent way.

They leave separately, moving quietly along the side of the building, weapons non-visible. Angel is on one side and Ashton on the other.

"Do you see them?" Ashton asks Angel through her earpiece.

"I think so. They're loading some black cases onto their jet," Angel responds.

"Where is she and her posse?" Ashton asks.

"We really have to update your slang," Angel pokes fun at her sister. That's the only way she can make it through these situations.

"Ha! You're funny. Just tell me where she is!"

Angel peaks around the corner a little more. "She's near the truck with that guy who took the money."

The anger Ashton felt when she found out her money was gone has resurfaced and has turned into fury. "Good."

"Ash. Ash! What are you doing?!" Angel peaks out from cover and sees Ashton leaving her post and heading straight towards Jordan. She quickly comes out from her post to stop Ashton before she gets herself killed.

Jordan instructs her team on how to load their product onto the jet, not noticing Ashton quickly approaching her.

"Make sure those are locked and secured," Jordan instructs. "I can do without the captain nagging me today."

As Jordan turns around, a knife flies centimeters from her face and lands in the chest of one of her agents. She even felt the strong wind through her hair. Ashton quickly walks towards the truck with Angel not far behind. Ashton has her knives at her side and Angel aims her guns at Jordan and Donovan. Jordan's agents, along with Donovan and Charlie, as if on cue, get ready to fire their weapons at them.

"It's okay," Jordan says, holding up her hand to let her team know they're fine. She keeps her eyes locked on the rage-filled teens in front of her. "Well, it took you long enough. You're late." Jordan mocks the situation, removing her black aviator sunglasses and tucking them in the inside pocket of her designer blazer.

"You're pretty confident for someone who was very close to losing an eye." Angel tightens her hands around her guns. Jordan shrugs her shoulders nonchalantly.

"Comes with the job," Jordan replies.

"Who are you?" Angel exclaims.

"Excuse me, my apologies, my name is Jordan Knox. Lieutenant Jordan Knox." Jordan knows getting these girls on her side will be a much harder task.

"Lady, I don't care who you are! But I do know you're going to give us our money or things are going to get real bloody, real fast," Ashton says, fearless with rage.

"Try it," Donovan protects his boss and team, stupidly daring Ashton to make a move.

"You need to watch your mouth, Wall Street," Ashton now threatens Donovan, pointing her knives at him, ready to launch them. Strangely enough, Donovan, as young as he is, does look like he should be working in lower Manhattan, with his crisp clean designer suit.

"That's enough!" Jordan shouts at everyone on the tarmac, knowing nothing is going to get resolved if they all keep yelling at one another. "Donovan, drop the gun." Donovan and Jordan's agents do as she says, but she doesn't control Angel and Ashton. "Everyone, get on the plane. I need to talk to them alone," she says. For Jordan, it's imperative that she has all four girls working for her.

"I'm not leaving you alone with them!" Donovan moves closer to Jordan.

"Agent James, get on the plane, now! Please," Jordan demands, but with sincerity.

"I agree with your lapdog. That's not the best idea," Angel snaps at Jordan.

"Just…go, I'll be fine," Jordan calmly said to Donovan. Everyone gets on the plane. Now Angel and Ashton have their weapons locked on Jordan. "Okay, they're gone. It's just the three of us. Let's put away the guns and the knives and talk like three civilized adults," Jordan says, trying to neutralize the situation.

"You really have no idea what's going on," Ashton laughs, but this situation is far from a joke.

"I actually know pretty much," Jordan replies. As Angel watches the exchange between Jordan and Ashton, she observes Jordan, trying to find any evidence of deception. Jordan could be trying to gain their trust and then as soon as they drop their weapons, they're dead.

"If you're a lieutenant, then why tase us to the point of almost killing us?" Angel asks, defusing the situation. "I'm pretty sure that goes against everything the job entails."

"It was the only way I could get you to come find me and talk to me. You were never going to give it away freely," Jordan says, moving closer to them inch by inch.

"Are you kidding me?! Give three-quarters of a million dollars away, just like that?!" Ashton exclaims.

"And talk to us about what?" Angel asks.

"About joining my team."

"Them? I don't think so," Angel points her gun towards Jordan's agents on the plane.

"No. My lead team. A team where you can use your powers freely," Jordan moves closer to them.

Angel and Ashton look at one another, their confidence and anger turning into fear. The last time someone knew about their powers, it involved their parents dying.

"H-How do you know that?" Angel stutters.

Jordan attempts to walk closer, raising her hands up slowly in surrender. They hold their weapons tighter. Angel's palms begin to sweat.

"I can't disclose that information, well, at least not right now," Jordan says, "but if you join me, I promise I will tell you everything…eventually."

"Ang, she's lying. Let's just get the money and go." Ashton is anxious.

There's a feeling about Jordan that Angel can't shake; it's a tingling feeling she usually has when she's close to a vision.

"Ashton, you're a TK, and Angel, you're an Astral," Jordan whispers. This isn't how the plan was supposed to go, but time is wasting, and she needs them. Angel believes Jordan enough to drop her guns. Ashton doesn't like the thought of someone she's never met knowing about the most private thing about her. She raises her knife towards Jordan, ready to launch. Angel lowers Ashton's hand. "I don't know how strong you are, but I know you're gifted, and your talents can help a lot of people," Jordan feels it's safe to approach them.

Angel holsters her gun. She isn't sure if this is a sign, but she's willing to take the risk. "Does the job pay?" Angel asks.

Ashton can't understand how Angel could fall for Jordan's lies. She paces back and forth, shaking her head and getting agitated listening to the exchange between them.

"You'll go through rigorous training in the beginning and then once that's completed, depending on level, we'll work out a stipend." It seems Jordan is finally getting through to them until Angel looks over to Ashton, wanting her support.

"Are you crazy?!" Ashton screams. "You don't even know who this woman is!"

"Ashton, I promise this is completely legit," Jordan tries to reassure her.

"You promise?! I don't know you! The first time we met, you almost killed me!" Ashton shouts at Jordan.

"Ash…," Angel rests her hand on Ashton's shoulder, wishing she would calm down. Ashton snatches her shoulder away.

"No, Angel! You're so desperate to leave this life behind that you're willing to trust someone who just robbed us! You can stay here and listen to this, but I'm taking my money and leaving." Ashton doesn't wait for Angel's response. She draws her knife towards Jordan, walking towards her with aggression and rage. "Where is it?!" Ashton forces her knife on Jordan's neck. Jordan is relaxed as Ashton presses the tip of the knife deeper into her jugular. Jordan could easily confiscate the knives from Ashton, but she refuses to hurt her.

"In the trunk," Jordan answers.

Ashton keeps her focus on Jordan. She opens the trunk, puts her knife away and leaves the tarmac with the four duffle bags in hand.

"I know it's hard when the ones you care about don't understand you," Jordan says, empathizing with Angel.

"Look, there may be some truth to what you're saying but leave my sister out of it."

"Okay, but Angel, you have skills that took my men years to develop." Jordan moves closer to Angel, establishing trust. She reaches into her blazer pocket and gives Angel one of her black cards. "Take my card and come find me at this location," Jordan says. "If you find it, then I know you're ready." Angel tries to process everything that just transpired.

"And I'm just supposed to trust you?" Angel asks.

"That's up to you," Jordan says, walking away. She gets on her plane, leaving Angel to study the blank black card in her hand.

Chapter 9

Daniella lays down with her back against a bookshelf in the rear of the detention center library. She's not supposed to be here, but when has Daniella ever listened to anyone? She always comes here to think, escape to another world away from her own reality. Daniella tries to focus on her reading but can't help thinking about Jordan and her offer. Using the black business card as a bookmark, she moves the card around the pages.

"What are you trying to do?" she says quietly to herself, knowing Jordan must be up to something.

Suddenly, she overhears two whispered voices outside the library. She can't make out the voices or their looks from where she's hiding, so she quietly eases her way through the aisles of the library to get close enough to observe. Standing near the entrance of the library is Warden Perry and C.O. O'Neal. Daniella kneels and peaks through a set of history books as the two men stand close to one another, keeping their conversation private.

"And you're sure they're going to pay us when we make the drop?" C.O. O'Neal asks Warden Perry.

"Once we put Vega on the van for transport to the facility, that'll be the delivery. They'll stop the van on the way and take her. All we have to do is report that she tried to escape, and we had to shoot her down. It's simple and we get paid," Perry explains.

"Good. We need this," C.O. O'Neal says.

"Make sure this stays between us. I don't need Campbell finding anything out about her golden child," Warden Perry says.

C.O. O'Neal nods. "I'll go make the call." He leaves first with Warden Perry waiting a few moments before he follows.

Just as he leaves, he senses someone watching. He looks behind him, scanning the room. Daniella quickly lays down on the floor, hiding behind all the books on the bottom shelf. She takes in a breath, not making a sound. He eventually leaves, thinking he's being paranoid.

Daniella lays on the floor a few minutes more before coming out of hiding. She paces the aisle anxiously, biting her lip and shaking the sweat off her hands. Warden Perry has always had it out for her. He hates how Sergeant Campbell comes to visit frequently to check on Daniella, giving her special treatment and undermining his authority in front of his officers and the other girls. Daniella can't understand how the men who have been chasing her all this time have found her. Why do they want her so much? she wondered. Daniella knew she was never safe in here and she needs to find a way out now. She instantly thinks of the black card Jordan gave her and the school pamphlet with a number on it. She takes both the card and the pamphlet out from the inside of her forest green jumpsuit, finds the number, and makes her way behind the desk of the library to use the phone. Daniella dials the number, and it takes a moment for the line to pick up.

"Hello?"

"President Knox?" Daniella cautiously says Jordan's fake title.

"Daniella?" Jordan is only a little surprised to hear from her so soon. She sits in the back of her private jet for privacy.

"Yeah…bet you didn't think I would call so soon?"

"Honestly, I didn't think you would call at all. What's going on? Did you change your mind?" Jordan asks. Daniella peaks at the entrance, making sure no one appears.

"I can't talk about it right now, but yes, I accept your offer." Daniella taps her foot and bites her lower lip nervously hoping Jordan didn't change her mind.

"That's great Daniella, but are you sure?"

"Yeah, yeah, I'm sure," Daniella says, peeking towards the entrance once more. "So, umm…How soon do you think I can get out of here? You know – with my record cleaned like you said."

"Umm…Just a phone call away. I can have it wiped by the end of today," Jordan says, worried something is off with Daniella. She's talking a lot more than when they met, more troubled.

"Cool. Thanks. That should work."

"Daniella, are you sure everything's okay?"

"Oh yeah. Just ready to get out of here, you know?" Daniella said.

"Okay, then. Just make sure you're ready. That's the only way you'll find the location."

"Of course. I got to go. Talk to you soon." Daniella quickly ends the call with a bit of hope that maybe Jordan can protect her. She safely puts away the pamphlet and the black business card. She sneaks her way back to her cell, freezing C.O.s along the way.

Ashton is leaning on the driver's door eating her leftover sandwich.

"I thought you were leaving," Angel says, though she knows Ashton would never.

"Trust me, I thought about it. Even put the keys in the ignition, but you owe me gas money and if Gigi found out, I'd never hear the end of it," Ashton says. Angel dismisses her sister's smart aleck remarks as she unloads the clips from her guns and stores them in the trunk.

"Let's just go home," Angel says. They leave the airport. The silence and tension in their car is so thick you could – well you know the saying.

They drive to their "home" in Boston, Massachusetts. In a dark, suburban, residential area, Angel and Ashton walk into an old home with a foreclosure sign on the front door. This home is vacant, but one wouldn't know by the freshly cut grass and neatly trimmed bushes. The neighborhood is quiet and there aren't too many people – mostly elders, so it's quite peaceful. Angel and Ashton don't come back here often, but when they do, it's always at night so as not to draw attention. The house next door is owned, but the residents don't live there anymore; they died tragically.

Angel and Ashton walk into the home they obviously don't own, arguing.

"The fact that you're even entertaining this woman is blowing my mind," Ashton expresses as Angel tries to ignore her while they walk into the 'home' they call their own. The house is fully furnished, but the home is empty – empty of love and warmth from a family. This is just a home to sleep in.

"What if she's telling the truth? We can both get something out of this. We're going to get paid for the exact same thing we're doing now. Don't you at least want to hear her out?" Angel wants to take the risk and follow Jordan up on her offer, but only if Ashton is by her side.

"No, what I want is my money! You might not care, but I like what I do, Ang. I can do and get anything I want with the flick of my wrist! Literally! I like the chase; I like the rush. Why can't you see it my way!?"

"Because there's more to life than stealing!" Angel says. "You're 18. It's not even possible to do this your whole life. You're going to get caught eventually." Angel throws the duffle bags on the old kitchen table.

"So, you can trust a woman who almost killed us, but I can't steal money that's already stolen?!"

"What!? Are you even listening to yourself!?" Angel always knew Ashton liked to rob, but she never would have thought it would become an addiction.

"Me!?" Ashton speaks sharply. Angel and Ashton continue to argue, walking upstairs. Angel goes into her room, Ashton following behind her. "You are trusting a complete stranger!" Ashton shouts.

"She knows our names and she knows about our powers. That doesn't sound like a stranger to me." Angel sits on her bed.

"And so did the people who killed Mom and Dad." Ashton tries to get Angel to understand why she doesn't trust this woman. This argument is getting out of hand, and Angel needs to tone things down and speak to Ashton like the adult she tries to be.

"After everything that just happened with that last job… yeah, we got away, but barely. Next time it might not turn out that way," Angel speaks to her softly.

"But now we know what to expect, for next time." Ashton knows Angel hasn't been as enthusiastic about these last couple of jobs as she used to be when they first started. She feels Angel is slipping away from her, but Angel has reached a breaking point. She's trying hard to hold it together, but it doesn't take long before all her emotions just start flowing out.

"Next time?! Ash, I can't do it anymore!" Angel cries out. Ashton can't believe they're back on this, but this time is different; Angel is serious. "It's too much," she cries. The room is silent. They realize the conversation has taken a turn and neither can go back.

"So, this is it." Ashton realizes it's over. They're parting ways for the first time in their lives.

"Tomorrow I'll be leaving, and I would really love for my sister to be right there with me," Angel says, hoping something will get Ashton to change her mind.

Ashton stares at Angel, eventually walking out of Angel's room in a sullen state.

Chapter 10

I can't believe you're leaving me!" Michelle rummages through Blair's organized closet, helping her pack. She doesn't like the idea of her daughter leaving the nest so soon, but she is overjoyed Blair is taking part in such an amazing opportunity.

"Mom, I'll be fine. I'll meet new people and I'll learn… new things." Blair is in her upstairs bedroom packing for the job she has with Jordan, but to her parents she's packing to leave for boarding school today. Samuel gave Blair her room back the night she decided to go to the 'academy' with 'President Knox'.

"I know. I just didn't think you would want to leave so soon. School doesn't begin for another four months," Michelle says.

"Well… I want to get used to the place, find my classes, meet my professors, that sort of thing," she's trying her best to keep up with the secrecy.

"And she's ready to apply herself, change for the better." Samuel stands in the doorway of her room. For the first time in a very long time, he's proud of his daughter.

"That I am, Dad," Blair is sarcastic in her tone.

"You've really made your mother and me proud," Samuel walks into her room and grabs Blair's face and kisses her forehead.

"You know I will always love you; you know that?" he says sincerely, in his own way. Blair nods her head in this awkward exchange. Her father trying to show any sign of sincerity makes her skin crawl. She hugs him back, hoping the moment will quickly pass.

"I figured it was time to focus less on my abilities and more on my studies." She continues packing, making sure not to make eye contact. "And President Knox made a good argument. Plus, after that voicemail you sent, it really put a lot of things in perspective."

Michelle has not a clue about the voicemail Blair mentioned. "I'm sorry, sweetie, but I never sent you a voicemail. I figured you would've calmed down and come back home like you always do," Michelle says, puzzled.

Blair realizes this has Jordan written all over it. She probably switched her phone at some point when they were talking at the pub. "Oh… umm... I probably had a dream about it or something," Blair tries to revert the conversation.

"Will Ms. Knox be sending a driver for you?" Samuel asks.

"No, I called a car and she'll pick me up at the airport," Blair's lies continue to grow. This is becoming a bit too easy. More like a habit, but she doesn't know where Jordan is or how to get in contact with her.

"That's really nice of her," Michelle says. Blair checks the time on the clock above her canopy bed. She still hasn't figured out the location of the agency Jordan mentioned, and she has to be there soon according to the mountain of lies she's already told her parents.

"So…I'm really glad to have you guys in here to help me, but since I won't see my room for a couple of years, I'd like to be alone with…you know…everything," Blair rushes her parents out.

"We understand. Just don't leave without saying goodbye to your brother and sister," Michelle caresses her cheek, feeling honored to be her mother.

"I left a gift for you on your desk. You can open it now or when you're on the plane," Samuel pats her on the shoulder. She watches as her parents leave the room. Closing the door immediately, she stops packing and goes over to her desk to fiddle around with the black business card Jordan gave her.

"Okay, I'm ready, I'm ready," Blair repeatedly says to the card thinking something would appear, but nothing. She looks at the card for a while but gets antsy, so she lays it down. Blair sees the expensive velvet black box her father left for her. She opens it to find a solid gold bracelet with jaded beads. The jade stone is from her father's country. It's rare and precious and she's always loved the color. Why would he put so much thought into this gift? It isn't like him, but she loves it. Tears begin to fall but she wipes them away. She carefully puts the bracelet on and picks up the black card once again. She stands and holds up the card towards the light and sees nothing. She then takes a penny and tries to scratch the location off and once again, nothing. Blair paces back and forth in her room. She's getting agitated. Blair balls up the card and throws it on her desk.

At that exact moment, she happens to glance and the film on the card pokes out. She bends it back to its original state, removing the film to reveal text that reads:

'Place on Wall'

Blair follows the instructions and places the card on the wall nearby and it sticks on the wall like a small projector screen. Light shines and a hologram of Lieutenant Jordan Knox is revealed.

"Great, so if you're watching this it means you've fiddled and worked your way through my card long enough to realize you're ready for something new."

"Wow, she was serious," Blair realizes everything Jordan said was true.

"Come to this location and begin your new journey," hologram Jordan points down to a holographic address located in Chicago.

Blair quickly types the address in her phone and puts the black card in her pocket. She closes the last of her suitcases and makes her way downstairs. "Mom! Dad! My car is here!" Blair shouts. She hugs her siblings and leaves her home for an interesting new adventure.

"Blair!" Michelle runs out of her front door to catch up to Blair opening the back passenger door of a Lincoln Continental.

"Mom, what's wrong?" Michelle hugs her daughter once more, this time so Blair can hear her next words. Michelle turns her back to the front door where Samuel stands.

"Be careful. I know who she is," Michelle whispers in Blair's ear. Blair tries to break away, but Michelle only holds her tighter. "Listen to me Bibi. I need you to remember everything I've taught you. Stay focused, stay calm and you will be in control. You are stronger than you think." Michelle releases her hug and holds Blair's face in her hand. "I'm so proud of you." Blair gets in the back seat of the car, unable to comprehend how her mother could have known about Jordan. It's only another secret coming out from the Hahn family.

Daniella lays on her bunk for a final time. She looks over every inch of this room, reminiscing about most of the time she spent crying in her bunk, punching holes in the walls by the door and staring blankly out the small window, dreaming about a day like this when she's free.

"Vega!?" A correctional officer comes to take her out of her cell, "Time to go," she says. Daniella grabs her notebook and rushes to the door with her hands stretched out, waiting for her to slap the cuffs on one last time.

"Not this time," the C.O. says with a hint of a smirk almost spreading across her face.

Daniella is surprised but she won't argue and walks away with the C.O. She can't help but glance back at her cell one last time. Finally, out of her every day, hideous, green jump suit, Daniella makes her way to the entrance of the all-girls Rochester Juvenile Detention Center. She's dressed in the same clothing as when she first arrived. Black high-top sneakers, worn out dark blue jeans, a wrinkled black t-shirt under a red bomber jacket, small gold hoop earrings and a gold chain with the letter "D" charm. The clothing is slightly loose since she didn't eat as much while being here and had some added stress.

"Is there someone here to pick you up?" the clerk asks as Daniella signs the last of the paperwork.

Daniella nods and a smile slowly spreads across her face, "Yeah."

The clerk returns the smile, understanding how Daniella feels in this moment, and gives Daniella the book bag she first arrived with. "Don't come back."

Daniella turns away from the clerk's window to exit. As quickly as the smile came upon her face, it quickly vanishes as she sees who is leaning against the entry doors.

"I didn't think you could do it," C.O. O'Neal says, standing upright and approaching Daniella with such intimidation. Daniella refuses to reply as she tries to move around him to leave, but he only blocks her path. He discreetly takes her arm and pushes her out of the building into the vestibule. Once they're out of sight, Daniella snatches her arm away from him. "I don't know how you got Campbell to get you out of here, but you'll be back." His expression is mean, surly. He lowers his voice to a whisper, "You think we won't find you? We know everything about you."

Daniella, as always, doesn't speak. She learned some time ago that the moment you speak is the moment trouble comes. She stares at him, her rage slowly taking over. Daniella wants to shut him up with her fists but he's an officer and she's a foot away from never seeing this place again. Also, over his shoulder is Erica Campbell pulling up to the entrance.

"This-"

"O'Neal!" C.O. O'Neal is interrupted by the sound of Warden Perry standing inside the doorway of the vestibule. "Leave her be." O'Neal stares down at Daniella, reminding her that she'll never be as free as she may think. He walks away and Daniella immediately leaves, not looking back. She opens the door but not until Warden Perry has the last word.

"Good luck, Miss Vega. We'll see you soon," he says in a sneering tone.

Daniella exits the building, not putting much thought into their empty threats. Taking her first steps outside, it's as if no one is around. Peaceful and content, Daniella closes her eyes and embraces the fresh air for the first time in four years. She's been let out for recreational purposes before, but nothing compares to the strong winds, the sounds of house sparrows flying through the sky and the sun beaming on her butterscotch skin. Sergeant Campbell leans against her car enjoying the calmness she sees come over Daniella.

"So, this is it?" Campbell says.

"I guess so."

They get in her car and drive away from the detention center, never to see it again.

"You look happy." She's never seen Daniella this relaxed, this open.

"…I am," Daniella smiles.

"What were O'Neal and Perry talking to you about?" Campbell asks.

"Oh that? O'Neal was just upset that he won't have anyone winning his boxing matches anymore."

"I thought we agreed you would stop that," Campbell said.

"Yeah, well, it was an easy way to keep the guards off my back."

"You don't have to worry about that anymore." They glance at one another and smile.

They drive in silence for a moment.

"You're not even going to ask me how I got out with a clean record?" Daniella knows Erica Campbell; she's nosey and loves to keep tabs on her. Sergeant Campbell keeps her eyes on the road and a smile slowly creeps across her face.

"No. I know the lieutenant or at least know of her and when you have been in my line of work for as long as I have, you learn not to ask…certain questions," Campbell says, remembering her private call with Lieutenant Jordan Knox just before talking to Daniella that night in the mess hall. "But I trust that whatever the Lieutenant has you doing, it will be good for you."

"You never stop surprising me," Daniella says, and they both snicker at the comment.

"I want to thank you," Campbell says, continuing to drive.

"For what? I should be thanking you."

"For trying something new. I know how hard it was for you to take that meeting."

"You have no idea," Daniella whispers to herself.

"Well, you'll be missed," she smiled. Daniella, even though she's never said it, is grateful for Erica. She would have never thought the woman who found her hiding in a closet that horrendous night would still be by her side today. "Oh, I have something for you. It's in there." Daniella opens the glove compartment and pulls out a small, thick, white envelope.

"What is it?" Daniella asks.

"Open it." Daniella opens the envelope and takes out a large sum of cash -- $3,000. Daniella flips the cash through her hands. She must be hallucinating; she's barely had $30 in her pocket, and now she has $3,000. "You've been through a lot, being taken away from your parents, going from foster home to foster home and then to juvie. Anyone would have gone mad or just given up," Erica continues as she parks in front of a shopping district. "I tried my best to be there to help you, but you didn't need me. You've stayed strong, and I am so proud of you. I figured this was the least I can do." Daniella is at a loss for words. No one has ever cared for her as much as Sergeant Erica Campbell, and because of this it's hard for her to express every emotion she is feeling at this precious moment.

"Thanks. I mean thank you…so much. And I promise I won't let you down." Daniella doesn't do the hugging thing, but Campbell knows she's grateful.

"So, am I taking you to the airport?" Campbell asks.

"You know what? That's okay. I haven't been outside those four walls in years, I just need to take it all in for a second. I'll find a way soon. Plus, I need some decent clothes." They both laugh. This is true for Daniella. She hasn't seen the outside world in a long time, but she hasn't found the location from this blank card yet, so she doesn't even know where she's going.

"You can just drop me off here." Daniella gets out of the car in front of a small boutique. "Well. This is it," Daniella says knowing how much she'll miss Campbell.

"No, I'll see you soon, but if I don't hear from you, I will hunt you down," Campbell said. They have one last good laugh with each other before they go their separate ways. "Just do me a favor and please be careful. Call me if you need anything."

"I will." Daniella steps back from the car and watches her leave. As soon as she's far enough away, she takes the black card out of her pocket and tries to find the location of the agency. "Okay Knox, just tell me where to go," she says to the card as she walks down the congested sidewalk. She gets annoyed and puts it in her pocket, but she's bumped by a pedestrian on their phone. A large breeze blows it out of her hand and Daniella chases it down an alley behind a restaurant. When she picks it up, the card is damaged; it's ripped and covered in dirt. She wipes away the dirt and then sees a piece of film. She removes it and reads the text:

'Place on Wall'

She checks her surroundings and places the card on the wall within the alley. The holographic image of Jordan appears, telling her to come to the address in Chicago. "Not what I expected, but okay." Another shocking discovery from Jordan, but Daniella will take her word for it. Removing the card from the wall, Daniella makes her way to a small boutique to purchase new clothes and a duffle bag to put them in. She then calls a cab.

"Airport."

"Where to?" the cab driver asks.

"You wouldn't believe me if I told you," she replies.

Angel barely slept last night. She tossed and turned. She and Ashton argue but this one was different. She gets up from her bed, hoping Ashton is awake and has changed her mind, but when she opens the bedroom door Ashton is nowhere to be found. It's as if Ashton never slept there last night. Angel rushes downstairs to see if Ashton's car is in the garage, but that's gone, too. A feeling of frustration and maybe some regret comes over her. How could Ashton just leave and not even so much as give her a goodbye?! At this exact moment, Angel realizes her relationship with her sister might never be the same. She remembers the talk with Gigi. She must move on with her life no matter how much Ashton might hate her now. Angel goes to her barely furnished room and starts packing. She packs all her clothes, which isn't much since she and Ashton are always on the go. They tend to keep the materialistic items to a minimum. Angel, with her bags, leaves the house. Coming down the porch steps, Angel hears a familiar voice at the home next door.

"Yes Gigi, we'll be gone a while. I'm not sure for how long. Yes! I'll apologize." Ashton sits on the trunk of her car, feet dangling. Angel cautiously walks to her, not knowing what to expect. "Here she comes now," Ashton puts the phone on speaker for a confused Angel to hear.

"I want to hear from you both every day," Gigi says. Angel looks to Ashton, trying her best to contain her excitement. "I don't care if it's a call, text or letter. I need to know you're okay or I'll find you and we don't want that. Take care of each other because all you have is each other. I love you."

"We love you, too," Angel and Ashton say together as they hang up the phone.

"It's about time you woke up," Ashton says to an excited Angel. She loves that Ashton finally listened to someone other than herself.

"Does this mean what I think it means?" Angel grins from ear to ear, waiting to hear Ashton say she was right. Ashton hates Angel's 'I told you so' demeanor.

"I listened to what you said, and you were…" Ashton struggles to say it.

"Go ahead, say it," Angel says, still grinning.

"You were right, I need to start doing better and I want to help you," Ashton puts Angel's bags in the trunk.

"Aww…you're growing up." Ecstatic, Angel grabs her little sister's face and starts kissing her cheeks. Ashton tries to push her off.

"Get off of me!" Ashton playfully pushes her sister away. Angel laughs as they get in the car.

"Did you get everything out of the house?" Angel asks.

"Every weapon he left," Ashton says speaking of their father. "Where are we going anyway?" Ashton continues.

"She said when we're ready to leave, the card will reveal the location." Angel takes out the black card Jordan gave her.

"Oh great, an undisclosed location, I've always wanted to go there," Ashton says in her own irreverent way.

"I'm sure it's fine, we just have to sit here and…wait." That's a bad idea since Ashton is incredibly impatient. They wait for several minutes, Angel flipping the card back and forth, around and around, trying to trigger something, anything.

"Let me see this." Ashton snatches the card out of Angel's hand, her lack of patience getting the best of her.

"Ash! What are you doing!?" Angel exclaims as she watches Ashton take out her knife and place the card on the dashboard, banging the butt of her knife on top of it. "Seriously!" Angel snatches the card back.

"You weren't doing anything," Ashton says. As Angel inspects the damage Ashton made on the card, she sees a piece of the card torn at the top. At a closer glance, the layer of film is shown. She pulls it back and it reveals the text that says:

'Place on wall'

They quickly get out of the car and go inside 'their' home.

This home is the house next door; the home of the residents that died tragically. This was once the Cross family home until that tragic night. Angel and Ashton made a vow to keep it in the family no matter the cost. They took it upon themselves to purchase their home, making a promise to their parents that they'll always be together. Every room is pristine, not an ounce of dust on the coffee table or art hanging on the walls. Before Angel and Ashton go further into their home, they take off their shoes at the front door, leaving them on the large 'Home, Sweet, Home' mat. They place the card on the wall of the foyer. The card sticks and light shines from the card revealing Jordan.

"Angel. Ashton. I'm so glad you've decided to join me. If you're watching this, it means you've fiddled and worked your way through my card long enough to realize you're ready for something new." Jordan then points to the address of the location. "Come to this location and we can begin." The card abruptly closes. Angel and Ashton are silent, both amazed.

"I…guess we should go then," Angel says. They rush to get in their car, but before Angel leaves their home, she breaks a piece of wood from the door frame of the house. She takes it with her so she can always watch over this home. It means a lot to both her and Ashton. The fearless but stubborn girls are ready to take this new journey with Jordan, but is she ready for them?

PART II – Welcome to Exodus?

Chapter 11

Underground in a suburb just out of the busy city of South Side Chicago, Illinois, lies Exodus, although no one would ever know. Exodus is a new and improved sub-division for the CIA. It's only been two years since its opening and not much has been accomplished. Prior to her opening, Jordan put all her focus, time and energy into finding Angel, Ashton, Blair and Daniella. They are the sole reason this Exodus exists. The agents who previously worked for the CIA aren't as skilled as Jordan would like for them to be and the new director pressuring her for results isn't helping matters either. Unfortunately, she has other problems to handle, like figuring out when it's the right time to tell her now co-director, Captain David Lawrence, she's bringing in four girls with psychic powers to work for them. Unknown to Jordan, the new director will make a surprise visit to the newly designed agency.

Inside his office of the Exodus Agency is Captain David Lawrence. He stands tall in front of his full-length mirror. He can cast a shadow that could fill a room. He's in his modern office, as sophisticated as only he can be, adjusting his designer tie while practicing a speech.

"Hello Director Warren, thank you for seeing me—" he says to himself. "No, no. Welcome, ma'am. As you can see, Exodus is doing very well since you last saw us and—" He tries to continue. Everyone plays their role. Jordan handles the espionage and operations, and it's clear Captain Lawrence handles the politics, which is a job no one wants. If the director does not like what she sees, Exodus could be over before it even starts and then Jordan would be back to square one. "No. Hello, Director, the agency is thriving in more ways than one—" he says to himself until medical genius Dr. Seth Nolan bursts into his office, interrupting his nervous speech.

"Captain, the director is here," Seth said, brushing off his wrinkle-free, blue cardigan vest.

"Thank you, Seth." Captain Lawrence adjusts his tie up to his muscular neck one last time. He then grabs his black suit jacket from the couch arm nearby and puts it on, his brawny physique showing through. They make their way through the agency, which is filled with the most technologically advanced equipment the government's money could buy.

"All agents have passed their physicals, sir," Seth says, hurrying alongside.

"Did you check their tags?" Captain Lawrence asks, looking at the tablet Seth gives him.

"Yes. Everyone should be able to enter the facility easily, but there is a problem with their detection option."

"All right, well, get it done," Captain Lawrence commands.

Seth Nolan is a 17-year-old medical genius, graduating at the top of his class at Johns Hopkins University at just fourteen years old. The CIA then recruited him to join their medical facility and Jordan had to have him on her personal team. He was ecstatic to join.

"Yes, sir. But Captain, do you mind if I ask you a question?" Seth asks nervously. "That depends," he answers.

"Do you think it's an appropriate time for the director to be here? We just opened and we haven't been on that many missions, and the agents we do have aren't as skilled as the lieutenant would like for them to be and…" Seth quickly spoke.

David stops and places his hand on Seth's shoulder to relax him. Perspiration begins to appear from his jet-black curly fade to his light caramel forehead. "Seth, the lieutenant and I are handling everything, but right now all I need from you is to do your job and let us worry about keeping that woman happy."

Seth is relaxed and he continues to follow Captain Lawrence down the hall. "Okay sir, but I do have another question, i-if you don't mind?"

"Yes Seth, what is it?" Captain Lawrence exhales.

"Does the lieutenant know you're meeting with the director today?" This catches Captain Lawrence's attention. Jordan and himself haven't been on the best of terms since he left her behind to go work for the CIA again. He never stopped thinking about her and when he found out she wanted to reopen Exodus, he wanted to be a part of it. Thankfully, she agreed, but both had different reasons for him coming back into her life.

"No and it is best for all of us she doesn't," he says looking around hoping she isn't near.

"Yes, sir. Good luck," Seth says, walking away from the conference room.

David wipes the shine from his brown, bald head with a handkerchief he pulled out of his suit jacket. He pulls his shoulders back and stands tall. "Welcome, ma'am," he says, walking into the large conference room, able to fit more than a dozen people.

"David, I told you about calling me ma'am. I'm not my father," she says, not facing him. "Only he liked the pleasantries."

"My apologies, Crystal."

Director Crystal Warren, daughter of the late Director Radcliff, has an intimidating presence about her, like Jordan. She holds a lot of power, and everyone knows it, but outside of the designer dresses, she's quite sympathetic. She stands bold, looking out the large bullet-proof glass window surrounding half of the conference room, which overlooks the operations floor of Exodus. She wears a designer forest green dress that accentuates the curves of her body and brightens up her fair olive skin tone. Heels make her five inches taller than her normal 5"5 height and gold jewelry reveals her luxurious lifestyle.

"David, I hope my money is being put to good use here," she says.

"Absolutely. The agency is thriving. Our agents are improving every day and-" Captain Lawrence says, reciting the speech he practiced repeatedly, but Director Warren isn't pleased.

"I would like to believe that David, but the rest of the board and I aren't seeing results," she says, now directly facing him.

"Director, I can reassure you, you haven't wasted your time with us, but it does take time training the new agents you and the board recommended," Captain Lawrence explains. When Director Warren and the CIA board gave Exodus new agents, David and Jordan expected them to be top notch, the best of the best, but unfortunately all they were good for was aiming a gun. They would have been better off at a training facility, but unknown to David, Jordan needed this as a cover-up for the girls. These agents are expendable.

"This agency was not built as a training center," Director Warren exclaims.

"I know that, and you know that, so what is the problem?" Captain Lawrence's frustration is beginning to take over.

"When you came to the board wanting to reopen an agency that was in shambles, they all thought you and Lieutenant Knox had lost your minds, especially my father," Director Warren continues. "No one trusted you to uphold an agency, but then Lieutenant Knox," Director Warren points down to operations where Jordan is directing and commanding people to do tasks, "gave me a proposition that I couldn't deny, and I fought everyone to help you open this place.

Now I refuse to have my reputation and name tarnished because you can't do your damn jobs."

"I understand, but the lieutenant and I are doing great work here. You have to trust us on this," he says, approaching her near the window.

"Right now, trust is wearing thin." Director Warren walks towards the intercom on the wall. "Lieutenant Knox, come to the conference room, please."

Jordan, being the boss, is giving orders to different agents and scientists in operations. Located on the main floor of the agency, it holds a very large screen, about the size of a jumbotron, showing data about the crimes going on in the world.

"Not now," she answers, not paying attention to who called her name. "I'll get to you when I can."

"Lieutenant! Do you realize who you're talking to?" Director Warren shouts over the intercom. Jordan stops and looks up to see Director Warren with a stern look. Jordan nods in agreement and leaves but can't help to give more orders.

"I want those labs on my desk, now!" Jordan walks into the conference room, surprised Director Warren is here.

"Good afternoon, Director." They all sit at the large, polished-wood, oval table.

"Lieutenant Knox. Captain Lawrence and I were just discussing the future of this agency," Director Warren says.

"Okay…and what's in the future for us?" Jordan puzzled.

"That's for you to explain to me."

Jordan glances over at David and, as always, he says nothing as she takes on all the problems.

"Director, it's simple," Jordan says. "You and I both know there are ruthless and malicious enemies out there in the world that the

CIA can't touch. The government has no time to deal with these issues and frankly they can't handle these enemies," she continues, "and that's why you need Exodus. We can get in and get out, undetected. I mean, isn't this why the board brought me on to Phantom in the beginning? Now Exodus is new and improved, operating with the most advanced technology and equipment of any agency under the National Intelligence Agency, and we have highly skilled agents arriving soon that will take this agency to a whole new level." Jordan takes command; it's what she does best. Director Warren gives the smallest smirk in her direction.

"David, do you mind if I have a moment with Lieutenant Knox?" Director Warren asks.

"Sure. Not at all," Captain Lawrence says, not wanting to leave.

Director Warren and Jordan wait for him to exit before they discuss anything further.

"Chris, what the hell are you doing here?!" Jordan exclaims.

"What? I can't come visit my pain-in-the-ass best friend?" Crystal jokes, her dominating presence switching in a matter of seconds.

"Not when you're risking our cover," Jordan sits closer to her longtime friend.

"I'm a professional. He didn't suspect a thing," Crystal says, playfully brushing off her shoulders.

May 27th 2012

"It feels like it's been years since I last saw you," Crystal said to Jordan. Both talk privately in Crystal's backyard patio cabana. She poured them each a glass of vintage white wine, while they sat in their all-black dresses, relaxing after a long day at Director Radcliff's funeral.

"Five years to be exact," Jordan smiled.

"How have you been? I heard you and David had to shut down Phantom," Crystal said.

"Unfortunately, but it was only a matter of time. It was only a decoy," Jordan said.

"And how is that working out for you?"

"We're doing good. We'd be doing better if I could get things back to the way they used to be," Jordan expressed.

"You know I can't come back. Not now," Crystal said, remembering her time working alongside her dearest friend.

"I know, but what I really need is for the CIA to approve Exodus. I'm so close to getting what we need. That's why I put in another request."

"I heard about that. That's all people are talking about down at the NIA."

"It would be nice if they'd stop talking about it and actually approve it," Jordan said, annoyed by the board's constant disapproval of Exodus. "But enough about me...how are you?" Jordan quickly switched the conversation from being about her failures to Crystal's troubles. Initially Crystal was confused by Jordan's question and sudden change in the tone of her voice but slowly realized what she meant.

"Oh, you mean this...I'm fine. My father practically planned his own funeral. He planned everything in his life," Crystal sipped her wine.

"Yeah...that sounds exactly like him." They laughed.

"You know what's funny? He's fought war after war and crime after crime all his life, but it took a heart attack to kill him," Crystal said somewhat sadden.

"I'm sorry, Chris."

"Really, it's fine. I guess it's not all that bad. He did leave me the house in Bora Bora and a seat on the board." Jordan's eyes grew wider, realizing her best friend could possibly be the answer to all her problems.

"Are you serious?!" Jordan exclaimed.

"Yes. My father left me his seat. I am the new director of the CIA," Crystal smiled at Jordan's excitement.

"Chris, that's great!" Jordan congratulated and excitingly hugged her friend. "But do you know what this means?!" Jordan said.

"I'm going to be stuck in a room full of snob politicians every day?"

"No!" They laughed. "You can approve Exodus," Jordan said.

"Of course, I'll help. I was just waiting for you to ask," Crystal smiled.

"Really? Just like that?!" Jordan's surprised it didn't take more begging, being that's all she's been doing since Director Radcliff denied her.

"You saved my life a thousand times over when we were deployed, working in the CIA and even Exodus, and I'll never forget it. I'll do what I have to do to help you. It's the least I can do."

"Thank you," Jordan smiled as they hugged.

"It might take some time. My father wasn't the easiest person to disagree with and the board always followed him."

"I don't have time," Jordan said to herself, sipping the last bit of her wine.

"Why is it so important to you that Exodus be involved with the CIA? I thought you found what you needed on Leviathan?" Crystal asked. Jordan contemplates if she wants to tell Crystal the whole truth.

"*Do you remember Dr. Maxwell Hawthorne?*" *Jordan says, speaking in secrecy.*

"*Yeah, he was the lead scientist at the CIA – a genius,*" *Crystal replied.*

"*Apparently, he was doing side experiments on...psychics,*" *Jordan said.*

"*Like crystal balls, seeing into the future type psychics?*" *Crystal said puzzled.*

"*A little more complex than that. He found psychics with abilities we've never heard of. Do you know he found a young girl that could create a hurricane when she wanted to?*" *Jordan exclaimed. She's very much invested with the research Dr. Hawthorne left her on these young girls.*

"*Wait, young girl?! Was he experimenting on kids?!*"

"*It was all harmless and he got the approval from the parents before he started any work,*" *she said, defending her late friend.*

"*Okay...but what does all of this have to do with you?*"

"*Before he died, he gave it all to me. The names, the research,*" *she continued.* "*I'm even raising his daughter,*" *she murmured.*

"*You're what?!*" *Crystal surprised.*

"*Another one of his wishes before he died. He made me the godmother and I know he would have wanted me to.*"

"*That's great and all, but do you think you can handle that? It's been six years since...*"

"*I'm fine...,*" *Jordan interrupted Crystal, not wanting to go deeper into the conversation.*

"*Okay...where are these psychics?*" *Crystal asked, quickly changing the subject.*

"That's one of my many problems. I don't know." Jordan has been working day and night to link the bios Dr. Hawthorne had on the girls with their possible locations, but she's come up with nothing.

"And if you don't find them?" Crystal asked.

"They'll be in trouble. They are in trouble," she continued. "Maxwell told me, or rather a video of him told me, that people will be after his experiments including these girls, and if these so-called people get a hold of his work, that could be trouble for all of us," Jordan stated. Crystal doesn't speak for a moment. She needs to ask her next question with Jordan cautiously.

"I can understand you don't want to talk about it, and I'm not going to force you to, but should you really be putting all your time into finding these random girls when your girls are still out there?"

Jordan looks straight out into the yard. Mixed feelings of rage and guilt course through her veins; she can barely face Crystal. "There's nothing I can do for them right now; I can't help them. I've done enough damage to my family. I don't even know what they look like, Chris." Jordan stops as she feels a lump forming in her throat and her eyes begin to water.

"Hey, you did what was best to save your family and I'm not going to let you feel guilty about that," Crystal reassures her, but Jordan doesn't feel any different. Crystal knows how much Jordan hates these mushy moments, especially crying. She quickly changes the subject. "You know the board is going to have a field day with this one," Crystal heaves a heavy sigh, processing Jordan's information.

"No. The board can't know about this. Not yet. I haven't told that many people," Jordan whispered.

"How many people know?" Crystal asked.

"Including you and me? Three. Maxwell's assistant Martin Edwards knows, but I haven't been able to get in contact with him since the break-in at Phantom."

"Things just got a lot harder for both of us." Crystal is nervous about risking her job.

"I'm on the verge of finding the girls really soon and once I do, everything will go according to plan. I'll find them, stop Leviathan and get my family back...wherever they are. I just need you to be patient with me," Jordan said genuinely.

"Okay, but we need to act fast."

"If I don't come check on you, then the board will think I'm giving you a pass. I still have to do my job," Crystal says.

"I get that, but why are you really here?" Jordan asks. Crystal pauses. She knows Jordan isn't going to want to hear what she has to say next.

"You are very close to being shut down. We've given you assignments and they've come back declined each time," Director Warren continues. "They want to know whether you are running an agency or a training facility."

"They're new, practically babies. I can't just send them out there in the field when I know they're not ready," Jordan exclaims. "They sent me these recruits. If they would have let me pick my own, we wouldn't be in this situation."

"Well, you better figure out something. What happened to the girls you found?" Crystal asks.

"They're supposed to be here. It's just a waiting game at this point." Jordan leans back in her chair, exhausted, with her head leaning down inside her hand.

"I don't know how much longer we'll be able to keep this up and I don't know how long I'll be able to let you keep this Exodus open," Crystal says.

"Don't you think I know that? You think I want this to be the quickest opening and closing of an agency? I'm so close, Chris!" Jordan exclaims. "Just trust me, okay? They'll be here." Jordan has had a lot on her plate, from getting this agency open, to finding Angel, Ashton, Blair and Daniella, to even searching for a missing friend, Dr. Martin Edwards.

"I trust you, you know that. But maybe you're spreading yourself too thin. You need help. Have you talked to David about this?" Crystal asks, worried.

"No, he's not ready. But I will."

"I think you should. You know that man loves you," Crystal smiles like a teenage schoolgirl teasing her friend.

"That's what I'm afraid of."

"I can hold the board off for a little bit longer, but you have to start showing results, like yesterday," Crystal says as she stands from her seat.

"Thanks, Chris," Jordan smiles.

"That's Director to you!" Crystal pokes fun at Jordan.

"I'll see you soon, *Director*," Jordan says sarcastically, standing as she leaves. Director Warren leaves and Captain Lawrence approaches the door, standing up from leaning against the wall nearby.

"David, nice meeting with you," Director Warren says in her now professional tone.

"You too, Director." It's an awkward silence between David and Jordan. He knows he was wrong for not telling her the director was coming today. He tries to handle most of the business himself because of how hard Jordan works.

"So, telling me the director was going to be here just slipped your mind?" she asks, crossing her arms.

"I didn't tell you because there wasn't a need to," David says, sitting on the edge of the conference table.

"There wasn't a need too?! David, this isn't the CIA. This is my agency that you asked to be a part of. You have to start including me on these types of things," Jordan expresses herself anxiously. She's always dealing with a heavy load of problems, but she always keeps a level head. These two have a very complicated relationship. David is more willing to share how he feels about her whenever he gets the chance, unlike Jordan, who would rather not reveal those emotions, and when she does it all comes spilling out. David stands to comfort her, his hands on her forearms, looking down into her big brown eyes like pools of honey.

"I'm sorry. I will make sure I include you in all the joys of politics," he says.

"Thank you. That's all I ask," Jordan smiles up at him. She can't stay mad at him for too long.

"Wait, you're disciplining me about my secrets, but who are these agents you have coming here?" Captain Lawrence says, realizing Jordan is keeping things from him too.

Jordan steps away from him. "You know what? I just remembered I have to go check on some tests in weaponry," she looks down at her watch.

"Don't change the subject, J!" David shouts as Jordan rushes out of the room, leaving him to worry.

Outside of the conference room, Jordan makes an urgent phone call and quickly makes sure no one is around listening. "Hey, do we have any word on the girls? Yes, we need them…now!"

Chapter 12

She wanted us to come here to do what?! Go shopping?" Ashton yells, driving down the streets of a south suburban town outside the city of Chicago, then passing by small shops in a local downtown area. After a long drive from their home in Boston, Angel and Ashton finally make it to the location Jordan gave them. They pull up to a small boutique clothing store.

"I guess we'd better find out," Angel says.

Ashton parks the car along the curb directly in front of the store. Exiting their car, Ashton turns around to see a black Lincoln town car drive up behind them and then a cab drives up behind the Lincoln. She puts her hand on her knife tucked in behind her jacket, ready for whatever may come her way.

"Looks like we weren't the only ones she got to," Ashton whispers to Angel.

"You think they're like us?" Angel asks. She and Ashton haven't met anyone like them. They always thought they were the strange ones living in a world that would never understand or accept them.

"You mean… confused, misunderstood, in hiding… possibly," Ashton jokes and Angel rolls her eyes.

Daniella pays her driver. "Thanks," she tells him. Watching the other girls, she knows this will be harder than she thought.

Blair takes her bags out of the car and notices Angel and Ashton. She walks over to introduce herself.

"Hi, I'm Blair." She reaches out to shake Ashton's hand, but Ashton stares at it.

"Hey, I'm Angel and this is my sister, Ashton." Angel shakes Blair's hand, interrupting the awkward exchange between the two.

"She got you guys too, huh?" Blair asks.

"Were you guys asked here, too?" Daniella approaches, showing them her black card.

"Looks like it. Hey, I'm Blair."

"Daniella."

"I'm Angel and this-"

Ashton interrupts the meet and greet, exclaiming, "Great! We've all met. Now, can we please see why this woman wanted us all here?"

They walk into the boutique – Ashton going in first, with Angel, Blair and Daniella not too far behind.

"Well, isn't she just a ray of sunshine?" Blair speaks about Ashton.

Blair stands next to Daniella, waiting for her to agree, but Daniella isn't sure how to respond. Her social awkwardness is taking over.

"Uh…yeah sure." Daniella replies, moving away.

"Right. You can handle this, Blair. Everything will work out fine," Blair says to herself as she stands alone by the front door of the shop.

Entering the boutique, they can see it's small and quiet with only two employees working the front counter. The girls walk around with not a clue as to why they are there.

"Hi! Welcome to Fantasy Apparel! Can I help you beautiful young ladies with anything?!" a woman shouts. They turn around to see a loud and perky woman with bold and bright clothing that matches her bright pink hair, standing behind the counter.

"Umm…hi, we received a…letter to meet someone here." Angel doesn't give this woman too much information because she's not entirely sure if this is the right address.

"I'm sorry sweetie, you sweethearts are my first customers of the day," the woman replies.

"Why am I not surprised?" Daniella murmurs, looking at the out-of-date boho style clothing.

"I'm sorry, what is your name?" Angel asks.

"Oh, the name's Charlotte dear!" Charlotte says, ever so chipper.

"Okay…Charlotte, maybe I need to be clearer. We're looking for a woman, her name is Jordan Knox. She told us to meet her here," Angel hopes they didn't come all this way for a hoax.

"Hmmm…Nope. Haven't heard of her, but can I interest you in our new sweater collection," Charlotte ignores Angel's questions.

Angel knows what she saw when Jordan's hologram gave them the address. She should be here and refuses to believe otherwise. "I don't want a sweater! You-"

Ashton steps in to help her sister. "Ang. It's okay, let's just go. We were played." It's clear to Ashton that Jordan was just messing with them. Ashton takes Angel away, being the reasonable one for once. She looks at Blair and Daniella and they're just as disappointed. She feels bad for them too, even when she doesn't care to get to know them. Ashton saw this coming – the exact reason she doesn't trust anyone – but she sees how bad Angel wanted this and only wants to be there for her sister.

"Thank you for stopping by! And hey, if you need any help with your wardrobe, I'm always available and I'm always around!" Charlotte shouts.

As they exit the shop, flustered by Charlotte's perky, happy go-lucky attitude, Blair stops when she hears Charlotte's last words *'I'm always available and I'm always around,'* She's heard those words before. She rushes back in.

"Changed your mind, sweetie? Found something you like?" Charlotte asks, organizing the cheap jewelry display case.

"No, but I do know Lieutenant Knox because…she's always available and she's always around," Blair says to Charlotte. Blair remembers those exact words when they first met in the pub that night. It couldn't have been a coincidence when Charlotte said it. Angel, Ashton and Daniella follow Blair back into the shop.

"She said you guys would get it," Charlotte, in an instant, changed her perky tone to something more vapid. It's like her entire persona changed. "When she told me, 'these girls are the real deal' I didn't believe her because she's been saying that about all the newbies lately," Charlotte talks quickly. She takes the girls to the back of the store to what looks like a fitting room. Puts them in two separate rooms.

"Wait, wait, there's more of us?!" Angel asks, wanting some answers because this entire situation shifted within the blink of an eye.

"Are we in here to try on those rags you call clothes?" Blair points to the run-down clothes.

"No, but you'll see," Charlotte closes the fitting room doors. Angel and Daniella are in one room; Blair and Ashton are in the other. Charlotte then slides open a hidden door on the side of the fitting rooms and it reveals a highly advanced keypad. The girls stand in the fitting rooms with mixed emotions about what's going on. A TV screen turns on inside the rooms, revealing Charlotte. "Good luck guys, and please keep all hands and feet inside until the ride is over," she said.

"What?!" Blair and Ashton yell.

"Kidding," Charlotte chuckles and disappears from the screen, "Gets them every time."

They wait for something to happen.

"I cannot believe I agreed to do this," Ashton says, wishing she would have stood her ground and stayed home.

"It could be worse. We could've gotten kidnapped," Blair says, trying to make light of the situation, but it only annoys Ashton even more.

Suddenly, the room begins to spin around 180 degrees. They are now in what looks like an elevator with glass doors, and outside those glass doors is a tunnel. The elevator descends.

"So, what did she say to get you here?" Angel asks, trying to break the ice with Daniella, knowing they'll spend a lot of time with one another.

"Told me I needed to make a change in my life and that this will be my best option," Daniella continues.

"You?"

"Same. Let's hope this opportunity is as good as she says," Angel replies.

The elevator abruptly stops, and the girls slowly exit. They're standing in a dull white and grey room in front of a woman at a desk.

"Hello, you must be guests of the lieutenant. My name is Jamie, you can follow me." The secretary leads them down a secured hallway. She's dressed in a slick black dress with four-inch heels that don't make her any taller and a slicked-back bun.

"Does anybody want to talk about what just happened?" Blair asks. "I mean, we were literally in a dressing room that turned into an elevator!"

"You don't get out much, do you?" Ashton mocks her.

"She did say she ran a secret organization," Angel says as she stares at the circular symbol on the wall behind Jamie's desk. The Exodus logo on the wall has the words 'Exodus' and 'Central Intelligence Agency' surrounding an eagle – wings spread out and its claws holding a scrunched-up USA flag.

"This is too much crazy for me in one day. I need food," Ashton says.

"Right this way," the secretary takes them through security, but not like airport or mall cop security. These officers are trained; they're the first line of defense.

"Step in the pod," the guard commands Blair.

"For what?!"

"Step in the pod," he repeats.

"It's protocol. Everyone that comes through must get scanned for security purposes and decontamination," the secretary explains.

"It wouldn't be an elite agency if there wasn't security," Blair says stepping into the pod. The white metal pod wraps around her body, only her head visible.

"She isn't going to melt or get a really bad tan, is she?" Ashton watches the pod as it rumbles and beeps.

"It hasn't happened…yet," the secretary teases.

One by one each of them steps into the pod as it scans them for anything out of the ordinary, external or internal.

"Yep, that was totally normal," Angel says stepping out of the pod.

"Place your right hand here," the guard guides them to a box with a slot; it's a scanner.

"What is with you people and placing body parts in enclosed areas," Daniella says feeling like she's back in juvie.

"It's a biometric scanner. It will put your prints in the system so that you can enter and exit throughout the agency," the secretary explains. "Not everyone here has this access. The lieutenant must really trust you all."

"Or she just wants to keep tabs on us," Ashton says, waiting behind Daniella. They place their hands into the slot as the scanner scans their prints into the system. "Anything else? Blood, loc of hair," Ashton says.

"No, that is all, Miss…"

"Hunter," Angel replies. Luckily for Angel and Ashton, Gigi legally changed their last names to hers when she adopted them. No one should suspect a thing.

"Well, right this way, Miss Hunter." The secretary takes them to an elevator at the end of the hallway. She opens the keypad on the wall, punches in a code and scans her hand. "Since we are underground, the numbers go down instead of up," the secretary explains.

"So, we're on the first floor now?" Angel asks.

"Correct. Take this elevator to the second floor and the first door on your right is the lieutenant's office. You'd better hurry. She's been expecting you for some time."

They enter the elevator. "I never got the royal treatment before," Blair says, enjoying herself no matter how secretive or dangerous this situation may be.

Lieutenant Jordan Knox's office is furnished with the finest luxurious furniture, only fit for the queen. Her light grey walls brighten up the room, and the expensive and exquisite painting of *African Warriors: The Agojie Women*, stretching out behind her desk makes a statement on its own.

"You made it," Jordan says to them, leaning against the front of her desk. "I was beginning to worry," she continues.

"Yeah, you made it really easy to get here," Ashton says with a smart aleck tone.

"Hello to you too, Ashton," Jordan says, knowing Ashton isn't willing to trust her too soon. "Please, all of you, sit down." She motions them to sit in the sitting area with two grey, gold-trimmed love seats facing each other. There are two crisp, cream, custom-designed armchairs with an oval, glass coffee table in the middle. Jordan can sense they aren't as happy to see her as she is to see them.

"Where exactly are we?" Angel asks.

"Exodus," Jordan cuts straight to the point.

"You definitely weren't kidding when you said secret," Blair says, still reeling from the elevator ride, security check and medals of honor hanging on the walls.

"This is a secret bureaucratic agency under my leadership," she said to Blair.

"And why exactly do you want us here, you know, besides the obvious?" Blair asks. The other girls wait for her response as they want to know as well.

"Honestly? You all have abilities that aren't the norm in our world. You're each one of a kind," Jordan equivocated. "And there are a few people out there who know of those abilities. Being a part of my team will give you the chance to use your powers freely without the fear of someone tracking you down and exposing them."

The idea of their psychic powers being exposed is quite scary for them. They know first-hand how people will handle it and what they'll do.

"Are we supposed to use our powers to stop criminals or something?" Ashton asks, slouching in the armchair next to Jordan. "Because I could have done that at home."

"You could have, but your last job has you on the brink of the Most Wanted List. I'm pretty sure I'm *all of you* guys' last option to a semi-normal life," she says, putting Ashton in her place. The girls look at one another and then at Jordan and realize she's right. They have nothing stable to go back too.

"When do we start?" Angel says, stepping up, asking the tough question they want to ask.

A sense of satisfaction comes over Jordan; she has them. "Training begins in just-"

A young girl comes rushing in, tripping over herself, and fumbling around with paperwork in her arms. She rushes over to the group. "Agent Hawthorne, glad you could join us," Jordan says, happy to see Natalie.

"Thank you for having me," she says, smiling towards Jordan and glancing over at the girls in front of her. Finally getting herself organized, she sits next to Jordan, excited to see them.

"Agent Hawthorne runs the engineering and tech department here."

"She's a kid," Blair says, watching a doe-eyed Natalie fumble around with paperwork.

"I'm actually sixteen, not that much younger than you," Natalie whispers, pushing up her circular rimmed glasses.

"I can assure you Natalie is the best there is and she will be showing you where you'll be staying," she says, defending her goddaughter.

"You were saying something about training," Daniella says.

"Training will begin shortly, but we'll get more into that once you all get settled in."

"I guess we should get started. I'll show you where you'll be staying," Natalie stands, brushing her long, wavy, auburn hair behind her ears.

"Someone has already taken your bags to your rooms," Jordan says. "Oh, and Ashton," Jordan stops her before she leaves the room, "we'll need your keys to move your car to a secure area." It's clear Jordan doesn't know the girls all that well. If she did, then she would know never to ask Ashton for the one thing she holds dear.

"No one drives or touches my car. Just tell me where to go and I'll park it myself," Ashton says with such cynicism.

Jordan compromises with Ashton and presses the intercom on her desk. "Jamie, can you show Ashton where she can move her car, please?"

"Yes, Lieutenant," Jamie replies.

"Jamie will meet you where you came in," Jordan says.

Ashton walks out of Jordan's office. Just as Jordan thinks all the girls are gone, Angel comes rushing back in.

"Lieutenant?" Angel says, timid.

Jordan is startled, quickly turning around from reading files about the girls on her desk. "Angel, what's wrong?"

"You said there were a few people who knew about our powers. Do they know we're here?" Jordan can sense the concern in Angel's voice. She must have faced Leviathan without knowing who they truly were.

"No, not at all. This is an underground facility, undetectable, no one knows you're here and they can't know. This is the safest place you can ever be." She reassures her she's made the right choice in coming here and Angel is coming around to believing her. "Oh, and don't worry about Faye Welsh. I have my men taking care of her as we speak," Jordan adds. Angel smiles with a sense of relief that her problems are fading away.

"Thank you," Angel smiles.

"You're welcome," Jordan says, watching her leave her office.

April 13th, 2018

Richton's Maximum-Security Prison houses the most dangerous criminals in the country. Assassins, mercenaries and drug lords have been put away in this prison by every agency within the NIA, including Phantom. Jordan is here to visit a menacing and conniving man: Tobias Vaughn, also known as Midas. Four heavily armed guards walk her down to the lowest part of the prison, passing heckling inmates along the way. They enter the basement with dim lighting and no sunlight. Five inmates are housed down here and they barely know the time of day.

"I want all of you armed and ready for anything," Jordan said, walking with the guards.

"Lieutenant, these inmates do not come out of their cells. No matter what. You'll be perfectly safe," a guard said, holding a rifle.

"That's great, but I want to talk to him face to face." The guards can't understand why she would want to see him. Midas is one of their most dangerous and lethal prisoners.

"Lieutenant, I'm sorry, but we can't let you do that. He's too dangerous," he said.

"Trust me, I know that all too well. I'm the one who put him in here, but I still want to speak to him."

"We understand, ma'am, but I'm afraid we can't do that," he said. Jordan didn't want to show her superiority, but she's done asking. There isn't time to go back and forth with them.

"I don't care what you can't do. I want to speak to him now and not through a slot in the door. I don't care how you set it up, but I want you to do it now or you all will be on suspension for disobeying a superior's orders," Jordan barked. The guards take into consideration everything she said, still not wanting to risk Midas escaping or even hurting them, but they have no choice. They do what she says.

"There's a interrogation room just down the hall. We don't use it often, only when one of the directors needs to come in and speak to one of the inmates but that rarely happens," the guard said nervously.

"Thank you," she said. She doesn't enjoy exercising her authority, but sometimes it's necessary. They finally approach the locked room holding Tobias 'Midas' Vaughn. the sounds of loud grunting and punching come from inside. Two more guards stand at attention outside of his room.

"We're opening him up," the lead guard said to his men. Four guards with armor on top of armor and rifles in hand take aim as the other two open the cell door. "Vaughn!" the lead guard shouted through the slot. Midas continued to punch and kick his handmade punching bag made of his mattress and sheets. Sweat is dripping from his low-cut fade to his overly ripped chest. "Stop fighting the mattress and lay on the ground. You have a visitor," he said.

Those last words catch his attention. He stopped using his martial arts techniques on the handmade punching bag and does what he's told. Usually, it takes three guards and a taser to get him to do anything the first time. They slowly open the door and the guards rush in, restraining him from head to toe. These aren't the normal restraints they use on regular inmates. They're made of solid steel and can only be unlocked by a device the lead guard carries. They walk him out and he sees Jordan standing outside his room. He gave her a menacing smile as he walked past because he knew exactly why she was there to visit.

Jordan and two guards are outside the interrogation room watching as the other guards securely seat Midas.

"How long do I have?" Jordan asked, knowing the restraints holding Midas down won't last long.

"Five to seven minutes top before they reset," the lead guard said.

"All right, I want men surrounding every inch of this room." She knows she can handle herself, but it will be a problem if he escapes.

"Yes, Lieutenant." The lead guard then orders his men to guard the front door outside of the Interrogation Room, the Observation Room on the other side of the two-way bullet proof mirror and inside the Interrogation Room.

Jordan enters the brightest room of the basement with only a table and two metal chairs. Midas sits chained to the chair, giving her the most disturbing smile as she takes a seat in front of him. "Tobias Vaughn," she mocked him. "Are you ready to talk?" she asked.

"How about we don't get into…names, Lieutenant Jordan Knox. We don't want to reveal anything," he said taunting her back. "Now, what is it that we're discussing today?" he asked.

"Don't play games with me Tobias. Why were your bullets found at Phantom the night a group of men came in and shot up the place?"

"How do you know they were mine?" he smiled.

"The bullets were solid gold, and no one walks around showing off their hardware as much as you."

Midas is your typical muscular and rugged looking criminal on the exterior, but internally he's very conniving and uses his charm and wits to lure his prey to do his bidding. Also, with the right amount of money offered to him, he's practically ready to do anything.

"I do live a promising lifestyle," he said, using his charm on her.

"If you think so. Now tell me why you were there that night, or I promise, you will suffer every single second you're in here!" Jordan had reached her breaking point with Tobias.

He lost the charm, becoming more menacing; he doesn't take threats too kindly. He leans in closer to her. "Lieutenant, you are a very, very beautiful and smart woman which makes me wonder how you haven't figured it out yet," he said. "We know more than you think and yes, I was there that night, I'm not going to deny it."

"And where was Silas Clay?" she asked.

Unknown to Tobias, she doesn't care whether he was there or if he killed dozens of agents, what she does care about is ex-agent now rogue, Silas Clay, and his location.

"Your concern should not be who was there, but for finding those precious little girls of yours," he disturbingly smiled at her. How could Midas of all people know about these girls, she thought. "Ah, there we go," he noticed the sudden change in Jordan's facial expression. "Dr. Hawthorne's experiments weren't so much of a secret as he would've liked them to be. There are more people who know about these psychics than you know of," he continues to speak to her as if he's reeling her in, ready to devour her at any moment.

"Well, it's apparent you do, so enlighten me, who are these people?" she asked him calmly.

"That's not for me to say, but you should find those girls soon because there are people who want them and who would do anything to have them," he leaned back into his chair, "and I can't say whether I'll be a part of that…danger that's coming to them."

"How do you know I didn't already find them?" Jordan tested him in return.

He knew her game and refused to continue this conversation. "You might want to tell your minions to put me back into my cell before the time is up on these restraints or there might be some blood on your hands," he said. They stare at one another for a long moment, trying to figure out the motives of the other. Eventually Jordan ordered the guard to take him back to his cell.

"You can take him," she said, standing from her seat and watching the four guards stand Tobias from the chair, taking him out of the Interrogation Room. She watched as Tobias left. There's a lot

more he's keeping from her. Tobias may be working with Silas Clay, but he answers to a much higher power.

"Wait," she said to the guards before they put him in his cell. She approached Tobias, they are now face to face, closer to each other than they were before. "I don't know why, but I know you're protecting someone, whether that's Clay, a government official, whoever. But whatever you have planned, trust me, I will make sure both of you will rot under this prison before I let you anywhere near those girls," Jordan said, using a malevolent undertone.

He gives her a sinister smile. "Have fun, Knox. If that's your real name," he says, and they walk him back into his cell where he continued his martial arts techniques on his hand-made punching bag. Jordan watches him from the slot outside the door.

"We call it The Penthouse," Natalie said, showing Angel, Blair and Daniella where they'll be living for the duration of their time here at Exodus.

"Aren't penthouses usually at the top of the building?" Blair asks. They've entered onto the last floor of the agency, Floor 5, where there is nothing but a long hallway and a door.

"I think you'll have a different perspective on the word, once you enter," Natalie said, typing in a code and using facial recognition to enter the penthouse. "It's important to the lieutenant and captain to have a high-level security system. It's the best. You'll be able to enter the same way as well," Natalie said, opening the heavy steel door. The girls walk in and are astonished. It looks like a penthouse you would see in downtown Chicago or New York City. The cream and wooden walls make the underground penthouse bright as if surrounded by windows. The furniture is as luxurious as the furniture in Jordan's office. "There's a fully stocked kitchen, you're standing in the living room and there's an advanced telecommunications system, which I designed," Natalie continues as the girls walk around the penthouse admiring its glamour. "Oh, and I think you all will like this one – your very own personal training center," Natalie says, rushing over to a black and purple back room with state-of-the-art workout equipment and martial arts mats laid across the floor, but no one is paying attention.

"This place is…amazing, but how are we supposed to know when it's day or night?" Daniella points to a blank wooden wall behind the glass dining table. She's worried she has herself stuck, just like juvie.

"The walls are set on a timer to synchronize with the weather outside," Natalie begins to touch buttons on her digital watch and the walls start to fade in and out like a theater screen showing various types of weather, "and right now it is bright and sunny outside," she said.

"Wow, that's different," Ashton says, walking through the door, watching as Natalie flips through the different weather settings.

"Ashton, nice of you to join us," Natalie greets.

"Wish I felt the same," Ashton says in her nonchalant tone.

"So, we basically can imagine what's outside instead of actually going out there?" Daniella wonders.

"Yes, only because we are an underground facility. But you have free will. You can go outside anytime you would like, but Lieutenant Knox would prefer you focus on your training for the next couple of weeks," Natalie says. "Speaking of which," the girls follow Natalie up the stairs onto a balcony overlooking every inch of The Penthouse, "each of your bedrooms is designed to accommodate your abilities."

"Where were you?" Angel whispered to Ashton.

"I had to go park the car in a very secret underground lair," Ashton jokes. "No, but seriously, you should see the vehicles they have here, it's like *Batman* meets *Fast and Furious*!"

"Your luggage is in your rooms along with the training attire Lieutenant Knox would like for you to wear in…the next hour," Natalie says, looking at her watch.

"We just got here!" Blair exclaims, feeling like she's been wide awake for the past three days.

"You were actually late," Natalie says pushing her glasses on her nose.

"Yeah because of your 'you can't get in unless you know the password' nonsense upstairs," Ashton exclaims.

"Again, for security purposes," Natalie whispers to herself.

"What type of training will we be doing?" Angel asks, directing the focus away from Natalie.

"I don't particularly know; the lieutenant usually comes up with her exercises at random, but she wants you to be ready for phase one of training right away," Natalie says, making her way down the steps. "I'll just be down here when you all are ready to go or if you have any questions." The girls cautiously open the doors to their rooms, each room designed specifically for them.

Blair's room has a thermostat separate from the rest of the penthouse to monitor her sometimes-uncontrollable weather manipulations. There's also a yoga mat to continue practicing her tai chi.

Everything in Daniella's room is designed for her not to explode the furniture.

Ashton's room has her furniture bolted to the floor, something she's not too happy about. That quickly changes when she walks over to the wall by the closet, where she sees a shelf holding a variety of military-grade knives. "I think this place is growing on me," she says to herself, admiring the knives.

Nothing much was done for Angel's room except for the fully furnished meditation area for her to stay calm with her abilities. She looks at the white and silver track suit with skintight black leggings still reeling from the conversation she had with Jordan moments ago. She vowed to herself and Ashton that they will never face those men who broke into their home and killed their parents so long ago. Maybe this is the safest place for them to be.

They put on their training gear to begin the next phase in their lives.

Chapter 13

Jordan, Captain David Lawrence and Exodus' head agent, Donovan James, observe from the sky box balcony of The Arena, a place to watch trained fights between the agents, like a large boxing arena.

"They moved our deadline up," Jordan says to them. "If we don't start separating the weak from the strong, we'll all be out of a job," she continues.

"And we don't need another shutdown," David says.

"We have ten potential agents down there. All recruited from MIT, Georgetown, of course including your new recruits," Donovan takes a jab at Jordan's decision to bring in random girls. She stares him down, intimidation bringing his tall frame down a couple of inches. He quickly gets back on track.

"How soon do they want us to be ready?" Donovan asks.

"By the end of the month," she says, knowing that's a lot for just the three of them.

"We should get started," David says, looking down from the balcony. "Who are these special agents you brought in?" he asks her.

Jordan hesitates. They look over the balcony at the girls and newly recommended Exodus agents.

"Them," Jordan points to Angel, Ashton, Blair and Daniella standing in a small group away from everyone else. They're not standing together because they may have developed a friendship with one another, but because of the comfortability of knowing they're the only ones like each other.

"Your special agents are kids?!" David exclaims, surprised that Jordan has been keeping an unnecessary secret.

"They're not that much younger than the potential agents we have down there, and they are just as skilled – maybe better."

"She's right sir, as much as I would like to deny it," Donovan glanced down at them, especially Angel and Ashton. He'll never forget how they first met.

"We're putting the stake of this entire agency into the hands of teenage girls," he says, not fully comprehending Jordan's plan. "Lieutenant, what aren't you telling me?" David continues.

"Have I ever steered you or this agency in the wrong direction?" she asked them. "Just trust that I know what I'm doing."

David doesn't speak for a moment. He knows she's hiding something from him, but she's right, she's never failed him. "Fine, but don't expect me to wait forever," he says.

"Should we start?" Donovan interrupts them. Jordan nods, giving him the clearance to begin.

"These suits are so tight," Daniella says, trying to stretch out her leggings.

"I think they look pretty cool," Blair admires the suit.

"Anyone have an idea what type of training we're supposed to do?" Ashton asks.

"Looking at that very large glass boxing arena," Blair points. "I would say a fight to the death." This brings a smirk across Ashton's face, with a chuckle almost slipping out before she composes herself.

"Am I the only one feeling kind of weak?" Daniella asks.

"I have been feeling kind of empty, like the air is thin down here," Angel replies.

"I feel fine," Ashton says.

Jordan, David and Donovan approach the edge of the balcony as the agents in training or, as Jordan likes to call them, initiates, talk amongst themselves.

"Listen up!" Jordan shouts, bringing the busy room to a halt with everyone looking up to pay attention. "You are initiates, agents in training. You will go through a series of phases to test your strength, agility, logic and whether you are able to withstand unpredictable situations," she continues. "You fail these phases, you leave. The CIA may have brought you into this agency but let me make this very clear: you run nothing. You do not control or dominate anything here. Leave your egos elsewhere. You are fetuses and will be treated as such until we believe you've earned it," she looks indirectly to the girls, and they aren't too happy about it. "You break any guidelines and you're gone. I don't care how good you may think you are... Other than that, welcome to Exodus."

Donovan steps up, "You will be separated into two teams: Alpha and Omega. Your suits will reveal which team that is."

The initiates look at their sleeves and on their wrist is a flashing bracelet revealing a light, either red or blue.

"We will begin Phase 1: Basic Combat. You and your opponent will enter the ring and fight. You have two minutes to get your opponent down and tapping out within ten seconds," Donovan says with superiority in his tucked-in, black, button-down shirt and pants. The initiates are ready for phase one, excited to show their talents. Angel, Ashton, Blair and Daniella, not so much. "Head over to your designated area and good luck." Donovan, Jordan and David take their seats as they watch the initiates scurry around the room.

"Of course, she would separate us," Ashton says as her wrist flashes with a blue light and Angel's red.

"It was only a matter of time," Angel said, glancing up at the three bosses. "Just remember what we were taught and if they make us fight each other it will be like when we were kids again," she continues.

"I don't think you want that, especially since I'd beat you every time," Ashton reminisces.

"Sure, you did!" Angel laughs. "See you on the other side."

"You bet," Ashton replies. They do their special handshake before they go their separate ways. Ashton notices Angel's Ouroboros ring still on her finger.

"Hey, make sure you put that in a safe place. You know you can't function without it."

Angel looks down at her hand and takes it off, placing the ring on her dog tag chain and tucking back inside her suit. "Thanks," Angel smiles at her sister, grateful that she's on this journey with her. They then go to their designated teams.

The teams separated into two teams of five, some mentally and physically preparing themselves to enter the arena. Ashton and Daniella are on Team Omega while Angel and Blair are on Team Alpha. It's time to begin the battles.

"They could have at least put me on a team with people who are on my level," says one of the guys on the Omega team. "Obviously I'm the best here." He stands behind Ashton. She tries not to turn around and throw him across the room.

The first battle is displayed on the large screen hanging from the ceiling. It's time for Blair and her opponent, Initiate Mark Parker. "Looks like I have to show you guys how it's done," Mark says in such a cocky tone. Ashton turns and realizes Blair's opponent is the dumb jock that swears he's a professional UFC fighter. He walks in between Ashton and Daniella, bumping them as he goes.

"That dude is on strike two with me. One more and I'm very likely to cause some damage," Ashton says, wanting to punch Mark in the face repeatedly.

"I don't blame you," Daniella agrees. They glance at each other, trying to figure the other one out.

On the Alpha Team side, Angel stands in a corner leaning against a wall, arms crossed, paying close attention to everything in the room. She watches Jordan and her team in the balcony, and she studies both the Alpha and Omega teams, making certain nothing is out of the ordinary. She even notices when Donovan tries to discreetly watch her from the balcony. It's obvious he doesn't want her and Ashton here.

"This is kind of strange, isn't it?" Angel looks up beside her and sees a guy with broad shoulders and slicked-back brown hair. She has to do a double take at him; she didn't notice how handsome he was prior to him approaching.

"What do you mean?" she asks.

"This," he points and looks around the room, "all of this. We're in a super underground agency, competing to be secret agents. I mean I might be too excited, but you must admit it's pretty crazy."

Angel keeps her focus on Blair and Mark preparing to enter the arena. "Yeah, it's not something you hear about every day."

"Hi, I'm Ethan. Ethan Carmichael," he says, flashing his pearly white smile, hand stretched out for Angel to shake. Angel hesitates, then stands straight up to face him directly. She plays off the sudden fluttering feeling she feels in her stomach once she's face to face with him.

She shakes his hand and introduces herself, "Angel."

"Nice to meet you, Angel." Ethan has had his eyes on Angel from the moment she walked into the arena. She's gorgeous. He doesn't know much about her, but he knows she's different from the others.

A slim young woman comes up from behind them. "Aww how cute," she says. Angel and Ethan quickly drop hands. "Maybe instead of making puppy dog eyes at each other, you should pay attention."

"Kate, relax," Ethan says.

"What?! I'm only suggesting she should focus on the fight; she might need the extra help." Kate giggles, standing close to Ethan and taunting Angel. Angel nods her head and smirks at Kate, keeping the peace. Stooping down to Kate's level will only cause unnecessary drama. Also, Ashton isn't too far away to witness the exchange. Angel steps away and goes back to her peaceful corner to observe Blair in her match.

Blair Hahn v. Mark Parker

Mark confidently walks into the middle of the arena, ready to fight. It doesn't matter that Blair is a girl, and he's twice as strong as her. Blair is quite nervous even though her mother taught her how to defend herself since she could walk. She never thought she would ever have to fight anyone. She thought her powers were enough.

"Don't worry, I won't take it easy on you because you're a girl," Mark says, trying to throw Blair off.

"Begin!" the automated voice on the flat screens surrounding the room says.

"Okay Blair, it shouldn't be too hard. Just blast him with a fireball or ice him. Simple. Just get it over with," Blair thought to herself.

The battle begins, Blair and Mark in the middle of the ring. He jumps at her, attempting to scare her. Then he throws a punch, but Blair blocks it. Blair stands there wanting to hit Mark, but too nervous to do it. Mark throws another punch, but Blair blocks it once again. This only upsets Mark.

"Hit me! You coward!" he shouts.

He then kicks and punches, throwing different combat combinations at Blair, but she continues to dodge them. As fast as he's moving to knock her out, Blair is quickly matching his movements.

"Don't think you will win this way," Mark says, huffing and puffing. Sweat pours down from the top of his forehead down to his face. He's right, she must do something, especially with Jordan watching. Jordan traveled around the country looking for her, so she must think Blair is something special.

"You're right," Blair says, slightly out of breath. She stretches out her hand and gets ready to ice him, so he'll fall back. Then nothing, nothing happens at all.

Mark, the other initiates, and some Exodus guards laugh hysterically. "What were you going to do? Blast me away, Iron Man?" he says, mocking her.

Blair is aghast as she studies her hand, wondering what is going on with her powers. She glanced up at Jordan, who just watches the match with no emotion. She then reads the large screen above, and it reads 1:00. As Blair looks back at Mark, he comes rushing towards her, hitting her straight in the face. She falls back.

"That's your special agent," Captain Lawrence asks Jordan with such sarcasm.

"Just watch, it's not over," she says, confident in Blair's abilities. Blair quickly stands, wiping the blood leaking from her lip. She really has no choice now but to fight, and she will. Mark tries to land another punch, but Blair swiftly dodges it and grabs his wrist, pausing him mid-swing. She uses his arm as an anchor and gives a roundhouse kick to his face. He falls on to the mat. He struggles to get back up, but that doesn't stop her. She gives one good, hard punch to his face, and he falls back on to the mat. With thirty seconds left, everyone, including Blair, waits to see if Mark will stand, and slowly he does, but it's too late.

"Time's up!" Donovan shouts.

Blair and Mark wait in the ring while Donovan, Jordan and David deliberate.

"Initiate Parker. Pass." Jordan says over the speakers surrounding the room. "Initiate Hahn." Blair holds her head down, embarrassed. "Pass." Jordan stays emotionless, but she's proud. Going back to their designated teams, Blair is praised while Mark is strongly disliked.

"Good Job, Blair," Angel congratulates her.

"Thanks, but I barely made it through. I don't know what's going on with my…you know," Blair says quietly to Angel.

"I'm feeling a little strange myself and it wasn't until we came down here that I felt it," Angel replies.

"You think Ashton and Daniella are having the same problem?"

"I don't know. I hope not," Angel says.

On the Omega side: "Do you think the lieutenant has something to do with Blair's powers not working?" Daniella whispers to Ashton.

"I don't know, but there's a way to find out," Ashton says, staring at a pen inside Captain Lawrence's suit jacket and trying to lift it with her mind.

"What are you looking at?" Daniella asks.

"Shhh…I'm trying to concentrate." She focuses harder and harder, straining her eyes, but nothing happens. "There's definitely something going on," Ashton says.

"So, we're doing this the old-fashioned way…great," Daniella says.

"Looks like it and it looks like you're next," Ashton points to the screen reading Daniella's name.

Daniella Vega v. Ben Chase

Daniella enters the arena, pulling her hair back into a ponytail. Being in juvenile hall for so long, she's developed a bit of paranoia with fighting. She has competed in numerous boxing matches set up by the correctional officers and she's undefeated.

"You sure you want to do this? This isn't a fight on the playground," Ben taunts Daniella. Ben reminds Daniella of those preppy, stuck-up, daddy-buys-me-everything type of boys she had to deal with in the little time she attended school. Daniella ignores him and focuses on what she must accomplish. The round begins with Ben and Daniella landing punch after punch to one another's face and body; it's a tie at this point.

"You can kiss the lieutenant's ass all you want, but you will never be at our level," Ben snaps at Daniella. In this moment, Daniella feels like she's a little girl again being degraded by her father or one of her many foster parents. All she sees now is Ben and rage stirs in her veins. Everything surrounding her is no more. Daniella lunges for Ben, kicking him in the face, quickly jumping on top of him as he lays on the mat. She punches with all her strength again and again and again. Ben tries to block the punches, but Daniella is coming at him too quick. He frees one of his hands and taps out, but Daniella keeps going.

"That's enough!" Donovan shouts.

Daniella doesn't stop and Ben is bleeding profusely.

"Okay, that's it. Guards, tear them apart, please," Jordan says.

The guards rush inside the ring to separate them. Daniella struggles with them to break free. She wants to hit Ben some more, it feels good to her, but they have a hold that's tight. They take Daniella out of the ring and a medical team takes Ben out of the arena. Ben's blood is left on the mat and on Daniella's hand.

"I'm impressed. Thought you were going to bomb that one," Ashton congratulates Daniella, well, kind of.

Daniella ignores her and sits on a nearby bench, eyes closed, doing the ten second countdown Sergeant Campbell taught her.

"If you don't mind, I need to examine your hand," Seth kneels beside her.

"I'm fine."

"Of course, you are. It's clear you can handle your own and you have no problem standing up for yourself, but I just want to make sure your hands are as strong as they need to be." Daniella lets Seth examine her hands; he wraps bandages around the scarred knuckles. "And between you and me, Initiate Chase is a pretentious jerk, so, thank you," he smiles up at her, trying to create a newfound friendship. Daniella returns the sincerity. It's nice to make a friend. She's never had that in the past. As he finishes bandaging her scars, she wants to ask him about her powers not working, but that would involve revealing she has powers, putting herself, Angel, Ashton and Blair at risk. "We're finished here," Seth says.

The speakers in the room come to life. "Initiate Chase. Fail." Donovan speaks, "Initiate Vega. Pass." Daniella can hardly believe it.

"Hey, you made it through!" Seth congratulates her. "You could soon be a regular around here," Seth said.

"I guess I'll see you around," Daniella gives him a small smile.

Ashton Hunter v. Kate Thomas

Ashton's name, along with Kate Thomas, is displayed on the arena's screens. "Let's get this over with," Ashton sighs heavily. She would rather be somewhere eating a pizza and playing video games. She doesn't have a problem taking part in Jordan's unnecessary training exercises, but she does have a problem with Jordan interfering with the one thing that makes her Ashton.

"Take notes, people," Kate shouts to her team. "You'll need them." She smirks and glances at Angel as she passes.

"Will do," Angel replies, smiling, trying her best not to laugh. Ashton and Kate enter the ring. Ashton stares at Jordan hard as she goes to her designated side of the ring. She's trying to keep her cool and not make a scene, but she wouldn't be who she is if she didn't.

"I know what you're trying to do," Ashton calls out to Jordan. "They may not know but I do, so I'll play your game." Shocked murmurs and indistinct voices are heard all over the room. No one can believe she was bold enough to shout at the lieutenant. Jordan lets Ashton vent, giving her no reaction.

"Stand down, Initiate!" Donovan yells at Ashton. He's not too fond of Ashton and Angel after their standoff at the airport hangar. Jordan signals to Donovan to sit down.

"Okay, then let's see how well you *play* the game," Jordan calmly says to her, continuing to relax in her comfy armchair, leg crossed over the other.

The battle begins with Kate and Ashton sizing each other up. Ashton now must go back to her roots. Looking at Kate, Ashton knows she can win. Kate throws the first punch. Ashton blocks it by spinning her around and kicking her in the back, knocking her against the ropes. The weight of Ashton's boot along with the power of her kick has Kate struggling to leave the ropes. Ashton rushes towards Kate, pulling her off the ropes. She grabs her and begins punching her like a life-size punching bag. She throws combinations so rapidly Kate can't keep up. Angel watches from the sidelines, grinning from ear to ear. Ashton throws Kate like a rag doll. She knew this match would be easy, but she didn't think it would be so easy she wouldn't have a scratch on her. Kate has barely touched her. Kate, in the ring, struggles to stand. Ashton's mission is to make this a quick round. Ashton gets ready to knock Kate out cold.

"Please! Please!" Kate stops her punch in mid-air. "I haven't even been in a fight before! I'm a computer geek. I-I'd rather be in the lab." Although Ashton may seem ruthless and selfish, she'll never hurt someone who can't defend themselves. Angel wants to help her sister; she knows Kate is lying.

Ashton steps back from her and turns towards Jordan, Donovan and David. "I guess that means I won." Remembering the rules, her opponent technically tapped out so it's a forfeit, right? The arena is quiet. Jordan, Donovan and David continue to watch the unfinished round.

"Ash!" Angel shouts from the Alpha side.

Ashton turns and to the side of her is Kate coming towards her, instantly gaining her strength back. Kate uses all her force to run, leaps from the ring and punches Ashton straight in the face, knocking her onto the mat. Kate played Ashton to her advantage and Jordan knew it. Time continued to run. Standing up with rage steaming from her eyes, Ashton wipes the blood from her nose. She begins to lunge towards Kate.

"Time's up!" Donovan shouts.

"Initiate Thomas. Pass." Jordan speaks and Ashton is livid.

"What!? Are you serious!? She got one punch off me!" Ashton shouts at them.

This time Jordan stands from her seat looking down to Ashton, not needing the speakers. "You underestimated your opponent; she studied you until she found an opening and you fell right into it. Played you at your own game," Jordan said. Ashton's anger grows as Jordan talks down to her. Kate stands by, enjoying how Ashton is being chastised. "This agency is looking for highly skilled agents who can handle themselves in all aspects of the field, not just someone who can throw a couple of punches," Jordan continues, this time speaking to all the initiates in the room. She sits down and speaks into her microphone as if the confrontation with Ashton never happened. "Initiate Hunter. Pass." The murmurs grow louder from Jordan's decision. Even Ashton can't understand how Jordan allowed her to continue.

Ashton goes back to her team. Seth tries to approach Ashton, but she swats him away. "It might be really smart for you to get away from me right now," Ashton threatens.

"You need to get that checked out before it causes an infection," Seth points nervously to Ashton's bloody nose. Ashton calms down slightly and realizes her battle isn't with this kid, but with Jordan.

"Fine, let's go," Ashton says following Seth to the bench.

Ethan Carmichael v. Darren Peters

"Looks like I'm up," Ethan says. "Have any tips for me?" He looks past Blair standing in between himself and Angel.

"And why would you want tips from me?" Angel asks. "I haven't gone yet."

Blair, standing in between them, moves her head from side to side watching the exchange, not sure if she should comment.

Ethan gives Angel a flirtatious smile. "I know a skilled fighter when I see one." He walks away leaving her wondering.

Just as Blair opens her mouth to speak Angel holds her hand up, "Don't."

Ethan steps into the ring and instantly gets into defensive position. Darren follows suit. The fight begins as both throw standard punches at one another. It's pretty boring as everyone watches on, almost as if they're watching a simple sparring match. Jordan watches the fight closely. It may look like a boring fight to everyone else, but she sees one fighter purposely prolonging the fight. Ethan blocks a few of Darren's martial arts techniques as he spins his leg in the air trying to knock Ethan off balance. Once the clock hits one minute, something clicks in Ethan. Darren throws a punch centimeters away from Ethan's face and he catches it directly in his palm. Ethan encloses Darren's fist in his hand and slowly brings him down to his knees with just one hand. Darren's face strains and veins protrude from his forehead. As Darren tries to free his hand from Ethan's restraint, Ethan pulls his fist back and with full force knocks Darren out cold, breaking his jaw in the process. The room is silent. Ethan stands over Darren, who is lying face down onto the mat. Ethan comes back to reality as the room speakers come to life.

"Initiate Carmichael. Pass." David speaks. "Initiate Peters. Fail."

Darren's limp body gets carried away by the medical team and Ethan makes his way back to his team. On his way back, he glances over at Angel looking for any reaction. She keeps her focus on the ring.

Angel "Hunter" v. Amos Jones

Angel sees her name on the large screen.

"Good luck," Blair says, hoping Angel does better than she did.

Angel doesn't have her powers and she has to fight using plain old skills. Amos enters the ring along with Angel and nods to her as a sign of respect. The round begins. Angel and Amos fight a fair fight. Amos lifts his leg to kick Angel. She dodges it by going under it and kicking him in the other, tripping him and making him fall hard onto the mat. Angel gets a little excited because she's winning without the use of her powers, but she can't help but wonder why this is so easy. Amos lies on the floor for a moment, groaning, until Angel comes rushing towards him, putting him into a UFC trained ju jitsu head lock with her legs. Amos quickly taps out, gasping for air. Jordan, David and Donovan observe Angel's fight. They are not accepting of the outcome.

"Initiate Jones, do you want to be here?" Donovan asks over the speakers. Angel doesn't understand his question. It takes a minute for Amos to answer as he holds his head down in shame.

"No, sir."

"That's what I figured," Donovan sighs in frustration and holds the bridge of his nose. "Initiate Jones. Fail. Initiate Hunter. Pass." He announces Angel's win so nonchalantly, it annoys her. She speaks up. Donovan is disapproving. He knows Angel did not deserve the win. Amos is escorted out of the arena by Exodus guards and Angel stays in the ring.

"Is there a problem?" Angel asks Donovan.

"Excuse me?" Donovan asks, asserting his authority.

"You've had this smug look on your face since the moment I walked in here and now you won't even give me the credit I deserve."

"You deserve nothing because you didn't win. He let you win," Donovan snaps. "But because of the rules, you passed by default."

"I don't want it, it wasn't a fair fight, so I don't accept it," Angel snaps back.

"No, you're going to accept it because this time you don't control the outcome," Donovan speaks subliminally.

"Then give me someone else to fight," Angel demands.

"Initiate Hunter, the phase is over and there's no one else for you to battle," Jordan steps in.

Angel refuses to leave the ring without fighting in an actual battle. "Then I'll fight you. You be my opponent," Angel points to Donovan. He confidently stands from his seat and unbuttons his crisp black designer shirt. The room comes to a sudden halt. The agents are in awe. She challenged *the* best agent in the agency – not only the best but the head agent. Donovan says nothing as he prepares to battle Angel. He's waited for this moment since the first day they met. He takes off his shirt, revealing a very chiseled, caramel glazed chest that has most of the women in the room hypnotized. Jordan steps in, ruining the moment.

"We're not doing this. No one is proving anything today," she says.

"Lieutenant, it's fine. Sometimes you have to teach these initiates a lesson in respect and…discipline." He leaves the balcony knowing without a doubt he'll win this battle. He's going to put Angel in her place and hopefully her sister will get the message too. "You know this wasn't the smartest choice, right?" Donovan says, following Angel around the ring.

The battle begins. Donovan takes the first swing, Angel blocks. They swing and kick at one another, each one getting blocked and dodged by the other. At this moment, Donovan realizes Angel is a much tougher opponent to face than he thought and everyone in the arena can witness it. Angel, on the other hand, is only focused on one thing: winning. After a minute or so of neither one hitting the other, Donovan does a quick combo – too quick for Angel to react to. Angel tries to block it but fails and he knocks her up against the glass wall of the ring, face slammed on the wall. The hit was hard and Angel struggles to pick herself up. He then comes up behind her and wraps his large bicep with veins protruding around her neck. Trying to get Angel to tap out, he squeezes tighter and tighter. It's working. Donovan is so much taller than her, six feet two inches tall, she needs to be smart about her next move. Angel braces herself and quickly head-butts Donovan; he never saw it coming. His grip around her neck loosens and he struggles to focus. Angel uses the wall of the ring as her base and backflips over him, landing behind him and breaks free. The initiates are stunned. As Donovan tries to focus from the head butt, Angel spins and kicks Donovan as hard as she can on the side of his face. He falls on to the mat, not moving for a moment, but slowly stands as blood begins to show from his eye.

The match is over and some agents in the room applaud her. Even Jordan hides the smallest smirk. Angel enjoys the applause. She's never had people cheer for her before, it just makes the decision she made to come here that much better, but her happiness soon leaves when she looks at Donovan. She has not a clue as to why she wants his acceptance, but she does. Donovan walks away embarrassed internally and visibly angry.

"Agent James." Jordan stops Donovan. He knows why she stopped him; she taught him to give the credit and respect where it's due.

"Congratulations, you were an exceptional opponent," Donovan professionally shakes Angel's hand. Angel leaves the ring satisfied.

"You all have successfully completed Phase 1. We started out with ten of you, now there are only seven. This is only the beginning. Phase 2 begins soon, until then, prepare yourselves." Jordan says.

Jordan, David and Donovan exit the arena. The room begins to clear out of guards, medical staff and the remaining initiates. The girls are the last to leave.

"You killed it, Ang," Ashton congratulates her sister.

"Yeah, he'll think twice before challenging you again," Blair amused them.

Angel laughs, "I don't think our judges felt the same way."

"Trust me, I think they noticed," Daniella says.

"The phase was fine and all, but am I the only who wants to know what happened to the main reason we were brought here?" Ashton interrupts the conversation.

"Yeah, I don't like being played," Angel replies.

"Okay, let's just retrace our steps. When did we all notice they were gone?" Blair asks.

"We don't need to retrace our steps. We know who took them. It was Miss Lieutenant. I knew I couldn't trust her," Ashton says, remembering her hatred for Jordan.

"We don't know for sure she took them," Daniella says.

"But we don't know she didn't either," Angel replies, "It's too much of a coincidence."

"Can we ask her now because I'm feeling like someone threw a brick at my head?" Blair places her hand on her forehead, trying to soothe her pounding headache.

The girls exit the arena and make their way to Jordan's office to get some answers.

"You know you have a target on your back now, right?" Ashton says walking with Angel.

"How do you figure that?" Angel asks.

"You challenged the strongest guy here, he's Knox's right hand, and won. I mean, you're not me, but you are the one to watch," Ashton expresses.

"One, we're twins so I think I am you, and two, I'm not the one to watch because Jones let me win and Donovan was stronger than anyone I ever faced," Angel downplays her skills.

"You acting like you're not awesome right now makes me question if we're even related."

"How about we focus on getting to Jordan's office? I think Blair is on the verge of passing out," Angel says.

They walk through the agency's hallway but suddenly are stopped when Ethan approaches them. "Hey, Angel."

"Hey," Angel greets him blandly, hoping the other girls, especially Ashton, don't catch on to the way Ethan makes her slightly flustered.

"Don't want to introduce us to your new friend, Angel?" Ashton turns on the sarcasm.

Angel sighs, wishing Ethan would just leave. "Ethan, this is my sister Ashton. Daniella, and you met Blair. This is Ethan Carmichael."

Ethan flashes that same pearly white smile to them all, "Nice to meet you."

Ashton side eyes him. He glances back at Angel for a moment and takes in her beauty.

"Did you need something, Ethan? We're in a bit of a hurry," Daniella asks as Blair tries to hold herself up against the wall near the elevator.

"I-I just wanted to know if I could talk to Angel for a minute. I mean Angel, i-if that's okay, I would like to talk to you." For a guy that has so much confidence and as strong as he is, Angel makes him feel like a 12-year-old boy trying to ask out his first crush.

"I don't think so," Ashton says speaking for her sister. A part of Angel doesn't want to talk to Ethan because she wants to keep her focus on doing well in these upcoming phases, but the other part of her really wonders why he's being so nice.

"It's okay, I'll meet you guys in the office," Angel says.

"Fine," Ashton says, glaring at Ethan as she goes.

Ashton, Daniella and Blair get on the elevator, leaving them to talk privately.

"Your sister, huh? That makes so much sense now," Ethan says.

"And what is that supposed to mean?"

"It means I can see the similarities when you fight. Personalities are different, but you both fight with precision like you're thinking two steps ahead of your opponent." Ethan smiles down at her and Angel tries to hold strong as her back leans against the hallway wall. "And it took all of your strength not to laugh when Kate got beat to a pulp."

Angel smiles, holding her head down, giving a small chuckle under her breath remembering the beating Ashton gave to a disrespectful Kate. She quickly brings herself back to focus on Ethan. "Why are you here Ethan?" Angel asks.

"I just wanted to congratulate you on your win against Agent James. I respect it."

"It's not a big deal. I just did what anyone would do when not given a fair chance."

"Understandable, but I saw the way Agent James was looking at you. It was like…you didn't deserve to be here, or he didn't want you to win," Ethan continues. "You proved him wrong."

"You don't know me, so how do you know if I deserve to be anything?" Angel asks.

"You're right, but you're different from the rest of us and what you did in the ring today only proved me right," he steps closer to her. His chest inches away from meeting her crossed arms. Heat begins to flood Angel's cheeks and that same fluttering feeling appears in her stomach. She feels a little uneasy as to what Ethan means by saying she's different.

"Don't take this the wrong way but trust me when I say I don't need you to tell me what I deserve and I'm not here to prove anything to anyone except the lieutenant." Angel walks around him and leaves him with his foot in his mouth, but there's something else she needs to know. "What's your motive?"

Ethan titters at her question, "What do you mean?"

"Why are you being so nice to me? You don't know anything about me, and we only met a couple of hours ago." Ethan may be nice to look at, but Angel won't let that cloud her judgment.

"You know…I just…and when you-" he can't sum up the words that he's only being nice to her because she's attractive. Clearly, Angel isn't going to get a clear answer from him right now. Angel returns his smile, thinking he's kind of cute when he's skittish.

"Bye, Ethan Carmichael," Angel walks away and makes her way to meet the other girls. Ethan watches as she struts away, believing she knows the truth about his true intentions.

Chapter 14

David's office is tense as he sits at his desk and questions the decisions Jordan has made for the agency. Jordan and Donovan stand in front of him arguing back and forth over the challenge against Angel.

"When I tell you to stand down, you stand down!" Jordan shouts.

"She called me out. What would I look like in front of them if I didn't step up?" Donovan defends himself.

"You would look like the leader I thought you could be."

"And I've proven that time and time again."

"You have, but down there you proved nothing other than the initiates can do what they want and get away with it." She tries not to turn into a motherly figure, but she can't help it. She's taught him everything he knows about being an agent. Donovan realizes he made a mistake with fighting Angel and hates that he let his emotions get the best of him, but it's going to take some time to put his trust in them.

"I'll make it right, Lieutenant," he says, exiting the office, disappointed in himself.

There's a moment of silence as Donovan leaves.

"Can I ask you something?" David interrupts, wanting to express his thoughts.

"Sure," Jordan says, allowing herself to open to him. "What is it?"

"Why do you want those girls here?" She can't believe they're about to have this conversation again. She'll let him finish, but after this she's not speaking about this again. "I understand wanting to open Exodus. I'm just as happy as you are but having those girls here who are undertrained and underdeveloped is only putting us at a greater risk of being compromised. I think we should keep the recruited initiates and agents the CIA sent over, get rid of these phases and train them as we take on missions. We don't need a bunch of teenage girls from off the street." Jordan lets him finish before she explains to him her reasonings.

"Do you know Agent Morrison?" she asks him.

"Of course I do. He's been with us since the very beginning," he replies.

"Agent Morrison joined Phantom when he was about 20, had no clue what it meant to be an agent, and didn't even know the difference between a Smith & Wesson Shield and a Walther P99." Jordan calmly proves a point.

"What does that have to do with anything?"

"The point I'm making is that several Exodus agents were underdeveloped when they first started, and to be honest they still are," she puts emphasis on her statement, making sure David understands. "Those girls down there are ten times more intelligent and experienced than our own agents ever were, specifically those I hand-picked myself."

"Those girls you brought in undermine authority, have no self-control, have egos as big as the earth and don't get me started on the girl who thought she could win a battle by blasting her opponent away." David takes his frustration out on her.

Jordan doesn't want to hear anymore of David's complaining and she can't understand how he has such a lack of faith in her after all this time. Jordan can see she's only good enough for him when he needs the support, but she'll never receive it in return. Being the mature person, she stands from her seat before she says something that could ruin their relationship.

"So that's it. You're not going to say anything, not even consider my opinion?" David asks her.

She stops at the door before exiting. "You know, I've never questioned any of the decisions you made, no matter how stubborn and egotistical they were and trust me I've disagreed with 90 percent of those decisions." The disappointment in Jordan's tone gets louder. "But the one time I need your support, the one time I need you to just have my back and not question every little thing I do, you can't do it." The only thing David can do is listen to the heartbreak in her tone. "I am going to train them the way I want to, and I'll decide who stays and who goes, and I don't want to have this conversation again…I won't have it again." Jordan tries to leave his office, but David stops her.

"J, you know I support you and I have your back 100 percent."

"Then act like it," she says, leaving him in his office to rethink how he hasn't been the most supportive friend and partner.

Hearing a lot of commotion in Lieutenant Knox's office, Angel abruptly opens the door and sees Ashton forcefully pushing Natalie towards a wall, Daniella and Blair standing by trying to talk Ashton out of whatever she's about to do.

"Why did you do it?! Why did you take them?!" Ashton shouts at a terrified Natalie.

"Leave her alone!" Daniella shouts at Ashton.

"Can we all just calm down?" Blair says, wanting silence for her headache.

Angel rushes in. "Ashton, what the hell are you doing?!"

"We came in and saw Bambi over here looking at our pictures on that screen with our training suits matching our profiles," Ashton says, not taking her eye off Natalie.

"I-It's not what you think!" she shouts, terrified.

Angel looks at the large screen behind Jordan's desk. It wasn't there the first time they all met in here, so it must have been hidden behind that large painting. The screen shows suit modifications done on each girl based on their significant abilities. Angel moves closer to the screen and sees Jordan knows more about them than she led on.

"Answer me. Answer me right now!" Ashton is losing her patience.

"I-I-I can't tell you right now," Natalie's words tremble as she tries to speak.

"Ashton! Let her go!" Daniella shouts.

"Not until she gives back what she stole," Ashton says. Natalie's body shakes as she's being held up against a wall. The girls argue back and forth about Ashton's actions and the information they see on screen. "She's been lying to us the entire time," Ashton says.

"There must be a reason for all of this," Angel says. "Natalie, are - " Before Angel could ask Natalie anything, Ashton shouts in pain, holding her head in her hands, quickly backing away from Natalie. The fear in Natalie caused her to panic; she wanted to break free from Ashton and all she did was touch Ashton's arm. "What did you do!?" Angel shouts at Natalie.

"I-I," Natalie barely able to speak looks down at her trembling hands. "I-I didn't mean too. I'm sorry."

"Natalie are you…" Daniella wants to ask but can see Natalie already knows the question.

"I don't care what you are, help her!" Angel is now upset her sister is hurt and she is no longer the calm person in the room.

"I-I don't know how. It will wear off soon," Natalie says. Blair stands in the corner barely able to stand on her own two feet as the rest of the girls continue to argue.

"Guys," Blair whispers, trying to get someone's attention.

"All of this wouldn't have happened if Ashton wasn't so set on fighting everyone!" Daniella shouts at Angel.

"Guys," Blair tries to speak louder.

"I would watch the next thing I say if I were you," Angel confronts Daniella.

"Or what?! I've only known you for a day and can see you never tell her when she's wrong!"

"Guys!" Blair gives one last shout before Angel and Daniella turn to her with anger steaming from their heads and Natalie fearfully standing in the background hoping Ashton is okay.

"What?!" Angel and Daniella shout at her.

"I think I nee…" Blair slurs her last words and falls limp onto Jordan's couch.

"So much for keeping a low profile," Angel says.

At this moment, Blair and Ashton are injured inside of Jordan's now unorganized office. Angel knows they have to get out of here before someone finds them and has questions.

"What are we going to do? We've got to get them out of here," Daniella says.

"I don't know, Daniella. Unfortunately, I've never been in this situation before," Angel says in an acerbic tone. Daniella uses the little bit of patience she has to not jump over the chair and lunge towards Angel.

"I know someone who can help," Natalie didn't want to interrupt them and doesn't know if they want her help at all. Angel kneels close to an unconscious Ashton, rubbing her head and hoping she feels her presence.

"Who? Someone to come help finish what you started?" Angel snaps.

"Let's just hear her out. What other choice do we have?" Daniella takes over the position of being the calm one in the room.

Natalie takes out her phone and calls that someone. "Hi, I need your help in the lieutenant's office, can you get here…fast, bring the preservation pods…oh, and Seth, can you keep this quiet, please?" Natalie hangs up the phone and helps Daniella and Angel prep Blair and Ashton to be taken to the medical wing.

When Seth and his assistant arrive, Natalie, Angel and Daniella help them quietly roll Ashton and Blair in two preservation pods down the agency's hallway.

"Should I even ask what happened in there?" Seth asks Natalie.

"Not if you don't want to be involved," Natalie says, looking down at her trembling hands. Seth can see just by looking at her something is wrong; he knows her too well.

"Did you have…you know…an episode?" Seth whispers to her like it's been a secret just between the two. Natalie stares at him and fiddles around with her hands. "Really?! You haven't had one in months?" Seth says in shock.

"I know Seth. I feel bad enough," Natalie says, disappointed in herself.

"Nat, what happened in that room?" Seth is concerned for his friend.

"Can we focus on getting them some help, please?" Angel interrupts Seth and Natalie's not so secretive conversation.

As they take the elevator down, the four of them finally make their way to the agency's medical wing. Angel and Daniella have never seen so much high-tech equipment all in one room. The medical wing looks as though CSI: New York City Crime Lab and Grey-Sloan Memorial had a baby. The medical wing at Exodus is one of the most predominant medical centers in the country, run by the youngest and one of the most profound biochemists, Dr. Seth Nolan. Angel and Daniella wait outside the operating room, Angel becoming tense as lab technicians poke and prod at her sister. Natalie looks back at a frantic Angel through the glass window.

"Seth, please tell me she's going to be okay," Natalie pleads.

"We just have a few more tests to take, but they're going to be fine," Seth reassures her, but can tell it's not helping her as much as it should. "Hey, it's not your fault," he places his hand gently on her shoulder. "You couldn't have known this would happen…it was just an accident." Natalie, feeling surer of herself, helps Seth with further testing.

"Somebody better have a damn good explanation as to what the hell happened here," Jordan rushes in, furious to see the agents she fought so hard to find laying on a procedure table.

"Umm..I-I'm going to go finish tests…the tests…I'm going to go finish the tests," Seth says, mixing up his words.

Jordan is a very intimidating person, and Seth tries to avoid this side of her as much as possible. "Natalie…," Jordan begins. Natalie is fearful as to what Jordan's reaction will be once she tells her the truth.

"I tried to stop them, really," Natalie says as the truth comes exploding out of her mouth. They walk to a nearby office for privacy.

"What do you mean you tried to stop them?" Jordan asks.

"I was in your office running updates on their suits and they all came barging in, asking who took their powers a-a-and I didn't know what to say b-because you told me not to say anything and then the next thing I know Ashton is throwing me up against a wall," Natalie spills out her words frantically and Jordan tries to keep up.

"Nat, breathe…just breathe." Natalie takes a breath, finally dealing with the aftermath of her actions. "Now why are Ashton and Blair lying unconscious?"

"I'm not 100 percent sure why Blair passed out, but Ashton…" Natalie paused afraid to tell Jordan her episodes have come back.

"Natalie, what happened to Ashton?" Jordan worries something permanent is wrong. She can't afford to be losing any of them.

"I had…my…my powers are back," Natalie says as her voice breaks and tears begin to coat her face.

Jordan knows now what happened in her office as Ashton lays on the table. She wraps her arms around Natalie, pulling her close to her and brushing her hair with her hands. "It's okay… I'll fix it and everything will be okay."

Pushing Jordan away from her, Natalie snaps, "Everything is not okay! Do you know what it feels like to not be able to touch someone because you're afraid you might hurt them or kill them?"

"Natalie, I know it's hard and I'm trying my best to fix this, to fix all of this, but until I do, everything we do has to be done delicately." Jordan tries to calm her. "I promise you I will find a way to help you gain control, you just have to be patient with me." Natalie gives a slight nod, only able to be seen if you were close. Seeing Angel and Daniella through the glass window of the lab, Jordan hates the way she came into their lives and caused disruption, if she hadn't then this wouldn't have happened.

"Good news," Seth says as he slowly enters the office. Jordan and Natalie quickly direct their attention to him. "They're going to be fine." They feel a sense of relief. "Getting Ashton into the preservation pod restarted her brain, giving her a burst in adrenaline and Blair she just had a simple complication with her suit." Seth gives them the good news while gazing at Natalie letting her know she can stop blaming herself.

"What's the recovery time?" Jordan asks.

"They should be awake and responsive within the next few hours," Seth says.

"Thank you, Seth," Jordan replies. Seth leaves the office, leaving Natalie and Jordan alone to take in all the events that transpired. "Everything is under control now; we just have to be more cautious." Jordan makes light of the situation.

"I understand always wanting to fix everything and everyone. That's who you are. But if you don't start being honest with people, especially them," Natalie says looking at Angel and Daniella, "someone's going to get hurt and you might not be able to fix it." Natalie leaves the office to help Seth in the lab. Natalie is right and Jordan knows it, but she can't help it. Her life has always been about fixing people, fixing situations, and keeping secrets. She walks out the back of the lab, attempting to avoid Angel and Daniella.

"You're just going to leave? You're not even going to tell me what's going on?" Angel blocks Jordan's path.

"Angel. Ashton is going to be fine, it was just an accident," Jordan avoids the question.

"You know that's not what I'm talking about," Angel is becoming more furious by the second. Jordan is out of options, trying everything to avoid telling the truth. By telling Angel some of the truth she hopes maybe that will keep her away for some time.

"The suits you're wearing look just like everyone else's, but with modifications."

"What type of modifications?" Daniella asks, approaching them.

"The suits were designed by Natalie and my partner, LIS. They suppress your powers."

"You came and found us. We didn't come find you. You said you wanted us because of our powers and now you're saying you took them away because of what, you realized we were too much of a hassle for you?" Angel says.

"I had to see how you would handle situations if your abilities weren't a factor. Like I told you before, this is the safest place you could ever be. I'm only doing what's best for all of you and my agency," Jordan says with the sincerest tone she can summon. She wants them to trust her; it's the only way to keep them safe. Jordan moves around them, but she has the final word. "And I didn't take your powers. You still have them. Just take off that bracelet," Jordan says, pointing to the attached silver bracelet on their suits. "…But you are going to have to eventually stop depending on them." She leaves.

Daniella is beginning to believe coming here was not the right decision. All the kept secrets, and the people around here are so angry, she's bound to lose her temper again. Angel is torn; a part of her believes she should have thought over Jordan's offer before accepting it so quickly and that maybe Ashton was right. The other part of her wants to give Jordan the benefit of the doubt. Deep down, and she doesn't know why, but there's something about Jordan she trusts.

Angel rushes down the hall to catch up to her, "Look, I understand you're just doing your job, but we haven't had the most trustworthy people around us, so you can understand why we feel the way we do."

"I get it and I know that I just barged in on your lives, but you can trust me, Angel." Leaving the girls, Jordan calls LIS. "LIS, any information on Clay's location?"

"I have found him in five possible disclosed locations, Lieutenant."

"Download those coordinates to the main hub…my star pupils are getting impatient."

"Right away, Lieutenant."

Seth and Natalie finalize testing on Ashton and Blair so they'll be back to themselves. "And one last shot of epinephrine for Blair and we're done." Seth finalizes his workup. He watches as Natalie looks out the glass wall separating them from Angel and Daniella. "You can go tell them they can come in if they want."

"I don't think I'm someone they want to talk to right now," Natalie says, picking and poking at Seth's medical equipment. Seth finishes giving Ashton and Blair their medication and comforts Natalie.

"All you can do is try. What's the worst that could happen?"

"Well, Angel could basically make my vision worse with a single punch," Natalie pushes her glasses up on her nose.

"See, and nothing could be worse than that," Seth tries to make her laugh, and it works.

"Fine," she says walking towards the glass window. "You guys can come and see them," Natalie says peeking out of the doorway. Angel rushes in, Daniella not far behind. "They only sustained minor injuries and should be back to themselves in no time," Natalie says, attempting to break the tension. Ashton and Blair lay on the preservation table, consciously asleep.

"When will she wake up?" Angel asks, rubbing Ashton's large hair. She'll freak if she wakes up and one hair is out of place.

"It should be in a few minutes," Seth says as the monitors beep periodically. "I'll give you guys some privacy." Seth leaves as Natalie stares him down, not wanting him to leave her alone with the other girls, but he leaves anyway.

"It's okay, Natalie," Angel says as she watches the exchange and an uncomfortable Natalie. "I know it was just an accident. I've been through it before…sort of still going through it now."

"Same," Daniella agrees.

Natalie is grateful. It's comforting to know they're just like her and are going through the same issues.

"But from what I've seen, Ashton doesn't look like the forgiving type," Daniella says.

"Unfortunately, you're right," Angel says.

Natalie's smile quickly fades. Angel continues to rub Ashton's hair, waiting for her to wake up.

Daniella sees Blair moving. "Hey, look," Daniella says. Blair slowly wakes, unaware of what happened.

"What's going on? Where am I?" Blair asks looking around the medical wing.

"You're in the East Medical Wing on level 3 of the agency," Natalie says.

"You passed out," Daniella says.

Blair, confused, tries to sit up. "All I remember is Ashton throwing you up against the wall," she says to Natalie. Natalie wishes everyone would forget that humiliating situation.

"Someone say my name," Ashton says, slowly awaking.

"Ash!" Angel shouts. Even though Natalie and Seth told her Ashton would be fine, it's nothing compared to hearing her unique voice.

"Why are you yelling?!" Ashton slowly opening her eyes. "What's going on?" she asked. Everyone hesitates.

"You don't remember anything?" Angel asks.

"I remember talking to…" Ashton pauses trying to remember Natalie's name, "her." She points to Natalie, who is peeking from behind Angel and Daniella. "And then everything pretty much goes black after that," Ashton steps down from the table, fully regaining her energy. The room is awkwardly silent. "So is anyone going to tell me what the hell happened?! How did I get here?"

"You passed out," Angel speaks up. "I walked in on you yelling at Natalie and then you just passed out…it was like…" Angel tries to come up with a stretched-out truth, "you were dizzy. Did you eat today?"

"Actually no, I feel like I haven't eaten in days." Ashton's only worry now is to find some food. Ashton makes her way to the door to leave. "Ang, let's go. I'm hungry." Angel knew that would switch her focus off a confrontation with Natalie.

Angel catches up with Ashton and secretly gives Natalie a slight nod. "Hopefully we can find something in this god forsaken place." The girls leave, following behind Ashton and leaving Natalie alone.

Chapter 15

A clean shaven, hair freshly cut Silas Clay paces in his home office, that even the President would be jealous. He walks back and forth, and back and forth, figuring out his next move. He slumps down on his state-of-the-art sofa and lays out plans with his counterpart, William Mitchell.

"All we need is them," he says, pointing to the information he has on the four mysterious girls.

"We don't even know where they're located. We've searched every corner of this country," Will says, being the realistic one of the two.

"They're kids! They don't just disappear," Clay raises his voice.

"I know. We almost had them."

Clay takes a minute to calm himself before he becomes more aggressive, the red on his olive skin fading away. He's been working on his anger. It causes him to lose focus, which he can't have if he wants his plan to succeed.

"We are this close to having everything," Clay says, slightly closing his index finger and thumb together. "We have the men, I have a shipment of biochips on the way, we just need the serum."

"They approved it already?!" Will asks surprised.

"No, but our meeting should go according to plan. We have Director Mills on our side, and we have votes from two other directors," Clay says. For his superpowered army militia to be a success, he needs to show he has allies.

"Mills isn't easy to persuade. How do you know he'll agree to this?" Will asks cautiously.

"Mills is all about personal gain. If it's beneficial for him–which it is—he'll do what it takes to make sure we succeed."

"And Jordan?"

Clay closes his eyes and relaxes himself before he blows up at Will for mentioning the woman he despises. Will only wants to make sure Clay has thought of everything and has a backup plan if they come across trouble along the way.

"What about her?"

"If she finds out about this meeting, which she will, she is going to do everything she can to stop it from happening. She has a vendetta-"

"That will cloud her judgment," Clay interrupts him as he goes on and on about the revenge Jordan may seek. According to Clay, he knows Jordan better than she knows herself. "Let's say she finds out where the meeting will take place. She will be so concerned with preventing it from happening that she'll put them in the crossfire." Clay points down at the holographic table showing digital prints of information on the mysterious girls.

"But-," before Will could interject his worries once again, Marissa Mitchell and Alexandria Clay enter.

"Mom! Get over yourself," Alexandria shouts like an annoyed daughter.

"You do not leave this house, Alexandria, and I won't say it again!"

Alexandria aggressively turns to face her mother. "I went for a walk, to get air! Excuse me for not wanting to be cramped up in Clay Manor all day!" This is a continuous argument for Marissa and

Alexandira which explains why Clay is ignoring them. "Dad!? You can jump in at any time!" Alexandria shouts at the back of Clay's head.

"Don't bring your father into this," Marissa demands.

"I don't understand why it's such an issue with me leaving. I'm 21 years old! You have two kids and you only let one go off and do whatever he wants! Why?!" Alexandria is beginning to break down, becoming increasingly angrier. "Uncle Will, tell them!" Will throws his hands up in surrender. Alexandria knows she's different from most people because of the powers and all, but she can control them more now than ever. Her so-called parents have always "protected" her from the outside world out of fear of what people may find out about her and, even worse, take her away; well at least that's what they've always told her.

Clay has had enough of the back-and-forth bickering between Marissa and Alexandria, and he's especially had enough of Alexandria's constant complaining. It's the same question every day: why can't I leave? He quickly stands from his seat and aggressively approaches Alexandria, staring down at her, piercing her with his forest green eyes. "Because your brother can't manipulate anyone he lays his eyes on. He is out there handling business, and you can't even do the one simple task I ask you to do!" His voice grows louder. Alexandria has always been intimidated by her father; he strikes fear in her and anyone he speaks to. But she respects him, strangely. Clay calmly pulls back from her and takes his seat. "You will not leave this house until I approve it." Alexandria wants to cry, but she balls up her fists by her side and sucks it up.

"How are the subjects?" Clay asks.

"They are under my total control," Alexandria says, fighting hard to hold back her tears welling up, filled with anger.

"Good, go make sure of it," Clay says. Alexandria quickly walks out the office, but her feet stop at the door. "And Alex," Clay stops her, "we won't have this conversation again, correct?"

Alexandria continues to face the door, not wanting to show the weakness that sits upon her face. "Correct," she says and leaves. She walks quickly to the basement of her family's compound, her suspicions heightened. This can't be a normal life, this can't be it for her, she thinks. She's always felt like she didn't belong to this family. She has a blue eye and a grey eye, her father and brother have green and her mom, brown. It may not seem like a big issue, but it was the first of many questions raised as Alexandria grew up.

"Was all that really necessary?" Marissa asks, sitting next to her husband. She is just as mean and surly as him. Her build of a model is thin but she's athletic and can hold her own.

"You want her to walk all over you, go ahead, but I raise my children how I want to," Clay says, stopping the conversation before it goes any further. Marissa is fuming at the ears but holds back her tongue and lets Clay continue with his power trip.

"So, what's our next move?" Will interrupts the tension between his best friend and wife, an everyday occurrence between the two.

"We move forward with having everything in place for the meeting," Clay says.

"And her?" Marissa points to the holographic information on Jordan Knox.

"I'll deal with Jordan myself," Clay says, almost forgetting Marissa and Will are in the room.

"Are you sure?! Because as long as she is still breathing, our problems don't go away!" Marissa shouts, hoping it will get through Clay's thick skull. "We need to take her down now." Marissa has despised Jordan for a long time. She needs for Clay to succeed. If he succeeds, Leviathan succeeds.

"You worry about the assignment I give you," Clay asserts his authority once again, "and that is finding me more men. You let me worry about Jordan and those girls."

Marissa approaches Clay, trying to intimidate him just as he did with Alexandria, "You got it… boss," Marissa says as she leaves the office, shoving him in the process. Will exhales out of frustration. Why can't we have one normal day where everything runs smoothly, he thinks to himself.

"We will have everything. We will end her, get those girls and I will have my day," Clay expresses. Will thinks Clay is talking to him, but he's really talking to himself. Like a self-affirmation he would do in the mirror.

Below the compound is a very efficient and upgraded lab. A discombobulated, pale and lanky man scatters around the main lab, overseen by one of Clay and Marissa's Milita Men. This man is Dr. Martin Edwards. "Leviathan will rule, Leviathan will rule," he says to himself repeatedly as he mixes different chemicals together looking for a reaction. The chemicals produce a bubbling purple liquid. Picking up a syringe that lays on a tray with two others, he looks over his square-rimmed glasses and injects the liquid into the syringe and lays it back on the tray. "I-I need to give the subject their feeding," he says to the Milita guards standing near a glass box the size of a standard bedroom. It can weather any natural disaster. Martin holds the steel tray filled with syringes as the guard unlocks the main door to the room that contains the glass-boxed room. The Milita guard opens the second door and Martin enters the room. A man sits in a corner along the wall. He's chained to the floor and his feet and wrists are shackled, too. From the length of his legs stretched out across the floor, you can see he's a tall man, maybe six foot three, but he's withering away. In his past life he once was a very strong man, mentally and physically. He could take down anything and survive everything, but it's a new day. Clay has put him through it all and this scientist has tested every serum created on him for the past nine years. He's a prisoner who was taken from his family years ago. Martin approaches the prisoner carefully; any sudden movements will put the prisoner on edge. He kneels in front of the shivering man, only a pair of navy-blue sweatpants keeping him warm. The prisoner's sunken brown eyes look up at Martin as he wipes away the sweat dripping down on his cold and clammy brown skin.

"Everything will work out in the end," he says softly to the prisoner as he lifts the tatted arm to insert medications to keep the prisoner stable and alive. The purple liquid alters the prisoner's reality; it increases his emotions. He is cold to the touch, but on the inside, struggling to show emotion, he is heated. Inserting the syringe with the orange liquid will create rage in his eyes, only able to see this strong emotion in the world. Everyone he sees he hates and wants to do bodily harm. Inserting the clear liquid makes the prisoner vulnerable to Alexandria's memory and emotional manipulation. The prisoner breathes heavily, in and out, as Martin lifts the syringe with the purple liquid. The prisoner gains enough strength to take the syringe from the scientist and lunge towards him. Martin lays on the floor, his heart leaping from his chest as he stares above at this grungy man. Two Milita guards rush in to hold the prisoner down as he struggles to break free. He can't take any more of the medicine being dripped in his veins.

"Dr. Edwards, are you okay?" one of the guards asks.

Martin gathers himself and quickly inserts the last two serums. "I'm fine, and please call me Martin."

Once struggling to break free from the chains and guards, the prisoner becomes limp and passes out on the cold, white, tile floor. The guards drop him and exit the box.

"Don't worry. You'll be with your family soon," Martin says quietly as he cleans up his tray of syringes. Leaving the box, he approaches the Milita guard who is guarding the door. "I will need to examine him further before we give another dose." Martin goes back to his lab table and carefully cleans his syringe tray. Taking the syringes one at a time and putting them in a container for later use, he holds on to the syringe with the purple liquid. He refills the syringe and slowly injects it into his right arm. Martin has lost most of his touch with reality. Struggling with knowing what his life used to be, he takes the serum to forget. Fighting the pain from the serum as it moves through his veins, which lasts for seconds, he focuses and then relaxes his mind. He's free and realizes this is the place he's meant to be.

Chapter 16

Daniella sits in the living room, feet propped up on the coffee table watching cartoons in comfy sweats. Blair moves around the kitchen in jeans and a rock t-shirt attempting to fix herself something to eat. Angel and Ashton work out in the penthouse training room in their training suits. Ashton does combinations on a boxing punching bag and Angel does sets on the leg press.

"How are you feeling about all of this?" Angel asks.

"I mean I wish we went on an actual mission, but it's whatever. I'm going with the flow," Ashton breathes heavily.

"I get it. It's been a week and Jordan hasn't told us much since we got here. She went through all the trouble to find us just to tell us if we fail one of her phases we're out," Angel grunts as she presses harder on the leg press.

"She's hiding something and not just from us. Did you see how everyone was looking at Blair at the arena? Like she belonged in a looney bin." Ashton rapidly throws punches as the bag swings back and forth.

Angel stands from the leg press. "I did. Reminded me of how the employees at Gigi's B&B used to look at us."

"And then Gigi fired them all," Ashton grins. Angel chuckles as Ashton throws a harder punch grunting. "And don't get me started on her lackies?"

"Donovan and the captain?"

"It's obvious they don't like us. How are we supposed to work here when the boss's right and left hands want us out?" Ashton stops.

"You're right. Especially Donovan. He's been trying to get us out of here since we walked through the front doors." Angel sits on a workout bench. "But we just have to prove them wrong, all of them. That starts with you not just going with the flow and actually taking this process seriously."

Ashton smirks and shakes her head as she removes her boxing gloves. "How am I not taking this seriously, Ang? Please indulge me."

"You're walking around here mad at the world and pissing off everyone you meet," Angel says.

"I have done every stupid exercise that woman has given us for the last week."

"With an attitude," Angel rebuts.

"But I do it and I've kept this stupid bracelet on that takes my abilities away. So don't tell me I'm not taking this seriously. Don't forget why I'm here in the first place." Ashton walks away with boxing gloves in hand.

In the kitchen, Blair has successfully made turkey sandwiches. "Hey, do you want one?" Blair asks Daniella with a stuffed mouth, holding up a bitten sandwich.

"Sure," Daniella turns her attention away from the TV and sits on the bar stool facing Blair. "Thanks."

"No problem. It's about the only thing I can make," Blair jokes. They eat in silence for a moment. "So…how are you liking Exodus?"

Daniella finishes chewing before answering, "It's fine, I guess, still getting used to the whole government secrecy vibe."

"Same. Just the other day I saw Natalie building a human size robot."

"That's definitely not something you see every day," Daniella says.

Blair smiles and they laugh. "Can you believe Jordan had us running a full obstacle course wearing bookbags the size of a toddler?" Blair comes around the kitchen island to sit next to Daniella.

Daniella is uncomfortable at first but can sense how much Blair is trying to be her friend or at least be cordial. "Said its purpose was to test our agility and stamina. The lieutenant is over the top, but I respect it." Daniella says.

"Ditto." They smile, continuing to enjoy each other's company.

Angel and Ashton walk out of the training room together.

"Hey guys, you want a sandwich?" Blair spins around in the barstool to face them.

Angel and Ashton pause by the steps, unsure if they should. "Sure," Angel makes her way towards Blair and Daniella but not before looking back over her shoulder to see Ashton still standing by the stairs. Angel widens her eyes at Ashton and points her head towards the kitchen.

"No, I'm good. I'll be in the shower." Ashton leaves them, not wanting to do the whole bonding thing. Angel meets Daniella and Blair in the kitchen, standing behind the island.

"Sorry about that," Angel says grabbing a sandwich. "My sister doesn't do well in social situations."

"No excuse," Daniella doesn't look up from her food, not realizing what she said. Awkward silence fills the room.

"You're right and it doesn't give her the right to treat you guys that way, but that's Ash," Angel explains. "She's been this way since we were kids. There's nothing I can do."

"It's okay. I mean none of us fit in the category of 'normal'. We have our own way of getting to know one another," Blair says. Angel gives Blair a half smile, wishing she didn't always have to defend Ashton.

"Sorry," Daniella says to Angel, knowing it's not her fault Ashton acts the way she does. Angel nods, accepting the apology.

"See! Look at us bonding," Blair breaks the tension the only way she can. They all let a small laugh.

"Those were some pretty nice moves you guys did in Phase 1. Where did you learn them?" Angel asks, truly wanting to get to know them.

"My mom taught me tai chi when I was about six," Blair says. "It's supposed to be some family tradition. My grandfather taught her, his father taught him, but I must be special because neither of my siblings have trained."

"Maybe she taught you to help with your powers," Angel suggests.

"And you would be correct. Unfortunately, I barely have control most days," Blair says, opening and closing her hands, hoping random ice crystals don't form.

"The Sergeant who raised me taught me some skills and when I ended up in juvie…the C.O.s would organize boxing matches between me and the other girls," Daniella explains with caution.

"Let me guess. You would always win?" Angel asks, making Daniella feel comfortable with confiding in them.

Daniella gives a one-sided smile, "Something like that."

"What about you? With the skills you and Ashton have, being here should be right up your alley," Blair says.

Angel takes a second to respond. She leans back on the kitchen counter behind her. "Our parents," Angel says. "Dad was ex-military turned police officer and my mom…she stayed at-home. They taught us when we were around four. Our dad…he wanted us to be able to defend ourselves. Not everyone is accepting of a kid with psychic abilities."

"You are right about that," Daniella says, remembering the men who were trying to kidnap her not that long ago.

"We also were only allowed to use our powers in our house, so that helped."

"And did you?" Blair asks.

"Of course not," Angel laughs. Daniella and Blair join in.

Ashton watches from above, standing inside her bedroom doorway as they all bond with one another. She hates herself for being this way but it's the best way.

Natalie comes into the penthouse, multitasking – tablet in one hand and an advanced cell phone that she clearly designed herself in the other. "Hi, I hope you all are ready. Lieutenant Knox would like you ready and in your team vans in ten minutes," Natalie says to the girls, not looking up from her phone.

Blair groans. "Does she know the meaning of the word 'break'?"

"No. She actually despises the word," Natalie replies, not realizing it was a rhetorical question.

"I guess that means I should head down then," Angel says, already dressed in her training suit.

"I'll go with you," Natalie follows behind Angel. "Please be prompt." Natalie gives one last command to the others before exiting the penthouse.

Blair is in her room changing, dreading the next phase. Daniella lets out a heavy sigh and marches towards her room to change clothes as well, passing by Ashton on the balcony.

"Hope you enjoyed your bonding time," Ashton mocks. Daniella pauses in her walk, closes her eyes and exhales. She doesn't want to snap at Ashton because there's clearly something deeper going on.

Daniella turns to face Ashton. "Why are you so angry?" she asks.

Ashton instantly stops in her tracks as she walks down the balcony stairs. How could Daniella have the audacity to ask her something like this. She respects it, but still, she doesn't know enough to question her. Frankly, Ashton doesn't even know how to answer.

Ashton turns around and walks back up the stairs to approach Daniella. Ashton begins chuckling. "You're bold. I like it." Ashton leans against the balcony, speaking softly so that only Daniella can hear. "That is the question I have been trying to answer for myself for most of my life." Daniella thinks Ashton is just being her irreverent self but then realizes this anger has bothered Ashton for some time. "Honestly, I wish I had an answer. Some concrete, straight-to-the-point answer because then everything would make sense, you know? And I would have a reason for feeling this way and doing the things I do," Ashton continues staring out onto the balcony, forgetting for a moment Daniella is standing by. Daniella knows all too well what Ashton is going through. Anger is a powerful emotion, and it has taken over her life, and apparently Ashton's too. "But that's neither here nor there. So how about we end this therapy session, okay? You go your way and I'll go mind," Ashton finishes. She stands from the balcony and walks down the stairs to exit the penthouse. Daniella watches as she leaves and realizes they may have more in common than she thought.

Blair eases her way out of her room after eavesdropping on their conversation. She pokes her head out, making certain Ashton and Daniella have gone their separate ways. "Talk about awkward tension," she says to herself as she leaves the penthouse.

Team Alpha and Omega drive in two separate vans down a deserted road, only passing corn fields and random tractors. Jordan, David and Donovan are not too far ahead in their black SUV. They sit in awkward silence for most of the ride. Jordan does business on her tablet. Donovan stares out the window with his designer shades, thinking of his recent actions and, well, David is trying his best to fight the urge to tell Jordan how he feels about their last conversation.

"I heard there was a problem in your office a few days ago," David interrupts the silence.

"And I took care of it," Jordan gives him the cold shoulder, continuing to work. He can't fight the passion he feels for her and quickly checks to see if Charlie the driver, and Donovan are listening.

"I know there is a reason for everything you do, and you always have good intentions and I...," he pauses, then continues to speak to her quietly, "... apologize for not trusting in you." Jordan pauses working. He's saying all the right things to make her forgive him. He always says the right things at the strangest of times. But there's nothing wrong with making him sweat a little more. She goes back to work. "Everything has changed since that break in, especially between... us. We used to be on the same page and now you're there and I'm here. Is it wrong of me to want things to go back to how they used to be?" He waits for an answer, but nothing. Jordan looks up from her tablet and stares back at him through her slick designer shades. David continues, "But I know when you're ready you'll tell me everything, so I'll step back and let you handle it like you always do." He puts on his sunglasses and faces forward, giving Jordan the same treatment she's giving him.

And there it is, Jordan thinks to herself. David Lawrence is a different man from Captain Lawrence. David wears his heart on his sleeve and isn't afraid to express his feelings. Captain Lawrence is just that... a captain. He's all about business and nothing more. If it doesn't abide by the law or follow direct orders from his superiors, he wants no part of it.

Back in the vans, the initiates have not a clue where the lieutenant might take them. Team Omega's van holds their remaining three Initiates: Ashton, Daniella and Mark. The Alpha Team van is calm. Ethan and Kate sit in the front conversing quietly.

Angel and Blair sit next to one another. "Do you have any clue where we're going?" Blair asks.

"Nope, but if it has anything to do with Jordan, we're probably doing something that involves almost killing each other."

"I don't understand why she has to be so secretive. I mean I get that it comes with the whole secret government agency situation, but she did come to us. She could at least give us something," Blair says.

"Trust me, I have tried on several occasions to get the slightest bit of information, but I guess she'll tell us when she's ready," Angel says.

The vans make a sudden stop. "I think we're here," Angel says. Everyone takes their time exiting.

The vans have parked in the middle of a deserted field. Here there aren't any houses or any signs of life. The teams stand before Jordan, Captain Lawrence and Donovan and wait for their next instructions.

"You have made it to Phase 2," Jordan says to both teams as they squint their eyes from the sun. "You'll be working as a full team in a game I like to call 'hide and seek'." Jordan smiles, thinking how this was her favorite game as a child and that the initiates have no idea what's in store for them. The initiates stand, puzzled, and some are annoyed by the thought of playing games like children.

"Standing behind me is a building that burned down years ago. Both teams will secure an object hidden inside. You will have exactly seven minutes to retrieve this object and defuse the bomb," she explains. "And to make things interesting, Exodus guards will be a part of each team."

"You have one minute before we begin," Donovan says as he looks down at his watch. "I suggest you prepare your teams and appoint a leader. Gear is located on the tables near your teams' designated areas." Each team gathers in their own areas and discusses their plan of action.

"I think Angel should be our leader," Ethan suggests.

"And I think I should be leader," Kate says, a bandage under her eye.

"Why would you think that?!" Blair shouted, recalling her fight with Ashton. "Angel should be leader," Blair continues as she encourages Angel to step up.

"I'm not disagreeing with her, but I don't need to be the leader," Angel says.

"The way you handled yourself in Phase 1 makes you the perfect person for this," Ethan expresses.

Kate rolls her eyes, but not too much. She's still reeling from the pain of Ashton hitting her repeatedly. Angel takes a second to think about it. She's never led anyone beside her sister, and that's a challenge on its own.

"Okay. I'll do it, but we have to work together," Angel gives a quick speech. "We have no room for egos." Angel glances over at Kate. "We need to separate, keep them distracted. Blair and I will go get the device, and Ethan, you and Kate will hold off Omega."

"I don't think so," Kate refuses to follow Angel.

"I don't trust either of you so I'll go with Blair and you can stay with Ethan. I'm sure you like that anyways." There is only so much patience Angel has before Kate has another bruised eye.

"Kate, really? Can you cooperate for once?" Ethan says, preventing Kate from going any further.

"It's fine. Whatever Kate. You and Blair can go get the device." Angel walks away to gear up, Blair not too far behind her. Team Alpha is ready to follow Angel to the finish line.

Team Omega has their own agenda for winning. "I'll take lead on this, I'll move faster if you two stay out of the way," Mark says gearing up, disregarding how Ashton and Daniella may feel about him taking point.

"If you think you can get us a win, then do it," Daniella says, "but we're not just going to be standing around."

Mark lets out a heavy sigh realizing he can't succeed without some form of assistance. "We get them before they get us," Mark explains his plan with such arrogance. "If we attack them first, they won't have the chance to get the object, then I can walk in and retrieve it." Mark stands firm in his plan. Daniella stands back and goes along with it. Ashton is over it with this team and she refuses to follow an idiot.

"Time begins now! You might want to hurry. Cleaning body parts wasn't on my agenda today," Jordan shouts.

"Was that necessary?" David asks.

"I couldn't help myself," Jordan laughs, watching as both teams grab their guns and go to separate sides of the building.

Jordan, David, and Donovan walk towards a tent near their SUV, holding monitors they can watch as each team moves throughout the building. The building is worn down with the roof almost completely torn away. On the outside it looks as though this used to be some sort of factory. Once inside there are flipped-over desks and chairs. Broken windows and elevators with no power. This looks like an old office building. Covered in soot and dust is a painted globe on the ceiling. Mark guides his team quietly and swiftly through the burned-down room behind broken desks as Angel guides her team carefully up broken stairs to a squeaky balcony.

"We couldn't have found a better and safer place to fight them," Blair says, moving quietly alongside Angel.

"If we attack them from above, we have better visual over them. Now be quiet," Angel whispers.

Team Omega has secured their positions behind broken desks underneath the balcony.

"You take point," Mark orders Ashton as he kneels.

"You wanted to be leader, you take point," Ashton snaps back.

"I am taking lead and I order you to go!"

On the balcony, Angel and her team crouch down for a better visual of Team Omega. She motions Blair and Kate to move forward toward securing the object. Mark comes out of cover and sees Blair moving across the balcony behind Kate. He aims his gun and fires. BANG! Mark shoots the first shot. Team Omega, Ashton, and Daniella follow along, shooting at Exodus guards on Team Alpha.

"Ahhh!" Blair falls to the ground rushing back to move out of sight. She looks at her bruised arm and is surprised she isn't bleeding. She wasn't shot by a normal gun. The agency has provided the initiates with highly upgraded dart guns. They shoot and have the same effect as any normal pistol or rifle. Angel rushes to Blair, pulling her out of the line of fire.

"Are you okay!?" Angel asks, concerned.

"Yeah, I think so."

Angel nods at her and goes back to shoot over the balcony, hitting Mark in the process.

"Damn it!" He falls to the floor in pain, holding onto his shoulder.

"SHOOT THEM! SHOOT THEM NOW!" Mark yells at his team, trying to quickly recover.

Team Omega takes cover and shots are fired towards Team Alpha. Each of them goes back and forth, taking one another down, one by one.

"Take them out from the left," Angel instructs some of her Exodus Guard teammates to move near the left of the balcony where Exodus Guard teammates from Team Omega have taken cover.

"They are taking us out!" Ashton shouts at Mark. "You wanted to be leader, now lead!" Mark aims his gun and quickly takes down two Exodus guards without a thought.

"You want directions," Mark aggressively approaches Ashton, "shoot them and keep moving!" Mark continues to shoot at Team Alpha, not focused on leading his team. Ashton wants to turn her gun towards Mark but stops herself.

"This is fun, huh?" Ethan smiles at Angel as they shoot in sync at Team Omega Exodus Guards.

"What? Shooting at people?" Angel replies, not focusing on him because those eyes and that smile are a major distraction.

"You, me, enjoying each other's company…and shooting at people," he gives her a slight smile keeping his forest green eyes on Angel as he aims and shoots an Exodus Guard, then winks.

For a moment, Angel glances over at him but a shot zips past her face, bringing her back to reality. Mark takes the opportunity of a taken-down Team Omega Exodus Guard shot by Ethan to move in and out of cover behind the desk to get better view of Team Alpha on the balcony. Ashton and Daniella keep up with Team Omega.

Ashton realizes time is running out and Mark has no clear plan on how to speed this up. She also has no idea where he has run off to and doesn't care. She'll take matters into her own hands. Ashton moves out of cover and sneaks away from the team.

"What are you doing?!" Daniella asks, noticing Ashton's attempt to exit. She's been around Ashton long enough to know that she'll do what she wants to do.

"Nothing that involves you!"

"Look, you don't like me, and I definitely don't like you, but whatever you're doing, it's only going to make things worse," Daniella says.

"If you think for one second that I will ever listen to you, you are sadly mistaken," Ashton continues. "So either get out of my way or you can show me how much you don't you like me." Ashton stares Daniella down, ready for whatever she chooses, but Daniella only backs away.

"Whatever. Do what you want. You'll regret it," Daniella runs back to help her team, who's now holding their own against Team Alpha.

Ashton stands frozen, her anger rising. She ignores the comment and moves to secure the object on her own. Angel and Blair are working side by side taking down Omega Guards. Angel sees to her right Ashton moving swiftly through the room. She knows immediately what Ashton is doing and it has nothing to do with the plan of her team; Mark isn't that smart. Angel contemplates shooting Ashton for the sake of her team, but she's still her sister; she could never bear to do it. She wishes Ashton would stop having the need to do what she wants.

"Give them all you got, they're almost down!" Angel shouts to her team as the bullets ricochet off the walls. She ducks down, grabbing ahold of the balcony as another shot flies past her face. Suddenly, Angel feels a rush within her body and begins to hold her forehead tightly. She feels a pounding over and over in her head and she can barely open her eyes. She leans against the barely sturdy balcony and stands, stumbling to a nearby corner and braces herself, until the excruciating headache leaves. Ethan watches Angel struggle not as if he's concerned for her well-being but more so curious at what could take place once the headache passes.

Ashton makes her way through the rundown office building, following the coordinates of the device using a tracking system that has been placed inside her training suit. She's cautious as she walks downstairs, guns drawn, ready for what may try to attack her. Turning down a mildly lit hallway, the tracking system in her suit sporadically beeps near an opened room. She walks in and it's a room inside of a room. The first room has TV monitors and cameras surrounding the outside. This must have been some sort of security room, she thought. She stays focused and walks into the next room, where there is broken glass and old medical papers thrown everywhere. This room is the most untouched compared to the rest of the building. She walks around the island and sees dusty beakers and tubes. This used to be a lab. Ashton stops her curiosity and gets back to business, looking in cabinets and drawers, and she finds nothing. She's getting frustrated when suddenly it comes clear to her the object is hidden, it wouldn't just be in a simple drawer or cabinet. She glides her hand along the walls and feels a hole near a torn picture of a human brain. Carefully reaching her hand inside, she finds a rod-shaped device with time counting down from 3:00 on the side. Ashton smirks; of course she would find it with ease. The moment she turns to leave an Alpha team member stands firm with her gun aimed at Ashton.

"Hand it over," the team member says, wearing a black mask that disguises her voice, making it sound distorted.

"If you want this, you'll have to take it," Ashton threatens. She feels something poking her back

"And we will. Drop it now." It's another Alpha team member, who is wearing a similar black mask. He snuck his way through the back door behind Ashton and it's now two against one. "Now you're going to follow my directions," he presses the gun harder on her back. "Place your gun on the floor, slowly," he continues.

Ashton does exactly what he says, but she has her own agenda on how this standoff will end. "Now give over the detonator," he orders as his fellow teammate stretches her hand out to Ashton. Ashton stands there, her hand wrapped tightly around the detonator and does nothing. "Give it to her now!" he shouts. Ashton looks down at the time that now reads 2:30 and she knows just how much time she has to knock these two down to the ground.

"I really don't do well with orders," Ashton says.

The Alpha team member places his finger on the trigger, but he's too slow. Ashton spins around and kicks him across his face, knocking his gun out of his hand and he falls to the floor. She quickly reaches out and with all her power punches the other Alpha member, making her lose her balance. Coming from behind is the male Alpha team member. He kicks Ashton in her back, and she falls on to a counter with a large beaker. She grabs the beaker and slams it on top of his head. Once again, he falls to the ground, unconscious. It's just her and the other Alpha team member. They land punch after punch, kick after kick, until Ashton sweeps her from under her feet. The Alpha member falls to the ground, trying to stand but not before Ashton grabs her gun and shoots her three times, knocking her out cold. Ashton takes a minute to catch her breath, wiping the small drop of blood from her lip on to her training suit sleeve. She grabs her gun and checks the time for the detonator. It reads 1:00 and she holds the device tightly in her hand, head held high, and lifts her thumb to press the button. She's going to win this whole thing for her team - The Team of Ashton.

The male Alpha team member slowly stands behind her, forehead dripping with blood and lifts the butt of his gun above her head, knocking her out cold. She falls to the ground with the detonator rolling out of her hands. "That'll teach you," he says picking up the device that reads :55. He presses the button and the alarm sounds. He helps his fellow teammate to stand, passes her the device, and they exit the lab leaving Ashton lying unconscious on the floor.

Both teams instantly stop shooting. "Damn it!" Mark shouts, appearing out of nowhere and breathing heavily. "They won again!"

"Well, if you came up with a better plan or even a plan at all, we could have won," Daniella replies, noticing him swiftly tossing an object behind an overturned desk. Mark storms off, frustrated by his team.

"Did we win?" Ethan asks Blair.

"I don't know, but by the looks of the Omegas' faces, I think we did," Blair says.

"Where's the leader you all begged for?" Kate asks, limping towards her team, knowing she was right all along. "Has the meaning of 'leader' changed or is the leader supposed to run off and let their team fend for themselves?"

"Don't you have to go call daddy or max out a credit card or something?" Blair, in her own way, tells her to shut up.

"I think what you meant to say was 'thank you'," Kate holds up the device. "Instead of worrying about me, why don't you figure out what's going on with your buddy?" Kate has the last word. She leaves with Ethan and the Exodus Guards follow, leaving Blair to look for Angel on her own.

Searching upstairs on the balcony, Blair finds Angel sitting crouched down, eyes closed and leaning against a wall in the corner. "Hey!" Blair projects.

Angel opens her eyes slowly; her painful headache has gone away. "Huh? What's wrong?" Angel asks softly.

"Is this what you call leading?" Blair asks. Angel realizes she passed out.

"Wait, what happened?!" Angel asks frantically, leaning over the balcony, looking for the other team.

"The phase is over. An alarm went off. And everyone is waiting outside. What is going on with you?!" Blair stays on the topic at hand. "It can't be your suit. Natalie fixed them." Angel wants to explain her reasoning for disappearing, but she can't tell everyone everything.

"Nothing," Angel walks away.

"Nothing?! You went MIA and I found you in a corner sleeping, so unless you're just super lazy, this isn't nothing," Blair follows, pushing for an answer.

"Look! I was tired of carrying the team on my back and needed to see you guys pick up some of the slack. I can't do everything for everyone!" Angel hates that she had to lie but protecting her and Ashton is all that matters.

Blair thought some weird friendship was developing between her and Angel after their bonding session earlier, but all she can see now is how much the twins are alike.

"Okay, I get it, you don't want friends, but at least be honest with yourself," Blair says, exiting the building. Angel watches as a disappointed Blair walks away. When her headaches first began, her parents made her keep it a secret from everyone. Her father always told her, 'The less people know, the safer you and your sister will be.' Was he right? She exits the building, sunlight beaming on her face. Ashton comes limping behind her.

"I'm really getting sick of this place," Ashton says, rubbing her neck.

"What happened to you!?" Angel asks.

"Your teammates caught me off guard."

"Well maybe you shouldn't have gone off by yourself," Angel chastises her.

"I had it under control."

"Congratulations. You all barely made it through Phase 2," Jordan condescends, "but there were those who did worse than others…" Jordan hates her next words but there are rules. "Initiate Ashton Hunter. Fail." Angel, Blair and Daniella look over at one another and then at Ashton. They are in disbelief that Jordan is sending Ashton home. Ashton never wanted to be here but for a moment she can't process Jordan's words. She instantly walks away from the group. "Team Alpha, you have won…again. Team Omega, I suggest you get yourselves in order and fast," Jordan continues.

"Rest up. Phase 3 will test your limits," David says.

Jordan, David and Donovan leave the remaining Initiates to take in what just transpired. It should be a celebration.

"We should have won," Mark says, raging with anger.

"You needed to have a better plan," Daniella says.

"My plan would have worked if we were all on the same page!" he shouts at her. He turns his attention towards Ashton who is sitting on a nearby rock, rubbing the back of her head. "This is your fault!" Mark yells, lunging towards Ashton.

"Okay, at this point you're just testing my patience," Ashton sits calmly. She's trying with everything in her to keep calm before she kills this man. It's like he wants her to act out. "Get away from me…now," she continues, standing from her seat to face him.

"Or what? You're going home anyway, you have no one protecting you." Mark moves aggressively closer to Ashton. He's looking down on her, trying to show superiority. Everyone watches the exchange between the two. Kate watches with the widest grin on her bruised face. Angel stands close by – not too close, but close enough so that if she needs to step in, she can. Daniella keeps her distance. She tried to warn Ashton something like this would happen, but Ashton had her own agenda, so now she can handle this all on her own, too.

Ashton takes her time responding as Mark tries to intimidate her. She gives herself another chance to dismiss the situation. Who is she kidding? She's Ashton! She tightens up her fists and gives Mark the strongest punch across his face, sending him stumbling back, his left eye bleeding. As he steadies himself, there's a gash she didn't notice before beginning to leak from his forehead. Like the gash she gave the so-called Alpha team member in the lab. The teams are in an uproar, some are encouraging the fight and Ethan and Angel attempt to separate them.

"I will kill you!" Mark shouts. Ethan rushes in to hold him back as he pushes towards Ashton.

"Do it!" Ashton lunges forward, getting another hit off Mark.

Angel jumps in. "Touch her and I will end you!" she snaps at Mark.

"I'll take the both of you!" Mark shouts.

"That's enough!" Ethan shouts. "All of you need to stand down! Parker, get on the van!" Mark stands there, eyes piercing Ashton and chest pumping in and out. "Go!" Ethan moves in front of his view of Ashton. He glowers at Mark, speaking to him through his facial expressions. Mark walks away before he does something he can't fix. Everyone stares at Ashton, not knowing what to do or say.

"What are you looking at? It's over! Leave!" Angel shouts at everyone standing idly by. They all do as she says and make their way towards their van. Ashton is now in a state where all she wants to do is hurt anyone in her path. She kicks the dirt, grunts loudly and makes her way towards an open field. Ethan and Angel remain at the scene of the fight.

"Crazy, right," Ethan says quirking up a smile.

"Next time, stay out of it," Angel says, frustrated by him. She swiftly makes her way to talk to her sister.

"I was only trying to help!" Ethan shouts, watching her walk away.

Ashton paces with her hands locked behind her head, a tool her dad taught her to use when she feels like she can't control her emotions.

"What is going on with you!?" Angel chastises Ashton.

"Me?! I just got attacked!" Ashton snaps back.

"You've been attacking everyone since we got here! Jordan, Daniella, Blair, Natalie-"

"You are not about to blame everything that has happened to us here on me! I never wanted to come here!" Ashton's voice rises. She paces back and forth again, hands locked behind her head.

"Then why did you?!" Angel shouts.

"Because of YOU!" Ashton yells, stopping to face her sister. "Do you think I wanted you to leave?! You're my sister! Basically, the only family I have left! But obviously you don't care about that," Ashton starts to release all those pent-up emotions, but Angel isn't buying it. Ashton does this all the time when she doesn't get her way.

"Well, it doesn't matter now, does it Ashton? We're going home anyways."

"What are you talking about? I'm going home."

"Oh, shut up. You know I'm not just going to let you leave like this…not without me."

Ashton exhales, cooling down enough to talk Angel out of the stupid decision she's about to make. "You're not leaving. I messed up, okay, like I always do. You don't need me; you stay here and do what you do best."

Angel can't tolerate this conversation with Ashton a minute longer. "And there you go again, only thinking of yourself." Angel leaves her sister, prepared to leave the Exodus agency. Once they get back home, it may be time to do things separately for a while.

Unknown to Angel and Ashton, Jordan watches their exchange from afar. She doesn't confront them, but a part of her feels like she needs to fix them. Maybe she made the wrong decision with failing Ashton. She doesn't know why she feels close to them, but it's time to find out.

Chapter 17

In the conference room, Angel stands at the oversized window looking over operations, knowing this will be her last day here at the agency. The argument she had with Ashton replaying in her mind, she uses her sleeve to wipe the tear stains from her cheeks. Agents move swiftly throughout operations like a beautifully arranged orchestra. It's relaxing. She loves Ashton, yet she can't help but want to do what's best for her life. Her dad comes to mind. If he could see her and Ashton now, it would disappoint him. Something needs to change, but where does she start? Maybe if she could find out the secrets Jordan is hiding from them, everything could become clearer. Then she could make Jordan let Ashton stay.

"It looks like I'm not the only one that comes up here to think." Ethan leans against the doorway, showcasing that magical smile and moving his silk hair away from his taunting eyes.

"And you're still the only one. I was about to leave." Angel holds her guard up.

"But yet you're still here." Ethan stands next to her, watching the agents. He must be careful. She's fragile. Any sudden movements will cause her to run away.

"Then you see my problem." Angel takes a step away. "Are you stalking me now?" she asks him.

"Me? No…we're just two people who happen to be in the same place at the same time."

"Oh, is that what they're calling it now?" Angel remains facing forward.

Ethan shrugs, letting out a light chuckle. "Not exactly...but, I mean, would it be such a bad thing?"

"Uh, yes, it would be a very bad thing. One, it's illegal. Two, the last guy who tried to stalk me is currently ten feet under."

"Oh. Ouch." Ethan clutches his chest as though he's wounded. The silence is loud, as neither wants to leave the room. Ethan notices the distance between them but doesn't acknowledge it. "So… you and Ashton… fraternal twins?" Ethan asks awkwardly, breaking the silence.

"Really… did you figure that all on you own?"

"Come on! I'm trying my best here," he laughs.

It's time to stop taking her anger out on people who are just trying to be nice. The only loyal friend Angel has had is Ashton, and it's time for new beginnings. Turning to finally face him, she says, "Yes, Ashton and I are fraternal twins. I'm older by five minutes."

"Whoa, the big sister. That's an enormous responsibility," Ethan tries to ease her.

"Not really. She does what she wants, and I do the same," Angel says subliminally.

"That can't be a good relationship."

"Yeah, well, we all don't get to choose our family," Angel goes back to staring out the window.

"I understand. I've only known Ashton for two seconds and can tell she is not the easiest person to live with. She has some stubbornness about her."

"See, you were doing good just standing there with your nice hair and cute smile, but I will not let you talk about my sister… that's my job." There's tension between them for a moment.

"So… you think I'm cute…and nice." Ethan gives a big grin.

Angel playfully rolls her eyes. He does have nice teeth, they're practically perfect, and she hates it. "It's clear we're two very different people." Angel quickly changes the subject.

"Well, I think we're more alike than you think."

"And how is that?" Angel says, calling his bluff.

"I have a sister, an older sister and she's just as overprotective of me as you are over Ashton, and I'm sure Ashton is the same way over you like I am over my sister."

"That's…really nice of you to say, but I doubt your relationship with your sister is anywhere similar to mine," Angel walks away.

"Wait…Angel," Ethan comes rushing behind her, gently grabbing her wrist. They're closer than before – now practically chest to chest. "I may not know or understand what you've been through, but I want you to know I'm a great listener, probably the best," Ethan takes the discreet flirting up a notch. "So, if you need someone to just listen, I'm your guy."

Angel is speechless as she looks up and falls deeper into his eyes. Why does he care so much? It's nice to have someone other than Ashton looking out for her, yet she doesn't know him; therefore, she can't let him in. Angel gives a closed-lip smile, releases her wrist, and walks out of the room. Ethan isn't sure whether she'll ever take him up on his offer, but he knows he broke down some type of barrier between them.

Roaming through the accessible hallways are Exodus guards and agents taking a break from a heavy day. Natalie, young and innocent, rushes through the hallway with stacks of papers and a box of newly tested, secret, bureaucratic phones. She moves in and out of agent crowds, excited by her new findings, and can't wait to tell Jordan. As she takes out her phone and dials, she runs into a group of recognizable Initiates. Natalie falls to the floor along with her work.

"Hello, Agent Hawthorne," Mark stands over her.

"Um…I'm sorry, I-I'm really, really sorry," Natalie fumbles around the floor trying to quickly pick up her mess so that she can get out there.

"She looks like a little fish out of water flopping around like that," Kate laughs as Natalie moves around the floor.

"Do any ass kissing today?" Mark mocks her. Natalie ignores them and picks up the last of her work off the floor. She tries to move around them. "Why don't you tell me the lieutenant's plans?" Mark steps closer to Natalie.

"I-I don't know what you're talking about."

"Yes you do. What is she doing with them?" Mark asks.

At a distance, Ashton leans against the wall watching the exchange; she despises a bully. Ashton walks towards them. Mark and Kate are instantly on guard. "If you want to know about me, you just have to ask. Doesn't mean I'll tell you, but why don't you take a shot at it?"

Mark gives Ashton a mischievous smile. He's not going to waste his time with her; she'll get what's coming to her soon enough. He moves in closer to Ashton. "It's okay, Ashton, you'll find out soon enough. You're not as strong as you think you are."

Ashton steps in closer. "You give a lot of threats, you know. Empty promises. If you want to kick my ass, do it. There's nothing but space and opportunity," Ashton says with such composure, ready and wanting, more like pleading for Mark to make a move. He leaves, not wasting another second on these inexperienced girls.

"Enjoy your ride home," Kate waves goodbye as she follows behind Mark like a puppy. Natalie is relieved Ashton was there to help before things turned bad.

"Thank you," Natalie pushes up her glasses.

"It was nothing. I hate Mark and I got to tell him off twice in one day," Ashton brushes off the good deed.

"I appreciate it. No one has stuck up for me like that…well, besides Jordan," Ashton rolls her eyes at the name. "And even she isn't there all the time," Natalie expresses.

"Really, it was no problem. Let it go." Natalie does as Ashton says and together, they walk through the fourth level hallways near the barracks and training center. "Okay, I just have to know: how did you get involved with all…of this?" Ashton addresses the agency.

"What do you mean?"

"I mean, you're clearly not the most athletic and you're like queen of the nerds when it comes to tech, so how did the lieutenant find you?" Natalie swallows like a pebble is stuck in her throat. She doesn't want to tell Ashton the reason she's there. What if Ashton treats her like all the other agents when they found out Jordan is her godmother?

"Ummm…due to contracts an-an-and files, I'm not obligated to discuss that," Natalie lies. Ashton can see right through her.

"All right," Ashton says.

"Really! I would tell you, but un-under law, I-I can't," Natalie continues.

"Natalie, it's fine, you don't have to tell me if you don't want to," Ashton relaxes her. "Unless you're trying to hide the fact that you're just like me."

Ashton clearly has a secret to reveal, but Natalie is clueless. "I don't understand," Natalie says.

"You know," Ashton flashes her ten fingers as if she's blowing someone away and whispers. "Abilities."

Natalie is still, unable to move. "I-I-I don't know what you're talking about," she trembles. Ashton pulls Natalie aside, far enough away so no one can hear.

"Calm down, I'm not going to do anything to you," Ashton says.

Natalie is relieved. "Did Angel tell you?"

"No, I knew when I woke up. At first, I wanted to punch you in your throat," Ashton says, as Natalie takes a swallow and rubs her neck. "But it wouldn't have solved anything, and I knew it was an accident. I'm not as mean people make me out to be."

"Ashton, I'm really sorry, I haven't got complete control of my powers," Natalie explains.

"You strike a mighty blow," Ashton jokes. "You have all this power. Why do you let them mess with you?" Ashton asks. Natalie has always asked herself that question, but she could never answer.

"I don't know. I guess because I don't know how to use them," Natalie says.

"Well, we'll just have to work on that now, won't we?" Ashton suggests.

"You're going to help me?" Natalie asks.

"Don't sound so surprised. I know how hard it is to control these types of things." Ashton takes Natalie's phone from her hand. "Here," Ashton puts her number in Natalie's phone. "Call me any time and we can meet up to train you. That is if the overseer lets you out." They both let out a light laugh.

"Thank you," Natalie smiles, internally jumping with joy. Natalie is always helping someone else, but the help is never reciprocated.

"It's not a problem, but let's just keep this between us. I don't need the lieutenant questioning me." Natalie smirks and then her watch begins to beep.

"Speaking of Jordan, she wants to see you immediately," Natalie says cautiously to Ashton.

"For what?!" Ashton snaps. "You know what? Don't even worry about it. I've been wanting to talk to her myself." Ashton walks away like she's ready for a mission. "Just me and her," she whispers to herself.

Following the directions Natalie gave her, Ashton takes the elevator down to the third floor. She makes her way to a secluded training room across the hall from Jordan's office. Opening the door, Ashton is expecting Jordan to be in her elegant business suit and ready to give a long monologue about Ashton's failures. Ashton walks into a well-equipped room full of workout equipment, punching bags, a small shooting range, and a large UFC octagon, not as big as the arena but big enough to fit a suitable match. Ashton is intrigued; she's a kid in a toy store. She shakes off the feeling and makes her way to the octagon in the middle of the floor.

"Excuse me, ma'am, I'm looking for a lieutenant," Ashton says irreverently. She sees Jordan in the octagon without her business suit, but in an exclusive, slick, black training suit custom-made just for her showing every curve and rock-hard ab. Jordan is ignoring the smart remarks, continuing stretches. "Because the lieutenant I know wears these pant suits that were probably made by a well-known French designer," Ashton says in a terrible French accent stepping into the octagon.

"Are you done?"

"With you personally? Yes. Messing with you? No." Ashton jokes, although she would rather starve than be in the same room with this lady. Jordan smirks in an irritated way. Trying her hardest to deal with Ashton's irreverent manner.

"You are something else," Jordan says, wrapping her hands with boxing hand tape.

"Thank you. It's a gift." Ashton turns up the sarcasm. "You want to tell me why I'm here? And can you make it quick? I need to get on the road," she continues.

"You know, I saw you fighting in there, inside the lab, taking matters into your own hands and fighting two against one. It was impressive," Jordan congratulates, finishing wrapping her hands.

"Of course it was, until they caught me off guard," Ashton says.

"That easily could have been avoided."

"And how do you figure that? This is real life, not some how-to paperwork given by the government or CIA or whoever you work for," Ashton snaps.

"See that's your problem," she steps in closer to Ashton.

"And what is that?"

"You have a problem with underestimating your opponent," Jordan smirks at Ashton and swiftly drops down, swinging her left leg, sweeping Ashton off her feet and landing on her back. Ashton winces in pain; it's the stun gun situation all over again.

"What the hell is your problem?!" Ashton shouts.

Jordan stands without a breath lost or a hair out of place. "I got a proposition for you," she gives her hand to Ashton, who swats it away.

"What?! I'm not taking anything from you!" Ashton struggles to stand, somewhat impressed Jordan could do a move that smoothly and swiftly.

"Just hear me out…let's have a match," Jordan smiles, knowing Ashton will pay attention.

"Really?!" Ashton is confused, not because of Jordan's offer but because she didn't think it would be this easy to get back at Jordan for tasing her and taking her money.

"You versus me," Ashton laughs, more like cackles. "Okay, I'm listening."

"You beat me, I double the money I took from you, and you and Angel get to stay," Jordan has Ashton's complete and undivided attention.

Ashton couldn't care less about the latter offer, but she knows how much Angel wants to stay. She wonders if Jordan is playing her by simply offering her so much money without a second thought.

"That's over a million dollars. How do you even have that kind of money?"

"Don't worry about it. I'm good for it," Jordan says confidently.

"Okay…and if you beat me?"

"You tell me why you came here." Jordan wants to get as much information out of Ashton and the other girls as possible.

"Ummm…okay…I thought that was obvious, but if you want to give me tax-free money, I won't turn it down," Ashton takes off her leather jacket and stretches, ready for the battle she knows she'll win. "Plus, I've been waiting on my payback."

Ashton and Jordan stare at one another, following each other around the ring with their backs protected. Ashton charges, throwing the first couple of punches. Jordan dodges them like a bee. Ashton begins to kick and punch repeatedly, giving Jordan multiple combinations, but Jordan…she's too fast, not breaking a sweat. She's not throwing a single hit at Ashton. "I thought this was supposed to be a fight," Ashton huffs and puffs as she tries to catch her breath.

"Seems like one to me. What's wrong? You can't keep up?" Jordan begins to toy with Ashton. Ashton starts to throw every skill and combination she knows at Jordan. Jordan continues to block every blow; it's like she knows every move before Ashton throws it. Ashton then jumps to swing and kick Jordan on her side. Jordan grabs Ashton's right ankle and with her leg, sweeps Ashton's left leg out from under her and slams her to the ground. Ashton shouts in pain. You would think she just finished a boxing match with the world's greatest. As for Jordan, you would think she just went jogging.

"Who are you?!" Ashton winces in pain, holding her lower back.

"Someone that can help you," she gives Ashton her hand again. Ashton hesitates but takes her hand.

"Help me with what?"

"Your skills."

"My skills are fine. You're just this mutant who has superpowers or something."

"That would be cool, but I'm far from that," Jordan jokes.

"Then how do you do it, are you…" Ashton looks around to make sure no one else is listening, "you know, just like us, with powers?"

"No, I'm not. I've been trained since I was a kid. Five to be exact."

"Okay…so you cheated. It's not a fair match. The deal is void," Ashton says.

"No, I won that fair and square. You just couldn't keep up." Ashton steps up closer to her, ready to throw a punch while she's off guard.

"If I would have known you were a trained fighter, I would have had you," Ashton says.

Jordan steps closer too. Their noses are practically touching. "Right now, all I hear is would of and could of. In the field, we don't have time to guess the skills of our opponent, we just do." She lets Ashton know her tough girl exterior won't work with her.

"Well, it's a good thing we're not in the field," Ashton says as she quickly throws a punch, but once again Jordan blocks it without moving an inch and continues to look straight at Ashton. Jordan swings Ashton around and bends her arm behind her back.

"Ashton, you are a very skilled fighter," she says as she holds a tight grip on Ashton. "I've seen you myself, but you have to learn to separate your feelings from the goal." Ashton finally frees herself from the tight hold, but only because Jordan loosened the grip.

"Feelings?!" Ashton shouts. "I feel nothing!"

"Oh, give it up!" Jordan snaps back. "You've hated me since the first day you met me."

"You tased me, lady! I don't know what part of that you don't comprehend!"

"And that's why you lost," Jordan says.

"Oh my god, here we go," Ashton knows a lecture is coming. "How is that?"

"You are so focused on trying to get back at me, you can't follow a simple task," she says trying to get her point across. Ashton leans against the octagon caged wall letting Jordan get all she needs to say out. Maybe she'll shut up more quickly. "I said let's have a sparring match. Simple. And if you win, I will double the money that I took from you and you can stay, right?" Jordan asks.

"I was there," Ashton says annoyed.

"See, if I was given that deal, I would use my mind instead of the feelings I have for my opponent and get my money," Jordan says. As Ashton listens, she doesn't know whether she wants to continue to hate Jordan, take her advice or find a way to hurt her permanently. She's mixed with many emotions and isn't sure how to handle them.

"And how should I do that?" Ashton says, giving up.

"Come here and I'll show you." Ashton stands, facing Jordan, ready to learn.

"When you're on one of your jobs, why don't you kill the robbers and take all the money for yourselves?" Jordan asks, already knowing the answer.

"Because we have to keep a low profile, taking half the money and leaving the rest for the police takes the pressure away from us and on the robbers," Ashton explains.

"So, killing them would deviate from the plan, right?" Jordan asks.

"Right."

"And you would lose the money and risk going to jail?"

"Yeah…" Ashton's trying to figure out what Jordan is getting at with all the questions.

"Even though these criminals try to kill you?"

"Yeah, but the goal is to not kill them but-" Ashton pauses, she finally gets it. Jordan can see it all making sense to her. "To get the money," Ashton says, recognizing.

"Exactly," Jordan says. "Don't let your emotions take over. If you just focus on the task at hand, the main goal, you'll be so much greater." At this moment, Jordan isn't trying to get information from Ashton. She sees so much potential in her and wants to help. "Let me show you something," Jordan says. She leaves the octagon and goes to a nearby wall case filled with tactical knives. "Do you know what this is?"

"It's a ballistic knife," Ashton is in awe, practically drooling, "first developed in Russia when they wanted to kill their enemies quickly and quietly."

"Wow, someone knows their stuff," Jordan is impressed.

"They're amazing. The blade releases like a bullet. It's not even legal in the United States. How do you have this?!"

"There is a lot you don't know about me. You want to try taking it from me?" Jordan asks. Ashton can see Jordan is really trying to help her. She nods and prepares to spar. Ashton throws a punch, but of course misses. Jordan flips the knife to where the blade is near her forearm, "You still see it?" Ashton does a jump kick, and it doesn't land. "Deal with your anxiety, Ashton." Ashton throws a quick combo. "No, no, no, I haven't done anything yet," Jordan says. Ashton is in her fighting stance, her chest pumping in and out, why can't she get it? She thought.

"Ashton, relax. If you continue to respond to the 'what if,' you'll always lose and you'll always be in trouble. Breathe," Jordan teaches. "If you move too soon you miss out. Pay attention to the goal."

Ashton takes a breath and focuses on her goal, getting the knife. Jordan throws the first punch, knife in the other hand, and Ashton dodges it. Jordan then throws a quick punch and kick combo, and Ashton quickly dodges it again. She focuses more on the goal than her anger towards Jordan. Secretly, Ashton is enjoying this moment. The last time someone took the time out to train her was her father.

"Follow my movements," Jordan says, guiding her. Ashton keeps her focus on Jordan. She swings on Ashton, but Ashton blocks. Then she quickly tries to grab Ashton's shoulder but Ashton swats her away and spins around to the opposite direction. Jordan's back now facing Ashton, she swings her leg around to hit Ashton, but Ashton grabs it and slams her to the ground. "Good Job," Jordan says lying face down on the ground. Ashton is kneeling on top of her and grabbing the knife in the process.

"I'm a quick learner," Ashton helps Jordan stand, "even though I already knew what to do."

"Of course," Jordan agrees to disagree.

There is a moment of awkwardness. Ashton is struggling to say thank you and Jordan doesn't want to make the situation uncomfortable by becoming emotional. "I guess I owe you $750,000," Jordan says unwrapping her hands.

"No. Keep it. You can make it up to me while I'm here," Ashton slightly extends the olive branch.

"Okay," Jordan smiles, proud of her. "I guess that means you want to stay."

Ashton shrugs. "This place is…all right. Free food, luxury apartment and I get to kill for a living. I can get used it." Ashton gives her knife back.

"Keep it," Jordan says.

"Are you serious?!" Ashton can't believe Jordan would trust her with such a rare object, let alone let it out of her sight.

"Sure. I can trust you right?"

"Yeah, but I think you better hold on to it…I don't trust myself," Ashton gives it back.

"All right. I'll see you at the next phase," Jordan says as they walk out of the octagon.

"It won't involve any bombs or kidnappings, will it?" Ashton asks.

"Now you know I can't tell you that," Jordan jokes.

"Right…I forgot, secret government agency." As Ashton begins to leave, she realizes Jordan isn't that bad of a person, she still has her guard up, but now she knows Jordan really is trying to help them. Ashton decides to take the next couple of steps in building a semi-relationship with Jordan; instead of being enemies they can be acquaintances.

"Angel," Ashton says stopping and looking back at Jordan.

Jordan looks up at her, confused. "What about her?"

Ashton walks back to her. "You asked me why I'm really here, well, its Angel," she says, sitting on the bench next to her.

"She made you join?" Jordan asks.

"No, never," Ashton says, reinforcing that Angel doesn't run her life. "My parents supposedly died when we were nine and it was just me and Angel. We didn't know any other family members outside of our parents. So, Angel stepped up. We're only five minutes apart but she's always been that big sister to handle everything. She got us through school, protected us when Child Protective Services were looking for us, and she found places for us to live. They weren't the best, but we were safe."

"What type of places?" Jordan sincerely asks.

"Well, the first placed we lived was in an old janitor's closet in our elementary school," Ashton says, making it seem as though it wasn't a big deal. "Angel even stood by me when I wanted to keep robbing," Ashton chuckles as she reminiscences. "I can't tell you how many times she wanted to quit, but she knew I was happy doing it," Ashton says she was happy, but the expression on her face says different. "So, this is why I'm here at your agency. It's her. If she's here, I'm here, and if I leave, she leaves." Ashton doesn't look at Jordan as she tells her story.

"You were never going to leave," Jordan says, glancing over at her. Ashton looks over to Jordan with her brows knitted. "I have eyes everywhere. I saw Kate and Mark attack you in the lab."

Ashton balls her fist tightly. "I knew it. I knew it when Mark got in my face, and I saw the gash I gave him from the beaker."

"I'm sure you've realized by now that you and the other girls don't have too many fans," Jordan says.

"Yeah, I'm starting to sense that."

"Agent James is delivering the news to them now that they will no longer be a part of this agency," Jordan continues. Ashton is content with Jordan's decision.

"Good, because I was liable to kill one of them, maybe both."

Jordan shakes her head and chuckles. "I do want to thank you for sharing your reason for staying here," Jordan says.

"Well…I never go back on my word; bets…I never go back on bets." Ashton stands to leave, having slightly enjoyed her conversation with Jordan and ready to make things right with Angel.

"Hey, Ashton," Jordan stands, stopping her from leaving. "You said your parents *supposedly* died."

"And?"

"And…usually someone knows if their parents died or not," Jordan says. Ashton is going to stop this conversation before Jordan ruins the moment.

"Lieutenant, if you haven't noticed, and I'm pretty sure you have, trusting in others runs very thin with me," Ashton says, stepping closer to Jordan respectfully. "And I've already told you more than I've told anyone, so be grateful with the information I gave you and don't ask me any more questions."

Jordan steps back with her arms raised as if she's surrendering, "All right."

Ashton leaves the training room satisfied with her and Jordan's newfound semi-relationship. She's leaving the room with some of her heavy past off her shoulders. She hates to admit it, but it felt good expressing her feelings to Jordan. It was nice to get it out and she learned new fighting techniques along the way.

After hearing Ashton's story, Jordan feels closer to her. So close, she feels as though she's known Ashton and Angel in the past. It sounds crazy, but Jordan's gut feelings have never steered her wrong. Fortunately, Phase 3 will give her some clarity.

Chapter 18

The penthouse is gloomy with the girls keeping to themselves, scattered throughout. Daniella sits by the window, feeling alone once again, wishing she would have set herself free from jail and maybe life would be different. Blair watches television, fiddling around with the jade bracelet her father gave her before she left home. She feels free from her father's restraints but wished she could have left with some closure between them. Angel is in the kitchen discreetly stirring a concoction that helps rid the migraines in her head while keeping her powers steady. Taking a yellow pill from the pill bottle near her glass of water, she cracks it open and blue powder pours into the glass. She stirs the mixes, and a once light-blue glass of water turns clear.

Ashton enters a quiet and dreary penthouse. No one pays her any attention, not even Angel. She knows they will eventually have to discuss their argument. Ashton comes marching into the open kitchen, staring at Angel as she drinks her medicine. Angel ignores her like any big sister would do. Ashton reaches over Angel to grab a bag of chips. Leaning against the island, she watches Angel from behind, waiting for her to make the first move. She pops open the bag and crunches on the chips loudly, hoping it will hit a nerve, but Angel's been handling Ashton's attitude for far too long. Nothing she does for attention phases her. "So, are we going to talk?" Ashton asks, continuing to crunch.

Angel finishes her drink. "Are you going to stop being a brat?" she asks and leans against the sink.

"Touché," Ashton says.

They're facing one another, waiting for the other to make the first gesture.

"You wanted to talk, so talk," Angel says wanting Ashton to take responsibility. Ashton struggles with her words, so she stuffs her face with potato chips. "Typical," Angel says, rolling her eyes as she walks away.

"I get it, okay?" Ashton stops Angel from leaving, gulping her chips down so she can speak. "I can be nerve-wracking sometimes, but it's only because I want the best for the both of us and I don't trust anybody to help us," she says, finally expressing her thoughts.

"I know you do, but Ash, you have to let your guard down sometimes," Angel leans next to Ashton.

Let your guard down. Those words are piercing to Ashton. The last time she let her guard down someone she loved and trusted broke her.

"I know I'm asking for a lot but—"

"No, you're not, I'm going to… I have been working on it."

Angel can see the change slowly coming over Ashton and she's proud of her. "Thank you," Angel says with a sense of relief. "Now you just have to make it right with them." Angel turns around, nodding her head towards Blair and Daniella.

Ashton knows she never gave Blair and Daniella a chance when they first met but making it right would mean she was wrong. "And I'm doing this because…"

"They're just like us. We all came here for the same reasons and whether we'd like to admit it or not, we're all we have," Angel says.

"I guess," Ashton dismisses the comment.

"You just said you were going to let your guard down, like 30 seconds ago."

"Give me a chance to process it." Ashton stands straight, shoulders back and exhales as Angel pushes her towards the living room. "I'm going!" Ashton says to Angel.

"We have something to tell you guys. Daniella, can you come here, please?" Angel says standing next to Ashton, who's fidgeting with her fingers.

Daniella unwillingly joins the group, sitting on the arm of the couch.

"What's going on?" Blair asks.

Angel waits for Ashton to speak up. She looks over and Ashton is looking everywhere but towards Blair and Daniella. Angel elbows her in her side.

"Ow! All right!" Ashton steps forward so that she can face everyone. "I want to apologize for the way I have been treating you both. I took my anger out on you and I was…" Ashton struggles to take ownership for her wrongdoings, "…wrong."

"It's okay. This change hasn't been easy for any of us," Blair says, understanding.

"I appreciate it, but does it matter at this point? Both of you are leaving," Daniella says.

"Oh! I knew I forgot something. I had a one-on-one with Jordan and she said we could stay," Ashton responds

Angel is in disbelief after hearing Ashton's news. "How did you get her to do that!?"

"Right! You guys are like oil and water," Blair says.

"It was Mark and Kate who jumped me and apparently Jordan hates a cheater. They basically gave her a reason to keep us here," Ashton says.

Angel is internally elated she gets to stay and thankful for her sister for making things right.

"Wow, she must really need us," Daniella says.

"I'm starting to see that, too," Angel agrees.

Suddenly, their bracelets flash and beep rapidly.

"Well, that's new," Ashton says, not surprised. Of course, it's Jordan putting them in another unpredictable situation.

"I think it's the next phase," Angel says.

"Something interesting is definitely about to happen," Daniella says.

Natalie enters the penthouse, phone in hand. "Hello, I hope you guys are rested," she says.

"Hey, what's going on with our bracelets?" Angel asks.

"Does it mean they're broke, because I've been itching to throw something… or someone?" Ashton asks, missing her powers.

"No, they are in great working condition. It's time for the next phase," Natalie says, "and you all are up next."

"What do you mean we're up next? We're not getting tortured or given shots that make us turn on one another, right?" Blair says frantically. They all give Blair a confused look.

"You had an odd childhood, didn't you?" Ashton asks.

"No, it's nothing like that. It's a random routine for every Exodus agent. Everyone has already gone and you're the final group to go, along with Agent Carmichael," Natalie tries to settle them.

"Wait, Ethan's on our team now?" Angel asks, annoyed, but she's only masking the fact that she hopes she runs into him again – and reject him.

"What are we supposed to be doing?" Daniella asks.

"Unfortunately, I can't reveal the nature of the phases," Natalie says.

"Of course, you can't." Daniella isn't surprised by all the secrets in this place.

"You'll see once you get there." Natalie motions them to the door.

"Round 3," Angel says, slightly drained from all the tests.

"Here we go," Blair agrees.

They walk through the hallways following behind Natalie. Focusing on where they're going, Angel doesn't notice Ethan behind her.

"Hey. Miss me?" he asks, flashing those pearly whites.

"Not really," Angel says, trying to mentally prepare herself for the next phase.

"It's okay, you don't have to tell me. I already know how you feel about me," he says.

"Oh, you do?"

"Yep."

"And how do I feel about you, Carmichael?" Angel asks curiously.

"You'll just have to meet me in the training room tomorrow night to find out," he smiles, hoping she'll consider. Before Angel can reply, he continues "You don't have to answer. I'll just see you tomorrow." He winks, walking away and heading to the front of the line. Daniella watched the exchange between the two and can see the spark.

"What?" Angel asks Daniella as she smirks at Angel.

"Nothing," she laughs.

In front of them, Blair and Ashton are trying to elicit information out of Natalie. "You really can't tell us anything?" Blair asks desperately.

"The phases are strictly confidential," Natalie says sternly.

"I need to prepare myself if I have to kill someone or if that someone is going to kill me, especially after that last phase," Blair continues anxiously.

"Blair, you're going to be fine," Natalie nervously continues to walk facing forward, afraid they'll detect there's more she's not telling them.

"Nat, come on, think of it as a… favor for a favor, a friend helping a friend," Ashton says. Even she knows that sounded weird coming out of her mouth.

Natalie exhales, not wanting to break the rules, but Ashton agreed to help her control her powers, so she owes her at least that much. "You're going to see the agency's top qualified therapist," she says cautiously.

Ashton and Blair are bewildered.

"I'm not seeing a shrink," Ashton forces.

"That's exactly why I didn't tell you," Natalie says to herself. "She's only going to ask you a few questions to find out if you're ready to be a part of Exodus," Natalie explains.

"So, we're just sitting on a couch talking? Okay, this I can do." Blair is relaxed.

"It's always a trick with you people," Ashton is frustrated, but she's trying to do better for herself, so she'll do the phase and complain later.

They've entered level two, but this area of the agency doesn't resemble the rest. The group has entered an area that hasn't been seen or used in years. The concrete walls are cold and the single placed light bulbs barely light the hallway and cobwebs cover the corners of the ceiling and walls.

"This is…nice," Ethan says, taking caution of his surroundings.

"You have got to be kidding me," Blair says.

"Something is definitely up," Angel says, looking around the hallway.

"Yeah, you're right…keep your guard up," Ashton replies.

They stop in front of an all-black door. "Hmm…let's see who's first, shall we?" Natalie scrolls through the tablet that never leaves her side. "Initiate Carmichael, you're first."

Ethan confidently steps forward, not at all worried about what might be behind the door. "See you on the other side, ladies," he smiles and gives a playful salute as he leaves them.

"Your boyfriend annoys me," Ashton says to Angel.

Angel scowls at her. "He's not my boyfriend."

"I see the way you look at him and I need you to be careful. Something isn't right with him," Ashton expresses. Angel understands Ashton's concerns; she doesn't like any guy Angel has connected with in the past.

Once inside the darkened room, Ethan sees a single throne-like chair in the middle of the floor with a spotlight shining down on it.

"I'm assuming I should sit in this chair?" he asked aloud. "This very strange chair," he says to himself. As he sits, wires with suction plates on the end come out of the chair and hook themselves on to him. There are four wires hooked on the back of his head, his hands, palms and legs, and metal covers placed over his feet. He moves around trying to break free.

"Hello, Initiate Carmichael," a voice projects out over speakers.

The concrete wall Ethan is facing dissolves and lights up like a high-tech projector screen. "Uh…hi. What's going on?" He settles down. Looking closer, he realizes the wall has turned into a window with Donovan standing next to a slender woman with blondish-copper hair sitting behind a high-tech operations table.

"Welcome to phase three. We will ask you a series of questions and all you have to do is answer them truthfully," the woman says, pressing a nearby intercom button.

"Okay, simple enough."

Donovan snickers. "Yeah, that's what he thinks," he says to the woman.

"Let's begin," she says.

Ethan prepares himself for what's to come by becoming comfortable in his chair.

"What was your reasoning for joining Exodus?" she asks.

"Oh…um…well," Ethan begins to squirm in his seat.

"Is there a problem, Carmichael?" Donovan asks.

"No," Ethan leans down as far as he can to sneeze in his hand. "Just allergies. There's a lot of dust in here."

"You're allergic to dust?" Donovan asks.

"Yes, some people are allergic to dust, Agent James. Do you mind if we proceed?" the woman interjects. "Ethan, what was your reason for joining Exodus?"

"When Captain Lawrence recruited me from CIAU, I knew I wanted to learn and fight with the best," Ethan answers poised and self-assured, yet his facial expression and body movements speak differently. Donovan studies him for a moment. He sees Ethan is sweating profusely. His eyes are tearing up, turning red and he's gripping the arms of the chair so tightly as if they can be ripped off. The one observation that has Donovan's internal detector going off is Ethan's index finger pressing tightly on top of his thumb; it begins to bleed.

"Carmichael, are you nervous?" Donovan asks as he signals to the woman near him to let Ethan speak.

"Uh…yeah, I think anyone would be in this situation, right?" he gives half of a smile.

"That is true, but you seem more agitated, and we haven't done anything. If you're going to be a part of Exodus, you'll have to be a force of nature -- an unstoppable force."

Ethan proceeds to stare at the celling, unwilling to look Donovan in the eye. Something comes over him. He's not the playful, always smiling guy but someone who is filled with hatred. "That I am, Agent James."

Donovan and the woman detect the sudden change in the tone of his voice. Before proceeding with more questions, Jordan speaks through Donovan's hidden earpiece. "End it. He can go."

Donovan presses the intercom button, "Agent Carmichael, you have made it through."

"What? That's it?" This brings Ethan back to reality.

"You answered our question truthfully, that's all we required."

"Oh, okay," Ethan says as Exodus guards come to escort him out of the chair. He isn't sure what is going on. That test was too easy. Something must have triggered them, Ethan thought.

Seth approaches Ethan, guiding him to his workstation outside the interrogation room on the opposite side of the room. "Okay, you're bleeding pretty bad here," Seth says as Ethan sits in front of him. He examines Ethan's bleeding thumb and fingernails.

"I'm sure you can handle it," Ethan says, staring up at Seth.

"And you would be correct." Seth cleans Ethan's cut, wiping away the blood. "Is this a nail?! I know the chair is ancient, but I'm most certain Natalie refurbished it inside and out when she built that room." Seth holds up a half inch nail he found inside Ethan's thumb, covered in Ethan's blood.

"I guess I was more nervous than I thought," Ethan jokes.

Seth responds with a nervous laugh. Unknown to Seth, Ethan gives him a hostile stare as Seth resumes treating Ethan's wounds. "That should do it," Seth says, snapping Ethan out of his trance.

"Thanks, Doc." Ethan slaps Seth's shoulder before walking away.

Back in the hallway, the girls lean against the wall and pace the halls waiting for their turns. "Initiate Hunter, you're up." Natalie looks up, waiting for Angel to open the door, but the twins are lost as to which one she's talking too. "Oh right, twins, my apologies. Angel, you're good to go." Angel stands ready.

Angel opens the door to the room that looks like the scary hallway she just left. Once inside, she sees the single throne-like chair. Slowly walking towards the chair, she examines it. Is it an electrocution chair? Does it strap you in while you're getting tortured? Or is it just a rusty old chair? These are the questions that run through her head. "Here we go," Angel lets out a large sigh, believing Jordan has already put them through it all. She gently sits in the chair. Suddenly the same wires that strapped Ethan in come out of the chair and hook themselves on to Angel, adjusting to her height and weight. Angel struggles to move. "Hello?!" she shouts into an empty room. For a moment no one answers. Angel continues to look for a way out of the chair.

"You can stop now," Donavan says as the concrete wall lights up.

Angel is startled and stops moving. Looking closer, she realizes the wall has turned into a window with Donovan and the same composed woman.

"What is this?" Angel asks.

"This is phase three. We'll ask you a series of questions and all you need to do is answer them truthfully," Donovan says sternly, speaking through an intercom.

The woman takes over the intercom. "Hi, excuse Agent James. He takes his job way too seriously. I'm Dr. Lucy O'Connor. We just want to ask you some questions to get to know you better. It's best you answer them truthfully so we can see if you're the right fit for Exodus." Lucy is the best of the best and has treated the worst of the worst.

"And strapping me in a chair is how you find your answers?" Angel stands her ground.

"Precisely," Donovan forces.

"You won't get anything from me," she snaps.

"We'll see about that," Donovan motions Lucy to begin.

"Is your last name Hunter?" Lucy asks. Angel says nothing, staring straight at the wall, making no eye contact with Donovan or Lucy. "Angel, we're trying to help you. Just answer the questions," Lucy says.

"Asking me about my personal business is not helping me nor is it any of your business, so again, no I will not be answering your questions," Angel shows no fear.

Lucy gives Donovan a nod to precede. Donovan presses a button on the operations table, and it lets out a vicious electric charge into the chair through the wires and into the suction plates connected to Angel. She screams in pain; the chair lets out a high voltage shock so powerful it feels like she's been tased multiple times. Angel's chest pumps in and out, her face starting to drip with sweat.

"Is your last name Hunter?" Lucy asks again.

"So…this is…how…you get your answers," Angel breathes heavily. "Okay then…let's do this," she continues, smirking. "Yeah, Hunter's my last name." Donovan and Lucy look at the readings on the operations table and they indicate Angel is telling the truth.

"Okay, why are you here?"

"Because Natalie dragged us here," Angel says, still breathing heavily, but that wasn't the answer they were looking for and the chair shocks Angel once again.

"AHHHHH!!!" she cries out.

"Try again," Donovan says in a condescending tone.

"Why are you here, Angel?" Lucy asks again.

"Gave…me…something…to do," Angel is pouring sweat, but they won't break her. The readings on the operations table are spiking off the charts: Angel is lying. Donovan shocks her again. The pain is becoming overwhelming, but Angel will continue to fight. Lucy touches Donovan's hand and he moves his hand away from the button.

"Okay, Angel, can you tell me how you got your powers?" Lucy asks. This surprises Angel. She thought the only person who knew about her powers was Jordan.

"Where did you hear that?" she asks, angry.

"Answer the question," Donovan interrupts.

"Please answer the question, Angel," Lucy calmly says.

"Then you might as well kill me now because I will tell you nothing!" Angel shouts. Donovan shocks her once again.

"All right, Angel, you're free to go," Lucy says, watching the timer on the control room table count down to zero. Guards come in to carry out a weak Angel and they take her to Seth, who gives her a powerful adrenaline shot.

Jordan and David watch as the initiates go through Phase 3 on Jordan's oversized flat screen behind her desk. "You're reasoning behind this phase is what exactly?" Captain Lawrence asks, keeping it strictly professional between the two of them.

"I need to see the power of their mental strength. Their loyalty," Jordan says.

"And electrocuting them is the best way to test them?" he asks, concerned.

"As long as they hold out until the seven minutes are up, I'll know only the best survive, and so far, Angel is the only one that has made it through successfully," she says.

"Understood. You're the boss," Captain Lawrence says, using a snarky tone.

Blair, Daniella and Ashton wait for their turn. "Angel's been in there a while," Blair says, pacing the hall. "And what happened to Ethan?"

"Trust me, Angel can handle her own," Ashton responds.

"Initiate Hahn, you're next," Natalie says.

"Wish me luck." Blair walks to the door.

Cautiously walking into the room, she sees the same throne-like chair. "Hello…" she whispers in the dark room. No one answers. "This is not the therapist's office I had in mind," she whispers to herself. She contemplates whether she should sit in the intimidating chair.

"Hi Blair," Lucy says, revealing herself and Donovan along the wall on the other side of the window.

"H-Hi." Blair looks bewildered. The wall was just a simple wall a second ago.

"Can you sit in the chair, please? We would like to ask you some questions," Lucy asks.

"I thought therapists were supposed to be in a nice office with a comfy couch. I can't lay on this," Blair says.

"I'm…unlike other therapists."

"I can see that," Blair lets out a sigh and slowly sits in the chair. "Here goes nothing." Suddenly the suction plates attach to her. "You have got to be kidding me!" she shouts.

"Answer these questions truthfully and everything will be fine," Lucy tries to calm her, but it only makes her more anxious. "Why were you kept hidden?"

Blair is taken aback by Lucy's question. "What?"

"Your father kept you hidden. Why?"

"My powers," Blair says, "but I don't see why that matters."

Lucy and Donovan look at the readings and they reveal Blair isn't telling the complete truth. "And…"

"What do you mean? There's no other reason," Blair says, frustrated.

"Your powers weren't the only reason you were kept hidden," Donovan says sternly.

"There isn't another reason!" Blair shouts, wanting them to move on from the question. Donovan presses the button, sending shocks through Blair's body. She screams in agony. "That's what those are for," Blair breathes heavily, trying to catch her breath, her pupils becoming dilated. "Is this how we're doing things?!"

"We need you to be truthful with us, and by that, I mean revealing the entire truth," Lucy says.

"I told you why. If that's not good enough for you, then that's your problem," Blair gains some confidence and makes herself comfortable in the chair, knowing this will take some time so she might as well relax.

"If you say so," Lucy says. "Are you forcing yourself to be happy?" Lucy continues the phase.

"Isn't everyone?! What are you getting at?!" Blair snaps.

"We know your powers work based on your emotions, so again I ask you, are you forcing yourself to be happy?"

"Seems like you know everything about my powers, so why don't you tell me?"

Donovan, with no hesitation, presses the button and shocks Blair once more. Blair grunts in pain. She wants to cry but refuses to let Lucy and Donovan see her weak. Blair's hands start to shake and she's dripping with sweat.

"Have you ever thought about killing your parents, Blair?" Lucy continues to slam Blair with question after question.

"What…does…that have to do…with anything!?!?" Blair groans in pain, trying to hold on.

"So, you're admitting to wanting to kill your parents?" Lucy taunts her.

"Wha-no! I would nev-" Before she could finish her sentence, Donovan shocks her again. This shock causes Blair to become unconscious. The guards carry her out and just like Angel, she passed the phase.

"Jordan picked some tough girls," Lucy says to Donovan.

"Yeah, but they haven't shown they can be trusted yet," he says, still wishing Jordan never went to find them.

"I understand you're apprehensive, but they could be a great asset to the team. They're already showing they have the skills of an agent, maybe better skills than you."

"You're kidding, right?"

"I remember you didn't make it past three minutes."

"Well, don't get too excited. We've only seen two of them and we're about to get the worse of the four," Donovan says, agitated.

Moseying along the hallway are Ashton and Daniella, waiting for their turn, not knowing what's waiting for them on the other side.

"Natalie, what's going? Every time someone goes in that room, they don't come out. I'm not in the mood for games today," Ashton says, frustrated. "Especially when I haven't had dinner."

"It's almost over. In fact, Daniella, you're next," Natalie says.

Daniella takes a deep breath and walks into the dark room, only lit by one light hovering over the chair. She can tell something isn't right. She's seen this far too often in juvie. Unknown to anyone outside of those juvenile walls, the correctional officers would strap Daniella in a similar chair that would mildly shock her when she would continuously defy them, when she wouldn't fight for them. She walks to the chair and her hands touch the cold metal. Those painful memories run through her mind.

"Hello, Daniella," Lucy and Donovan reveal themselves.

Daniella doesn't respond for a moment, distracted by her thoughts. "I'm guessing you want to see how much pain I can handle," Daniella says nonchalantly.

"We only want to ask you a few questions. You answer them truthfully, you'll have nothing to worry about," Lucy says.

"That's what they all say." Daniella sits in the chair and the suction plates latch on to her. She sits comfortably.

"Daniella, why were you separated from your parents?" Lucy asks. Daniella slowly stares her down, wondering how she knew about that part of her life. But she won't give them the satisfaction. She sits with ease as if she's in a spa waiting for her cucumbers and facial masks.

"Daniella? Do I need to repeat the question?" Lucy waits for an answer and Donovan watches, puzzled.

"Why were you separated from your parents?" she asks again.

Nothing, Daniella says nothing. I wish they would get on with it, Daniella thinks to herself. Lucy gives Donovan the signal and he shocks Daniella. She handles the shocks better than her pervious counterparts. She lets out small grunts and clinches her teeth. She doesn't scream. Lucy and Donovan are amazed. "Really, that's it?" Daniella taunts them. "I have to give it to you. It hurt like hell, but I've been through worse."

"Okay, Daniella, were your powers the cause of you being separated?" Lucy continues to question and Daniella refuses to answer. Daniella sits quietly but only this time staring directly at Donovan and Lucy. Donovan shocks her once again, this time longer so she can truly feel the pain.

"I can go all day," Donovan speaks over the intercom.

"I guess we have something in common," Daniella snaps back.

"Daniella, what happened to your mother?" This question makes Daniella tense; it struck a nerve. Her rage increases and she's trying hard to get out of the straps and break free. "Daniella, calm down," Lucy says. Donovan is ready to increase the level of the shock. Lucy, using her own skills, tries to calm an aggravated Daniella while also holding off Donovan's hand as he gets ready to press the button once more. "Daniella! Look at me. I want you to focus on what's making you angry and count to ten." The directions are going in one ear and out the other for Daniella. She's blinded by rage. Lucy has no other choice but to shock her. She's shocked and becomes limp. Guards come in and carry out an enraged Daniella, passing the phase. "That had to be the worst, right?" Lucy asks Donovan after the tiring session.

"Not even close," Donovan says.

Ashton waits in the hallway impatiently. "Is the therapist just hoarding everyone in her office?" Ashton asks Natalie.

"You can go see for yourself," Natalie says, motioning Ashton to the door.

Ashton arrogantly walks to the door. "About time."

Walking into the dark room, she's instantly frustrated that Jordan keeps putting her in these ridiculous situations. She walks towards the chair in the middle of the floor. "All right! You can come out now!" Ashton shouts to whoever could be listening. The room is silent. Ashton has her guard up like always. Behind the hidden wall, Lucy and Donovan watch an anxious Ashton.

"So, this is her?" Lucy asks him.

"Yep, the most arrogant and egotistical person I have ever met."

"Okay then…let's get to it," Lucy says bracing herself. Lucy and Donovan appear along the wall.

"Hey! Wall Street, I haven't seen you since my sister whooped your ass," Ashton mocks him. "And who are you?" she asks Lucy.

"I'm Dr. Lucy O'Conner, psychotherapist," Lucy introduces herself proudly.

"Now we're psychos?" Ashton says, flustered.

"I'm actually a cognitive psychology and neuropsychology therapist, but psychotherapy is easier on the tongue," Lucy tries to ease the tension between them.

"Yeah. Okay," Ashton dismisses her. "So, what am I doing?" Ashton asks impatiently.

"We're going to ask you a series of questions and all you have to do is answer them honestly and you can be on your way," Lucy explains.

"And if I don't?" Ashton challenges her.

"You have no choice, Initiate. Now get in the chair!" Donovan takes over the intercom. He's had enough of Ashton's disrespectful remarks.

Ashton gives him a smug smile, taunting him while she sits. As the wires strap on to different parts of her body, reality sets in for Ashton. This is more than just asking a couple of questions. "What is this? Huh? If I don't answer your questions, you torture me?!" Ashton yells.

Lucy ignores her and begins the questioning. "How strong are you?"

"Strong enough to come out of these restraints and beat both of you senseless," Ashton threatens Lucy and Donovan.

"Try it and the restraints will be the least of your worries," Donovan challenges her.

"Let me rephrase the question: how strong are your powers?" Lucy asks again.

"Take me out of this chair and I can show-" Donovan shocks Ashton before she can finish. Ashton feels the voltage throughout her body. The pain is like nothing she's ever experienced.

She breathes heavily. "This is what…you did to…everybody else," Ashton struggles to speak, but is still confident in every way. "Okay."

Lucy continues, "What happened the day your parents died?"

Ashton is frozen. No one knows about this, except for the only person she told: Jordan. "Who told you about that?" Ashton's rage appears over her face; she's out for blood.

"Just answer the question," Donovan demands.

"What happened, Ashton?" Lucy asks once more. Ashton refuses to answer. She sits quietly, trying to relax herself. Donovan shocks her and she tries to hold in the scream. "Ashton? Do you want to kill me right now?" Lucy asks boldly and Donovan's eyes grow wide in surprise that she would ask the question.

"You…and so many others," Ashton says, wanting the words to pierce Lucy. "Now let me out!" she demands. Donovan shocks her again. The shocks go through her body like hot metal. This only makes her blood boil.

"That's not an option," Lucy says.

"LET ME OUT!" Ashton shouts so loud she shakes the room. Ashton uses all her strength to release some of her power even though she has on the suit and bracelet which hinders her from doing so. She's trying hard to release herself, grunting and trying to snap the wires off her hands.

Lucy and Donovan watch, uneasy. "She can't actually break free, right?" Lucy asks Donovan.

"No, it's impossible. The chair is made of pure titanium. There's no way she's breaking out of…"

Ashton lets out a battle cry. "AHHHHHH!" She breaks her right arm free.

Jordan and Captain Lawrence watch the situation take a turn for the worst.

"How was she able to do that?!" David says, becoming increasingly concerned and standing from his seat.

"I-I don't know," Jordan had no idea Ashton was strong enough to break through her suit. It's designed to keep powerful supernaturals like herself under control. She steps in before David becomes even more suspicious. Stepping to her desk, she presses a button allowing her to speak to the guards in the room with Ashton. "Bring her down, now."

Ashton still struggles to release herself fully, the left side of her body still attached to the wires. Lucy is nervous and Donovan gets ready for a fight, placing one hand on his holster. The moment Ashton stands from the seat, a guard sneaks up behind her and grabs her arm. Ashton swiftly snatches her arm away and kicks him. Donovan knows this is a problem he must solve. He runs out of the detection room, gun in hand. Ashton struggles to fight off the guards single handedly.

"There are three of you and she is one girl with one capable arm! Put her down now!" Jordan yells at her guards through their earpieces. They do as they're told. A guard takes out a baton and, pressing the button on the side, he electrocutes her in the neck, knocking her unconscious.

"Stand-" Donovan bursts into the room a second too late. "Take her to medical," he says, watching the guards unhook a limp Ashton.

Jordan and David sit in silence as the video showing phase three goes dark. He sits in the chair like the vigorous man he is, ready to give Jordan her 'I told you so' moment.

"I have been patient, I have been calm and I have been understanding, but you are really making it hard to trust you," he asserts.

Jordan leans on her desk in front of him, arms folded, letting him release it all. "You know what, David? Please explain to me what I have done to you for you not to trust me?" Jordan asks, at her breaking point.

"What have you done!?" He's done being the nice guy and says, "You started this whole initiate program against my better judgment, you bring in these random girls without my knowledge and one of them just broke free from the most advanced polygraph test in the world and took on three highly trained guards with one hand tied behind her back, and you're wondering why I don't trust you?!"

"I'm sorry you haven't been able to serve your ego by not being the glorified captain everyone knows you to be," Jordan snaps back. He should be grateful. She gave him free reign and let him believe he's a partner in this. "But you want to know the truth, David?" she walks towards him. "The truth is I run all of this! I don't have to tell you anything! I tell you what's going on because I want to, I respect you. Unfortunately, lately I don't know what to think or do with you anymore." Jordan goes to sit at her desk to work, no longer acknowledging his presence. He storms out, filled with so much anger. He loves Jordan, but he realizes if they're working together they could never truly be together. He rushes pass Donovan and Lucy, overlooking their presence.

"Is everything okay? Do you need us to come back?" Donovan asks Jordan before entering her office.

"It's fine. Come in." She motions them in. Donovan closes the office door behind them.

"Thoughts?" Jordan asks Lucy.

"Nothing much other than you were right," Lucy says as she and Donovan sit in the armchairs facing Jordan's desk.

"Aren't I always?" Jordan smirks as she sets her work to the side.

"Those girls are truly remarkable," Lucy continues, amazed at what she witnessed from Angel, Blair, Daniella and Ashton. "Their tenacity, their fortitude at such a young age, is nothing short of amazing."

Jordan looks over to Donovan, his hands folded in his lap. "Agent James? I'm sure you have something you would like to share," she says to him.

"Although I believe their presence will cause nothing but trouble for our team and this agency, I agree with Dr. O'Connor their skills are those of an Exodus agent," Donovan says.

Jordan leans back in her desk chair and smiles, knowing how hard it was for him to give them credit. Lucy catches a glance from Donovan and gives him a warm smile, placing her hand in his and squeezing tightly.

"What they've overcome in such a short period of time will only accentuate their strength for Exodus," Lucy says.

"So, we're doing better than expected," Jordan says aloud, but internally checks off the items on her mental list.

"Exceptionally," Lucy agrees.

"And Agent Carmichael?" Jordan asks.

Lucy and Donovan glance at one another, uncertain of Jordan's reactions when they tell her what they witnessed from Ethan. "He exhibits signs of trauma and some psychotic behavior," Lucy explains.

"How did you come to that conclusion?" Jordan asks.

"Aside from him obviously lying on his test, I'm sure you saw," Lucy says.

"Seth brought this to my attention," Donovan takes out the half inch nail Ethan used to press into his fingernail, setting it on Jordan's desk.

Jordan picks up the nail, toying with it in her hand.

"He found it inside Carmichael's thumb," Donovan says.

"Well, whatever he's hiding, this shows he'll do anything to keep it from us. Let's continue to keep an eye on him, but not too close. We don't want him to suspect anything."

"Yes, Lieutenant," Donovan agrees as Lucy and himself stand to leave.

"Great work, you two," Jordan says. "Now when can I expect an invite to the wedding?" Donovan and Lucy stop in their tracks.

"Lieutenant…umm...I'm not sure…," Donovan clears his throat, attempting to explain.

Jordan gives a light laugh. "Donovan, it's okay. I'm only messing with you."

Lucy places a comforting hand on his shoulder and looks up at him, addressing Jordan. "We aren't sure what you mean, Lieutenant."

"You two aren't as secretive as you think, but I'll play along. Just make sure whatever you're doing, it's worth it. Our jobs are not the easiest, trust me I know," Jordan gives them advice she hopes they follow.

"Understood, Lieutenant," Donovan says as he holds the door open for Lucy and follows her out.

Outside of Jordan's office, Lucy presses Donovan up against the wall, lightly brushing her hand on his shirt, feeling for his toned chest.

"Looks like our secret is out," she says. "

No, Jordan is just that good. It's extremely difficult to hide anything from her."

"Well in that case," Lucy presses a soft kiss to his lips, "have dinner with me?"

"See you tonight," Donovan gives her a soft smile as she walks away. Once out of sight, the smile quickly vanishes. He's having doubts. Maybe this thing he has with Lucy will only hinder him from doing his job. Jordan was right. This job is too risky to involve oneself in unnecessary relationships.

Chapter 19

The following night, attempting to relax in the penthouse, the girls tend to their wounds received from phase three. Blair sits on the couch with her feet on top of the nicely polished coffee table, an ice pack on top of her head, shoulders and legs. Daniella sits near her, taking aspirin and placing an ice pack on her head. Angel and Ashton are in the kitchen.

"There was a reason you told her," Angel says, referencing Jordan.

"Yeah, to extend a freaking olive branch. And there was a bet involved," Ashton says, wrapping her left arm after injuring it in the fight.

"Ash, come on, you and I both know you wouldn't have told anyone on the streets as much as you told Jordan," Angel says, turning into the big sister with all the advice to give. "You told her because you're starting to like her or at least respect her. It's fine," she says, grabbing a water bottle out of the refrigerator.

"Are you crazy?! Me, like, and her are words that do not belong in the same sentence," Ashton says.

Reading her pill bottle on how much she should take, Angel pops one in her mouth. "All I'm saying is, if you didn't trust her, then why would you tell her? You could have told her anything, so you can't get mad at her for telling the information you gave her." Angel drinks her water and makes her way to the living room, but not before she gives her little sis one last bit of advice. "And you didn't even tell her anything, at least nothing important, so chill," she says, leaving Ashton to feel slightly stupid for making a big deal out of nothing.

"I feel like a construction drill is in my head," Blair moans, holding the ice pack to her forehead.

"I'm surprised you aren't passed out right now. What is that? Two days in a row you've had a piercing headache," Angel says, slumping down on the couch with her large bottle of water. They sit in the living room together relating their pain to one another, not realizing this is the first time they've come together to share similarities.

"At least you only have a headache," Ashton says, referencing the bruise on her arm that's limiting her movement.

"I still can't believe they electrocuted us repeatedly," Blair says.

"It's only been two weeks and I'm already used to Jordan's antics," Angel says. "That should be concerning, right?"

"It's actually not that bad after the first time," Daniella says, fiddling around with her ice pack, believing she thought this statement in her head. Daniella looks up and Blair, Angel and Ashton are looking at her like she's crazy. "I-I mean after the first shock," she tries to make a smooth recovery.

"Are you saying you've been through this?" Blair asks.

Daniella wonders if she should dive this deep with them, but they are the only ones who might be able to understand her. "I…spent some time in juvie and when the guards found out I was a fighter they would take me down to…to the basement and pit me against the other girls. They placed bets."

"Wait, they had cage matches, like you were a dog?!" Ashton says, shocked at what Daniella had to go through.

"Yeah, and when I refused to fight, they would sit me in a chair and…" the memories are hitting Daniella all at once and she's trying her best not to cry, "strap me in and shock me." She's hoping they don't place judgment on her.

"I'm sorry you had to go through that," Angel says.

"That's horrible, no one deserves that," Blair says.

"That's really messed up," Ashton says, showing empathy in her own way. "See! They're asking us all these questions, but when we want to know why they're sitting us in a glorified electric chair, the only answer we get is, 'We can't reveal protocol'," Ashton says, mocking the leaders of Exodus. The girls give a slight chuckle at Ashton's comment.

"Right! Do you know they had the nerve to ask me if I ever thought about killing my parents?!" Blair sits up.

"Well, have you?" Ashton asks, being nosey.

"Who hasn't?" Blair says, trying to justify herself.

"Sane people," Ashton jokes.

"Okay, well if your parents ever locked you in the basement of your own home for literally half your life, only to release you to go to church, you'd be pretty unstable too."

"Why'd they lock you up?" Daniella asks, concerned.

"My powers," Blair says, scared to tell her whole truth. "And…because I started crushing hard on this girl in my class, so my dad made me drop the course to keep me away from her."

"He kept you hidden because of a crush?" Angel asks.

"Well, we were kind of dating and him catching us making out in the school parking lot didn't help either."

"Still doesn't justify locking you up, trust me," Daniella states.

"They must really want to know who we are because they asked me when I first discovered my powers," Angel relates.

"And they asked me whether my powers were the cause of being separated from my parents," Daniella says, agreeing with them.

"Looks like our powers cause more problems than they fix," Ashton says. They reminisce to themselves about how their abilities have controlled much of their lives.

"We've known each other for almost a month now and we still don't know what we all can do," Angel says to them, trying spark up a more intimate conversation.

"Then, I'll go first," Blair says eagerly, "I'm an environmentalist."

"So…you can talk to trees?" Ashton asks.

"In a way. I can control the weather and manipulate the environment. Make it rain, snow, create fire and thunderstorms, that type of stuff," Blair reveals her true self, hoping they accept her.

"That is…amazing!" Ashton says, astounded by Blair's abilities.

"Okay…I don't think I can top that one, but I'll try," Angel jokes. "I'm an astral. I can see into the future."

"I thought that was a psychic?" Daniella asks.

"Yeah…just let her finish," Ashton whispers to Daniella, letting her know she's in for a surprise.

"I can see into the future and…go to the future – well, my spirit self does."

"You can just go, like right now?" Bair asks, shocked.

"Not exactly. I have to touch an object related to a specific time in the future and even that sometimes doesn't work," Angel continues.

"Yep! She's a super psychic," Ashton says sarcastically. "My turn!" Ashton says energetically. "I'm a TK. Telekinetic. I can move and bend people and objects." Ashton is excited to talk to other people about her powers without the risks of causing trouble. "And if I weren't wearing this stupid bracelet, I could show you this artistry." Ashton waves her hand in the air like she just presented a masterpiece.

"You guys have great abilities. The only thing I can do is blow up objects and freeze time," Daniella says, brushing off her abilities as if they're nothing compared to the other girls'. The girls sit quietly, amazed and shocked at her powers.

"The fact that you're saying that like it's not a big deal says everything about you," Blair jokes and they all laugh.

"I remember my dad telling us that we had to go see this doctor to help us control our powers," Angel reveals to Blair and Daniella, "and that seeing him would make all of our problems go away."

"And did they?" Blair asks.

"Nope!" Ashton jumps in, eating a slice of pizza. "Because the dude just disappeared and then we were on our own."

"I saw a doctor like that too when I was about five. My mom took me, said the doctor would be able to help with my powers and…anger," Daniella says.

The look on Blair's face says these stories aren't that much different from her experience. "And what was that doctor's name again?" she asks.

"Harper or Thornwood or something. We were about five when we met," Angel says. "Oh, wait," she runs to the kitchen counter to grab her pill bottle. "He wrote me this prescription to help with the headaches and visions," Angel says, bringing over the pill bottle. "Uh…Dr. Maxwell Hawthorne," Angel says.

"I feel like I've heard that name before," Blair says.

"Uh…yeah, from the doctor that apparently treated all of us," Ashton says.

"Hello, initiates," Natalie says, coming into the penthouse.

"Hey, Natalie," Angel says.

"If you're here to tell us we need to get ready for another phase, you might as well turn right back around because I'm not going," Ashton says.

"Ignore her," Angel says, knowing Ashton is all bark and no bite. "what's going on?"

Natalie sits in the single chair facing all the girls. "Because of your success with all of the phases, you all are now officially agents of Exodus," Natalie happily gives each girl a burgundy jewelry box. They take out a sterling silver digital watch with a black and red globe with the letter 'E' in the center, all surrounded by an Egyptian ouroboros digitized on the face of the watch. Their names and agent credentials are engraved on the back.

"I am starting to hate this agency a lot less," Ashton puts on the exclusive watch.

"The lieutenant had me customize them specifically for you," Natalie shows them Jordan isn't as bad as they want to make her out to be. "It has all the functions you need to be an agent, with some newly added functions," Natalie explains.

They play around with the watches and Daniella accidently hits a button that brings up a holographic image of the earth with red dots. The girls are speechless as to what they're witnessing. "Looks like the lieutenant pulled out all the stops," Daniella says, mesmerized.

"This is an image of the various crimes that are ongoing around the globe," Natalie shows them how it operates by standing and touching the holo planet Earth. "We have satellite imaging from every location to every corner in the world. There's nothing we don't already know," Natalie says proud of her work.

Blair sits quietly trying to figure out where she's heard the name Hawthorne before; she knows she's heard it recently.

"Natalie, what is this symbol?" Angel asks, pointing to the logo on the watch, noticing how different it is from the symbol she first saw when arriving to Exodus and how similar it is to the ring she wears on her index finger.

"Jordan hasn't spoken about it much to me other than it symbolizes resilience and unity. As far as what the symbol is, you would have to discuss that with her," Natalie answers.

"Oh, I have some good news," Ashton tells the group. "I'll be teaching this powerful being how to control the beautiful gift within her," Ashton says, irreverently discussing Natalie's powers. Angel and Daniella burst out in laughter.

"Natalie, are you sure you want this one helping you?" Angel jokes about Ashton but is so, so very serious.

"I think she can do it," Natalie says, confident in Ashton's abilities to help her.

"I'm a mentor; don't hate on me," Ashton says.

"I barely know you and find that hard to believe," Daniella laughs.

It feels good to be around people that understand her, and she hasn't truly laughed in years. Blair, on the other hand, is in her own world. "Hey Natalie?" Blair gets everyone's attention. "What is your last name again?"

Natalie wonders why she wants to know. "Haw-Hawthorne, my last name is Hawthorne," she says nervously. The girls look at Natalie with an abundance of emotions.

"I knew it!" Blair shouts.

"Wait, your father is Dr. Maxwell Hawthorne?" Angel asks anxiously.

"Y-yes," Natalie confirms.

"Your father is a psychic enthusiast, and you don't know how to control your powers?" Ashton gives her a perplexed look.

"Well, he died when I was two," Natalie hates reliving how she never had the opportunity to know her parents. Jordan constantly says he was the smartest and most loving man anyone could have known.

"Did he know about your powers?" Daniella asks.

"I'm not sure. I don't really know much about him and the things I do know…Jordan tells me." This remark sparks something within Angel. Here Jordan goes again, keeping things from them.

"Did Jordan know your dad personally?" Angel asks, hoping Natalie will be honest.

"Yes, they worked together at the CIA," Natalie replies.

It's clear Jordan knows a lot more than she's leading on. Angel doesn't know why Jordan won't explain everything, but Angel will confront her. "This woman never ceases to amaze me," Ashton says now, used to Jordan's secrecy.

Natalie recognizes their feelings. Jordan should have told them she knew the doctor that treated their powers.

"On the bright side, this agency upgraded to four badass agents," Blair says, excited about working for a secret agency and with this team of girls.

"That I can agree on," Ashton says.

"Me too," Daniella says, and the four of them give each other a high five.

Natalie enjoys seeing them bond, but they must know more about her father. Jordan only told her how he was as a father and a friend, but nothing more. Natalie needs answers. "Umm…since you all seem to have known my father more than I did, how was he? Like, was he a good doctor?" Natalie asks, hoping they have answers.

"I don't remember much about him, but he was really nice to us," Ashton says. "He helped me channel my powers, like they weren't something just given to me by accident, but they are me, they're what makes me…me." Ashton gives Natalie as much information as she needs. She knows how it feels to want to know about a deceased parent and she hopes this advice from Natalie's father will help Natalie control her own powers.

"He helped our parents understand that we were still kids, just with some enhancements," Angel smiles, remembering her parents.

Chapter 20

It's May 29, 2009. The Cross Family sat in the pediatrician's small office, which sat in a plaza between an old dry cleaners and a bagel shop. Elise and Aaron Cross watched as Dr. Maxwell Hawthorne tested their beautiful, melanated, five-year-old twin girls. Dr. Maxwell Hawthorne stood tall and sophisticated, dressed in black slacks, button-down shirt and vest.

"All right, little beauties," Dr. Hawthorne said to the busy little girls.

"I'm a race car driver," little Ashton shouted with her arms in the air, always the excited one.

"Sorry, her father bought her first pint-size car and now she never wants to come in the house," Elise said as the three of them laughed at the thought of Ashton whipping her little car around the driveway. Elise brushed a curl back into Ashton's hair and Ashton played with the braids hanging down in Elise's face.

"How can you deny those faces?!" Aaron pointed to a giggling Angel and Ashton.

Angel and Ashton are the spitting image of their father, Aaron, with some features resembling their mother.

"I have to agree with you. There's something about the love of a daughter you can't deny," Dr. Hawthorne smiled at them, but once he turned his back, his face changed quickly to despair. "I'm sure you'll be the best race car driver ever, Ashton, but do you know what a race car driver needs to drive?" he asked.

"Mmmm... a helmet!" she shouted, elated.

"That's right!" Dr. Hawthorne motioned his assistant to grab the petite-sized helmet and place it over Ashton's head. *"And we can't forget about our little princess here,"* he said to Angel, placing a helmet on her head.

"I'm not a princess. I'm the police," she shouted.

"Whoa," Dr. Hawthorne acted surprised for Angel. He surrendered with his hands up. *"You have some strong girls here,"* he said to Elise and Aaron.

"We sure do," Elise smiled at her girls and back at Aaron, but it's not a smile of the moment. Their smiles are of something more. They fought for their girls to be this happy. Once the helmets were tightly placed on Angel's and Ashton's heads, it's time to run the tests.

"My team and I will run tests to see the exact abilities your daughters possess. The test is completely harmless, and it will only focus on one specific spot in their brain." Dr. Hawthorne continued to explain the process to Aaron and Elise, trying to ease their worries. *"My assistant here will take you to get the DNA samples we need for the test."* He directed his assistant towards Elise and Aaron, who now are a little uneasy.

"Why do you need our DNA? No one mentioned this to us?!" Elise said on edge.

"We need DNA samples to determine if the abilities were genetically passed or the first-time shown," he explained.

"Doctor, I can guarantee you there is no one in either of our families with these abilities," Aaron stepped in to explain.

"And you could be right, but we not only need the samples for this, but to also treat these abilities, because they can eventually become unstable."

"Can we have a minute before you begin?" Aaron asked.

"Of course, but we have to start soon," Dr. Hawthorne said. Elise and Aaron step out and on the other side of the room is a small waiting area with a two-way mirror that has a view into the doctor's room where Angel and Ashton are being treated.

"Are you sure we should do this?" Elise asked Aaron.

"We don't have a choice. They're getting worse every day," Aaron tried to reassure her.

"Yes, but doing it this way...I mean, is this what she would have wanted for them?" Elise anxiously watched Dr. Hawthorne through the mirror as he set up the procedure for Angel's and Ashton's test.

"No, but she would want us to do everything in our power to protect them. I'm not losing them, too," Aaron expressed to her.

Elise contemplated if she wanted to take the risk. "You know if we do this, we're putting all of us at risk, even Savannah," Elise watched the girls, "wherever she is."

"That's a risk I'm willing to take," Aaron said as he walks out the room to tell the assistant they're ready to give their DNA.

In the doctor's office, Angel and Ashton are playing with the stuffed animals Dr. Hawthorne gave them to keep their minds on something other than the staff walking around the room and wires hanging from their heads. "Okay, girls are you ready to play a little game with me?" he asked, pulling up a rolling stool in front of them and sitting down.

"Yeah," they say at the same time.

"Great! Do you know how to play 'Go Fish'?" Dr. Hawthorne took out a deck of colorful, animal-filled cards.

"I know this game!" Angel shouted excited.

"Okay then. Let's get started." Dr. Hawthorne began by passing out five cards to each of them. "Ashton, do you have any 4s?"

"Go fish!" Ashton shouted like she'd already won.

"Angie, do you have any sebens?" Ashton asks her sister in that oh-so-sweet baby tone wanting to say seven. Angel unwantedly gives Ashton two 7s. Dr. Hawthorne glanced at the monitors behind the girls and sees that Angel's monitor displays increase wavelengths.

"Doctor, do you have any frees?" Ashton continued her winning streak.

"Nope, go fish!" Dr. Hawthorne says.

"Oh man!" Ashton said, disappointed. Her monitor showed wavelengths increasing at a rapid pace.

"Your turn, Angel," Dr. Hawthorne continued the game, hoping to get more of a reaction out of them.

"Do you have any 6s?" she asked him.

"Sorry Angel, go fish," Dr. Hawthorne says. Angel is visibly upset, she hated to lose, and Dr. Hawthorne is making sure they both lose to spark strong emotions, so he cheats. "Ashton, do you have any 5s?" Ashton gave Dr. Hawthorne two of her 5s. The game continued with Dr. Hawthorne winning. Angel and Ashton are sad they're losing to him and their vitals are increasing. "Ashton, do you have any 8s?" Dr. Hawthorne asked, finishing the game. Ashton gave him the last of her cards and he wins. "Looks like I win," Dr. Hawthorne said, taking Ashton's card and putting it with his other winnings.

"No, no, no!" Ashton shouted.

"It's okay Ashton, everyone can't win at everything," Dr. Hawthorne tried to calm her.

"I want to win!" She grew increasingly louder and more agitated. Watching Ashton's monitor, her vitals have become uncontrollable. "Ashton, it's okay, we can play another game."

It's too late. Ashton broke out into tears and the deck of cards begin floating in the air and the lights flicker. Dr. Hawthorne and his team are in awe but at the same time nervous about Ashton's capabilities. "Hey, hey, Ashton, it's okay sweetheart," Dr. Hawthorne took his time with relaxing Ashton. "Since you played a good game, how about a big, juicy, lollipop?" He gave her the biggest sucker she had ever seen, and she relaxed instantly. The cards drop to the floor, and she happily licks on her sucker, her face stained with tears. "Okay," Dr. Hawthorne exhaled, relieved he didn't see a more dangerous side of Ashton. "Angel, how are-" Angel stares at the wall in front of her, not blinking an eye or batting an eyelash. "Angel, are you okay? What's wrong?" he asked, waving his hands across her face. He glanced at her monitor and her vitals are just as bad as Ashton's. "Angel? Angel!?" Dr. Hawthorne continued to bring her back to reality.

"Sir, what do we do?" a team member asked.

"We wait," he said defeated.

Angel's astral body has gone in time. After waiting several minutes, Angel comes out of her vision but isn't feeling too well. Fortunately, her vitals were now stable.

"Ow, my head hurts," she said, rubbing her forehead.

"Hi Angel, can you tell me what happened?" he asked.

"You got hurt really bad," she said to him.

"I-I'm not sure I understand; how did I get hurt?" he asked, hoping to get more information. Looking around the room and seeing everyone watching her, Angel is fearful to give any more details. "Can you all leave the room for a moment?" Everyone leaves and Ashton continues to eat her lollipop while watching a cartoon a nurse set up for her. It's now Dr. Hawthorne and Angel. "Okay, sweetheart, you can tell me. Everything is going to be fine; I promise."

"You got punched and someone kicked you really hard and you were bleeding there," she says pointing to his head. This information takes him back. He doesn't know how to process it; is it true or is she having trouble putting the pieces together?

"Do you know when this happens?" he asks. She shakes her head, answering no. "Does someone help me get better?" he asked, realizing he was talking to a five-year-old. She shook her head again, unsure of her answer. Dr. Hawthorne had become anxious. Had his confidential work finally caught up to him? "Um...okay Angel, you did great today," he stopped the questioning. "Let's see what we can do about those headaches." He frantically moved throughout the room to a nearby cabinet that held various medications. He takes a pill bottle; his hands shake in the process as he breaks open a pill and pours it into a cup of apple juice. Stirring the mix, the only thing he thought about is his possible fate leading to his death. If what Angel said was true, he must prepare now. "Angel, drink this and you'll feel all better," he smiled. Dr. Hawthorne motioned his assistant into the room. "We're finished here. Monitor them while I go talk to their parents," he said, beginning to leave the room as if he's on a mission.

"Sir, before you go," his assistant stopped him with vital information, "you should look at this before talking to them."

Taking the folder, Dr. Hawthorne was surprised at their findings. Briskly walking to the waiting area, Dr. Hawthorne brought Aaron and Elise to his office.

"Doctor, what's wrong with our girls?" Aaron asked, getting straight to business.

"Well, first I must say you have extraordinary children, very intelligent. You've done an exceptional job raising them," Dr. Hawthorne said as he makes them feel they've done their jobs as parents.

"Thank you," Elise said, showing her brightest smile.

"You're welcome, but to get down to what your daughters are capable of," he begins to explain that Angel and Ashton are supernaturals and it's normal for girls to show signs earlier than boys. "Ashton is what is known as a telekinetic; she can manipulate and move objects with her mind."

"Okay, that makes sense. The first thing we ever saw her move was a spoon, but can she move heavier objects?" Aaron asked, concerned.

"I believe so. She's able to control multiple objects at a time and she's only five. By the time she's 16, she should be able to compress objects," Dr. Hawthorne said, intrigued by Ashton's abilities.

Aaron and Elise had looks of worry. How are they going to help Ashton through something they know nothing about or have no control over? "And Angel?" Elise asked.

Once he heard Angel's name he instantly reverted to their conversation and what she supposedly saw. "Angel is very special; she is an astral," he was hesitant to continue, but he had to help them. "She can not only see into the future, but her astral self, her soul, can go there."

"That would explain why she's been so distant from me for the past couple of days," Elise added, "but how do you know this for certain?"

Dr. Hawthorne contemplated whether he should mention the vision Angel had or should he continue to be professional and state the facts. "During testing, we have monitors to not only display brain activity but the patient's vitals," he continued. "While testing Ashton, her vitals were unstable, but we were quickly able to gain control and get her back. With Angel, her vitals became unstable and then..." he paused because he doesn't know how they'll react, "she flat lined."

"She what?!" Aaron shouted.

"How in the hell did that happen?!" Elise became angry as well, wanting to pin Dr. Hawthorne to the floor.

"I understand your concerns, but if you just let me explain," Dr. Hawthorne said trying to de-escalate the situation.

"You better have a damn good explanation," Aaron threatened, the vein in his neck protruding.

"She did flat line, but only in this reality," he said, but Aaron and Elise aren't satisfied.

"What are you saying?" Elise was confused and annoyed.

"Think of it this way, when your soul leaves and separates from your body, what happens? What are you?" he asked rhetorically. "You're dead. So, when Angel's soul left her body in this reality, she flat lined, she was dead, but her soul, which is still a part of her, is alive. It always comes back," he continued.

"But that still doesn't explain how you knew if she was dead or not," Aaron said.

"I knew Angel was still alive because I saw her breathing, I felt her breath. The only thing my team and I could do was wait until she came out of it." Aaron and Elise took a minute to gather themselves.

"Dr. Hawthorne...where do we go from here?" Aaron asked, hating that he didn't know for himself how to protect his girls.

"Well, it begins with you," Dr. Hawthorne said. "You have to understand that your daughters are still the precious little girls you've raised, and they'll always be," he sincerely explained. "The only difference is they have a slight enhancement. Think of it as a special gift, I mean we're all given one, right?" he smiled easing their worries.

"Thank you, Doctor," Aaron reciprocated the feeling.

"Earlier you said something about giving them medicine to help control these powers," Elise said.

"Unfortunately, that is another matter we have to discuss." He mentioned the folder his assistant gave him. Aaron and Elise begin to look skittish. Their hands become clammy and little specs of sweat begin to appear across Elise's smooth chocolate skin. "The results of the DNA samples revealed some...concerns," he said, approaching this situation delicately.

"Which are?" Aaron asked.

"Mr. Cross, you are 99.99% Angel and Ashton's father, but Mrs. Cross," he looked at Elise as she sits uneasy, "you are not the mother of these girls." The room is silent, no one knows what to say next. Aaron and Elise exhaled as if they're letting down their guard. If they want to continue receiving help for their girls it was time to be honest, in their own way. "Usually when I reveal DNA test results it's the father who's upset but being that you're not the mother, I'm sure you already knew this information," he said.

"No, I am not their BIRTH mother, but I have cared for them and protected them each day they've been on this earth, and I don't plan on stopping." Elise felt the judgment of her motherhood.

"I'm sorry I offended you, but I need to know the genetic history of both biological parents in order to finish the process."

"My..." it's hard for Aaron to speak about his past, "late wife passed away during birth. Our daughters never had the chance to meet their amazing mother. Dr. Hawthorne, I can assure you she never had any abilities, nor did she show any signs. I know this because she was never the one to hide information, not in our marriage, not ever. So, I am asking you, more like begging that...that you would please help our girls because for the first time in my life I don't know how to fix this." A strong, fearful, virile of a man poured his heart out to Dr. Hawthorne, hoping he would use all his resources to help Angel and Ashton.

"Mr. and Mrs. Cross," Dr. Hawthorne comes from behind his desk to sit next to them.

"Please, you don't have to be formal with us," Elise said knowing they've given each other enough information to become more than just patients.

"Aaron and Elise, I promise you I will do everything in my power to help your girls and care for them as if they were my own." They continued to discuss further the powers Angel and Ashton now possess and how to help them as they become older and stronger. "I can see Angel has these reoccurring headaches after she has a

vision, so I've set up a prescription that you can only get here," he showed them an address he's written on a piece of paper for them, 2860 St. Claire Ave., Chicago, IL 60462. "You pour this powder in any liquid drink and it should ease the pain instantly."

"And Ashton," Aaron asked.

"Because Ashton has shown signs of being very powerful for her age, it's best to keep her as calm as possible," Dr. Hawthorne stressed. "The more emotional she becomes, the harder it will be to control her."

Aaron and Elise took everything Dr. Hawthorne explained to them and thanked him considerably for all the information he had given. "You've helped tremendously. Thank you, Doctor," Aaron said, standing up to shake his hand.

"Yes, thank you for all your help. I hope we see you soon. The girls have become fond of you," Elise smiled.

"I would love to see them again as well, but if you don't see me, it means they're doing well, so let's not wish on a visit any time soon," he said lovingly.

They laugh. Aaron and Elise exit his office.

Aaron and Elise made their way to the office where Angel and Ashton were being checked.

"You laid it on pretty thick in there," Elise said, referencing Aaron's sob story about his apparent late wife.

"Whatever it takes, right?" he replied.

"I guess we got what we needed," Elise said.

"Except for the biochip," Aaron said.

"I wonder why he didn't mention it," Elise replied.

"I don't know. Maybe the girls aren't that far along. But as long as he doesn't figure anything out, we're fine," Aaron said seriously.

"You mean about Savannah? How long do you think we can keep up with me being their mother, Aaron?" Elise asked, concerned.

"We won't be getting DNA tests anytime soon so we're fine, plus you have similar features, and you love them and treat them like they're your own. That's why she chose you," Aaron said, grabbing her hands and gazing into her eyes, letting her know everything will work.

"All right," she said relieved. "Let's just do what we can to keep their powers hidden. We can't trust everyone."

"Of course," he said, kissing her on top of her head.

Dr. Hawthorne waited until they left the office to show is fear. He didn't want to mention what Angel told him because he didn't want to put any more pressure on them and he wasn't sure if it was entirely true. He doesn't want to take any risk of his experiment getting into the wrong hands.

PART III – YEAR 2010

Chapter 21

A year had passed since the events involving the Phantom agency - and the people who work for it - being destroyed. Not much has happened since then.

Major David Lawrence dreads the announcement he has to make to the rest of his officers today. After their disagreement on whether ex-agent Silas Clay acted against Phantom, Jordan barely showed up to work. She was taking some time for herself by handling her own mission, trying to find an elite assassin organization, Leviathan. Dr. Hawthorne quit Phantom and the CIA, the day after his wife passed, never to be seen again. Except for today when he gets a call from Lawrence to come clean out his lab.

No one had seen or heard from Computational Bioinformatics Analyst Martin Edwards since the night of the agency's break-in. Martin realized that, as much as he respected Dr. Hawthorne, participating in the heinous experiments that would be done on innocent children was morally wrong. Martin decided to move on.

The atmosphere of Phantom is different now. Normally, everyone is upbeat and ready to start their next assignments, but the remaining officers and agents mosey along, not knowing what the next stage in their careers.

In his office, David sat at his desk reflecting on the happier times he's had with the CIA and Phantom but he can't help but wonder all the ways he could have prevented the events that had transpired. There's nothing he can do about it now; it's clear Director Radcliff isn't changing his mind. David pulled himself out of his slump and packed up his office. He puts important paperwork in large file boxes on one side of the room and his personal items such as his many badges he received while working in law enforcement, pictures of his parents and a picture of the first day Phantom began on the other side. For a moment, he stared at the picture. He's satisfied with what he's been through with the agency and he can be content with the ending.

He continued to pack until a voice comes through from the intercom box on his desk. "Sir, Lieutenant Knox is here to see you."

He paused. He didn't expect Jordan to visit him.

"Sir?"

He quickly approached the intercom and directed his secretary to let Jordan come up. Jordan entered the office. When she enters a room, everyone pays attention. She has poise inside and out. When stepping towards her, he was cautious, not knowing whether to show affection or stay professional, so he takes his chances. He wraps his hulking arms around her waist pulling her close and gently kisses the top of her forehead. She hesitates before returning the affection.

"Where have you been? I've been trying to get in touch with you for months?" he asks.

Jordan pulls away from him, not wanting to tell him the reason she didn't keep in contact with anyone from Phantom. "I had important business to handle."

"And that kept you from answering your phone?" he asked skeptical of her story.

"Well, you know me, once I get caught up in a job, I lose focus on the real issue," she said. He realizes that was a remark made towards him. Jordan walked around the office and she didn't notice the emptiness at first. "What's going on with all the boxes? You going somewhere?"

"That's why I've been trying to get in touch with you. I need to talk to you about Phantom. The night you left, Director Radcliff didn't just come to see the damage, he came to let us know Phantom is the worst subdivision the CIA has put together."

"Of course, he did. The man is never satisfied."

"What we've done isn't good enough for him."

"Okay, David, what's the problem and why would you lie about something as small as that?"

His mind is telling him to protect her from the truth about the jeopardy of the agency, but his heart won't allow it. He's kept the truth from Jordan for the past few months and it ends today. "They're shutting us down."

Jordan braced herself on the couch behind her. She can't understand how this is happening. What was she going to do now? This isn't how the plan was supposed to go. Leviathan needs to be stopped. "Have you told them?" she asked about the agents and officers.

"I was on my way down to make the announcement," he said, sitting close to Jordan.

"They've been through so much," Jordan said, staring out into the bright blue sky of the large windows in the office.

David placed his hand on the upper part of Jordan's back, comforting her through this difficult time. They sit in silence for a few seconds until he tells her the other news.

"You know it's not all bad."

Jordan slowly looked at him to see what he had to say. "How can it not be?" Jordan said.

"Radcliff offered me my old position." He's proud. Jordan stood away from him and backs away, her sadness turned to anger.

"What!? So, you're telling me the good news is that you're not out of a job, but the rest of us are!"

"It's not like that, Jordan! You know that!"

"What is it like then, David?! Because what I'm hearing is you don't care what happens to any of them! I don't think you even care about what happens to me and then you lie to me for months!" Jordan pushed him with her shoulder as she walked around him to leave.

"I want you to come with me!" he shouted.

She stops in her steps and turns to face him.

"Come back to the CIA and work with me."

She purposely doesn't answer him, disapproving of his decision and upset her plan to destroy Leviathan and get her family back is falling apart. She left him standing, watching as she pulls herself together as though everything they've been through meant nothing. David rubbed his thick beard and then kicks a full box of papers. Maybe he shouldn't take the job, maybe he should quit the field, but he's worked too hard and would never be happy. He prepares himself to go explain to his agents how Phantom will no longer be in operation. He approached the silver box on his desk and commanded his secretary to send a message to everyone in the building to meet in the conference room in a half hour.

Dr. Hawthorne cleans up what's left of his lab. He doesn't seem as upset about the lab being destroyed or the agency folding, unlike everyone else. He's content with where his life is going since quitting. As he gets ready to enter his office, he hears a knock at the door.

"Knock, knock," Jordan said, happy to see him.

"Hey, how are you?" Dr. Hawthorne asked his good friend. They embrace one another, gaining back the time they've lost.

"How am I? How are you and little Natalie?" Jordan chuckled, it's been a year since his wife passed and he's asking how someone else is doing.

"We're doing wonderful. She's becoming more and more intelligent each day, just like her father if I say so myself." They laugh. "So, Phantom is shutting down." Dr. Hawthorne said cautiously.

"Yep," she confirmed. This may be the end for this agency, but not the end for her own.

"We all knew it was coming," Dr. Hawthorne said.

"Yes, but not this soon," Jordan said, wishing she had more time to follow through with her own plans.

"Well, if anyone is going to catch the people who did this, I'm sure you and David will."

Jordan stepped away from Dr. Hawthorne and begins to pace around the lab, struggling to tell him the problems she's having with David.

"What's wrong, Jordan?"

"Actually, me and David aren't seeing eye to eye right now."

"Trouble in paradise?"

Jordan spins around to face him, embarrassed by his remark. "What?!" Jordan said surprised.

Dr. Hawthorne snickered at Jordan being surprised he knew. "You two aren't as subtle as you think."

"Well, David is going back to work for the great CIA, so we won't be seeing each other anytime soon."

"You didn't expect him to not go back to work after this, did you?"

Jordan didn't answer him. She knew Dr. Hawthorne was right. She shouldn't have thought David would give up his career because of what took place. "As much as it pains us all to see the agency go, we have to move forward," Dr. Hawthorne said.

"Enough about him, what are you going to do now that this is all over?"

"Continue my practice."

"The pediatrics?" she asked. Dr. Hawthorne paused. He looked around the lab and directs Jordan to his computer in his office. "I wasn't necessarily running a pediatrics."

Why is everyone in a secretive mood today? she wondered. "What were you doing then?" she asked.

"The potential psychics I found were actually children, toddlers to be exact," Jordan is stunned that Dr. Hawthorne would even think about inserting chips into toddlers.

"Max, are you crazy?!"

"I know, but it's not what you think. I started the pediatrics to better help control their powers." Jordan was relieved to hear he hadn't been killing kids in his free time. "After dealing with the biochip and going home every night to Alexandria and seeing her precious face, I knew I couldn't go through with getting rid of her special abilities. She was my daughter for god's sake, so I helped other parents deal with the same issues I was going through," Dr. Hawthorne explained.

"Were you able to help them?" Jordan asked, hoping he would give her more information. Dr. Hawthorne gives her a smile stretching from ear to ear.

"Yes! I keep in touch with the parents to monitor the girls and-"

"They're all girls?" She was amazed at his findings.

"The strongest young ladies I've seen. Might be stronger than you." They joked.

"Ha, ha," Jordan said.

"These girls were my main patients. I studied them almost every week, trying to convince their parents that I could get rid of these powers. Some were willing, but others refused, and it wasn't until Alexandria was…gone I realized these powers were a gift and can be used to help a lot of people." Dr. Hawthorne is so proud of the work he's accomplished. He loves what he does and finally feels he's doing something great in the world, a feeling he hasn't felt in a very long time.

"That's amazing, Max. I'm really proud of you," Jordan said, congratulating him. "If they're as strong as you say they are, I have to meet them," she said, making her way out the door.

"Of, course!" Dr. Hawthorne said.

"I'll see you at the meeting," Jordan said, leaving the lab.

Dr. Hawthorne stayed to finish packing the last bit of work he had when suddenly he hears a sound from outside the lab. The noise resembled someone kicking over a box. He stopped packing to figure out who or what made the noise. "Hello?" his voice is shaking. "Hello?!" No one answered. He proceeded on with packing his last box. As he turns around to leave, he's frightened by Marissa Michell standing directly behind him.

"Hello, Dr. Maxwell A. Hawthorne," she said, smiling in the most conniving way.

"What are you doing here, Marissa?" Dr. Hawthorne said, surprised to see an old colleague.

"Why? I can't visit an old friend?" she asked, walking towards him as he moves backwards into the lab.

"No. Not when you're on the Most Wanted list of every agency in the United States."

"Maxwell, let's stop beating around the bush. You know why I'm here."

"Unfortunately, Marissa, I don't," Dr. Hawthorne said, fearless.

"Give me the experiment."

Maxwell paused for a moment as he replays the past events that had transpired and begins to piece everything together. He now knows Clay and Marissa are behind it all – the break in at his home and the disappearance of his daughter Alexandria - and he had to handle this situation with Marissa delicately. "I no longer have it."

The smile on Marissa's face fades. "Don't lie to me, Maxwell. You and I have known each other long enough to see when the other is trying to deceive," Marissa said impatiently.

"You're right, Marissa, I do know you and I also remember you being the top agent in the CIA and then going rogue because you wanted to sell secrets to our enemies."

"Then you understand that what I want, I get," she moved closer to him. "Now, give me the experiment."

Dr. Hawthorne grew increasingly angry. "I said I don't have it."

After a short silence, Marissa began to laugh hysterically. Dr. Hawthorne is puzzled at her sudden amusement during this situation. "Oh, I get it, you must think I'm asking." Her laughter stopped abruptly and she's back to herself. "Here's the deal, Maxwell, you're going to give me the experiment along with the research on those girls and you're going to give it to me in the next sixty seconds or more family members are going to pay the price for your arrogance. You've already lost two."

Dr. Hawthorne stood firm in his answer. "I'm not giving you anything. Now you need to leave. I'm sure you don't want anyone, including your husband, finding out about your new career as an assassin. Tell me, how is Leviathan treating you?" Dr. Hawthorne said courageously. Marissa pierced his soul as she stared deeply. She stepped away from him and began to walk towards his computer. "Get away from there, Marissa!" he shouted.

"Put him down," Marissa said as men dressed in all black, like her, came in through different entrances of the lab.

"Stop! What are you---" Dr. Hawthorne struggled as the men began to tie him to a lab chair wrapping his wrist and ankles with leather buckles.

"Search the lab from top to bottom, corner to corner. Anything that looks remotely close to an experiment, we take with us," Marissa demanded. "Download everything!" she said to one of the men as they searched through the lab computers.

"You're not going to find anything!" Dr. Hawthorne struggled to move.

One of the men standing over Dr. Hawthorne hits him hard with his fist, sending Dr. Hawthorne's head flying back. As he moves his head forward, his right eye is swollen shut and blood drips down onto his bright white lab coat. "Shut up!" the man said.

"I've been… hit harder… by my… mother," Dr. Hawthorne said as he begins to taunt the two men standing over him.

They enjoyed his comment and began to take turns punching him continuously in his face. "That's enough!" Marissa yelled as she comes from inside Dr. Hawthorne's office. They back away from him, obeying Marissa's every command. She kneeled in front of him, "I'm going to give you one more opportunity to give me Experiment X and those girls, and all of this will be over."

Dr. Hawthorne laughed maniacally, his face swollen. "I'll give you the names when you give me my daughter."

Marissa smiled, the only emotion she knows to give at this moment, but she is impressed at how quickly Dr. Hawthorne figured them out so quickly. At least now she doesn't have to kill Alexandria. "I don't know what you're talking about, but if I did have your daughter, Clay and I would be far better parents than you and that pathetic wife of yours."

Dr. Hawthorne threw out the largest glob of saliva onto Marissa's face. Her face is splattered with blood. The taste and smell of copper consume her. The entire lab becomes silent, the men abruptly stop what they are doing. She stood over him and wipes her face.

"Finish him," she said, so relaxed it was frightening. She walked away as five men unstrap Dr. Hawthorne from the chair and begin to beat on him, smashing their fists into every inch of his body. Their fists hit him like boulders as the cracks and shatters of his bones graze their fists. He moans and groans as they lay their punches. Then they begin to take their large, heavy working boots into his face and chest. Unknown to all of them, before they unstrapped Dr. Hawthorne, he hit the alarm button at the bottom of the lab table near the floor.

Upstairs inside Phantom's large conference room are the remaining agents, officers, technicians, engineers, and scientists, as well as Jordan. David stood at the podium explaining the events that brought them to where they are now. "As you all know, we lost many of our fellow agents a year ago, some of which we all consider not only friends, but family. But we've remained strong through adversity, as we always do."

"Sir, I don't mean to interrupt, but do we know who could have done this?" an agent asked.

"I've looked through the evidence we've obtained and have come to the realization that our number one suspect is Midas."

Jordan stood in the back of the room watching David, irritated by his continuous accusation that Midas did all of this when he knows it was Clay. She wants no part of this meeting. "Excuse me, sir," Jordan shouted from the back of the room.

"Yes, Lieutenant?"

"Since Midas was the cause of destroying the agency, what's the plan for going after him?" she asked obnoxiously. David lowered his head and let out a large sigh.

"Unfortunately, we will not be taking on this case. Phantom will no longer be operating; the CIA will take over this assignment." Everyone in the room began to panic, asking each other what they were going to do next, where they were going to go. "Everyone, everyone! Please calm down!"

"What do you mean calm down!?" someone shouted out.

"It's hard enough finding a job in this field," an agent said fearfully.

"I assure you all: everything is going to work out just fine," David said.

"Who are you to say that! Everything is going to work out for you. It always does with you people," an agent says angrily.

"I'm just like the---" before David could finish, his secretary comes rushing in.

"Sir! The silent alarm in the lab just went off!" Everyone turned to face her. Jordan stands from the wall.

"I'm sure Dr. Hawthorne triggered it while cleaning it out," David said, reassuring everyone.

"Sir, it was the motion alarm." Jordan and David look at each other from across the room. That alarm never goes off.

"Everyone take point. It looks like we've been breached…again," David said to his agents.

David and Jordan begin to rush down to the lab. "What do you think is going on?" David asked.

"I don't know. I just left him minutes ago and everything was fine."

"I guess we'll have to see for ourselves. Be ready," he said.

"I'm always ready," Jordan said, removing her guns from her hip holster and cocking her gun.

Chapter 22

D r. Hawthorne groaned on the lab floor, clutching his stomach, attempting to regain any strength he has left. One of Marissa's men guarding the lab doors comes rushing through the front door of the lab. "Boss, I heard some movement upstairs."

Marissa looked around the room, observing what information is the most valuable to take, and then looked back down at Dr. Hawthorne. She moved closer to him. "You know it's a shame Maxwell, you were one of my favorite people and I have very few of those."

"It will not be this easy… for you… they are… going to find out…what you and Clay did… and who… you are." Dr. Hawthorne coughs up blood, struggling to speak. Marissa chuckled, mocking his comment.

"It was a pleasure, Doctor."

One of her men approaches Dr. Hawthorne and aims his pistol at his head. As he becomes centimeters away from pulling the trigger, David and Jordan come rushing in through different sides of the lab, stopping everyone in the room, their guns pointed at the first men they see.

"Stop! Back away, slowly," David said, motioning Marissa's men away from Dr. Hawthorne. Most of the men had already left the lab to put the equipment and information they obtained in their vehicles, but by then the leftover Phantom agents had already stopped them, unknown to Marissa.

"Major David Lawrence, well, isn't this just a fun little reunion," said Marissa. She chuckled a bit at the thought of David and Jordan and how they can be so confident when it's clear they can't compete. It's two against her five.

"Marissa, why are you here?" David asked.

"That seems like the question of the day." Marissa stood without an ounce of fear in her body as Jordan slowly pointed her gun at her.

"David, you know her?" Jordan asked.

"I'm afraid I do."

Jordan kept her eyes trained on Marissa. She senses Marissa is not the type of person you want to trust. "Max, are you all right?!" Jordan shouted across the lab. She can't see him, and she needs to know if he's okay.

"You don't have to worry about him, hon," Marissa said with the snarkiest smile.

Jordan's blood boils. She hates terms of endearment like sweetheart or honey; they make her feel weak, like she can't take care of herself. "You're a real confident person for someone who has a gun aimed straight at their face," Jordan said.

"Jolie, no Julie, or is it Jamie," Marissa continued to taunt Jordan. "Well, whatever it is, you won't shoot me," she said with such cockiness.

Jordan holds her gun tighter, waiting for Marissa to make the slightest move so she can shoot one right between her eyes. "Want to bet?" Jordan replied.

"Enough, Marissa! It's over!" David yelled from the other side of the room, while still protecting Dr. Hawthorne from the man who was going to end his life. Marissa's men wait for her next command because clearly they don't have minds of their own. Just then a loud boom erupts outside. The remaining Phantom agents are outside the building, shooting bullet after bullet against Marissa's team. "Marissa, you are under arrest for the breaking and entering of this agency and the assault on Dr. Maxwell Hawthorne." David was confident in his approach, but Marissa and her men chuckled at his statement.

"That's never going to happen." Marissa said.

In an instant, Marissa leaps in the air and forcefully kicks Jordan on the side of her face knocking her to the ground. Marissa ran out the lab leaving her men to handle David and Jordan. The man near Dr. Hawthorne tried to shoot David but he knocked the gun out of his hand and lands his own punches, knocking the man back against the glass window of the lab office. When Jordan finally stands, she's confronted by two of Marissa's men: one just as tall and slim as her. The other is as big as a defensive tackle. The slender one tried to land a punch toward her face, but she ducked down and hits him right in his stomach. Jordan is very athletic and has been told on several occasions she has the strength of any man; a weapon in a business suit. The defensive tackle picked Jordan up. She flipped around to the back of his neck, where she sat on his shoulders and dropped down behind him and kicked him on top of the lab table where he burned his hands in mixed chemicals. The slender man approached Jordan from behind and wrapped his arms around her neck, attempting to strangle her. Jordan braced herself and head-butted him. She spun around to kick him with as much force as she could on the side of his face, causing him to tumble down on to the floor, unconscious.

On the other side of the lab, David continued to fight off the other two men who were trying to finish off Dr. Hawthorne, still lying on the lab floor. David and the men go back and forth throwing punch after punch, blow after blow. David is very skilled in these situations, but as he fights his way through, he thinks to himself, are these men too skilled for him? The men finally get David in a corner and begin to punch him forcefully. He knew he had to handle himself, but not until one of the men grabbed their gun and points it at David, seconds from pulling the trigger. Jordan glanced over to see David staring death in the face and rushed to aid him, but she's tackled by the defensive tackle. She gave him a blow to the head with her black heel to get him off her and she reaches for the gun Marissa kicked out of her hand and shoots him, killing him instantly. She jumps up from the floor and runs to snatch the gun from the man who is trying to kill David, but it's too late. The moment Jordan snatched the gun out of the man's hand, he shoots David in his shoulder. Once Jordan had the gun tightly in her hand, she quickly shoots the remaining men in the lab. She fired three quick shots and they fell to the ground.

The lab is quiet. She rushed over to David. "Are you okay?" she asked, cautiously touching his shoulder.

"I'm fine."

Jordan then rushed over to Dr. Hawthorne's side, kneeling in front of him. "Max! Are you okay?!" She struggled to sit him up on the floor against the lab table. He could hardly form a sentence.

"I-I-I'm s-s-sor,.." Hawthorne struggles.

"Don't try to speak. The medic is on their way," Jordan said, trying not to touch him. She looked at him with mixed emotions, his face swollen shut and his lab coat drenched in blood. Jordan is furious she let Marissa get the best of her; she had never let an enemy get away alive. She stood from Dr. Hawthorne and picked up her guns from the floor. She checked how many bullets remained in the clip and proceeded to go after Marissa. Jordan had only Marissa on her mind – it was tunnel vision. Jordan won't allow herself to see anything but her target.

David groaned on the floor from the pain of the bullet in his shoulder and tried to catch her attention. "Jordan." She can't hear him. "J!" David grabbed the nearest chair and brought himself to stand. Jordan stopped and turned to face him, but didn't respond.

"Don't let her get away," he said, out of breath but having faith Jordan will bring justice to Phantom.

She left the lab and swiftly moved outside to the back of the agency where she hears bullets flying from either direction. There's an even number of Marissa's men and Phantom agent casualties on both sides. Jordan jumped over broken crates and destroyed cars to get to Marissa. Marissa and some of her men rushed to a large black truck and began to drive away. When she looks back, she sees Jordan running after them. Marissa began mocking her persistence. This only made Jordan more enraged. She jumped inside the nearest car and quickly drove behind them. They sped up, trying to lose Jordan, but it's unsuccessful. Jordan sped up just as fast.

"Get rid of her, NOW!" Marissa demands, agitated.

Jordan chased them through the rugged terrain around the agency. Phantom is hidden within an old, abandoned building just outside of the city. To an outsider it's just an old, torn down factory that will eventually collapse. Jordan sped up next to them, ramming her car against theirs, attempting to steer them off the empty road before entering the city. They ram her once again. The truck is too big compared to the car she's driving. They ram her once again, this time with all their force, sending her spinning out of control, but she quickly regains her momentum, speeding up once again behind them. Immediately she grabbed her gun from her holster. At that very moment, as Jordan pulled out her gun, more of Marissa's men come hastily behind her. They shoot at the back of her windows; bullets begin to ricochet throughout her car. She's trying hard to keep her focus on Marissa, but she needs to get rid of these guys. She slowed down and switched into reverse and began speeding backwards. Both men lean out of their cars and shoot at her, but they miss. With one hand on the wheel, she uses the other to point the gun outside the passenger window and shoot the driver, causing the car to spin out of control in front of her. She then immediately points her gun through the driver's window and shoots the front tires of the other car. Both men's cars spin out of control and crash into each other, creating a fiery explosion.

Marissa looks out to see the explosion. She's sure it was Jordan's car that blew up. Unfortunately, it wasn't. Jordan sped out from the smoke, racing to catch up to them. By the time she catches up to them, they've entered the city and are slamming through cars. Marissa became troubled. "I'm really getting sick of her," she said to herself. She took out her phone and began talking to a mysterious figure. "Take her out, take her out NOW!"

Jordan is still on their tails. They sped down the busy streets. As Jordan followed Marissa around a corner, a black car in an alley crashed right into her, causing her to crash into the brick wall of a convenience store. A sense of relief comes over Marissa. She's escaped and is pleasantly satisfied Jordan could be terribly hurt.

Jordan gets out with minor injuries and finds the car that hit her. She runs over to open the door and no one is there, but there is a brick on the gas pedal. She sees Marissa and her men fleeing the scene; they're long gone now. She kicked the car, fuming. She wanted Marissa to pay and she wanted her to pay now. She held her arm in pain, her shoulder is dislocated. She braced herself and popped it back into place and walks into the convenience store. "Is everyone all right?" she asked the convenience store owner.

"What did you do to my store?!" he yells frantically.

"Sir, I apologize, but I need to use your phone," Jordan says. She is in a lot of pain and she's still infuriated with what just happened.

"You're not getting anything until you tell me how you're going to fix my store!" the convenience store owner shouted. Jordan is beyond annoyed at this point. The store owner continued to go on about his store and how it's all Jordan's fault. "I'm calling the cops!" he yelled.

She pulled out her gun and aimed it at him. It's not loaded; she wasted all her bullets on Marissa's men. "I am the cops, and I will send someone over here to assess the damages. Now give me the phone before…" Jordan struggled to get her words out due to the pain, "I have to pull it away from a dead man." Jordan struggled to get her words out due to the pain. The store owner does what she demands and gives her the phone. "Thank you…and sorry," she said as she walked away to find a private spot. "This is Lieutenant Jordan Knox, 2880, I need damage control and extraction," Jordan told a female operator.

"Right away, Lieutenant. Just give me a moment to pinpoint your location. Extraction will be available in approximately five minutes."

"Thank you." She returned the phone to the nervous store owner and exited the store. "Have a nice day," she said, trying to appease him.

As she waits for her extraction, she began to examine the car that hit her, examining every inch of it. She then checked the outside of the vehicle along with the trunk and she finds nothing. The car is spotless; nothing is out of place except for the broken windows and doors. She's missing something. Why can't she see it, she thought. Now able to stop and think, Jordan began to put the pieces together. She began her own organization long ago to protect those from her past, and to create a better future. Partnering with the CIA was only a decoy for protecting her own organization, Exodus. Jordan has been searching for the elite assassination organization, Leviathan, and tonight she may have become closer to the organization than she ever had before. Jordan's personal team gave her a lead that Leviathan had assassins undercover in the CIA. They must have heard of Dr. Hawthorne's experiments and made that their new objective. She goes to look again, but extraction and damage control have arrived to clean up.

"Lieutenant, what happened?" Agent Rogan asked, approaching her.

"Marissa had one of her guys ghost me. Never saw it coming."

He looked at her ripped and blood-stained clothing as she held her arm. "You need someone to check that arm out?" he asked, worried about her.

"No, I'm fine. How's everyone?" she asked.

"We lost a few, but most came out alive with minor injuries."

"David?"

"The shot in his shoulder did some damage, but it was an exit wound. He should be fine."

"And Dr. Hawthorne?"

Agent Rogan paused for a while, not wanting to give Jordan the news.

"Agent Rogan? How is Dr. Hawthorne?" she asked again. She needed him to answer.

"The doctors are saying he keeps coding…he's not doing well…"

Before Agent Rogan could finish summing up the status of Dr. Hawthorne, Jordan took his car and sped out into the city to check on her dearest friend.

Chapter 23

The east wing of the emergency room is frantic. They have blocked it off for the privacy of Phantom. Agents, scientists and engineers are scattered throughout the floors of the hospital. There aren't enough rooms to hold them all. The nurses and physicians patch up bullet wounds and splint broken bones.

In an exclusive room, David sat on his hospital bed at a loss, unable to explain what he's been through. He's failed as a leader – failed to protect his people. He reached for his crutches, leaning against his bed. Slowly he braced himself to stand, trying not to injure his sprained foot and wounded shoulder.

The hospital doors burst open, and Jordan comes rushing through. She grabbed her arm, wincing in pain, but she needs help finding Maxwell. A nurse watched as she held her arm. She quickly came to her aid.

"Ma'am, are you hurt?"

Jordan was not paying attention, needing to find someone she knows. "What? No. I'm fine."

"Are you sure? I can look at it for you."

"I said I'm okay!" Jordan became agitated. She walked to a very busy desk where nurses are running back and forth.

She tried to grab someone's attention. "Excuse me. Excuse me. I'm looking for a patient." No one is paying her any mind.

"Hello?! Can someone please tell me where I can find-"

"Jordan Knox?" Jordan turned around and sees a short, timid nurse standing behind her.

"Lieutenant." She wanted her respect; she's earned it.

"I'm sorry. Lieutenant Knox, Dr. Parker would like to speak with you."

Jordan followed the nurse, moving around the numerous agents. She felt bad for them but can only focus on her friend. The nurse and Jordan enter an unauthorized area down the hallway. Only a select few can enter. The area is protected by a heavy-duty steel door with the only entry being hand recognition. And if that wasn't enough, the door is guarded by two officers. Once through the door, the hallway is mildly lit, and the atmosphere is dreary.

There are three private VIP rooms. Dr. Parker stood waiting outside the first room. "Lieutenant Knox, how are you?"

"How is he?" Jordan bypassed the question.

"Dr. Hawthorne sustained serious blunt-force trauma to the head, causing severe internal bleeding." Dr. Parker gave this information to Jordan as delicately as she possibly could. Jordan slowly walked into Maxwell's room. She's afraid of what she might see. Dr. Parker continued to explain his condition, but she heard nothing. As she walked closer to Dr. Hawthorne, she sees he's connected to every machine in the room and has tubes inside his mouth to help him breathe. Dr. Parker walked closer to Jordan and explained further Dr. Hawthorne's condition. "He lost consciousness several times and then he suddenly became fully aware."

This statement brought Jordan back to reality. "Excuse me!?"

"He was able to communicate with us for a short period of time," Dr. Parker said, trying to keep her composure. Jordan can be intimidating at times.

"Then what the hell happened?!"

"We like to call it a surge. It's when the patient experiences a burst in brain wave activity before becoming incredibly worse."

Jordan collected herself. It's not Dr. Parkers' fault. She was the one who was too late. "So, he was fully aware – talking and moving?"

"I'm afraid so," Dr. Parker said. Jordan sat in the chair next to her dear friend, struggling to hold it all together. She hasn't felt these emotions in a very long time.

"What do we do now?" she asked.

"Well, after the passing of his wife, he listed you as his proxy."

Jordan glanced over Maxwell's lifeless body and knew what she had to do and what he would want her to do. "And there's no other way?" she asked.

"No, his organs are failing," Dr. Parker said. The room is silent for a moment. "Do you know what you want to do, Lieutenant?"

"Just…give me a minute," Jordan said, attempting to process the situation. She said nothing for a while.

Dr. Parker stood behind Jordan, waiting for a decision. As she sat there pondering, Dr. Parker picked up an envelope from the nightstand near the hospital bed. "Lieutenant, when Dr. Hawthorne was aware, he wanted me to give you this." Dr. Parker handed Jordan the large manila envelope. "I'll give you some privacy." Dr. Parker exited the room and orders a guard to stand by outside the door. Jordan opened the letter. It read:

Dear Jordan, for the past few years we have created a bond, a loyal bond, and therefore I must reveal things I've hidden from you for the past couple of months. I've revealed to you that I created a biochip to rid the supernatural abilities of youth, but many people did not believe in my research and the thought of kids having these powers frightened them, and I knew danger was sure to follow. A few weeks after setting up my private practice, the danger that I feared struck close to home. My practice that was once used for getting rid of these abilities became a haven for these children to find ways to control them.

Along the way, I met these young girls whose abilities were extraordinary, unbelievably the best I've ever seen at such a young age, but this was a dangerous discovery. People are very interested in my findings and now I must stop and turn over my work to you. Enclosed in this envelope is a key to my home as well as my lab, where all my research is located.

Natalie and I are leaving and I'm going to use my findings to bring Dria back to me. I know others have found out about my work and I must protect my daughter since I've failed to do so in the past. I consider you my dear friend, a part of my family. Finish my work, protect these girls. They may think their parents can protect them, but they can't, and I know you will. I know you Jordan, and I know YOU, Savannah and I know you'll find what you're looking for and I hope it's everything you ever imagined.

An overwhelming array of emotions come over Jordan as she reads Dr. Hawthorne's letter. She can't summon up the words. Dr. Hawthorne knew all along of her plan to stop Leviathan. He knew about her past, about her façade. If she stopped Leviathan, she would be one step closer to regaining her family. She stood over Dr. Hawthorne as if he was still alive, speaking to her. Jordan begins to cry, something she doesn't do often. "What have you done?" She began to lose her calm. "What do you expect me to do?! I don't know anything about this! I have enough to worry about." Jordan stepped away from him to gather herself and her thoughts. Once Jordan has returned to herself, she comes back to Maxwell's side. She stared at him for a while, as though they were having a silent conversation. "I guess I don't have a choice." She began to remember the good times they shared; a sense of peace comes over her. "You can trust me." She grabbed his hand and pressed the call button letting Dr. Parker and the nurse know they can take him off life support. "See you later," she said as her voice started to break.

Dr. Parker and the nurse began to release him. Jordan doesn't want to be comforted. She left the room quickly and caught her balance against the wall. She felt like she was holding her breath the entire time.

David limped through the unauthorized double doors showing his badge to the guards that stood in front. He sees Jordan outside Dr. Hawthorne's private room, unable to move; he knew the outcome of the situation. On his crutches, he limped over to her. "How is he?" he asked.

Jordan said nothing to him – just a look revealing her dear friend is gone. David saw her pain as she tried hard to hide it.

He stood against the wall next to her and grabbed her hand gently. "I'm sorry. He was a good man and a great doctor," he reassured her. He will always be there even if she doesn't want him to be.

"Yeah. Yeah, he was," she said. They hold hands for a moment until she lets go. She walked away from the room, to never look back. She left the hospital and got into her car.

While she sat in the hospital parking lot, Jordan opened the envelope Dr. Hawthorne had left for her and took out the keys to his home. She reached further into the envelope and took out a brochure she didn't see before. The brochure is for a gifted school located in Wales, United Kingdom. She's just as clueless as to what the brochure means as to everything else that took place tonight. She goes home, there was nothing she could do tonight.

Suddenly, her phone rings. "Hello?"

"Hi, I'm Natalie's babysitter and I was wondering when someone would be home. I tried to get in touch with Dr. Hawthorne, but he hasn't called me back."

Jordan didn't want to tell this young girl that someone she'd clearly known for some time was no longer alive.

"I've been here all night and your name is on the emergency contact list he left me if I couldn't get ahold of him."

"Thank you for contacting me. What's your name?" Jordan asked.

"Lucy. My name is Lucy."

"All right, Lucy, I'll be there in 15 minutes." She hung up the phone. She stopped and thought about the one person who should have been here, the one person who would have wanted to be by Dr. Hawthorne's bedside: Dr. Martin Edwards. She dialed his number and he doesn't answer. Jordan thought nothing of it, other than he probably got as far away from this cursed agency as he possibly could. She left the hospital and made her way to Dr. Hawthorne's condo.

That same night, Marissa and her men drove up to her new home, a secluded mansion hidden by a forest. It has castle-like features and the only way to enter is through the front gates. It's a craftsman style mansion, on a land all by itself and fully equipped with a staff. This is the "compound." Everything Clay needed to see his plan become successful was right there. Every room in his home is fully furnished, specifically the lab and armory located underground; one would have to go through tunnels to enter either one. Marissa and her men, in three other trucks, approach the extravagant mansion and are greeted by Will. Marissa and her men look like they've been through a struggle, well at least her men do. Marissa doesn't have a scratch on her. "I want all of that research sent to the lab now." Marissa said shouting out orders to her men as they unload their trucks and make their way behind the mansion to enter the lab below.

Will came running up behind her. "Hey, where were you?"

"Wouldn't you like to know." They walk inside the fancy mansion.

"I don't care what you were doing, but your husband has been on a rampage," Will said.

"So, it's been a regular day." She laughed.

"Yeah, you tell him that." Marissa and Will walked into the extravagant family room where Clay is playing toy trucks with his son.

Clay is rarely seen in this way, a father. He loves his son, but he will always be Silas Clay. "And where were you?" Clay asked Marissa without acknowledging her presence.

"I went to Phantom," she responded.

"Without me knowing?"

"I didn't think I had to let you know anything." She is the only person on this planet who could ever talk to Silas Clay in any tone she saw fit and that infuriated him.

"You didn't think you had to tell me you were going to take my men and ambush Phantom, practically exposing us all?!" Clay shouted.

The room is silent now. Will awkwardly sat with his godson as Marissa and Clay have a stare-down sitting across from each other.

"This is the thanks I get for cleaning up the mess you two created?! Clay, it is nothing but luck you got this far because that woman was not going to rest until you were either locked up or dead, and Will, you-"

"Hey, I was just doing what I was told," Will interrupted Marissa as she plays the blame game.

"Yeah because 'Objective B'," she said moving her fingers in quotes, "worked out so well."

"That was not my fault!" Marissa and Will begin to argue.

Clay had to get his team back in order before everything started to fall apart. "Enough!" He brought the room to a halt; everyone stopped. The maids stopped cleaning and even his son stopped playing with his toys. "Marissa, I understand your frustration and you had to do what was needed, but we aren't going to accomplish anything if we all aren't acting as one." Marissa and Will realized

Clay was right. If they want to see their plan through, they must be on each other's side.

"What did you find?" Clay asked Marissa.

"We took everything in the lab. When I got there, Hawthorne was packing up his office. He must have been leaving."

"Will, go oversee them unloading the research. I want to know everything they found." Will left the family room and goes to the lab below to watch the men organize the information they received at the Phantom lab. Clay and Marissa stay. "Everyone. Leave." Clay said, demanding his staff to exit the room and close the sliding double doors behind them. Marissa sat on the couch, holding her son.

"What's wrong now?" Marissa asked.

"I have something for you," Clay said with a smirk as he exited the family room and enters a small office located in the back of the room. Marissa continued to hold her little boy as he babbled aloud. Marissa sees Clay walking out hand-in-hand with Alexandria, Dr. Hawthorne's eldest daughter.

"Your surprise is the girl you kidnapped?" Marissa asked, confused.

Clay put his index finger on his lips, telling Marissa to be quiet and he looked down at Alexandria. "Alexandria, do you know who that is?" Clay pointed to Marissa. Alexandria, looked up at Clay and then Marissa.

She's hesitant to speak. "Mommy."

Marissa is dismayed that Alexandria called her mommy, and she's more concerned as to how Clay got her in this state. "Yes. I am, sweetie. Come here," Marissa said. Alexandria ran into Marissa's arms and hugged her. Marissa is happy; she's always wanted a daughter, but Clay refused to have any more children. "Hey, sweetie, why don't you go play with your little brother?" Marissa said. Alexandria nodded. Marissa walked both of her *children* to the maid standing outside of the double doors. "What did you do?" Marissa asked.

Clay pours himself a glass of whiskey at his mini bar. "I gave you the greatest gift imaginable. She will always remember the abandonment her birth parents made her feel. They didn't want her. They left her on the doorstep of a stranger's home and forgot about her," Clay said, fabricating a story as if he had this planned from the very beginning.

"You and I both know that's not the real story. So how did you really do it?"

Clay, with his drink in hand and smugness across his face, guides Marissa out of the family room. "Let me show you." He leads her down a set of secluded stairs deep underneath their home.

"Did we really have to have an entire lab in the basement of our home?" Marissa asked Clay as they walked through their exclusive, private, advanced science lab.

"I like to keep a close eye on my work," Clay smirked. They moved around the men unloading the information they received at Phantom. The atmosphere of Clay's lab is dark -- evil leaking through the walls. Clay guided Marissa into the main lab.

"Why am I down here, Clay?"

"You asked about Alexandria, so I'm going to show you." Clay pointed to a projector displaying research on a special serum showing how it works on the human mind, the side effects that take place and how humans interact once it has been inserted into their blood stream. Marissa moved in closer to the screen, her curiosity taking over.

"What is this?" she asked.

"This. This is the beginning of our future," Clay said as he swiftly moved behind her, wrapping his arms around her waist. "This serum destroys memories. Once injected, you forget everything you once knew or thought you knew for months."

"You injected this into her, and she'll have memory loss for, what? A couple of months?!" Marissa began to question her husband's behavior.

"That's what I thought at first, but then Will brought me him." Clay pointed to an average-height male, slim, with square-rimmed glasses rummaging through paperwork on the lab tables. He's very fidgety. Marissa recognized him but couldn't put a name to a face. They stood across from him. He doesn't even notice they're there; he's focused on finding something. "Marissa, this is Dr. Martin Edwards. He created the serum, but with some adjustments."

"How did you get Dr. Hawthorne's flunky to work with you?"

Clay gave a sneer smile and Marissa knew what he had done.

"Are you holding him against his will?" Marissa asked.

"I don't encage anyone. Everyone that works for me has free will," Clay said arrogantly.

Marissa knew that was a lie; it's always a trick with Clay. Marissa walks around the table closer to Martin. She wanted to see what happened to him. She moved in closer to his face, trying to look directly into his eyes. Martin continued to work frantically, searching for research. "Martin, why are you here?!" Marissa waited for him to answer, but he just mumbled to himself. Marissa snapped her fingers in his face, but she got nothing.

Clay stood across from them, watching the exchange. He enjoyed it. He finished the last bit of his drink and walked over to Dr. Martin Edwards and stopped him from fidgeting around with the research on the table. He had Martin face him. "Doctor! What is your purpose here?" Clay forcefully asked. Martin stared at Clay blankly for a moment. He showed no emotion; it was like he was in a trance, detached from the world around him.

Then he slowly spoke. "I'm here to…help you…build…your greatest weapon."

Clay smiled at him. Clay knew he had won, and everything was falling into place. Clay backed away from Dr. Edwards and let him continue to work. Marissa and Clay left the lab.

"You never cease to amaze me," Marissa said as she wrapped her arms around Clay's neck, her lips parting to meet his.

Back in the main lab, Martin fumbled around, searching for something in his research scattered throughout the lab. He mumbled the same words repeatedly. "Separate the Leviathan, separate the Leviathan."

Chapter 24

Jordan drove to a gated community with condos as big as mansions. This was her first time visiting Maxwell's new home. It's unfortunate she had to visit on these terms. She used the address Lucy sent her and waited to be buzzed into the condo.

"Who is it?" Lucy's voice came through the condo speaker box.

"It's Jordan, Lucy." Lucy buzzed her in, and Jordan made her way up the modern steps. A young woman, only 15, came to the door. Her honey blonde hair was pulled back into a ponytail and dressed in messy sweats.

"Hi. So, I've fed her, gave her a bath and read her to sleep."

Jordan hid her emotions. She acted as though everything that happened earlier with Maxwell never took place. "Thank you for everything, Lucy."

Lucy was appreciative and gathered her things to leave. "Just out of curiosity, do you know why Dr. Hawthorne didn't come home?"

Jordan's stomach twists, she tried to avoid this conversation.

"I'm just asking because he's never done this before and he usually calls me back."

"Lucy," Jordan stopped her and had her to sit down on the couch. "Dr. Hawthorne was involved in a fatal accident tonight."

Lucy's perky attitude quickly changes. "What?! Di-did he make it?!"

"No… I'm sorry." Lucy cried. Her family was close to Dr. Hawthorne. They live in the same building and Lucy was starting an internship at his practice soon. "Wh-what about Natalie? Sh-she has no one."

Jordan placed her hand on Lucy's shoulder, trying to console her. "Dr. Hawthorne was one of my closest friends, a brilliant doctor and a phenomenal father and husband. I will forever remember him for it and the day Natalie was born, he named me the godmother." Tonight, is the first time Lucy has met or even heard of Jordan, and if she is Natalie's godmother, why hasn't she been around, she thought. "Maxwell is… was an only child and Christine had no contact with her family, so I'll look out for Natalie," Jordan said, fully prepared and ready to take on the responsibility.

To Lucy, Jordan seems like a trustworthy woman, and if Dr. Hawthorne trusted her enough to put her name down in case of an emergency, she must be the real deal. "Okay." Lucy leaves the condo, convinced Natalie will be safe.

"Hey, Lucy," Jordan stopped her from leaving. "You can come visit Natalie any time." Jordan gave Lucy her address and number, something she didn't do for most. Lucy takes it and leaves the condo. She took some time to rid herself of all her feelings from tonight. She walked around Maxwell's home. It's pristine, nothing out of the ordinary or out of place, just a simple condo.

She walks upstairs to Natalie's room, a bright pink nursery with books covering a single wall. She watched over Natalie as she slept soundly in her crib. She's so precious and her little body is so peaceful; she doesn't have a care in the world. Jordan stayed with Natalie for a while, sitting in the rocking chair near her crib. She rarely gets these silent, peaceful moments. It's getting late and after everything that happened tonight, she decided to stay at Maxwell's condo and get some rest. She wanted a refreshed mind in the morning.

The next morning, Jordan is dressed in her casual attire rather than her exclusive business suits. "Take everything in here and put it on the truck. It needs to go to the storage unit." Jordan, back to her old intense self, gave orders to men who work for her personally. They take the modern furniture and put it on a truck parked outside behind the condo. As she gave orders, Natalie sat on her hip. Jordan is tapped into mommy mode – a mode she's never had the chance to experience.

Jordan takes Natalie to her room. The secret movers put Natalie's things in a box and wrapped her furniture. "Boss, will this be going into storage too?" one of the movers asked her.

"Umm…" She took a second to think about it. "No, put it on the other truck." She couldn't bring herself to get rid of the furniture Maxwell bought for Natalie.

The movers cleared out the room and Jordan finished putting Natalie in her car seat. Suddenly, she hears glass crack. "Are you serious right now?!"

"My bad, boss," the mover said nervously. The mover picked up the now cracked music box.

As he picked it up, she saw a black jump drive that must have fallen out on the floor. She quickly picked it up without him noticing. "Just finish up, faster, please." She waited for him to leave and examined it, but it looked like a normal jump drive you would get at the electronics store. "Well, it's just you and me kid," Natalie sat in her car seat babbling and moving around. Jordan smiled at Natalie. She's a mother now, let's see how this will turn out. She came downstairs to an empty condo. It's time to move on.

They exit and Jordan puts Natalie in her car along with some research and data she took from Dr. Hawthorne's office. The trucks began to drive past Jordan. She gives the thumbs up to the truck driver to proceed taking Dr. Hawthorne's furniture to the storage unit.

The truck driver with Natalie's furniture pulled in front of Jordan. "Hey boss! Am I following you?" he asked.

"I have some business to handle, so I'll meet you there. Just park it in the driveway," she said to him as he tipped his hat to her.

The trucks drive off and she gets in her car. She adjusted her rear-view mirror. "You ready to start our first mission together, Nattie?" Jordan asked, joyous to have Natalie by her side. Natalie replied in her own way, smiling and babbling. She took out the envelope Maxwell made for her, takes out the key to his home and made her way over there to find more information on this biochip and the gifted girls.

Moments later, Jordan approached Maxwell's home. She parked in the driveway and takes out Natalie's stroller from the trunk. Here comes the hard part. Jordan is a woman that can take apart and put together any gun within seconds, eyes closed, but a stroller – that's a different situation. She struggled for a few minutes, hoping the neighbors weren't watching the catastrophe. She finally gets the stroller up and puts Natalie inside.

She enters the home; she hasn't been here since that night. It's gloomy, only lit by the sunshine from outside. Dr. Hawthorne had all his family's belongings cleared out the day Natalie was born. "This is where your dad and mom used to live," Jordan said. They walked through the home to Maxwell's office. The past events that took place in this room play through her head – the blood stain of Christine Hawthorne still visible on the carpet. She shook the feeling off; she had a job to do. The office was as empty as the house. The only thing in there was the desk, and Maxwell's first stethoscope on the wall, engraved with, '*To the most amazing son any parent could ask for, love Mom and Dad*'.

Jordan turned the stethoscope, and the floor began to open. "Here we go," Jordan whispered to herself. Jordan and Natalie make their way down the steps and entered the most upscale and high-tech lab to date, the opposite from the office upstairs. She approached the door to open the lab, but it was locked. Dr. Hawthorne didn't give her a key or a code to enter. "Really?" she said, frustrated. Suddenly, she heard a voice call out her name, like an automated system.

"Hello, Lieutenant Knox." Jordan was startled as she pulled her gun out of her holster, thinking someone was there with her.

"Who are you?! Come out now!"

The voice spoke again. "My name is LIS. I am rather a very sophisticated Liason Intelligence System. LIS, an advanced artificial intelligence, spoke over a speaker somewhere within the lab.

"How do you know me?"

"Before Dr. Hawthorne's exit, he switched all control over to you."

Jordan puts her gun back into her holster. Once again, Dr. Hawthorne had secretly involved her into something she knew nothing about. "Ummm…ok, LIS, how do I get in here?"

"It's on the key." Jordan looked at the house key Dr. Hawthorne gave her, and it has a four-digit code: *2860*. Jordan typed in the code at the door, but another lock popped up. "The key code requires a retinal scan," Jordan said.

"That won't be a problem, Lieutenant." LIS overrides the scan for her. She and

Natalie enter the lab, putting and she put Natalie's stroller alongside the wall giving her a teething ring to keep her busy. She walked toward a large screen mounted on the wall. Different images appear: pictures of a male and female brain, past experiments on psychic abilities and how the mind works while handling these abilities. "LIS, what is all of this?" Jordan asked.

"Dr. Hawthorne studied the human brain and how it functioned when supernatural abilities were activated."

She swiped through the pictures and data. "So, is this a psychic brain?" Jordan asked.

"That is correct," LIS said. "This is the cerebrum of a young female. She displayed strong psychic abilities when emotions were activated."

Jordan was amazed at the advancement of this girl's brain, but she noticed these studies have mainly only been done on young girls. "Are females more dominant with these…powers?"

"According to Dr. Hawthorne's studies, two-thirds of psychics are females."

Jordan continued to swipe through the research. "LIS, are there any studies on the little girls Dr. Hawthorne found?"

"You're viewing them, Lieutenant." Jordan was impressed and even stunned these girls are so advanced at such a young age. Maxwell knew once she found out more about these studies and these girls, she couldn't put it down and she wouldn't stop until she found them. The research caught Jordan's attention and she wanted to know more. "Can you download these for me?" she asked LIS as she pointed to the four girls' studies.

"Certainly."

Jordan began to walk through the lab looking for more research and studies on Maxwell's work. "Alright, Nattie, let's see what else we can find." Natalie sat in her stroller playing and chewing on her teething ring. Jordan looked through the drawers and then through his computer.

"Lieutenant, will you be continuing the biochip project?"

"Is it necessary?" Jordan asked.

"Yes, Dr. Hawthorne created the biochip to remove the supernatural abilities from humans. Unfortunately, for reasons unknown he later altered the biochip's capabilities, causing the chip to give non-psychic beings these powers," LIS explained. For an AI, she showed serious emotions about Jordan completing this project.

"So, if I don't continue the project and it gets into the wrong hands…" she paused. "We're looking at potential war."

"Yes."

Jordan doesn't like that answer. She ran her hand through her large kinky hair and calmly takes the information in. "Where is the biochip?"

"It is located on the wall to your left."

Sitting at the computer on the lab table, Jordan sees a picture of a human's anatomy. She removes the picture from the wall, revealing a safe – more like a 12x12 steel door with a tiny hole in the middle of it. She touched the hole, and she needs a key to open it. "Uh…LIS, you happen to know how I can get this open?"

LIS doesn't answer for a moment. "Dr. Hawthorne never disclosed this information."

"Perfect," Jordan said, annoyed. Just another piece of information for her to find; she can add that to her long to-do list.

Two hours or so have passed since Jordan had been searching through Maxwell's lab, and Natalie was getting fussy. "Here I come Natalie." Natalie began to cry. "It's okay, it's okay." Jordan bounced and rocked Natalie back and forth to calm her down but nothing worked. Jordan realized the time and can't believe she wasted it all and forgot to feed her. She looked in the diaper bag and luckily finds a bottle. "LIS, I need you to download every piece of information Dr. Hawthorne found. I'll be back tomorrow and hopefully we can see how to get that safe unlocked."

"Yes, Lieutenant." LIS said.

Later that evening, Jordan, with Natalie in her arms, entered her home. It's a family-oriented home, the type of home most loving families could only dream of living in, with four fully furnished bedrooms, a living room, a family room and a large backyard big enough for multiple dogs, if only she had one. The only difference between an actual family living here and Jordan are pictures around the home to display the love they have for one another. Jordan doesn't have one picture of herself or her parents. She's a very secretive woman, never having many visitors in her home – except for Maxwell, but even he didn't make it past the front door. She puts down her bags and sat with Natalie in her family room, realizing it's time to make some changes in her life.

Later that night, Jordan is in her family room, her kinky hair up in a messy bun and in an old basketball t-shirt with sweats. She had files, papers, tablets and a laptop scattered on her polished wooden coffee table. She paced the living room, holding Natalie in her arms while feeding her milk in a bottle. "It's just you and me now. I've never had the chance to do this, so I don't know how good or bad I'm going to be…just bear with me," Jordan said gently. She sat on the couch with Natalie. "But I promise you, I'm going to be the best godmother ever." Jordan kissed Natalie on her cheek.

Sitting Natalie on the couch with her teething ring and her arms wrapped around her, Jordan shifted through the paperwork Maxwell left her, trying to find any clue as to where this mysterious key could be located. She opened her laptop, but Natalie started to fuss like any other playful baby. "Okay, okay, you can help me with these studies your father left me," Jordan said, putting Natalie in between her thighs. She began to read through some of the research, putting pieces together, while Natalie started to play and fidget around on the laptop. "Whoa. Kid, we're friends and all, but this is expensive," she said, laughing at the cuteness overload.

As Jordan moved Natalie away from the laptop, she looked up at the screen and saw a file with a link. She picked up Natalie and sat her in her playpen and attached her pacifier to her shirt.

Jordan clicked on the link and a video of Maxwell appeared. He's in his home lab. "During my earlier studies, I created the biochip to rid the abilities of supernatural powers," Maxwell said as he held a diagram showing how the biochip would transfer the powers. "Then these schematics showed that not only can I rid these powers, but I can transfer them into a powerless human being. Unfortunately, due to some very detrimental events recently, I've decided to change the function of the biochip." Maxwell held up the biochip. "The chip will no longer rid these powers but maintain them, suppressing the activity on the right side of the frontal lobe." The mood of the video instantly changed from informative to urgent. Maxwell leaned closer into the camera, making sure no one could hear him. "If you're watching this video, it's probably because I'm either in great danger or I'm dead and I've trusted you with this information. I've hidden the chip and the schematics for it right here in my lab. I've left the key with the one thing I hold dear to me. Protect it with your life," Maxwell looked into the camera, as though he's speaking right to her. The video ended and Jordan sat there replaying the last words Maxwell said. 'The key is with the one thing I hold dear.'

That could be anything, she thought. "The one thing you hold dear," she said quietly to herself. Jordan had no clue what that could be, she's back to square one, so she stopped, thought and reassessed the situation. Natalie started to fuss once again while playing. Jordan picked her up, "I think it's time for someone to go to sleep," she said, taking Natalie upstairs to her room.

Jordan's master bedroom is fit for a queen with its large canopy bed and warm colors on the walls. Natalie's furniture is still on the truck parked in the driveway. Jordan, being the independent woman she is, will set up everything herself in the morning. She took out an extra onesie from the diaper bag and changed Natalie into it. Sitting in a modern style rocking recliner in the corner of her room, Jordan rocked Natalie to sleep. She took some time to think about how her life had changed over the past couple of days, but surprisingly, she has no regrets. This is a life she always wanted but never had the chance for because of her line of work. Jordan looked down at Natalie and she's finally asleep.

She took the pacifier attached to the onesie and puts it in Natalie's mouth, but it pops out on to the floor. She laid Natalie in her bed, putting pillows all around her and goes to her master bathroom to wash off the pacifier. As she's washing it off, she feels something hard inside the round teat. "What is this?" Jordan said to herself. She grabbed a razor from her medicine cabinet and poked a hole in the teat and pushed out a mini rod with ridges on the side. She held it up to the light and smiled. "Max, you are one strange man. A genius, but strange." Jordan placed the key in her nightstand and laid in her bed. She gave Natalie a new pacifier and laid a blanket on top of her. They go soundly to sleep.

Chapter 25

The next morning, Jordan and Natalie are up taking their baths. They go downstairs for breakfast, watching BabiesTV and then they played with Natalie's flash cards. Jordan put Natalie in her playpen and brought in Natalie's furniture from the truck outside in the driveway. This work is simple for her. She's fought bigger battles.

After about three hours, she had finished setting up Natalie's room. It's bright yellow and when the sunlight hits the walls, it's as though you're looking up at the sky. Jordan changed her clothes into more of a casual attire. She already knew the outcome of Phantom, so she can lay the business suits to rest, but even with her casual attire she dresses with business on the mind.

She heard the doorbell ring, which rarely happens, and goes downstairs to answer the door. It's Lucy, Natalie's babysitter. "Hi, Lucy, thanks for coming by," Jordan said, welcoming Lucy into her home. This is one of the many steps Jordan is making to change now that she has a baby.

"Hi, Ms. Knox, thank you for calling me. I'm happy to help," Lucy said.

"Well, in that case, let me show you around and give you the rules of the house." She took Lucy through her home. "The kitchen is fully stocked, so you don't have to worry about food," Jordan said as they walked back to the family room. "Natalie's room is the first room upstairs on the left, my room… off limits. There are two guest rooms upstairs across from Natalie's. You can choose which one you want and use it any time. My office and the basement are NO ENTRY. You don't go in them under any circumstances, and no one is to step foot in this house, if it is not myself. Other than that, my home is your home."

That was a lot of information for Lucy to take in, but she could handle it.

"I should be home later on this evening," Jordan said, grabbing her expensive purse and keys to her luxury car from the table in the foyer.

"Okay, is there anything I should know about with Natalie?" Lucy asked, since Jordan gave her all this information about the house rather than Natalie.

"Ummm…I just fed her, and she'll probably need to be fed…again, but I trust your judgment. Bye!" she left Lucy and Natalie, got in her car and made her way to Maxwell's home to continue working on their research.

Jordan entered the lab. "Hey, LIS, I found the key. Now let's get to work," Jordan said, opening the safe.

"Right away, Lieutenant," LIS said.

Jordan opened the safe and took out a box the size of a bracelet box. She opens it and there it was, the biochip, along with a technical injector to inject into the body. She also took out the schematics for the device. Jordan read over all the information and was at a lost on what to do next. "LIS, did Dr. Hawthorne mention at all what he was going to do once he fixed the chip?"

"The four girls he discovered were going to be his first subjects, Lieutenant," LIS replied.

"So, in order to actually know if this thing works, I have to find these girls?"

"That is correct, Lieutenant."

She stopped and thought for a moment. There must be something she's missing. Then she remembers the jump drive she found in Natalie's room. She took it out of her purse and put it in the computer connected to the projector screen on the wall. There, popped up the four girls' files. "LIS, I think I found them," she said, relieved. She's one step closer to finding them. "Well, at least something about them." Now that Jordan had found this information, she had to figure out what she was going to do once she found them. "Okay, LIS, I'm lost here. We've found the biochip and we've found the information on the girls. What do we do next?"

"It's all in the research Dr. Hawthorne left for you, Lieutenant."

Jordan gave LIS a look as if she's standing right in front of her, confused as to what she is talking about. "That information he gave me made no sense. It was like I was reading an entirely different language. You have to know something else," she said, getting frustrated.

"Unfortunately, I do not, Lieutenant."

Jordan usually had an answer for everything. They don't call her the best for nothing, but this time she has not a clue as to what her next move should be. Suddenly, her phone rings. "Lieutenant Knox."

"Hey, Jordan." It's David.

She wondered what this call was about. She hadn't heard from him in a couple of days. "Hey."

"How are you?" They start the conversation very awkwardly.

"I'm good," she said.

"I would have called you sooner, but I didn't want to overstep and-"

"It's fine, what's going on?" Jordan interrupted him mid-apology. She knew he didn't just call to apologize and she wasn't in the mood to relive that night.

"Director Radcliff wants to meet with us as soon as possible."

"Now?!"

"Unless you're busy. I can cover for you, but I think it's urgent."

"No, no, I'll be there in 20 minutes," Jordan doesn't feel like dealing with the director today and, also, she really wanted to do more research on this experiment.

"See you there," he said.

"Bye."

"Lieutenant, should I put your work on hold?" LIS asked.

"Yes, thank you. I should be back later and hopefully we can find out what to do next." Jordan grabbed her purse and exited the lab.

Later, Director Radcliff and David Lawrence sat across from each other in an office within a tall building in the city, not speaking to one another. It's an intimidating silence between the two; they know what this conversation will be about. Jordan finally entered the room, and the men greet her. David eagerly stood to shake her hand, even though he wanted to do more. Director Radcliff stayed in his seat.

"I apologize for my tardiness," Jordan said nonchalantly.

"That is quite all right, Lieutenant," Director Radcliff said. "Let's just get to the business at hand, shall we?" The three of them sat in a business manner. "A lot has happened during these past couple of months regarding Phantom. The first attack on the agency was detrimental and I gave you plenty of time to shut down, but now we have another problem. Marissa Mitchell has resurfaced, and she targeted your agency. Why!?" Director Radcliff says, demanding an answer.

David and Jordan look at one another. Who is going to speak first and who ever does, will they give the right answer? "The reasons are unknown sir, but we believe it had something to do with Dr. Hawthorne and a secret project," David spoke up.

Jordan was worried David knew what the experiment was. Hopefully that was paranoia.

"I'm sorry for your loss, but this agency has done more damage than good. The opposite of why it was established."

David and Jordan have nothing to say. The director is right. It has been difficult keeping this agency up and running. "With that being said, I am shutting you down effective immediately," Director Radcliff said without a care in the world.

Jordan wasn't moved by his decision. She knew she would be fine with or without the CIA backing her up. She was concerned for the men and women who have nothing to fall back on.

"You're shutting it down now?! Today?!" Jordan asserted.

"Yes, I am, Lieutenant. Is that a problem for you?"

"Yes, actually. Have you even let the other agents that work for you and have given time to this agency know they'll be out of a job, not at the end of this year, but today?" Jordan respected authority and those who held a higher position than her, but she will stand up for what's right and she will never change, not for anyone.

"They all knew this time was coming. They've had more than enough time to prepare." She cared for nothing he had to say at this moment. "The NIA is growing and we're looking for the younger generation to take lead. The closing of Phantom was inevitable with or without the destruction caused by either Midas or Silas Clay," Director Radcliff said, showing Jordan and David statistics on the younger generation leading companies and working within agencies. "They're quicker, stronger and they require less pay," Director Radcliff said, proud of his findings. Jordan couldn't take the arrogance coming from him any longer.

"You're shutting us down because you want kids running an agency?" Jordan asked sarcastically.

"Yes, that's part of the reason."

David stepped into the conversation before it took a turn for the worse. "What will happen with Marissa, sir?"

"The CIA will be handling that case." Director Radcliff changed the topic, focusing on the business at hand. "Speaking of the CIA, David, are you ready to accept my offer?" David and Jordan know what he'll choose; they don't like the decision, but he just had to say it. Before he does, the director continued, "Lieutenant Knox, you've contributed much to Phantom. You gave us the idea and the board would like to offer you your position back at the CIA as well." Jordan was not surprised the director would offer her a position. "Of course, you would work under Major Lawrence once again," Director Radcliff said confidently.

Did he really say that? Jordan thought to herself. "I would need some time to consider, sir," Jordan said, just buying herself some time to think of a quick proposal to pitch to the director. She knew now what she wanted to do once she found these girls.

"Of course. David?"

"I accept your offer," David said, unsure of himself.

"Smart decision."

"Sir, I would like to propose an idea," Jordan said, interrupting.

"Lieutenant, I can't accept anything without the board present."

"I know, I know, just hear me out. Let me bring some young people in. We'll train them and educate them and-"

"And who will run or fund this?" Director Radcliff stopped Jordan before she went any further.

"Myself, of course, and I figured the board would help with the funding." The room became silent for a moment.

"No," he said bluntly. She waited for the director to explain further, but he said nothing.

"That's it? Just no?"

"Correct. The board will never agree to it and it's too soon to open another subdivision."

"But you wouldn't be opening another. Just don't close this one," Jordan explains.

The director has no response.

Jordan was frustrated the director wouldn't listen to her and David sat there and didn't back her up because clearly Director Radcliff will only listen to someone like himself. "Well, in that case, I will not be accepting your offer, nor will I work under anyone," she said as she headed abruptly out of the office. "I thank you for the opportunity and wish you both the absolute best."

As she leaves, David stopped her, not caring if the director would see the exchange. "J, don't leave like this. We all can work this out. I'll make sure you'll have a division to head," he said grabbing her hand gently.

Jordan cared for David, but it's time for her to move on; she has other problems to worry about. "It's over, David. There's nothing more either of us can do," she left him standing there, wishing there was more he could have done. "Now if you don't mind, I have a baby to attend to." She left him, knowing she may never see him again.

That same afternoon, Clay, Marissa and Will discussed the next steps of his plan in Clay's overly extravagant office. The wooden floors are so finely polished one can see him or herself as they walk through. The furniture comes from the most expensive shop in Milan.

The atmosphere of the office is serious; this is not a place for joking matters. Behind Clay's desk is a large computer screen displaying what looks like an unfinished biochip. "Based on the information we received from Dr. Hawthorne's home, we just need the device to insert the chip," Clay said, pointing to the screen.

"And who's going to be creating all of these?" Will asked.

"Dr. Edwards created the device alongside Dr. Hawthorne and he's already in the process of making a few. We just need a team to transport," Clay replied.

"Once we have the device, how will we get the NIA, especially the president, to back us up?" Marissa asked Clay, wanting to see if he's thought this plan all the way through.

"They'll have no other choice," Clay says as he smiles at the screen deviously. "Now if we-"

Before Clay could finish, Valentina, Marissa's assistant rushes in.

"They shut it down. It's over," Valentina is winded from running.

"Valentina, what are you talking about?!" Marissa shouted.

"Phantom, you asked me to keep track of them and I did. Director Radcliff shut them down today," Valentina said.

The information immediately grabbed Clay's attention. "And David Lawrence and Knox?" Clay asked.

"Lawrence went back to his position at the CIA and Jordan, well, I can't seem to find anything on her. It's like she's a ghost."

"I swear I hate that woman," Marissa said, irritated.

"Wait, hold on, how did you even know all of this?" Will asked suspiciously.

"I hacked into the agency's systems. They've planned on shutting the agency down for months, it's been a year, but after Marissa breached them, they made it official."

"But we've lost the one person who could ruin it all for us," Will said anxiously.

"No, no, that's okay, she can't do anything without a team behind her, let alone an agency. She's the least of our worries," Clay said.

"Are you sure?" Marissa asked, ready for a fight.

"Yes, and just to show you," Clay pressed the button on the black intercom box on his desk and spoke over a loudspeaker to his men. "Everyone, meet in the strategic room, now!"

All of Marissa's men, Will's team and the elite mercenaries Clay hired, gathered in a large room, the size of a warehouse. Clay stood on the balcony above them all with Marissa and Will standing on steps below him. "You are all here because you are the best at what you do, but we all want more. More power, more luxuries – and you will have it if you follow me. Phantom has sought out to take this power away and if it was not for me, they would have succeeded," Clay continued to make his speech with much authority. "Using the biochip the late Dr. Hawthorne created, I will build an army, and it will be the only army left standing and our world leaders will have no other choice but to follow our commands. It is time for us to take the lead." Clay finished his speech and his men applauded him; they are ready to follow his command.

"Nice speech," Marissa said.

"It's only the beginning."

Back at Hawthorne's lab, Jordan and LIS swiped through the information on the girls and Jordan took notes, but all she had on them were their age, race and the powers they possess, not one picture or where they could possibly be located. "LIS, can you open the first file?" Jordan asked.

"Yes, Lieutenant."

"Three years old, Hispanic and has something called molecular manipulation," Jordan said, trying to make sense of the information.

"She is able to decelerate, accelerate or stop the molecules of different objects and organisms."

The file said this special girl can freeze an entire group of people. Most psychics with this ability can't do this until they are well into their adult years.

"And the next girl?" Jordan asked.

"Four-year-old Asian-American female with the power to alter, sense and manipulate weather of all forms," LIS described.

"She can make it rain or snow if she wants to," Jordan said, intrigued by her findings.

Unlike the other girls whose parents and guardians were trying to help them maintain their powers, the parents of this four-year-old came to Dr. Hawthorne to get rid of her powers. Swiping to the last set of girls, Jordan is drawn to their file.

"These two are twins," she said and for many reasons this struck a nerve in Jordan, but she doesn't worry about it too much.

"Yes, Lieutenant. Fraternal, four years old and African American," LIS said.

"The oldest has astral premonition?" Jordan asked, puzzled.

"She has the ability to project herself into the future."

"Instead of just telling the future, she can actually go?"

"Yes, unfortunately her physical body must stay in the present time," LIS explained.

"And at just four years old, she takes time traveling to another level. What about the other twin?"

"She's telekinetic."

"Oh, that's when they can move and bend objects with their mind, right?" Jordan asked, confidently knowing at least one of the abilities.

"Correct. According to Dr. Hawthorne's studies, by the time she's sixteen, she will become the most advanced telekinetic of her time."

Jordan was in awe of all she had read on the girls. Their abilities are far greater than she could have ever thought. These girls are special, and she won't stop until she continued her friend's work. "Okay, we have one girl that can stop motion, another who can basically create a hailstorm if she wanted to and twins, one that can travel to the future and another who can move objects." Jordan went over her notes.

"What will be our next steps, Lieutenant?"

"Well, we have no agency to back us up and even if we did, we can't tell them about this, so for now it's just me and you, LIS. We'll find these girls and protect chip." Jordan's cellphone suddenly rings, but this was an unknown number. "Did you find him?" Jordan asked the person on the phone.

"We searched all the places you told us to and we can't find Dr. Edwards," the mysterious man replied.

Jordan had been looking for Martin Edwards since the night Maxwell passed. Martin hasn't always been the bravest person. When Phantom was breached, she figured he left immediately and decided to take a sabbatical. Jordan tried her best not to worry. Maybe he doesn't want to be found, but she can't help but think that something is wrong. Unbeknownst to her, Clay is doing a great deal of damage to Dr. Martin Edwards at this very moment. "All right, will you be able to make it tonight?" she asked.

"I can have everything cleared out and installed in your place by morning."

"Good. And thanks…for everything," Jordan said sincerely. "At least I'll be able to do one thing right."

"No problem, boss, and hey, we'll find them. Leviathan isn't as smart as they think they are. Just…be safe out there," the mysterious man said. "We can't wait for your return." He talked to Jordan as though he's known her for years.

"Same." She hung up the phone.

"LIS, we're going home."

"I'm not sure I understand, Lieutenant," LIS expressed.

"You'll be coming home with Natalie and me and you'll be programmed into a new server. We've got a lot of work to do, and you can start by calling me Savannah."

"Yes, Savannah," LIS responded.

The following night, Will and Valentina approached the home of Dr. Hawthorne. "So, this is where it all happened?" Valentina referred to the killing of Christine and the kidnapping of Alexandria.

"We didn't come here to talk about that," Will said, picking the backdoor lock to enter the household. "Clay thinks there's something here holding all of the information on these kids."

They enter the empty, foreclosed home. "What is with him and children these days? I mean, he's not really the fatherly type," Valentina expressed.

"The chip thing he's making can take the powers from psychics and implant them in…," he can't think of another word for non-psychics, "people who aren't psychic. Hence why he wants to build an army and needs the kids, so focus on that so I can go home," Will said, agitated.

Walking through the home with their flashlights shining brightly through, they make their way to Dr. Hawthorne's old office. Opening the door, Will and Valentina don't know what to make of what they're seeing. "You've got to be kidding me," Will said as he looked at an empty room. He called Clay and puts him on speaker.

"Did you find them?" Clay asked, answering the phone.

"It's gone," Will said.

"What do you mean it's gone?!" They can tell Clay's blood pressure is rising.

"All of it. The office is gone, it's empty. It's like it never existed!" Will said, his voice breaking. The used-to-be office is now a four-walled room with nothing more than just a floor and ceiling. No paint. No carpet. No furniture.

"An office doesn't erase itself!" Clay yelled through the phone.

"Apparently this one did," Valentina said.

There's silence for a long period of time. "Clay?" Will called out.

"Sir?" Valentina said.

"It's her," Clay said softly, yet sinisterly. Silence once again.

"Who is he talking about?" Valentina asked Will.

Will and Valentina then heard screaming and someone breaking objects in the background.

"Jordan Knox," Will said.

Clay is livid. He's lost to Jordan once again.

PART IV – This is my Exodus

Chapter 26

Are we the only ones Jordan chose for the team?" Blair asked.

"For the primary team, yes, including Agent Carmichael; she thought he would add some… testosterone to the team, but it's more for political reasons," Natalie explains.

Jordan truly wanted them and only them, but you can't beat politics.

"Hey Angel, are you still training tonight?" Daniella asks.

Angel stares down at Daniella, wanting her to shut up.

"What? Was I not supposed to say anything?" Daniella is confused.

"Who are you training with?" Ashton asks, wondering how she can go somewhere and not tell her.

"Umm… one of the guards said they wanted me to show them some techniques, so… I'm going to help them," Angel says slowly, making her way to the door before Ashton asks her any more questions.

Daniella realizes she should have kept that bit of information to herself. Ashton follows her.

"Helping huh?" Ashton says, not believing anything Angel says. "Natalie? How often does Jordan allow newly appointed agents to train her guards?" Ashton asks, keeping her eye on Angel to see if she's going to lie to her face again.

"She doesn't…Jordan wants her team solely focused on missions, so she has a high-level guard train them." Natalie hates getting in the middle.

"Would you like to continue, Ang?" Ashton says, antagonizing her.

"I'm not doing this with you right now," Angel walks away from Ashton.

"Doing what?!" Ashton snaps, tired of Angel blaming her for everything.

"Okay… do you guys want to thank Jordan? Because I want to thank Jordan," Blair says, interrupting the awkward moment. She, Daniella and Natalie leave Angel and Ashton to work out their differences, as usual.

"What am I doing, Ang? Asking you about the date you're about to go on?" Ashton says.

"No, I'm not going to listen to you whine and complain like the spoiled brat you always are," Angel walks away from her.

"Yeah, because you're not the girl that's fallen for the first big guy that smiled and batted his eyelashes at you," Ashton follows behind.

"Ash, I can talk to whoever I want to. Get over it," Angel says, irritated.

"You know what? I'm not even going to start. We've been arguing since we got here. You do whatever you want to, just know there will be a time when I get to say, 'I told you so' and it's going to be great, so have fun," Ashton says, letting her go and wiping her hands of whatever Angel is about to get herself into.

Angel checks her new watch and makes her way to the arena. She's hesitant to take this step with Ethan. What if she can't trust him? What if Ashton is right? But she can't always live her life looking over her shoulder.

Opening the heavy steel doors to the arena, she can hear loud rock music blasting through the speakers and someone grunting and punching an object. Walking through the arena, she sees Ethan shirtless, the bright lights reflecting off his soft peach skin as sweat pours from his forehead. Angel is intrigued at what she sees. It's clear he works out…a lot. He doesn't notice she's there. She steps into the ring as he practices advanced martial arts techniques on an automated robot.

"If you keep kicking with the bridge of your foot, you're likely to cause more damage," Angel says, trying to get his attention, but he doesn't notice her. "Hello! HELLO!" she shouts while tapping his shoulder.

"Wha-!" Ethan is startled, until he sees it's Angel and is excited to see her. "Oh hey, I didn't think you'd show up," he says, grabbing his towel and wiping the sweat from his face and body, Angel following along with her eyes.

"Yeah, well, I have to keep you on your toes," she says, and they smile at one another feeling the passion between them but afraid to tell the other how they feel. "So…why am I here?" she asks him.

"I think we need to see who's the most skilled fighter," Ethan says, as if he's giving her a present.

"You sure you want to do that?" Angel mocks him.

"Oh, I'm sure," he says stepping closer to her. "You may have beat the top agent here, but you have yet to face me and I'm pretty good…trust me," he continues looking down at her, gazing into her eyes. They're chest to chest. She rubs her hand down his warm arm and he follows her. The rematch is no longer a thought in his mind. It's her and only her he sees, until Angel quickly punches him in the stomach and as he leans forward, she wraps her arms around his neck and flips him over.

"Rule number one, never become vulnerable in front of the enemy," she says over him.

"Oh, you want to do it this way," he says, quickly standing and getting in a fighting stance. "Perfect."

Keeping their eyes on one another, they follow each other around the ring, waiting for the other to make a move. Angel jumps first, quickly throwing kick after kick at his face and using all the simple martial arts techniques she knows. Ethan dodges the kicks with his hands, knocking her feet onto the mat every time. "Come on, I know you can do better than this," he antagonizes her.

"If you say so," she smiles and takes the fighting up a notch. Angel swings her arm towards his face, and he dodges it, swiping her under her feet. She lands on her back. Quickly jumping back up, she realizes this is going to be more of a challenge. Lunging towards him, she throws multiple kick and punch combos, but he continues to block each one.

She swings her arm again. Ethan grabs it and swings her back towards him. "You know what your problem is?" Ethan whispers, lowering his head down towards her ear. They both breathe heavily.

"What?" she says, unable to look behind her.

"You move too quickly," he says.

"You expect me to move slow and get my ass beat," she jokes.

"No. What I mean is, you're just throwing whatever you want. You must strategize the hits; it's a game," he says moving hair from the side of her face to the back of her ear.

"You mean like this," Angel kicks him in his knee and quickly jams her elbow in his stomach. With Ethan still holding onto her arm Angel yanks her arm from him, spins around, flips him and places her knee on his chest as he lays on the mat trying to catch his breath.

"Not exactly what I had in mind, but good job," he says, grinning. They gaze at each other for a moment, waiting to see who's going to make the first move, but Angel only rolls over and lays next to him, trying to steady her breath. "Where did you learn that move from?" he asks.

"My dad. Me and Ashton were always fascinated with his job, and he hated when we snuck into his armory. So, to keep us busy, every day after school he would train us," Angel says, looking up at the ceiling and reminiscing. Ethan enjoys the way she talks about her family and how overprotective she is of them. Seeing her smile is a sight to see.

"And what did your father do?" he asks.

Her smile leaves. Should she tell him more or should she leave this situation now? Facing him, she reveals the truth. "He was Black ops, *the* sergeant," she says, putting emphasis on his skills.

"Is that how he died?" he asks sincerely.

Angel is taken aback by the question; she never told him her father died. "What makes you think he died?" she asks, sitting up.

"Well, you keep talking about him in the past tense like he's no longer here," he says, sitting up with her.

Angel thinks about it and for once someone has pointed it out to her that she does talk about him like he's dead. She was never truly sure if he was dead or not, but it's been nine years; he would have found them by now. "I guess you have a point. I've never really said *it* out loud," Angel reveals to him.

"And you don't have to," Ethan grabs her hand. and they stand together. "He lives…just in you." Angel hasn't felt this way with anybody. She wants to see what would happen if things went further. Ethan places his hand on her smooth mocha skin and she allows his warmth to caress her cheek. He leans in close enough, hoping she follows.

"Last time I checked this room was for training purposes and training purposes only," Jordan says, slowly walking in, interrupting their exchange.

Angel and Ethan jump apart.

"Lieutenant," Ethan salutes, attempting to take the focus off him and Angel. "I never got the chance to thank you for choosing me to join the team," he says, running towards her to shake her hand.

"Just don't make me regret it," Jordan says sternly, watching as Ethan lets his hand fall to his side. "And please don't salute me."

"Yes, ma'am," he says respectfully.

Angel is fighting the urge not to have the same conversation with Jordan, but she can't help herself. She needs to know the truth. "Ethan, do you mind giving me and the lieutenant the room?" Angel asks him.

"No problem," he says, exiting the arena and closing the door behind him.

Jordan sits on a nearby bench. "So, what is it that you want to talk about?" she asks.

"I spoke to Natalie tonight and she had some very insightful information," Angel says, sitting next to her, approaching the situation delicately.

"Yes, I'm sure she told you all about becoming agents here and the new watches she designed," Jordan says, steering the conversation in a different direction.

"You're really going to sit here and play this game with me…again?"

"I don't know what you're talking about, Angel," Jordan continues to act oblivious to the matter.

"Why did you bring us here?!" Angel shouts over her. Angel has been patient for far too long. She'll get her answers no matter what the cost. "And don't tell me you brought us here to protect us, because it's getting old."

"That is the reason, Angel. I don't know what else I have to say to convince you," Jordan hides the truth. It's too soon to reveal anything. She just needs a little more time to put everything in place.

"Who is Dr. Hawthorne!?" Angel stops Jordan from continuing with her lies.

Jordan never thought they would remember someone treating them 13 years ago. Jordan takes a moment to process this revelation. Angel's not going to stop asking until she gets her answers. "Dr. Maxwell Hawthorne is...was a great friend of mine," Jordan explains with the most sincerity. "And I'm sure you already know he is Natalie's father." Angel pays close attention as Jordan begins to reveal her story.

"I, Captain Lawrence and Dr. Hawthorne, even some of the agents here, all worked for a secret division called Phantom about 13 years ago. But there was an agent who went rogue, and he stole very important information on an experiment Dr. Hawthorne was working on."

"What was the experiment?"

"It was called Experiment X. It was meant to get rid of supernatural abilities in children before they became adults and were uncontrollable."

"And he planted something in us?" Angel asks, fearful she's been lied to all this time.

"No, not at all. After Natalie was born, he realized he wanted to do more. He created the pediatrics, which I'm sure you're familiar with, and instead decided to help parents help their children control their powers and deal with the mental struggles that go along with them because... let's be honest, the world isn't welcoming to those that aren't up to its standards."

Angel nods in agreement. She's met a few of those in her lifetime. "That still doesn't explain why you came looking for us," Angel says.

Jordan exhales. "Another rogue agent attacked our agency." Jordan remembers Marissa and her name still sends chills up her spine. "And unfortunately, Dr. Hawthorne didn't make it. When I arrived at the hospital, I was too late, but he left me a letter explaining everything he had done from the experiment to the pediatrics practice. He also told me that it was now my responsibility to find the four of you and protect you as well as the experiment."

"I can guarantee you we don't need protecting," Angel reiterates, "unless these people also have powers." Jordan is silent for a moment and Angel can see it all over her face, there's so much more to this story.

"Wh-what aren't you telling me?" Angel asks.

"Experiment X involved a biochip that would be injected into the supernatural's mind, suppressing their powers. Unfortunately, there were complications with the biochip that were never fixed," Jordan explains.

"What were they?"

"The biochip could get rid of supernatural powers, and it could give non-psychics abilities," Jordan cautiously tells her.

"What?! How!?"

"Taking the blood of a psychic and inserting it into non-psychics can jump start the biochip," Jordan explains. Angel stands, trying to comprehend everything that has been revealed to her.

"How can I trust you?" Angel asks.

Jordan stands near her. "Everything I've told you is true. There are people out there looking for you."

"Who are they?" Angel asks, hoping it's not the same people that came for her and Ashton and possibly killed her parents.

"His name is Silas Clay; he has an army, and he knows you all exist," Jordan tells her half the truth. She can't disclose anything about Leviathan without having more information.

"Why wouldn't you tell us this when we first met?" Angel asks.

"If I would have come to you and said there are men coming to kidnap you, drain you of your blood and you need to come with me so that I can protect you in my underground agency, would you have really come willingly?"

"Well, no, not when you put it that way," Angel says.

Jordan smiles at her, lighting up the mood. "I have no doubt you can protect yourselves but just consider being a part of this team as a safe haven; we depend on each other," she places her arm on Angel's shoulder. A connection has developed between them, and Angel hasn't felt this way in a long time. Strangely enough, she continues to have the feeling she's known Jordan all her life.

"Thank you for telling me everything," Angel says.

"You actually did me a favor. I was getting a little drained from holding in everything," Jordan says, relieved.

"Why did you hide everything for so long?" Angel asked.

Jordan lets out a large sigh. "I've learned keeping people in the dark keeps them protected."

"Well, I've learned it's best to at least tell the people you trust because they'll always have your back no matter what. I mean look at you and Dr. Hawthorne; its obvious you guys trusted each other and without trust you wouldn't have been able to find us," Angel smiles, giving the adult advice. Angel is wise beyond her years and would make an excellent leader one day. Jordan is proud.

"You are right about one thing. He was a great friend to me, and I trusted him, but he became so wrapped up in this experiment that we barely communicated," Jordan continues to reminisce as if Angel isn't in the room. "The last time I saw him he was showing me his progress on the biochips, and it always felt like he was preparing for something bad to happened, like someone gave him…information," Jordan begins to put the pieces together. She looks to Angel. "Do you remember telling Dr. Hawthorne anything about him getting hurt or the experiment when you would go to see him?"

Angel thinks to herself and tries hard to remember but unfortunately, she can't. "Actually, no. It's strange because I can't really remember anything before I was nine." Angel has never thought about it, but she can't remember too much of her life before her parents died. Relying on Ashton's memories is all she has lived by. "I mostly only remember *very* good things, which I don't think sometimes are true because whose family is that perfect?" Angel and Jordan laugh. They begin to bond with one another on a more intimate level. "What made you want to become a lieutenant?" Angel asks.

Jordan laughs with her head leaning back. It's a question she's never been asked. "Let's see, I…umm…never wanted to be a lieutenant, it kind of just fell in my lap, but I get to tell a lot of men what to do, so I guess it has its perks." She smiles with so much confidence, loving her job.

"But isn't that a hard job? Don't you get tired of always telling someone what to do?" Angel asks.

"No, not necessarily. Yes, you do have to make the tough decisions, but if you work with your team and take in consideration their feelings, everything just goes smoothly."

Angel nods.

"In my opinion, I think you would be a great leader," Jordan says, confident in Angel's abilities.

"Me?! No, I can barely lead Ashton."

"Okay, Ashton is not the best example you want to use," Jordan says sarcastically. They both laugh hysterically.

"Well, I should probably get back before Ashton throws one of her daily fits of rage." Angel enjoyed her time with Jordan.

"See you around," Jordan says, standing to exit with her. "Thank you for the talk."

"Thank you for being honest. I don't have too many people around who are like that," Angel says.

"I'm always around," Jordan says sincerely. Angel leaves the arena, happy to have Jordan as somewhat of a mentor; she hopes to learn much more from her. "Hey Angel," Jordan catches her before exiting, "since I revealed so much to you, don't you think you should return the favor?"

Angel, confused, turns to face Jordan, "Like...what?" she asks.

"You really thought I wouldn't find out your last name isn't Hunter," she surprises Angel once again.

Angel stands quiet, not wanting to continue with this conversation. If Ashton found out she told Jordan their true last name she would kill her. Not to mention the trouble that would follow. But Jordan has been honest with her about everything, more than she asked for, and she is in a safe place now, right? Maybe it is time to let the weight go.

"You're right. Our last name isn't Hunter. Our adoptive mother gave us her last name and it just stuck. Our birth name is Cross." Angel says hesitantly.

That name strikes at so many nerves in Jordan she can't comprehend where she is. The once strong and confident woman, able to withstand anything, becomes fragile and can barely stand. The room begins to spin, and she can barely keep focus on Angel.

"Wh-wh-wh-what did you say?" she stutters, unable to speak full sentences.

"My last name is Cross," Angel says again, worrying about Jordan. "Lieutenant, is there something wrong?"

Jordan doesn't respond for a moment. "Ummm…no, no I-I just have to go take care of something." Jordan swiftly exits the arena, leaving Angel to wonder what she did or said.

Wobbling to her office, Jordan holds on to the wall as she quickly pushes herself into her office. "LIS. LIS!" Jordan calls out in her office.

"Yes, Lieutenant?" LIS replies, speaking through the screen behind her desk.

"Pull up all the information we have on Aaron Cross. Old and new," Jordan sweats profusely as LIS pulls up the information. She takes off her suit jacket and throws it on the couch.

"Right away, Lieutenant."

"Aaron Cross, age 35, Boston police officer, deceased, cause of death homicide," LIS gives Jordan all the details she could find. "Government Black Operations," LIS continues.

Jordan begins to hyperventilate and must brace herself. She sits on her couch feeling nauseous and dizzy; suddenly she leans over and puts her head in a nearby trash bin, vomiting.

"Lieutenant, is this all you needed?" LIS asks.

"Yes LIS, but I need you to delete everything, your history, me even asking you to look it up," Jordan demands, wiping the vomit from her mouth.

"Right away, Lieutenant," LIS says.

Tears slowly start to stream down Jordan's face. She's about to face the one situation she can't fix.

Chapter 27

I expect our next shipment of biochips to be here by the end of the week," Silas Clay speaks to a cleanly shaven, model-type man on his large projector screen via video satellite located underground at his home, 'The Compound', in the lab.

"We're on schedule. The shipment will be here as planned. You just worry about payment."

"You should know me by now, Mateo," Clay says. "You will get your payment once I'm notified the delivery was successful."

"It will go smoothly so long as you keep Knox away from me and my men," Mateo says, determined but with slight fear hidden behind his eyes.

"Let me worry about her. She doesn't suspect a thing."

"Are you confident about that? I've heard far too many times where Jordan Knox has been five steps ahead."

Silas closes his eyes, suppressing his anger. "She is not the one you should be worried about. Now I said we're good. Just get it done, Mateo."

"If she messes this up, it's on you, and I want double with interest."

"You've got a lot of nerve when your men couldn't capture a simple teenage girl in juvenile detention and you of all people was bested by twins." Mateo falls silent, slightly embarrassed.

"She was obviously tipped off. How else could she have been

released that early? And I didn't know the girl was a freak," Mateo said, rubbing his broken arm inside of an arm sling.

"Knox needs to be stopped, and the biochip will do it," Clay says to Mateo but looks off into the distance as memories of the revenge he plans to get from those who have wronged him in the past flood his brain.

"It'll get done." Mateo abruptly ends the call.

Clay walks across the hall and enters the 'Preparation Room' where Dr. Edwards normally works. He approaches Dr. Edwards, who is frantically working with multiple serums at a lab table. "How are you, Doctor?" Clay asks. Dr. Edwards unintentionally ignores him as he works his way through the serums and mixes, producing different colors and reactions.

"See it through. See it through," Dr. Edwards repeats.

"Oh, I forgot, insanity has you pretty busy these days," Clay smirks, making his way to the large glass box on the far side of the room. "Open it," he directs one of his guards. They open the glass box for Clay and he enters the empty room holding a fragile, chained Aaron Cross. Clay walks over to Aaron, holding himself in the fetal position. "It's a shame, the once-great Sergeant Cross has become a weak, frail man. If I were you, I would hate for my children and wife to see me in this state. Lucky for you, you don't have to wait too long. Your wife and children will see you real soon and you'll be able to make Lieutenant Jordan Knox pay for what's she's done to you." Clay gives him a sinister smile. "I know, I know, you don't have to thank me. It's the least I can do for all the testing you allowed me to do on you." He's interrupted by a call coming from the cell phone in his slacks.

"Hello," he answers sternly.

"Clay? It's Samuel Hahn."

Clay loosens his tone, "Ah…Mr. Hahn, to what do I owe the pleasure?"

"I did what you asked; she has the bracelet. Can I trust you to get rid of her powers?" Samuel asks, speaking in a low voice as if he's in a rush and doesn't want to risk anyone catching his conversation.

"I have men in place who are ready when I give the word to bring her and others to me to rid them of these ungodly powers." Clay smiles, enjoying luring Samuel into his plans.

"Thank you. I don't know how to repay you," Samuel says, relieved.

"It's fine. I am only trying to rid the world of the inequities these powers involve."

"And you will bring her to me once you've completed the extraction?"

Clay pauses for a moment.

"Of course. Once the extraction is complete your daughter will be returned to you, powers gone like they never existed."

"Thank you, Clay."

"My pleasure." Clay ends his call.

Marissa sashays into the lab dressed in black leather from head to toe. She looks as though she came back from her own mission. "Lying to desperate parents now?" she asks Clay, watching him from outside the glass box.

He exits the box, swaying his hand towards the door for his men to lock it. "Whatever do you mean, dear?" he smiles coyly.

"Only that you'll be bringing his daughter to him in pieces rather than alive like he expects."

"If he's willing to sacrifice his own blood to benefit himself, what does it matter to me? Doesn't sound too godly now does it?"

"Point taken."

"Enough about him. To what do I owe this visit?" Clay asks, turning his attention away from the glass container holding Aaron and giving his wife his undivided attention.

"You're my husband. I didn't think I needed an appointment," Marissa says.

"Not when you're dressed like that," he grins, and she's unmoved by the compliment.

"Thank you, but I have a gift for you." She places a thick manila envelope in his hand. He raises an eyebrow, continuing to keep his focus on Marissa. She watches with pleasure as his eyes scan the pages.

"Savannah Taylor, born February 4, 1984, in Houston, Texas. To parents REDACTED. Says she was homeschooled most of her life. Enlisted in the military at the age of 22 and became lieutenant by 30." Clay continues to read on, unsure of the identity of this woman. "Why are you showing me this? Who is she, a new soldier? We have enough of those, put her file with the rest." Clay disregards Marissa's find, which frustrates her. He's so quick to dismiss everyone. If it doesn't benefit him, he wants no part.

"If it was just another expendable soldier, I wouldn't have brought this to you." She puts her hand inside the file before he can close and toss it to the side.

"Look," she flips over the pages and points to a black and white picture of a young woman no more than in her teens. She's dressed in a simple blue jean jacket, sneakers and jeans. She aims her pistol at an unknown mark.

Clay's eyes widen but once surprised, swiftly shift to a smile stretching from ear to ear. "Care to explain to me where you found this?"

"Does it matter? We have something that would put her away for good. Not to mention Savannah is on America's Most Wanted List," Marissa says, pointing to the papers in Clay's hands.

He stares at her for a moment, not believing she just stumbled upon this evidence. He'll play along for now. "This doesn't explain how she's been able to roam free without anyone noticing."

"It seems she has friends in very, very high places," Marissa says.

Clay takes a moment to process Marissa's findings. The mental gears turn as he plans his next steps. "Not anymore. Starting now, Lieutenant Jordan Knox is no more. Hello Savannah Taylor. Let's set up a meeting with the NIA."

Chapter 28

It was a cloudy evening in the summer of 2015 in Boston, Massachusetts. This neighborhood is always quiet and somewhat somber. Few people live here and those that do are mostly elderly. The Cross house sits farther back within the neighborhood. Trees surround the dusty blue and cream home, and a tan fence wraps around the yard more so to keep them in.

"Keep those hands up, Ash!" Aaron shouted at her. It's another day of training with their father in the backyard of their home. Angel and Ashton have never been typical nine-year-old girls. Playing with dolls, hair, or makeup has never piqued their interest.

"I am!" Ashton shouted back, trying to keep up with Angel. "Ang is cheating!"

"I'm not cheating. You're just slow!"

"Stop talking and stay focused!" Aaron shouts at them.

Angel and Ashton stand firm, facing one another, ready for another boxing round to begin. Ashton lunges for Angel, trying to throw a right cross punch, but Angel dodges it and quickly hits Ashton with a right and left hook. Ashton stumbles to the ground. A frustrated Ashton jumps up with the anger she can barely control.

"I win," Angel gloated.

"Angie, stop it. No gloating," Aaron said, holding Ashton back. "Go in the house and get yourself cleaned up for dinner."

Angel does as she is told, tossing the boxing gloves on the ground. Ashton watches as her big sister skips happily in the house, mocking her lost. She tries to break free from her dad's arms. "Hey, hey, calm down." Aaron kneeled eye level from her. "What do we say?" he said, calming her. Aaron takes her hand and wipes away her tears. "Come on, Bunny, what do we say?"

"Don't give up, no matter how hard it gets," Ashton said softly.

"And we fight harder and stronger." Aaron brought her chin up and encouraged her to stand tall with her head held high.

"I can't win!" Ashton said, lacking confidence.

"Look at me, you have more power in yourself than you know," Aaron said. "Trust your instincts and have faith in yourself and you can move mountains." Ashton slightly smiles. Her dad always knows the right things to say. That's why they're so close. Aaron loves his daughters equally, but Ashton always seemed to need more attention. "Come here. Let me tell you a story." Aaron stood up and grabs her hand.

"Dad...," Ashton said, not wanting to hear one of his long war stories.

"It'll be quick, I promise," he laughed. He guided her to the backyard patio seating area. "Your mom and I used to fight... a lot," Ashton looks surprised. She always thought her parents loved each other. "No, we used to box, wrestle, and spar," Aaron cleared up his statement and Ashton was relieved. "I used to get so frustrated because I could never beat her. Every time I thought I'd tricked her, it was like she was two moves ahead of me," Aaron smiled as he reminisced about his one and only true love.

"So, what happened?" Ashton asked.

"I kept fighting and fighting until one day I beat your mother," Aaron continued. "Your mother knew she could be beat me and it came to a point where she wasn't even trying; she underestimated me. I studied your mother's moves and when it was time to fight, I

used them against her. All that time we were fighting, I was learning." Ashton always thought her parents were amazing, but after hearing this story she's in awe of them and their relationship. "Bunny, don't give up. You may not get it now, but I promise you, you'll win soon," Aaron said, rubbing her fluffy hair. Ashton gives her dad the biggest hug, and he kissed her on the forehead. "Now go get ready for dinner," he said, watching her run away.

As he stood to go in his home, Elise stood in the doorway, apron wrapped around her thin waist and towel in hand; she's finished with dinner. Ashton gave her a fist bump before going inside. "Take those shoes off before coming inside," Elise said to her. Elise saw a surprised Aaron. "How long are we going to keep lying to them?" she asked him with concern.

"I'm not lying to them, their mother did beat me," he said.

"But when you say mother, they're thinking of me and not Savannah," Elise said, frustrated. Aaron stepped closer to her. They're both hiding under the door frame. He made sure the girls weren't nearby.

"That is what we agreed to. That is what we promised. We wait until they're old enough to handle it," he whispered.

"Old enough?! No one is prepared or able to handle something like this!" she whispered louder. "What, so we just wait until their 18th birthday and say, 'Happy birthday and oh by the way I'm not your birth mother and your real mother could be dead, but don't get upset because we've only been trying to protect you," she whispered sarcastically, hoping he gets the point she's trying to make.

"We will tell them when I feel they're ready," Aaron said.

"Mom! Ashton is sneaking food!" Angel shouted from the kitchen.

"No, I'm not," Ashton replied.

"Savannah is my best friend, and I would do anything for her, but you're the only real parent they have now. Just make sure you're doing this because you think it's what's best for them, not because its what's best for her." Elise left Aaron standing in the doorway, contemplating if he's made the right decision regarding what his wife had asked of him. He shook off the feeling and goes into the kitchen to have dinner with his family.

"Hey, look what I can do," Ashton sat at the table, staring at her fork as it twirls around and around in the air.

"Ash, no powers at the table," Elise said.

"Angel uses her powers all the time and no one says anything to her," Ashton talked back.

"No, I don't," Angel replied.

"Ash, do as your mother says," Aaron said with authority. Elise gave him a quick look, referencing the conversation they just had seconds ago. "Let's bow our heads for grace," Aaron said to his family, grabbing Angel's and Ashton's hands. "Dear Lord, thank you for another day of keeping us alive and healthy. We ask that you continue to protect us and give us strength. Help us to make the right decisions even though they may hurt us...Amen."

"Amen," the women in his life agree.

Aaron closed his prayer and Elise noticed he's been struggling to tell his daughters the truth for a long time.

"So, girls, how's school?" Elise asked them.

"Boring." "It's fine." Ashton and Angel gave their answers simultaneously.

"You're telling me you didn't learn anything today?" Elise asked them.

"I learned the food they give us tastes like dirt," Ashton jokes.

"Hey! We're eating!" Aaron shouted in disgust, but smirks at Ashton's sarcastic attitude. "One day you'll appreciate those lunches," he said.

"Yeah, right," Ashton disagreed.

The family laughed together and for a second the problems Elise and Aaron are dealing with are no more.

"Hey Angel, did you know Mom used to beat Dad in fights?" Ashton said, excited about how her mom is awesome.

Angel laughed, barely able to swallow her food. "That true, Dad?"

"It was most fights...not all," Aaron tried to ease his embarrassment.

The girls laugh uncontrollably, and Aaron can't help but to join in. He gave a chuckle and glanced over to Elise, hoping she'll say something to make matters normal.

"Yeah, your father was a pretty easy target," Elise joined in, *"and girls, just remember, you're stronger than any boy."*

"Haha, you girls are very funny tonight," Aaron cuts their laughter. *"Let's see how funny you are when your favorite contestant loses tonight on 'America's Greatest Warrior'."*

Ashton's face lit up with joy; her dad just mentioned her favorite show. "Can we eat our ice cream in front of the TV tonight?! Please!" she begged.

"If you two clean up the table, we got a deal." Aaron and Ashton gave each other their secret handshake. Angel and Ashton quickly cleaned the kitchen, throwing dishes in the sink and putting the leftovers in the refrigerator.

"Okay, Ang, which flavor ice cream do you want? Coco Crunch or Strawberry Delight?" Ashton asked her while standing on the kitchen stool with her head in the freezer. *"Please say you want strawberry,"* Ashton whispered to herself as she gets everyone's favorite flavor. *"Hello...Angel?"* Ashton doesn't get a response. *"Ang!"* She tried to get her attention once more. Stepping down from the stool, she saw Angel standing as still as a statue by the

kitchen sink with a plate in hand. "Dad! Mom! Ang is having a flashback again!" Ashton shouted, knowing this was a daily occurrence with Angel.

Elise and Aaron rushed over to aid Angel, not knowing when she'll come out. Elise rubbed Angel's long black hair, hoping Angel will feel she's there even though her spirit is gone now.

"It's okay princess, take your time," Aaron said, bending down in front of her, looking into her unexpressive eyes.

"Ash, go get your sister's medicine," Elise asked.

"On it," Ashton said as if she's on a mission.

"She's been in it longer than she ever has," Aaron said, worried.

"She'll be okay, she-" Suddenly, Angel began to blink her eyes and move her fingers. "There's my girl," Elise said, relieved.

"You're okay. Come here and tell me what you saw," Aaron said, picking her up and sitting her on his knee at the kitchen table. Angel was fearful to tell what she saw; she doesn't want to see anyone get hurt.

"It's okay sweetheart, you can tell us," Elise said, sitting next to Aaron and leaning in to rub Angel's hand.

"T-Th-There was these men and they came to the door," she said pointing to the front door, "and they w-wanted,,,". Angel began to cry.

"They wanted what, Angie?" Aaron asked, worried. Angel can't speak, she's too scared. "Angel, you need to tell me," Aaron begged her.

"They wanted me and Ashton." Aaron looked at Elise, fearful that this day had come.

"Okay Angel, when are these men coming?" Elise asked her.

Leaning up from her dad's chest as he comforts her, Angel said, "I-I don't know but it was dark outside. Are they going to kill us?"

Aaron could feel her trembling. "No, hey, look at me, no one is going to hurt you or your sister," he stared deeply into her eyes, letting her know he will never let that happen. "As long as me and your mother are here, you are safe." Angel nodded her head, agreeing, and Elise turned her around to wipe her tears.

"I love you," Elise smiled at her and they hug each other tightly.

As her back was facing Aaron, he began to take on the weight of the world. Knowing Angel's visions always come true, Aaron had to devise a plan to protect his family.

A knock is then heard at the door. The three of them were scared, each in their own way. Aaron made his way to the door; he wanted Elise to be ready for anything. Walking towards the front door, he stopped at the foyer table and pressed on the side to open a concealed drawer. Reaching in, he pulls out a .22 Glock and puts it at his side, out of sight from whoever could be at the door. The knock was heard again, and he slowly turned the knob. His gun ready and loaded, he opens the door and it's his partner, Shawn.

"Hey, what's up, Aaron," Shawn said, walking into his friends' home.

"Oh, hey Shawn," Aaron said, relieved, unloading his gun and putting it in the back of his pants.

"You expecting some company?" Shawn asked him, watching him put away his gun.

"Elise, it's okay," Aaron shouted to her in the kitchen, then turned back to Shawn. "Long story, but what's going on?" he asked him.

"I came to take my nieces to go get some ice cream," he said.

"No thanks man, they're actually about to eat ice cream. You can stay, though. We're about to watch America's Greatest Warrior," Aaron said.

"No, no, I'm okay I just wanted to give you guys some alone time," he said, nudging Aaron's arm, hinting at a romantic night for the two.

Elise chuckled at Shawn. "We're okay Shawn but thank you for taking that into consideration."

"Aw come on, when was the last time you guys spent some time alone," Shawn said, now forcing the request.

"Shawn. We're good," Aaron said, placing his hand on his best friend's shoulder.

"But don't you-"

"Shawn! They're okay...What's going on with you?" Elise asked, concerned.

Angel peaked her head out from the kitchen, watching the exchange between the three. Aaron could see the paleness in Shawn's face, his hands are shaking.

"A-Aaron, you really need to let me take them," Shawn whispered to him. This isn't a request anymore. It's a demand.

Elise's instincts guided her to the couch as Aaron and Shawn have their exchange. She moved the couch's pillow and reached in to grab her gun. Placing it into the back of her pants, she glanced over at Angel staring at her. She motioned Angel to go upstairs. Angel doesn't move, and Elise knows this is the vision she mentioned moments ago.

"I'm not giving you my kids until you tell me what's going on with you!" Aaron demanded.

"You have to give them to me, man. It's the only way I can protect us all!" Shawn pleaded to Aaron.

"What the hell are you talking about?! Protect us from who!?"

Shawn is unable to answer him. That's when three men approach the front porch dressed in military grade equipment. They grab

Shawn and hold him tightly; escaping is not an option. Aaron, within the blink of an eye, took out his gun, loaded and aimed it at the man walking towards him.

"What do you want?!" Aaron shouted at him as he held his gun tightly.

"I heard you had very special girls living here," the mysterious man said. He isn't dressed like the other men. His attire is casual as if he stepped out to hang with his best guy friends.

"You need to get out of our house now!" Elise commanded.

The man smirked at Elise. "Take him out of here," he commanded his men to take Shawn.

"Let me go! Aaron, I'm sorry!" Shawn said, struggling to escape from the overly powerful milita men.

Aaron watched as they took his best friend away. He hated himself for trusting someone with his girls. He promised Savannah he would always protect them, and he's failed them all.

"I've traveled a long way to be here. You wouldn't be so rude to not invite me in," he taunted them. His demeanor showed he's the one in charge.

"If I let you in, you won't be leaving the same way you came, so it's your choice," Aaron moved closer, his gun now placed on the man's chest.

"Hey, Clay, I found one of them."

Lowering his guard, Aaron saw a man holding on to a frightened Angel. He isn't dressed in military gear like the others. He looks more like his boss, Clay. Clay stood firm as Aaron continued to press the gun onto his chest. Clay fearlessly moved the gun pressing down on his chest and sinisterly smiled at Aaron and Elise.

"Excuse me," he said into Aaron's ear. He stepped towards Angel as tears run down her face, wanting desperately for her mom and dad to save her. "Hi, what's your name?" Clay asked her.

"Sweetheart, don't answer him," Elise shouted.

Clay moved closer to her, approaching her at eye level. "I heard you're a special girl," he said.

Aaron, wanting to protect his daughter, sprinted towards Clay, until he is stopped by the sight of Will flashing his gun holstered inside his jacket, warning Aaron if he takes another step he won't hesitate to use it on his precious little girl. Elise grabbed Aaron's arm, motioning him to step back. "I heard you have special powers...like a superhero," Clay continued to trick the truth out of her as her parents stood by, helpless. Angel stayed silent. "Oh, you're a very obedient young girl...but I think I can fix that," Clay smirked at her. "Will...scan her," he commanded.

Elise side-eyed Aaron, letting him know they have to get these men out of their house, but not until they protect their girls. Elise slowly made her way to the upstairs steps to go find Ashton.

"You just stay still. This won't hurt a bit," Clay began taking a phone-like device and hovers it over Angel's body, detecting any abnormal activity.

"You're not going to find anything," Aaron said, standing his ground. Clay ignored him, still determined to find psychic children. Aaron reassured Angel that everything will be okay by eyeing her intensely. Elise had almost made her way to the steps without Clay or Will knowing, but Clay stood from kneeling.

"Well, it looks like you were right. Your little girl isn't special," Clay mocked them. "But that doesn't mean the other one isn't. Go get her," Clay commanded Elise, knowing she was on her way to get her anyway.

Elise chuckles at his order, "Yeah, sure I'll go get her because I'm one of your pathetic little soldiers that follow you everywhere you go like a homeless puppy."

Clay laughed at her condescending attitude "That's a good one, but see you'll do as I say because my guys will kill your daughter, being that she isn't any use to me anymore," Clay said seriously.

"Touch my daughter and I will kill you with my bare hands!" Aaron stepped to him, so close Clay could feel the air coming from his nostrils. "Now I have told you my daughters don't have anything you want, so get the hell out of my house before I have you locked up under the jail," Aaron said, promising Clay.

"Will, let's go...we'll be back soon," he said hitting Aaron on his shoulder. Clay and Will walk towards the front door and Angel runs towards Elise, holding her tightly.

"Sorry it took me so long, I couldn't reach the shelf, but I found Ang's pills and the TV remote," Ashton said, coming down the steps unaware of what has taken place. Everyone, including Clay and Will, turns to see Ashton coming down.

"No..." Elise said to herself, watching as Ashton came down the stairs, the pill bottle and remote leading the way high in the air. Clay turned into a young boy who has just found a new puppy; he was right all along.

"Ash! No!" Aaron shouted at her. Frightened, Ashton drops the pill bottle and remote.

"Grab them," Clay commanded Will and the military men guarding the front door. Will and the guards come barging in. Aaron lunged towards Will using all his strength to give a hard-right hook. Will fell back into the two military men, and his eye began to bleed.

"Get them out of here!" Aaron shouted to Elise.

Elise ran into the kitchen with Angel and Ashton and hid them near the basement door. "Everything is going to be all right," she comforted them.

"Mom! I'm scared!" Ashton shouted.

"I know sweetie, but you're both going to be okay. I want you to go hide in the basement, okay?"

"Mom! No!"

"Yes, Angel, go in the basement and don't come out until we come for you." Elise pushed them downstairs, closed the door and locked it.

She makes her way back to Aaron, who's handling Will and the two guards on his own. They've been able to get a few hits on him because they have him surrounded. The heavy-set guard tried to grab Aaron from behind but Aaron head butts him and, with force, kicked him in his knee at the point of breaking. Will, tired of losing this battle, quickly pulled out his gun. He pulled the trigger and it fired towards Aaron. It hits the ceiling. Unknown to the rough-housing men, Elise came running in and kicked Will's gun away from Aaron. It's now Will versus Elise. Will tried to land a punch across Elise's face, but she's able to dodge it, shifting her body to the right as she grabbed his arm and flipped him forward, landing on the coffee table. Aaron continued to go back and forth with the two milita men, taking hit after hit as they ram one another into walls and knocking over furniture. Elise was quickly dodging the attacks of Will, taking him down every chance she gets, already breaking one of his arms. She ended her fight with Will by breaking his leg as he lifts it and tries to kick her into unconsciousness. As he screamed in agony kneeling on the floor, holding onto his arm and now his left leg, Elise landed a powerful punch across Will's face sending him unconsciousness on the floor. Aaron was holding his own against the attacks of the two militia guards. One guard picked Aaron up and slammed him onto the floor, but he gets them back by sweeping his feet under theirs and they landed on the floor just as hard as Aaron. Rolling over, Aaron lifted the guard's head and slammed it hard onto the wood floors. The last remaining guard took out his rifle and aimed it at Aaron as he wrestled on the floor with the heavy-set guard. Elise rushed over and tried to snatch the rifle from the guard. They wrestle, bullets began to hit the ceiling and furniture that isn't torn apart by the fighting. Elise elbowed him in his stomach, but it wasn't a strong enough hit to snatch the rifle away. He kicked Elise behind her knee and she fell over. He loaded his gun and fired at a helpless Elise. Just as he fired, Aaron came running over and slammed the remaining guard into the wall. Stepping back, Aaron took his gun out from the back of his pants and fired a couple of shots at the guard's chest. The guard slid down on the wall, blood following. Breathing heavily, Aaron rushed over to Elise lying on the floor, catching her breath.

"We got to get out of here," he said, helping her up.

"I know," Elise said. She knew giving Angel and Ashton a normal life was going to be a difficult task.

"I'll meet you in the garage," he said, walking towards the basement.

Elise grabbed the prepared bags in the hallway closet and then walked over to Will and the heavy-set guard, tying them together.

Waiting outside along with Shawn and three other guards is Clay. He listened to the gun shots and then nothing. "I'm tired of this," he said, waiting for Will to bring out Angel and Ashton. "Every time I want something done, I have to do it myself. What am I'm paying you people for!?" he shouted at the three militia guards. Clay rushed back into the Cross home and is infuriated at what he sees.

Aaron walked down the barely lit basement steps. "Angel? Ashton?" he called out for them. Turning on the switch lights the basement well, revealing workout equipment and a separate room hiding in the back corner storing Aaron's black ops gear and Elise's weapons. It's highly protected by a door code only opening through retina scan. "It's over guys, you can come out now," he looked over boxes and benches.

A door opens from underneath the basement steps, and Angel and Ashton come out of a small room. They run over and hug their father.

He held onto them tightly, savoring the moment. "We have to go, okay?" he said to them kneeling at their eye level.

"Where are we going?" Angel asked.

"I don't know, but there are bad men coming and we have to-" Aaron heard gun shots go off from upstairs and the rustling of people moving. He's terrified. He had to do the one thing he promised himself, Savannah and his girls, he would never do.

"Daddy, I'm scared!" Angel cried out in terror.

"I know, I know, but can you both do something for me?" he held their hands, being strong for both. "Can you protect each other?" Angel and Ashton nod, but they know where this is leading to. He reached around his neck and pulled out a long black chain with two black military dog tags hanging from it. "You need to go, run away from here," he said to them, trying desperately to hold back his tears.

"What?! Dad, no!" Ashton pleaded.

"You have to Ash, it's the only way to keep you safe," he broke his chain in two and placed the halves around their necks.

"I promise I will come back for you. Here, take this." Aaron reached into his back pocket and gave Ashton a combat knife and then gave Angel the gun he's just used on the men upstairs. "No matter what happens, you protect each other. You go and you don't look back," he said, expressing to them the seriousness of the situation.

Angel and Ashton hugged their dad, crying on his shoulders.

"I love you, too," he said as if it will be the last time he'll see them.

He pushed them out the back door of the basement. Closing the door, he paused, wanting to break down, but there's no time; he had to go protect a friend. He keyed in the code to the door of his armory and took out a rifle, loaded it and prepared to take out multiple enemies. He ran up the stairs on alert, ready for anything to come his way. The house is disturbingly quiet. He saw the prepared getaway bags on the kitchen table, but no Elise. He moved to the hallway where he fought and killed two guards, but they aren't there anymore. Moving to the living room, where Elise fought Will, he's gone too, but what he sees next is worse than what he could have imagined. Elise sat up against the couch trying to keep consciousness.

"Elise!" Aaron rushed towards her aid. "St-st-stay with me, okay? We'll get through this. Okay? We'll go get you some help and then we'll get the girls, and we'll go. We'll, we'll..." Aaron panicked, the emotions from his daughters leaving to this, is all too much for him.

"Shh-shh," Elise grabbed his hands and stared deeply into his eyes, slowing him down. Aaron took a breath and watched as Elise guided his hand to the left part of her chest. She struggled to speak. Aaron was speechless as he lifted his blood-stained hands.

"No, no, no, no, no...Elise, come on," he pleaded. "A-a-a-are they okay?" she asked.

Aaron nodded as tears trickle down his face.

"Th-that's good," Elise had accepted her fate. She relaxed her body and let nature take its course.

"Thank you...for everything," Aaron held her hand.

Elise smiled, "We-we-we're fam-family," she laid her hand on his face. "Go f-find them an-and t-t-tell Savan-Savannah...I love-" Elise's eyes slowly closed, and as she became unconscious, her hand went limp. Aaron broke down, crying next to his dear friend.

After crying for a moment, he gathered himself and prepared to go find his wife and children. As he stood, he becomes motionless, unable to move his legs. He felt a sharp, stabbing, unbearable pain in his neck. He can't move his neck and slowly collapses to the floor.

Clay came walking from behind. "I have to give it to you, you've taught your family well," Clay looked at his work laying lifeless against the couch. "Well, maybe not that well." The remaining militia guards came walking in. "Take him, we'll deal with this situation later," Clay commanded them.

"And her?" one of the guards asked, pointing to Elise.

"Not our problem," Clay said with such arrogance. They drag a limp Aaron out of his home and threw him in the trunk of their SUV. Hiding in the neighbors' bushes across the street are Angel and Ashton.

"What do we do now?" Ashton asked Angel.

"We go, like daddy told us," Angel said, assuming the role of leader and becoming the protective older sister. They watch as their lifeless father gets taken out of their home and their 'uncle' stands by doing nothing.

"It's all my fault!" Ashton cried out.

"You didn't know, Ash. It's okay, I'll protect you," Angel hugged her sister. She took her hand, and they left their childhood home.

Chapter 29

Unable to cope with the news, Jordan sits in the basement of her home. It has a secret presence about itself. Normal people store old Christmas trees and decorations and other junk in their basement. Jordan isn't normal. It's her own private lair. She has computer screens detecting suspicious activity, an armory and her own personal combat suit collection. This basement has all the equipment a former assassin would have… until they need it.

She sits at her desk, drinking vintage scotch and thinking about her past choices and how they've finally caught up with her. Continuing to pour her liquor, Jordan stares at two stuffed animals on her desk: panthers. "I left you and I never came back," she says, speaking to the… panthers, slurring her words. "You're better off without me. I'm a mess, a mess of a mother." Jordan breaks down in tears. The newborn babies she left behind to protect have been in her face for three weeks and she didn't know. Taking her drink, she walks to a wall across from her desk displaying images of the people that mean the most to her. Pictures of her military life with herself, Crystal Warren and her fellow team of soldiers enjoying a night on the town. Playful pictures with her best friend, Elise, in the same black and red leather combat suits. She looks further down the wall and stares at the many pictures of her and Aaron. They are the happiest they've ever been with one another. Riding camels in Dubai, drinking champagne in Sicily, kissing under The Bridge of Sighs in Venice and him kissing her enormous belly in front of their then-new home. She touches the picture, where her hand is placed over Aaron's. The love of her life is gone and maybe if she hadn't made so many enemies in the past, she could have had a normal life with her daughters and husband—a normal suburban life, where killing people wasn't a job. Jordan logs into her 90-inch computer screen and pulls up the past files on Angel and Ashton. "You were right in front of me, and I didn't even know." Jordan tears herself down. She scrolls down to their listed powers and instantly thinks back to her conversations with Dr. Hawthorne. He knew all along. He knew her daughters and husband were alive and said nothing. Jordan grew increasingly angry at the thought of her friend betraying her like this, so angry she throws her glass of leftover scotch at a nearby wall.

Huffing and puffing, she hears the doorbell. She takes a deep breath to calm herself and checks her security monitors; it's David. She isn't in the mood for his complaining. She tries to gather herself, becoming Lieutenant Jordan Knox once more, and goes upstairs to greet him. Opening the door, she sees that David is dressed in casual clothing, no suit, which is odd for him because he has enough suits to open his own warehouse.

"Hey, we need to talk," David says, inviting himself in.

"Umm…okay…come on in," Jordan says to a frantic David.

"Ok, I know we've had our share of problems, from me going back to work for the CIA, you not telling me about the new agents and running this new agency, but we weren't always like this," he says, moving closer to her.

Jordan is still dealing with the recent news and still feeling the effects of scotch, and all she can do is listen and become mesmerized by the strength and masculinity of the man standing in front of her now.

"I miss you and I…" he contemplates if he should take this first step in their relationship, "…love you. We're a tea-"

Jordan jumps towards him and wraps her arms around his neck, interrupting him with a kiss. David is caught off guard and pulls

Jordan off him. He looks into her eyes and notices she's not herself. "J? What's wrong?" he asks her, concerned about her well-being.

"Shut up and kiss me," she commands him. Unable to fight his feelings for her, David kisses her passionately and picks her up, like the king carrying his queen. He whisks her away to her upstairs room and they escape with one another as if they're escaping from their problems and the world.

After spending hours with one another, they lay close, feeling each other's warmth. Wrapped in David's arms, Jordan can't let go of her negative thoughts.

"We haven't done this in a long time," David lightens the mood.

"You've gotten better," Jordan says.

"Wow…I feel more confident," he laughs.

"As you should." Their laughter slowly turns into silence.

"I guess it's safe to say we moved up from formally dating to passionate lovers to something more…serious," David says hesitant.

Jordan gives no response, believing he's moving way too fast; for Christ's sake she just found out her husband is dead. David turns over, waiting for her response or some sign of agreement. "I wouldn't…say we're there yet," she says, leaving their island away from the world.

"What are you talking about? After everything I've said tonight, you still don't trust me?!" David says.

"I'm not saying I don't trust you. Believe me, I do, but-"

"But you just don't love me enough," he says, quickly putting on his clothes to leave.

"Don't put words in my mouth. I'm just saying we have too much going on to be prancing around, flaunting our relationship to people," Jordan expresses.

David stands by the opposite side of the king-sized bed, half dressed. Shirtless, with his pants and shoes on. "*We* have too much going on or you do?" he says, testing her. "You know what, J? I'll do whatever you want, and I'll give you time because it's clear something's been going on with you and not even just tonight when you're smelling like a walking bottle of liquor."

Jordan stands speechless. She knows she's wrong, especially since her relationship with David was never supposed to go this far.

Fully clothed, he walks to her, gently grabbing her neck and brings her forehead to his lips, "I won't wait long, though." He leaves her bedroom and Jordan is once again alone.

It has been a long and dreadful night. She lays back in her bed and pulls the covers over her head, escaping her problems. But she's still the boss and her work is never done. Her phone rings. "What?!" she snaps at the person on the other end.

"Ummm…hey Jordan, we're ready to begin," Natalie says.

With all that has gone on today, Jordan forgot about Phase 4. "All right," she lets out a heavy sigh. "I'll be there in 20 minutes." She forces herself to get out of bed, walks to her master bathroom and stands in front of the mirror for a moment. She must pull herself together. She can't go into that agency and see Ashton and Angel. She's strong, she's powerful, she's the lieutenant. These affirmations run through her mind, and she becomes Jordan once again.

Showering and washing away her face full of tears, sweat and of the alcohol seeping through her pores, she puts on natural make-up and takes out one of her designer business suits. "Hey, Charlie, I need you to come pick me up," Jordan talks on her cell phone.

"On my way, Lieutenant," Charlie says through the phone.

Ten minutes later, Charlie honks his horn outside. Sunglasses on, Jordan makes her way to the backseats of the jet-black SUV.

"Not feeling too well, Lieutenant?" Charlie asks, curious about Jordan wearing sunglasses in the middle of the night.

"I'm fine. Just didn't feel like driving, that's all," she says, deflecting.

"Well, you know I'm always happy to help," Charlie tries to cheer her up.

"Thanks, Charlie, it's just one of those days," she says, looking out of the tinted black window. "And all days," she says to herself.

"You need to hook up the converter to the power source so that we can get an accurate depiction of what will be going on!" Natalie orders her team of techs around in the Exodus engineering and tech lab, The Workshop.

"Hey, how is everything? Do you need any help?" Seth asks, coming to help his best friend.

Natalie lets out a large sigh of frustration. "That would be great. Everything needs to be set up perfectly before Jordan gets here and for some reason I'm working with a team of incompetents."

Seth helps connect cords to a large silver tube next to five 35" flat television screens. "Well, it is three in the morning. Maybe they're sleepwalking," he jokes with her, and Natalie's frustration turns into ease.

"Okay…we just need to adjust the portion size of the antibody and they can stay in the world a little longer," Natalie says as she takes a syringe and fills it with a bright green liquid the consistency of glue.

Walking in, barely awake, is Donovan James. "Natalie," he calls out her name while covering up a yawn, "is there a reason you called me down here at three in the morning?"

"Sorry, the lieutenant wanted you, me, Seth and the captain here for phase 4…it's a private matter," Natalie says, continuing to work out the kinks of her work.

"Phase 4?" Donovan says, perplexed. "This has to do with them, doesn't it?" he asks, referencing Angel, Ashton, Blair and Daniella.

"Ummm…I'd rather wait for the lieutenant to get here. She can explain everything," Natalie says, quickly taking the pressure off herself.

"Well, I hope she's honest with us this time. Ever since she brought those girls in here it's been one secret and drama-filled day after another."

Natalie continues working on her antibodies, trying to ignore Donovan's remarks.

"I hate to agree Nat, but Donovan's right," Seth says, finishing connecting the wires. "The moment they set foot through our front doors, everyone's been on edge. It's like a dark cloud hovering over us," Seth continues.

Natalie slams her syringes on the lab table, shutting them up. "If you two actually sat down and got to know them, then maybe you wouldn't think of them as dark clouds and troublemakers," Natalie protects her newly found friends. "They're not who you think they are…they're good people." She goes back to working as Seth and Donovan are silent. They know they're wrong for judging them, but who's to say Natalie is right?

"And who told you they were…the lieutenant?" They all turn to see Captain Lawrence in the doorway of the workshop entrance.

"Sir, sorry we didn't see you there," Donovan and Seth salute him and stand at attention.

"At ease guys, it's three in the morning," he says, still dealing with the emotions of Jordan from moments ago. "Natalie, how well do you know these girls?" he asks. If Jordan won't give him any information, he'll get it somewhere else.

"I haven't known them for long, but I can tell they've been through some things," Natalie says, knowing what he's trying to do. Jordan warned her about this.

"Ok, let's see if I can put this another way," David says, beginning to become more frustrated than he already is. "Why did Jordan bring those girls, specifically, here?"

Natalie feels pressured to answer. He is the captain and has more leverage than anyone here when it comes to the CIA, but Jordan is a much scarier beast to face. "Sir, I really think you should ask the lieutenant." The room is silent. Everyone can tell there's something off about the captain. "Now if you'll excuse me, I have to finish preparing phase 4," Natalie continues as she walks over to the flat-screen televisions. Seth follows her, comforting her along the way like any good friend would do.

"Are you okay, sir?" Donovan approaches him.

"Yes, I'm fine, Agent James, just tired of being kept in the dark," David says, leaning on the lab table, reflecting on his military and CIA days of always being overlooked.

The room comes to a halt. "Don't stop working because I'm here," Jordan says, entering the workshop slowly, aviators on.

Natalie rushes over with her tablet to give to Jordan. "Everything is set up."

"Inside voice, Nat."

"Oh…okay," Natalie speaks more quietly. "We had some minor technical difficulties with the converters connecting to the data routers, but everything is fixed."

"Are they ready go in?" Jordan asks, referring to Angel, Ashton, Blair and Daniella, as she looks through the schematics of Natalie's project.

"Ready as they'll ever be," Seth says.

"Why are we here, Lieutenant?" David asks. "I think we deserve to know that much."

Jordan takes off her sunglasses, letting out a long sigh and giving the tablet back to Natalie. "Okay, you know what, you want to know so bad, well here it is goes," she says, completely over David's and everyone's whining, constantly nagging her about these girls. "Dr. Hawthorne was working on a private experiment; he wanted to study supernatural abilities in children." Seth looks at Natalie, wanting to know if she knew this about her father. Natalie nods, reassuring him that it's okay.

"What do you mean 'private experiments'?! Was he doing this before or after we were breached?" David asks, shocked.

"Before. That's why Clay and Marissa came for him…but before he died, he wanted me to go find them and…" Jordan pauses for a moment. She thinks about the last thing Dr. Hawthorne said to her, 'I know you'. He had to know Angel and Ashton were her daughters and she failed them, immensely. "…Protect them. Do you honestly believe if I came right out and said to the director, 'the new, advanced agents will also have psychic abilities,' everything would be peachy, and we would all go back to our normal jobs?!" Jordan says, aggravated, but then closing her eyes tightly trying to ease the pressure of her headache. "Look, I didn't tell you everything because I wanted to protect you and them. The less you knew the fewer questions that would have been asked. So, I am asking you, not only as your lieutenant but your friend, to please keep this information between us," she whispers in the huddle they're in around the lab table. "I apologize for keeping this from you," Jordan says to the group, but mainly speaking to David. "I thought my intentions were for the best," she continues sincerely.

"You have my word, Lieutenant," Donovan says.

"Same," Seth says, placing his hand on Jordan's shoulder. She gives him a look of 'why are you touching me?' and he quickly takes away his hand.

She smiles at him. "Thank you, Seth," she says, placing her arm around him.

"I'm going to go prepare everything," Natalie says, saddened to hear once again of her father's work and other young girls experiencing his loving spirit. Jordan notices her sadness, but the best thing to do for Natalie is to let her be.

Once everyone walks away, it's only her and David left. She looks at him for some forgiveness and he gives her nothing. He stares at her and then walks away, leaving her with confusion and a semi-manageable headache.

"Nat, care to explain phase 4 to everyone?" Jordan asks, walking towards the flat television screens and tinted window.

"Of course," Natalie's attitude changes when discussing her favorite thing: tech! "Phase 4 is specifically designed for our five new candidates. The suits our girls were wearing during our pervious phases were lined with a material that suppressed their powers, but now we are unleashing their powers in a place I like to call," Natalie flips a switch on the silver tube next to the tinted black window and the flat screen televisions light up with vitals and the tinted window reveals a room where Angel, Ashton, Blair, Daniella and Ethan are laying face up on beds. "The LAND," Natalie says confidently.

"So, we're drugging them now?" Donovan asks.

"Yes," Natalie says, overly excited.

"Nat!" Jordan corrects her.

"I mean no, they're in a deep sleep, a REM sleep more specifically," she explains.

"We've placed them deeper into their dreams, with minor adjustments."

"What kind of adjustments?" David asks.

"I've created a dream sequence of an Exodus break-in," Natalie says with excitement. "We'll each sit at a station and monitor the progression and vitals of them." Natalie swipes through her tablet and guides them to their designated areas. "Captain, you will have

Daniella; Lieutenant, you will have Ashton; Seth, you will have Ethan; Donovan, you'll have Angel. And I will have Blair."

Everyone sits at their designated areas. "And I'm guessing we need these headsets?" Donovan asks.

"Yes, they're more like virtual reality sets, so you can see their dream as they see it. It will be reality to them, they'll feel every hit and every gunshot as if it happened," Natalie expresses.

"And if they actually get shot, then what?" David asks, knowing she probably didn't think this all the way through.

"Their vitals will go down and we would have to pull them out immediately," Natalie says.

"Basically, if they die in their dream, they die out here," Jordan says bluntly, wanting to move on.

"Let's begin." Natalie tries to contain her excitement. This is the first time her project is being used outside of testing.

The five of them strap on their headsets and phase 4 begins with their designated screens powering up.

"Natalie, it looks like your project is broken," Donovan says, viewing a black screen.

"I think he's right, Nat," Seth agrees.

"Just give it a minute!" Natalie snaps at them.

They sit in silence for a moment. "Nat, nothing is happening," Jordan says.

"This is ridiculous," David says.

"Wait! Just hold on for another minute," Natalie pleads.

"It's okay, Nat-" Seth comforts her.

"Wait," Donovan interrupts them, "something is happening on my end." His screen shows a horizontal blurred line, slowly opening and closing. "I think she's waking up," Donovan says as the blurred line opens further. He realizes this blurred line is Angel's eyes and she's waking up. Her eyes suddenly open abruptly. Donovan is now watching the screen from Angel's point of view.

Chapter 30

Angel awakens from what she believes was a terrible dream, gasping for air. It wasn't a dream; it was a vision. She frantically tries to make sense of what she saw and makes her way to her sister's room. "Ash? Ash!" Angel whispers loudly.

"Mmmmm…" Ashton groans, wanting whoever is talking to her to go away. Angel runs over to Ashton's bed and rocks her back and forth.

"Ash! Get up."

"Leave me alone," Ashton says putting her pillow over her head.

"I just had this weird vision," Angel says.

"That's what your medicine is for. Go take it!" Ashton says.

"No, it's not that. I saw someone trying to break in here," Angel says nervously.

"Okay, it's clear you won't let me get any sleep," Ashton gets out of her bed. "What specifically did you see?" she asks, pulling Angel up from her bed.

"On the other side of the front door there were three guys dressed in…" she tries to think of the right words, "all of this military gear, and they had guns pointed at the lock."

"And you're absolutely sure this isn't a future you're seeing that's going to happen months from now?" Ashton asks.

Their conversation wakes up Blair and Daniella. "I understand you guys are siblings and maybe it's just me because I'm an only child, but you should not be fighting this much and this early," Daniella yawns.

"She has a point. Maybe you guys should seek a therapist or go talk to Dr. O'Conner," Blair agrees.

"We're not fighting," Ashton says, annoyed by the three of them. "Angel had a vision that someone was going to break in here."

"You sure it's going to happen tonight?" Blair asks.

"I think I know my own visions; I've had them my whole-" They're interrupted by an alarm; the sound is faint being that they're in a highly secured room made of reinforced steel.

"What is that?" Daniella asks.

"Sounds like someone hit the alarm," Ashton says.

"Now do you believe me?" Angel says to them as she makes her way to the front door of the penthouse.

"The alarm going off means nothing. It's probably Jordan starting one of her tests," Ashton says as she follows Angel. Daniella and Blair aren't too far behind.

"If that's what you believe, that's on you," Angel says as she grabs her guns from underneath the coffee table.

"It's not that I don't believe you, it's just we've been in situations like this before," Ashton says as Angel continues to gear up. The alarm continues, and they hear a bang on the other side of the door.

"What was that?!" Blair asks, fearful. The colossal bang frightened them, and Angel just gives Ashton a look of 'I told you so' and walks to the screen displaying who is on the other side of the door. It's the militia men in her vision at the front door.

"I am not the one to say I'm always right, but I'm right," Angel says as she sees three dangerous men at their front door.

"We know you're in there, come out and this can all be over!" the leader shouts.

"Okay! Fine, I was wrong," Ashton confesses as she rushes to grab her knives from the training room.

"Wait, Angel, how were you able to see a vision clearly if Natalie suppressed them?" Daniella asks curiously.

"She only put them in our suits," Angel says, "which we're not wearing." Angel is surprised she didn't notice sooner.

"I do feel slightly stronger," Blair says, looking at her hands.

"If you won't come out, we'll come in!!" the man shouts on the other side of the door. The men take a large ramming pole to bust down the door, and the girls hear a continuous bang from their end.

"Open the door and I'll take them out myself, then I can go back to sleep," Ashton says with such arrogance.

"That won't work. As soon as we open the door, they'll have guns aimed right at us. You can't take down all three," Angel says.

"Who says I can't?!" Ashton snaps.

"We need to think of something now! That door will not last that long," Blair panics.

"I could do it. I could freeze them then we can sneak by and find the lieutenant," Daniella says.

"No, we're okay. I can handle it," Ashton says.

Blair and Daniella have slightly grown on Ashton to the point where she can tolerate their presence but fully trusting them with her life might take some time. The men ram on the door as they finally put a dent in it and a hinge falls off. "Guys! I don't care who takes care of it, somebody needs to before we're all dead," Blair shouts.

Angel loads her last gun and walks behind Ashton. "Ash, it's okay," Angel says.

"Ashton, I can do it," Daniella says, attempting to get Ashton to trust her.

"Fine."

"Get ready," Daniella says as the girls stand behind, covering her back. The men give one last ram on the door and it breaks down, falling in front of the girls. As the smoke clears, the men move toward them with their military-grade weapons in hand.

"Hands up!" the leader shouts.

"If you say so," Daniella says, doing as she's told. Giving them a smirk, she raises her hands and then snaps her fingers. Their guns burst into smoke, like a small explosion.

"Get them!" he shouts orders. Before they could rush towards her, with a flick of her wrist, she freezes the men in place. Angel, Ashton and Blair lower their weapons, impressed.

"All right …let's go find everyone else," Angel says, leaving the penthouse.

"You're awesome," Blair says, excitedly following behind Angel.

Ashton approaches Daniella and she's expecting a self-absorbed response. "You did good," Ashton smiles and runs out, catching up with Angel.

Daniella smiles at the thought of Ashton being nice to her for once. Maybe Ashton isn't as bad as she thought. Daniella runs out of the penthouse into the darkened hallway lit up by only floor lighting and the flashing red lights of the alarms.

"Why is it so quiet? Where is everyone?" Blair whispers.

Guns in hand, the four of them move slowly throughout the lower level of the agency. "Maybe it was just those three we had to worry about. Daniella, how long before your freeze wears off?" Angel asks.

"We have five minutes."

"That's not a lot of time. We need to move fast," Angel says as the other girls follow her lead.

They continue to move forward, checking rooms – the training rooms, the armory and the storage rooms – but they come across nothing.

They approach the elevator. "Jordan's not answering. What type of lieutenant doesn't answer her own-" Ashton says.

"Ash! Wait!" Angel interrupts her.

"Fine, I never knew you liked her this much," Ashton says with such sarcasm.

"No, someone's already on the elevator." Angel blocks Ashton with her arm. They all watch as the elevator's down arrow continues to glow, flickering as it reaches its destination. "Get ready," Angel says.

Angel, Ashton and Daniella ready their weapons and Blair panics, "What?! I-I don't know if I'm ready, I haven't fought anyone in like…forever!"

"Well, you better get ready," Daniella says.

They move back as the elevator gets closer to their level. The elevator stops and slowly opens. Ashton throws a knife quickly through the opening of the door, hoping to have struck one of the paramilitary men, but she doesn't.

"Hey!" Ethan shouts as he dodges the knife flying across the side of his face.

"Ethan?! What are you doing?!" Angel says, surprised he's come to find them.

"Besides risking my life coming down here, I came to find you," Ethan says to them, but directing his statement more so to Angel.

"Do you know what's going on?" Blair asks.

"They're everywhere in the building, searching for something called 'Experiment X.' I'm surprised I made it down here," he reveals.

"How did you make it down here?" Ashton asks curiously.

"I woke up to the alarm and when I opened my door there were two guys standing outside. I had to take them down and sneak my way past the rest of them to get to you."

"Did you see anybody else? The lieutenant, Natalie, Agent James?" Angel asks, worried they her and the others could be the cause of an army breaching the agency.

"No, I haven't seen anyone. I've only been on my floor. They all could be fighting them off on the operations level," Ethan says.

"Well, we need to figure out something. Those guys will wake up any minute," Daniella reminds them of the three men she froze.

"Even if we do find everybody else, how are we going to get rid of an entire army?!" Blair asks, panicking…again.

"We need to split up," Angel says, figuring out a solution. "We split up and take them down ourselves."

"Great idea. Me and Angel will take the stairs covering the outer regions and you guys can take the elevator clearing each floor, looking for the rest of the team," Ethan commands.

"Okay, when did we decide to make you captain?" Ashton snaps. She already doesn't like Ethan for obvious reasons, so taking orders from him is something that will never happen.

"I don't see you coming up with any logical ideas," Ethan says, stepping closer to Ashton. For a moment, Ethan changes, his witty and laid-back attitude quickly switching to intimidation.

"We don't have time for this right now!" Angel interrupts them, pulling them apart.

"You guys go throughout the agency and see if you can find anybody on our side. Ethan and I will clear out the garage and anybody else outside." Angel has a talent for taking a hectic situation and controlling it. They separate, Ethan and Angel taking the stairs down to the garage and Ashton, Blair and Daniella taking the elevator.

"Yeah, we don't mind getting killed," Ashton sarcastically says as Ethan and Angel make their way to the stairs. Ashton, Blair and Daniella ready their weapons.

"What do you think we'll find up there?" Daniella asks.

"I don't know," Ashton says, feeling her nerves taking over. She knows how to take down an incompetent robber, but paramilitary men with highly advanced tech weapons may be out of her league. "But expect the unexpected," she continues. They exit the elevator and begin searching through the barracks.

"So, Ethan and Angel, huh?" Daniella says trying to spark up a conversation at the most inconvenient time.

"What about them?" Ashton asks.

"They clearly wanted to be alone," Daniella says.

Ashton keeps moving throughout the floor, not wanting to dive deeper into this unwanted conversation. "If you knew Angel, you would know she would never fall for a guy like that, so I'm not worrying about their bizarre relationship and neither should you," Ashton says, continuing to lead the way. Blair and Daniella know there's more to this story and Ashton is refusing to accept it. But what can they do? She's not their sister.

"I just think you should give Ethan a-" Blair is interrupted by Ashton storming into the barracks, taking down two paramilitary men rummaging through lockers and beds. Ashton stretches her arms out and slams the men against the lockers, hard enough they could have gone through the walls. Approaching them, she takes her gun out and shoots them, making sure she doesn't have to deal with them later. "-chance," Blair finishes her statement in awe of what Ashton did to those men.

"Give him a chance?! I can barely remember his name," Ashton says, moving forward as if she didn't just kill two men in under thirty seconds. Blair and Daniella smirk at the thought of Ashton not caring too much for Ethan and his wannabe suave attitude.

"All right, it looks like there's no one else here," Daniella says.

"Yeah, let's head up to the labs," Ashton says as they make their way to the elevator. The elevator is quiet, you can hear the motors move throughout. Quietly exiting the elevator to the third floor, they sneak their way through the hallway. Crouching down with guns in hand, they look through the glass windows of the medical wing and tech lab. A large group of paramilitary men move through the labs, knocking over beakers, searching through cabinets and computers. Ashton, Blair and Daniella take cover outside the medical wing.

"What is Experiment X and why are we about to die over it?" Blair asks.

"Angel told me Experiment X was created by Natalie's dad, Dr. Hawthorne. He created it to get rid of the powers people like us have, but something went wrong and now people like them," Ashton slowly looks up at the men through the glass window from the hallway, "can be just like us."

"Okay, well there's clearly more of them than there are of us, so what do we do?!" Blair asks. "I didn't sign up for this. I didn't sign up to die on my first month here."

Ashton and Daniella watch as Blair begins to break down. They can't take it any longer; she'll get them all killed if she doesn't pull it together. Ashton scurries over to Blair, grabs her arm and pulls her over to a hidden corner. "Look, you have got to pull yourself together before we actually die," Ashton places her hands on Blair's shoulders and Daniella stands guard. "I understand you're scared, and all of this was just thrown at you, but there is a reason why

Jordan chose you and I really hate to say this, but she knows what she's doing." Ashton comforts Blair in her own way and Daniella and Blair like what they see.

Blair nods her head and exhales all her worries. "Okay, how do we take them down?"

"They're not in the armory because you need a code, retinal and thumb scan, so I say we take the stealth route, sneak in medical and take them out," Ashton says.

Daniella and Blair agree and they make their way to the side door of medical, crouching down and moving in and out of cover. Five men are searching through the lab unaware that Ashton, Daniella and Blair are hiding behind the desks and lab tables. Ashton gives Daniella and Blair a signal to hold their fire, but of course they have no idea what she's talking about. Ashton spots a shelf with pill bottles and other medical supplies behind two paramilitary men. With the flick of her wrist, she knocks over the shelf, startling the men. The men quickly take out their weapons, feeling like someone is in the room. They walk past the lab table Ashton is behind. As the heavy boots walk past her, she readies her knives and takes them both down with the quick sway of her weapons. She slices their legs and allows her weapons to cut deeply through their armor into their cold skin. Not giving them a chance to scream out in pain. Daniella helps her get them out of sight.

Daniella is highly impressed by Ashton's skills but now it's time to show her what she can do. Moving around the room unnoticed by the remaining three men, she quickly stands, grabbing their attention. "Excuse me?" Daniella says, toying with them.

"Hey!" one of the men shouts, unholstering his weapon. Before they could fire a shot, Daniella stretches her arms out and their gun bursts in their hands, knocking them out onto the floor.

"Okay! I see you," Ashton says standing giving Daniella a slow clap, extremely impressed.

"Two floors down, two more to go," Daniella says.

"Help." Ashton and Daniella turn to acknowledge Blair. She stands with an arm the size of her body wrapped around her throat and a Beretta 9mm pistol pressed against the temple on her head.

"I suggest you do the smart thing and drop your gun and leave her the hell alone," Ashton says, drawing her gun. Daniella does the same. Blair struggles to escape from the paramilitary man.

"Drop your weapons or I'm putting a damn bullet in her head," he says aggressively. "Drop them now!"

Ashton and Daniella do what he says, and they raise their hands in surrender.

"Now me and your friend here are going to leave. Since we don't have the real Experiment X, we might as well take one of you as collateral," he says, trying to intimidate them. But it's only making them angrier. Blair continues to struggle to escape and she's becoming more and more frustrated with herself for getting herself in this situation. "Follow us and she dies," he leaves the lab, dragging Blair with him as she kicks and punches him, trying to release herself. The harder he pulls, the more aggravated she becomes, and her body begins to rise in temperature.

Within seconds, Blair's overwhelming fear turns into anger. As she places her hands on the man's arm wrapped around her neck, her body becomes increasingly hotter. Her hands are scalding. Her hands begin to turn red and burn through his armor and onto his skin. He releases her, screaming in agony, holding onto to his left forearm.

"What did you do to me?!" he screams louder, sweat pouring from his face.

Ashton and Daniella come rushing towards Blair's aid, but soon realize she never needed the help as they watch smoke come from his arm and they notice third degree burns. Blair's hands continue to smoke and show signs of fire bursting from them. The paramilitary man, enraged, lunges for Blair, but he's too late. He's thrown against the elevator, chest caved in and disintegrating before their eyes. Blair breathes heavily as the red streak in her hair slowly turns back to her natural jet-black hair color and the body cools off.

"Hey, hey, you did good," Daniella says, helping her to calm down.

"That…was…amazing," Ashton says, excited. "You had all of that under your sleeve and you were scared of a little army. Could have fooled me."

Blair smiles and a streak of her hair begins to turn green. She is elated on the inside. The feeling of finally being accepted is the best feeling in the world and she doesn't want it to go away.

"Okay…so taking the elevator is out," Daniella says, looking at the burned paramilitary man stuck to the doors.

"Is it over?" a whispering voice asks behind them.

Daniella, Ashton and Blair quickly draw their weapons and Daniella takes a shot, startled. The voice they hear is Seth's, who is peeking his head out from the medical wing. He screams and dodges the bullet.

"Hey! Watch it!" he shouts.

"Seth?! Where did you come from?!" Daniella asks, lowering her weapon.

"I was hiding in the cabinets," he says. Blair looks him up and down.

"How did you even fit in there?" Blair asks as she and Seth are in their own one-on-one conversation

"It actually wasn't that difficult. The cabinets are bigger than you think. The outside is just an illusion, my own design, I might add," Seth continues rambling.

"Okay! Can you please tell us why there is an entire army trying to kill us? And where the hell is Jordan?" Ashton interrupts Blair and Seth's distracting conversation.

"Last time I saw her she was going to her office to secure some plans," Seth says. "The men are here for Experiment X and…" Seth takes a moment to tell them, knowing it will be a lot for them to take in.

"And what, Seth?" Daniella says.

"They're here for all of you," Seth explains. Daniella, Blair and Ashton all take a moment to compose themselves.

"Well, I'm not going down without a fight," Ashton says, putting away her knives and taking out her guns to load them. "You guys with me?" she asks Blair and Daniella.

"I got your back," Daniella says, reloading her gun.

"Me, too," Blair chimes in, picking up her gun from the floor.

"Seth, take us to the lieutenant," Ashton commands.

"What?! I-I can just stay down here until you all, you know, handle everything up there," Seth says, trying not to get himself killed.

"Seth, we'll protect you. Just stay behind us because if you stay down here, you're very likely to be killed," Daniella says with such confidence.

"Okay, fine, but we'll take the back door," Seth says, leading them to the back of the workshop. Continuing to move through The LAND unknown, Daniella, Blair and Ashton make their way to Jordan's office, hoping for answers and help.

Chapter 31

Ethan and Angel clear out the outer perimeter of the agency, where very few paramilitaries are stationed, and make their way to the garage. "Sorry you had to get between me and Ashton," Ethan says, taking lead as Angel follows behind, making sure no one sneaks up on them.

"Ashton is her own person. I don't control her, but I did tell you not to provoke her," Angel says.

"I didn't provoke her. I just told her the best route to take," Ethan says.

Angel chuckles as his statement. "There are very few people who can tell Ashton what to do, and by few, I mean my father and mother and they're both dead so…"

"From what I've seen, she listens to you," Ethan says as they walk through the lower level of the agency.

"She listens to me out of obligation," Angel says.

"Okay well, I'll do my best to steer clear of Ashton Cross," Ethan says.

"Thank you," Angel says, watching him from behind, mesmerized by his stature and confidence. Completely focused on him, for a moment Angel doesn't see Ethan looking back at her. She catches herself. "What?" she asks awkwardly.

"Nothing," he says, turning back around, excited to know there may be something between them. "So, this Experiment X. What is it and why are we risking our lives for it?" Ethan asks.

"Jordan said it gave normal people supernatural abilities," Angel explains as they approach the front doors of the garage.

"Like the ones you guys have?" Ethan says, stopping in front of the doors.

"Something like that." Angel moves up to open the door and hears footsteps inside.

"I bet that's nerve-wrecking. What type of abilities do you have?" Ethan says, not noticing how Angel isn't paying any attention to him. He moves closer to her, wondering why she's peeking through the doors instead of going through them. "What's wrong?" he asks. Angel quiets him, pushes him back, and closes the door.

"You want to know what I can do?" Angel smiles at him, knowing he'll be impressed within the next few minutes. She kneels in front of the doors and touches the floor. She becomes motionless and enters astral mode. Her astral body stands up and opens the doors to the garage. With everything moving around her in slow motion, she captures seven paramilitary men ready and equipped to catch whoever comes through the garage doors by surprise. Angel's astral body walks back to her physical self to prepare for a quick and easy fight. Ethan stands, unimpressed.

"Ummm… okay… you're kneeling is very nice," he mocks her.

She just smiles at him, readying her weapons, and kicks through the double doors. The paramilitary men come out of hiding and shoot, but not as fast as Angel. Knowing where each man is hiding, she takes aim and shoots each man with a quick and steady shot they didn't see coming. She shoots three men within seconds, but the others quickly catch on. Ethan takes cover next to Angel, infatuated with her skills. "Okay, now I'm impressed," he says, shouting over the ricocheting bullets.

"Thanks. Now can you be impressed and help me take out the rest of them?" Angel shouts back. He gets ready to stand, but Angel takes his arm and pulls him back down. "Wait. Behind the tank, behind the pillar on your right, inside the security room and one behind the pillar on the balcony," Angel says, giving him their hidden locations. As Angel gives him these locations, he believes there is a chance of falling for her sooner than he expected. Simultaneously, they stand and shoot their remaining targets. "See, told you I'd impress -"

Ethan takes Angel by her waist and pulls her close to him like there's no one else in the world that matters and presses his lips against hers. Angel takes it all in and embraces his warmth and for a moment they aren't worried about who's coming after them or any tasks needed to be completed. It's them and only them. They eventually pull apart, giving themselves a moment to understand what just took place, to breathe.

"I'm…sorry, I just…I saw you and-," Ethan rambles, continuing to hold Angel close.

She places her hand over his mouth to shut him up. "It's fine, let's just go find everyone else." Angel walks away from his embrace and leaves the garage. Ethan watches, memorized by Angel as if she's walking on water.

Back in reality, Jordan, Natalie, Donovan, Seth and David watch them move throughout the synthetic world, revealing more of their personalities, something they would never do willingly.

"This door leads right into her office," Seth says, walking behind them closely. Ashton pushes open the door and notices it has been tampered with, so she gives them the signal to be quiet as she slowly opens the back door. They creep their way in and see three men standing over Jordan and Natalie, who are tied up tightly to chairs.

"This could all be over if you just tell me what I want to know!" the man shouts in front of Jordan. He must be the leader of this army because he's dressed differently and exudes more confidence and strength than his soldiers.

"And I told you, I'm not telling you anything," Jordan shouts back at him.

One of his men searches through Jordan's office, ripping through files and trying to hack her computers.

"We don't have the experiment so why don't you just go. You're wasting all of our time," Natalie snaps in frustration.

The leader angrily grabs Natalie by her jaws and squeezes. "Now you don't expect me to believe that, do you?" He's condescending. "Your father created the experiment, and you and the lieutenant worked alongside him, so somebody better tell me something or Exodus becomes a morgue." He tosses Natalie's jaw out of his hand.

"How would he even know that?!" Daniella whispers.

"Doesn't matter, there's more of us than them," Ashton whispers.

They look behind them and notice Seth. "Okay, it's an equal amount. We can still take them," Ashton continues.

"I found something," one of the men says. He's found a hard drive that could include information on Experiment X.

"Now is our time," Daniella whispers, noticing the leader and his soldier walking away, leaving only one guarding Jordan and Natalie.

Crouching down and moving behind furniture, they split up in twos. "Seth, you go untie Natalie and I'll cover you," Ashton instructs.

"What?! Why can't you go?!" Seth whispers loudly, panicking.

"Because I'm the one with the gun and powers. I can't shoot and untie her at the same time," Ashton says. Seth realizes he doesn't have a choice. He takes a large gulp and prepares himself to scurry across the room to untie Natalie.

"What was that?!" the man guarding Jordan and Natalie says, aiming his rifle to the area he heard the sound. Ashton quickly reaches for Seth's belt and pulls him back behind the couch.

"What is it?" the leader asks. He draws his weapon and follows his soldier to the front door. The soldier notices the office front double doors are halfway open. With his gun, he slowly opens the door and looks out into the hallway, but no one is outside.

"False alarm. It's clear," the soldier says, coming into the office.

"No…it's not," the leader says, frustrated. He rushes towards Jordan and backslaps her across her face. "Where are they?!" he yells.

Ashton, Daniella, Blair and Seth watch the exchange between the paramilitary men and Jordan. Even though Ashton has her many problems and reasons to hate Jordan, something in her becomes outraged when he hits her. Ashton becomes so enraged she stands up and with her telekinetic abilities sends the leader flying across the room, landing on top of Jordan's desk. His soldiers quickly turn around to shoot Ashton. Just as they aim and fire, Angel and Ethan come storming in to help.

"Get down!" Angel shouts to Jordan and Natalie. With two quick shots, Angel takes down the remaining two soldiers. Everyone comes from out of cover, relieved it's all over. Daniella and Blair quickly rush to untie Natalie and Jordan.

"Are you okay, Lieutenant?" Angel asks.

"Yeah, I'm fine," Jordan says rubbing her wrist.

Ethan comes walking towards them with a barely conscious paramilitary leader. "What do you want me to do with him?" Ethan asks.

Jordan steps towards him, takes a moment to remember what all that took place, and gives him a right hook to the eye. "Take him down to lockup."

"What is going on?!" Daniella asks.

"We were breached. They were a secret paramilitary group looking for Experiment X, probably for themselves," Jordan explains.

"By the time we could shut everything down, they cornered us in here," Natalie continues.

"Me and Ethan cleared out the outside perimeter, lockup and the garage," Angel says.

"And me, Ashton and Daniella cleared out floors three through five," Blair says.

Angel looks around and doesn't see Ashton. "Ummm… where is Ashton?" she asks.

They all look behind them but Ashton is nowhere to be found.

They hear a small voice behind the couches. "It's okay, it's okay, it's okay," the voice says repeatedly and frantically.

Angel, Natalie, Jordan, Daniella and Blair rush over to the couches and see Seth frantically pressing his hands down on Ashton's left shoulder where she's been shot.

"Ash!" Angel cries out, running towards Seth on the floor.

"They must have shot her b-efore-ore you c-c-c-" Seth words begin to break, and his body begins to shake rapidly.

"What's going on?!" Angel shouts.

"Lieutenant!? Natalie?!" Blair says. She and Daniella watch as Jordan and Natalie stand in place and their bodies begin to shake and disappear like a glitch in a video game.

"Okay, I've always thought this place was weird, but this is on another level," Daniella says, watching as Seth, Jordan and Natalie's bodies slowly fade away as if they never existed, and the office fades with them.

"I don't care what's happening. Help me get Ash out of here!" Angel shouts, scared. Angel tries to lift Ashton by her shoulders, but she slips through. She looks down at her hands and they begin to fade. She knows she isn't entering her astral state, so it must be something else. "Th-this isn't right," Angel says confused. She turns to ask Blair and Daniella for help once more and see they too are fading away. "What's happening to us?" Angel whispers to herself as they all, including the Exodus agency, disappear into the light as if they never existed in this world.

Chapter 32

Frantically moving through the workshop, Natalie and Seth unplug Ashton from The LAND, checking her vitals. "Natalie, you said nothing would go wrong. What is happening?!" Jordan asks, suppressing her fear.

"It's fine. We just have to keep her stable long enough for her to come out of it," Natalie explains.

"She was shot. How can she even survive that, plus the strain on her mind?" Donovan asks.

"I said she can feel the effects of being shot, but in reality, temperature and pressure in the body go down significantly," Natalie continues to explain as she pushes a syringe into the IV in Ashton's arm.

"Vitals look stable. She should come out soon," Seth says as he runs a temporal thermometer across Ashton's forehead. "By the way, we're going to need to talk about the way you perceive me in your… virtual world," Seth whispers to Natalie.

Blair, Daniella, Ethan and Angel awaken from their slumber as if they've drowned and have suddenly been resuscitated. They wake up in pain, holding their heads and stomachs.

"What in the hell is going on?" Daniella asks in frustration.

"Where's Ashton?" Angel holds her stomach, lifting herself from the lab bed.

"Angel, you can't move," Natalie says.

"Where is my sister?!" Angel forcibly asks Natalie, in a way that anyone would do as she says.

"Angel, you, okay?" Ethan asks, worried for her well-being. Irritation runs across Donovan's face as he remembers the exchange between Ethan and Angel during The LAND. This is highly inappropriate, and he needs to intervene before their so-called developing relationship affects the team.

"I'll be okay once somebody tells me where my sister is." Fear increases Angel's tone.

"She's stabilizing. We're just waiting for her to wake up," Natalie says.

"Angel, she's right here," Jordan guides her to the bed at the end. Seth goes to examine Blair, Daniella, Ethan and Angel, making sure going into The LAND didn't throw them too much off balance with the real world. David watches from afar. He observes as Jordan oversees these girls and he wonders where he lost himself.

"I feel like somebody just ran me over with a semi," Blair groans.

"That's just the aftereffects. You guys will be fine in a couple of hours," Natalie explains.

"Hours?!" Blair exclaims.

"This is getting old," Daniella says.

"Why are you so loud?" Ashton whispers as she struggles to lift herself up from the bed.

"Ash!" Angel shouts, excited to see her moving and speaking. Ashton groans in pain, wanting Angel to lower her voice. Seth rushes to her aid, shining a flashlight pen in her eye.

"How are you feeling, Ashton?" Jordan hides her concern.

"I've been better, but what have you done to us now?" Ashton shoos Seth away from her face.

Upon waking up, believing she had dreamt everything that took place, the feeling of being shot made it more realistic than she had hoped. This is obviously one of Jordan's unnecessary tests.

"Natalie, care to explain?" Jordan asks, but more so telling.

"Not really, but okay," Natalie braces herself. "We put you through a virtual simulation that gave you the impression Exodus was under siege. We wanted to observe your full capabilities, including your special abilities," Natalie continues.

"Or you could have asked and we would have just showed you," Ashton speaks roughly.

"I'm with Ashton on this one," Daniella says.

"You're right, but I'd rather skip the pleasantries and get right to it," Jordan interrupts. "Plus, this was a much easier way to see you…honestly…at work."

"Wait, how did we even get here? I know I was asleep in my bed because it's almost six in the morning and I'm still in my sweats," Angel says.

Seth and Natalie give each other a look that suggests maybe they shouldn't tell them how they woke up in the lab. "We…entered your rooms and induced you with a substance that placed you into a REM sleep," Natalie fearfully explains.

"Oh, so you've entered the business of drugging people now?!" Ashton questions them.

"Drugging is a harsh word…it's more like a very peaceful day at the spa," Seth interjects, but they're not buying it.

"Okay, you saw what you wanted to see, now what?" Ethan asks. He's usually the one to observe rather than speak, but he's a part of this team now.

"Now, I know you guys are fully capable of being not only agents, but my agents for Exodus," Jordan says.

"Daniella, Blair…" she takes a moment to revel in the beauty of her daughters, "…Angel and Ashton, you can use your powers at will, if they're within reason."

"So, does that mean we have full access to…everything here?" Ethan asks.

"No, you don't," this catches David's attention, bringing him out of a sulking state. "There are restrictions for specific levels. You would be lucky if we let you hold a loaded gun," David storms out of the workshop.

"What's wrong with Buzz Lightyear?" Ashton asks.

"He's fine. The tough exterior is only for show," Jordan covers up their problems.

"I will see you all at nine for debriefing on your first mission," Jordan says, proud of them and remembering how a month ago they were four entirely different girls.

"That's in three hours," Daniella says.

"Then you better rest up," Jordan says, leaving the workshop. "Congratulations girls…and guy."

Leaving the kids to play, Jordan once again leaves to check on David.

"I thought I would feel different," Blair says believing she would have felt some type of accomplishment.

"Yeah, I thought I would feel important, powerful," Daniella agrees.

Donovan steps up. "You don't feel any different because you haven't done anything."

"Umm…excuse me Wall Street, we've done plenty. You should know. You were there at every one of our tortured sessions," Ashton says, hopping down from her bed feeling better.

"You showed us your skills, what you can do in a fight, and you've fought the fake bad guys. But you haven't been in the trenches where there are people out there who won't think twice about torturing or killing you," Donovan expresses to them.

"Wow, you forgot about us that fast," Ashton mocks him about the first time they met in the parking garage. "All of this fighting and the feeling of dying has my stomach talking. Let's go get some pancakes." Ashton leads the pack as they all, except for Donovan, bond for the few hours they have before going into their first mission. Who knows? It could be their last meal.

"Agent Carmichael, Agent Hunter, can I speak to you for a moment?" Donovan waits until everyone else has left the workshop so he can talk to Ethan and Angel privately.

"Cross," Angel says.

"Excuse me?" Donovan asks.

"My name…it's Cross, not Hunter. I'm not sure if Jordan told you," Angel politely corrects him.

"Well, Agent Cross, I don't know if Agent Hawthorne or Dr. Nolan have told you, but while you were in the virtual world, each of us out here were able to see everything that took place," Donovan continues to explain as confusion starts to enter the room.

"No, they haven't. But why is it important?" Ethan asks, not a fan of Donovan.

"I'm saying we saw everything from your plans, your routes, to you taking down the enemy, even your personal *conversations*," Donovan puts emphasis on conversation. Angel and Ethan know exactly where he's going with this conversation.

"Donovan, what are you trying to tell us?" Angel is annoyed by Donovan's condescending tone.

"This relationship needs to stop," he commands them. Ethan and Angel chuckle at his command and his thought of believing they would even consider doing as he says. And who said they were in a relationship? Angel steps to Donovan, ready to give him a piece of her mind, but Ethan, with his arm stretched out, stops her from going any further. He'll handle Donovan himself.

"I don't think that's any of your business…Agent," Ethan tries to intimidate Donovan, but he has no impact.

"It becomes my business when it starts to interfere with my missions and disrupts my agency," Donovan says, arms folded, leaning against the lab table.

"Oh, so now it's your missions and your agency. I don't remember Jordan telling us she was stepping down," Ethan responds.

Donovan says no more and walks away from Ethan before the situation escalates. "You either end it or I'll end it for you," Donovan says sternly. Ethan gets ready to attack Donovan from behind, but not before Angel stops him, pulling him back towards her.

"Leave it alone. He's not worth it," Angel says, calming him.

"I really hate that guy. He walks around like he owns the place," Ethan says. His anger and frustration are making Angel feel a way she doesn't think she ever felt before. She's warm inside and she has this weird feeling like butterflies are in her stomach. They've only known each other for a short time, but to see him protecting her, willing to fight for her, makes her overjoyed. She places her warm lips on his cheek, letting him know Donovan could never stop them from moving forward.

"We'd better go. Ashton hates sharing." Angel quickly changes conversation.

"You go ahead. I want the medics to look at my head. It's still kind of sore," Ethan says. As Angel leaves, Ethan never thought he would fall so deeply for her this quickly. He enjoys where this is going but he needs to be careful as it could ruin everything.

Continuing to go back and forth in conversation like an old married couple are David and Jordan. "I don't know why you can't just seem to understand why I couldn't tell you?!" Jordan shouts.

"Because I'm your partner, J! I could have helped you," David pleads to her.

"I know that," Jordan agrees, approaching him slowly and caressing his hands. "I know you would have done everything you could to help me, to help Maxwell." She lets her body touch his and begins caressing his masculine arms. "But you have to let others take the lead. If I would have told you back then what was going on, you would have been asked questions and then you would have been at risk of losing your job and I couldn't live with myself if I let that happen."

David tries to dismiss Jordan's advances, wanting to continue to be angry with her, but he can't. "Why is it that after every argument we have you always end up being the one who's right?" he asks, smiling down at her like she's the only person in the world that matters.

"It's a blessing and a curse," she says. They gaze deeply at one another.

"We'd better go prepare the kids for their first mission," David says, accepting the cards he's been dealt.

"I'll meet you down there. I have to grab some notes from my office."

As David leaves, Jordan stays back in his office and releases all the emotions she's been feeling for the past few hours. She breaks down. She just watched one of her daughters almost die and she can't find the courage to tell them the truth. "Okay, Savannah, breathe, you got this. Be ready, stay ready," she says, exhaling and pulling herself together, becoming the leader she's always known she could be.

Chapter 33

Has anybody ever been shot before?" Blair asks the group sitting around the operations floor.

"Does being shot at count?" Daniella replies.

Ashton snickers, "Not at all. I've been shot in the back of my calf and in my shoulder and, trust me, those are two completely different feelings."

"I've been shot in my thigh, and I still have random bursts of pain," Angel agrees.

Donovan stands nearby, separate from the group, but close enough he can hear the conversation.

"Yeah but being shot is quick. How about being stabbed and having the object left in your arm?" Daniella remembers her time in juvie. "It's slow and it's painful," she continues.

"You guys have had it rough," Natalie says as she sets up the screen for their mission briefing. She looks over to Seth who is close by, letting him know she was right. They're good people who just so happen to have been through more than the average teenagers.

"New York juvie, right?" Ashton asks.

"Yep. Rowdy Rochester," Daniella replies, "where you go in and never come out."

"You got out, so you must have done something right," Blair says.

"Yeah, I agreed to leave with Jordan."

Donovan, still listening to their conversation, joins. "Well, I commend you. It couldn't have been easy in there."

"I hate to agree with Wall Street over here, but I have much respect for you. I mean, I could never go to jail. I'm too cute for it," Ashton jokes. Everyone laughs at Ashton subliminally, lighting up the room. Even Donovan shows half a smirk.

"Hey, where's Ethan?" Seth asks.

"He had a headache, so he stayed back to get checked out," Angel replies. The room is silent for a moment as everyone looks at her.

"Of course, you would know," Ashton flippantly says.

Angel gives attitude towards her sister, wanting her to shut up.

"All right, team, let's get ready," Jordan says, marching in, commanding the room. "First off, congratulations and welcome to our new agents." Everyone in the room welcomes Angel, Ashton, Blair and Daniella to the team. They're happy to be a part, loving the idea of finally being accepted for who they are. "You have successfully passed every one of my tests. I'm proud of you…" Jordan says to them but discreetly smiling at her daughters. "… all of you," she changes.

"You sure? You don't have someone planting a bomb somewhere and then we have to go diffuse it?" Ashton asks with her irreverent tone.

"No, I don't, Ashton. Now you will only be doing missions I assign you," Jordan explains.

Ashton still looks at her, unsure she's telling the truth, but she'll go along with it for now for the sake of the "team." Jordan looks around the room. "Where is Agent Carmichael?" she asks.

"Angel knows," Blair jokes.

Angel pierces her eyes at her. "He wanted to get checked out by medical."

"Fine, we'll just have to fill him in later. Let's begin." Jordan uses a remote to navigate the enormous screen. "In four hours, every director of each intelligence agency in the United States will meet under one roof, here, at the National Intelligence Agency." She points to a picture of a layout of the NIA. "This man," the screen now displays a headshot of Silas Clay, "Ex-CIA and Phantom Agent Silas Clay, has summoned a meeting with the leaders of each agency and some members of the Executive Branch to get approval for his militia army," Jordan says, annoyed at the thought of Clay. "Our goal is to stop him from succeeding."

Angel studies the headshot of Clay on the screen. He has a sense of familiarity about him. She doesn't know where she saw him, but the memory isn't pleasant. Was it a past time, a vision or a dream, she thinks to herself. "Isn't this the man you told me about? The one who's trying to steal our powers?" Angel asks.

"Wait, what?!" Daniella has fought hard and for a long time to get away from the men who have been trying to get her. "You want us, who have been agents for not even a full day, to stop a rogue agent from creating a super army with our own powers?" Daniella continues, frightened at the thought.

"You won't be necessarily stopping him," David explains.

"Well explain, Captain, because I'm not too thrilled about the idea either," Ashton agrees.

"Stopping Silas is our secondary objective," David says.

"He's right. Our primary goal is to rescue and secure him," Jordan switches the screen to a headshot of a quirky man with square-rimmed glasses. "Dr. Martin Edwards worked alongside Dr. Hawthorne in the creation of the biochip. He was there from the beginning and Silas Clay has him…he's had him for some time now," Jordan remembers the days she searched for Martin and how hard it was to get him back. David notices Jordan struggling and steps up to finish explaining the mission.

"We assume Silas Clay will give a demonstration of the biochips at work," David continues commanding the room, doing what he does best, "and we need to stop that from happening."

Jordan gathers herself and takes back control of her briefing. Ethan quietly makes his way between the team circled around. "And this is where you all come in. We will take three points," Jordan gathers the team around the main operations table moving holographic images of the NIA building and schematics around. "Agent Carmichael, nice of you to join us," Jordan says.

Ethan nods.

"Captain and I will be in the meeting, so we'll keep our eyes on Silas. Angel, Blair and Daniella, you will be taking point on finding Dr. Edwards," Jordan stretches out a hologram of a room located a level beneath from where the meeting will be held. "You will secure him and bring him to transport. Ashton, Natalie and Ethan, you will take position here." Jordan shows a hidden road across from the entrance where Clay and his men will be located. "Clay never travels alone so I'm most certain that he will have his men on standby," Jordan continues.

"And Seth and I will be on standby in transport waiting for Dr. Edwards," Donovan interjects.

"So, we'll basically be doing all the work," Ashton says.

"Of course, it's the only way to prove yourself worthy of this team," Donovan patronizes her. Ashton disregards his comment, which holds little weight.

"The assignments I give you have nothing to do with who has more or less of the work. We're a team and that's what we're going to start thinking as - a team, we do what's best for the team and this way is what's best," Jordan expresses.

"May I suggest something?" Ethan asks with caution, not wanting to step out of place.

"Yes, Agent Carmichael," Jordan replies.

"Wouldn't it be best not to have half the team with superpowers in one place?" Ethan suggests.

"What do you mean?" David asks.

"You guys said he wants their powers. Sending three down there when we don't know what we're going to face is just giving him an advantage and for us, possibly three fewer team members," Ethan explains.

"So, what do you suggest we do…agent?" Donovan condescends.

"Let me go with Angel and Blair, and Daniella can stay with Ashton and Natalie-"

"Oh, here we go!" Ashton interrupts him, tired of him trying to push up on her sister. "I don't think it's the right time to be showing how much you want to stalk Angel."

"Ashton, quit it," Angel interjects.

"Unlike you, I care about what's best for the mission and the team," Ethan snaps back.

"That's enough!" Jordan interrupts the arguing. "Ethan, you will go with Angel and Blair, and Daniella you will take point with Natalie and Ashton. I don't want you guys at each other's damn throats and exposing us," Jordan enforces. "Be ready. We leave in an hour," Jordan says, leaving them surrounding the operations table.

"An hour?!" Blair says anxiously.

Jordan ignores her and continues walking. She has to go prepare herself; this will be the first time in 11 years she's going to be face-to-face with Clay and Martin. She wants to be focused and ready for anything. Clay will not get the best of her again.

"You guys can meet me in the armory for your new suits," Natalie says.

"Suits? We're not wearing the ones we've been wearing?" Angel asks.

"No, those were strictly for training, and it limited your abilities. With these suits, you'll have full control and some newly added upgrades," Natalie says, excitedly rushing to go prepare their suits.

"Right behind you, Nat," Seth says.

"Am I the only one who feels something is wrong here?" Blair asks.

"No, something is definitely going on, but we'll never find out," Ashton references the secrets Jordan keeps.

"You haven't gotten any visions lately?" Daniella asks.

"No, but we'll be fine. We've trained with Jordan and Donovan, and they know what they're doing. And we have something no one else has," Angel encourages her team.

"And that is?" Daniella asks.

Ashton, with the twirl of her wrist, levitates a pen in the air and flings it at the back of Daniella's head.

"Ow!" Daniella rubs her head, and they all start laughing, making their way to meet Natalie.

Donovan stays back to go over the mission briefing. He watches the developing camaraderie amongst the girls and realizes he never should have doubted Jordan. He can see they'll be a force to be reckoned with, unlike Ethan. There's something about him he doesn't like or care for, something is wrong. He especially enjoyed the way Angel brought them all together and eased their nerves. If she would focus more on her development as an agent rather than dating, she would be the best leader this agency has seen.

Chapter 34

The team makes their way on to the Tempest – a jet that is fully equipped with the top tech equipment only money can buy, but with a homelike environment. The size of the jet blew the girls away.

"I feel like I'm in an action movie," Blair says in awe. Blair and Daniella rush onto the plane, Ethan and Angel not too far behind.

Ashton stops at the entry to the hangar. She wants to move but can't. She stares at the size of the jet and her stomach drops.

"Hey Ashton, you ready to go?" Natalie comes from behind.

"Huh? Oh yeah, I'll be there in a minute. I was just checking to see if everything works in this suit," she gives Natalie an odd smile.

"Trust me, they do," Natalie smiles back and makes her way onto the Tempest.

Jordan enters the entryway as she goes over the mission details on her tablet. She looks up from the overflow of emails and sees a frozen Ashton. Jordan studies her for a moment. This could be the chance.

"Big, isn't it?" she says, moving beside her.

Ashton ignores her, continuing to stare at the jet.

"I remember the first time they brought it to me; I couldn't get on it for a week," Jordan tries to relate to her. "It's too much, you know? I like a simple ride…on the ground," she laughs.

Ashton hopes Jordan knows she's just wasting her time talking to her, so Jordan should just keep it moving.

"You haven't said more than a sentence to me since phase 3," Jordan says.

"That's more than you deserve," Ashton says, continuing to face forward, not acknowledging Jordan's presence.

"I didn't say anything to Dr. O'Conner," Jordan explains. "I had to see how strong you were. I only told her that your parents died, nothing more. She only asked you that question because she knew of your powers and came to her own conclusion."

Ashton is trying her hardest to ignore Jordan, but there's a voice in her head telling her to open a little and give people a chance. Angel's little pep talks are really aggravating. She turns to face Jordan. "Okay," Ashton slowly nods, believing Jordan's explanation.

"Okay? Just okay. No, 'I should kick your ass' or 'shut up lady, stop talking to me'?" Jordan says, surprised.

"Angel wants me to do this whole 'turn over a new leaf' thing and give people a chance or whatever, so I'm going to give you the benefit of the doubt and believe that's what happened. I still don't like you for it, but the very least I can do is give you a... chance," Ashton says, giving Jordan a pass.

"I guess...thank you," Jordan says, still slightly confused, but it's Ashton. Nothing is ever simple. They stand facing the jet for a moment until it becomes awkward. "So, you ready to go?" Jordan asks her.

"Yeah, of course, I'm just, you know," Ashton tries to come up with another excuse on why she's avoiding moving.

"Afraid of heights," Jordan reveals her fear before she tries to make another excuse for it.

"What?! No, I'm-" Just as Ashton is about to make yet another excuse, Jordan gives her a look that says, 'give it up'. "Yeah, I am."

"The fearless Ashton – afraid to be off the ground a few feet" Jordan mocks.

"One of my very few flaws," Ashton says.

"I promise it won't even feel like you're off the ground," Jordan reassures.

"Yeah, until I look out a window."

Jordan walks away laughing while giving Ashton some advice, "Are you really going to let your small fear stop you from taking down enemies like it's target practice?"

That does get Ashton excited. She takes a deep breath, exhales all her fears and makes her way on the jet where everyone is preparing for the mission.

"This isn't real. You have an entire living room on a plane!" Blair shouts excited. Cautiously walking onto the jet, Ashton is amazed at all the tech and equipment. It's the agency in the air.

"Hey Ash, I'm sorry," Angel says, leaving the excitement with Daniella, Blair and Ethan, forgetting her sister is afraid of heights and that she's normally the one to ease her fears and anxieties. "I saw the plane and got all excited about the mission. I just got distracted," Angel continues to spit out excuses, but Ashton knows her real distraction.

"It's okay, Ang, really, you were over there with your boy."

"Ash, what are you talking about that's not-"

"Angel…it's fine," Ashton walks away before she says something that will make her more upset than she already is, but not until she gives Angel some advice.

"I know you rarely take any advice that I give, but I'll tell you anyways. It's okay to have your guard up sometimes. Don't be so quick to trust everyone. Remember we learned that the hard way." Angel knows who she's referring to and she's right; she rarely takes her advice. Angel and Ashton join the rest of the team to relish in the joy of being on a private jet equipped with all the luxurious items a girl could only dream of.

"Every time I want to leave this place, it keeps pulling me back in," Daniella says, excited about what her future holds here at Exodus.

The team begins talking at once with excitement. Jordan watches from afar and enjoys the smiles on their faces. She's done something right.

"I definitely can get use to this," Ashton says, touching the large, digital, holographic table. "I can't wait to beat Clay and his men from here to mars," Ashton jokes, and everyone laughs with her, surrounding the table. For a moment, Ashton looks up and sees Jordan leaning against the Tempest's bar, staring and smiling directly at her.

Jordan knows she's been caught, so she diverts their attention. "If you think up here is cool, you all should go check out the armory downstairs," she says, approaching the table. There is something going on with Jordan and Ashton is noticing. She knows Jordan wanted to say something but couldn't. Natalie takes the team downstairs to the armory that houses every weapon she's created and designed and then some. Jordan keeps a professional smile on her face until they're all out of sight. She exhales deeply. If she doesn't focus herself soon, they will surely fail this mission. When would she tell them? Would they accept her? Thoughts spin through her head.

"We're about to land in a few minutes," David says, interrupting her thoughts.

"Okay…thanks," Jordan says.

David notices her deep in thought. "Are you okay?"

"Who me?! Of course, why wouldn't I be?" Jordan deflects the question.

"It's okay, I know what's going on," David says.

Jordan's stomach begins to turn into knots. What does he mean, he knows?! If he knows, then surely Angel and Ashton have their suspicions. "Kn-know what?"

"You're nervous to see Clay. We haven't seen him in years," David explains.

Jordan lets out a small chuckle. This secret is making her lose her mind – and how dare David think she could ever be nervous, much less nervous about Silas Clay. "I was just going over the plan in my head," Jordan reassures him, "and I'm fine. Clay should be more nervous about us." She pats his chest and walks away to go over the plan.

Downstairs in the armory, the girls and Ethan, along with Natalie and Seth, are prepping for the mission. "I want that one and that one, oooooo and that one, too," Ashton says, getting her pick of the melee weapons along the wall while everyone else chooses their gun of choice.

"What's with you and knives? Why not a gun? It's quick and at the right aim you can take out any man," Daniella says, examining a rifle.

"You just answered your own question," Ashton replies. "A gun is quick and easy, but a knife," Ashton runs her fingers across the blade of a US Military Bayonet, "a knife is personal. Your enemy suffers and when they're pleading for you to stop, that's when you know you've won," Ashton explains.

"Well, you know what they say, 'never bring a knife to a gun fight'," Daniella says.

"Oh, don't get it twisted. I can handle a gun when I need to," Ashton expresses. Strangely, Daniella and Ashton just connected in their own way.

"Are you doing anything for your birthday?" Seth asks Natalie as they test equipment at a nearby table.

"It's not a big deal. I have bigger things to worry about," Natalie says.

"It's your birthday?! How old are you going to be?" Blair is excited.

"Sixteen, like any other age," Natalie says nonchalantly.

"It's your sweet 16; you have to be doing something," Blair expresses.

"Nat, you only get one," Angel agrees.

"It's not a big deal. I never cared for birthdays," Natalie expresses.

"Well, I think you need to turn up one good time, loosen up, let down your hair, throw away the glasses," Ashton dances around Natalie.

"Let's just worry about the mission, okay?" Natalie says.

Everyone finishes prepping. They gather their specific weapons and tighten up their suits. Ashton reaches into her duffle bag and pulls out a pill bottle, tossing it to Angel. "Here, I almost forgot, you should take them before you have another episode."

"Thanks." Staring at the pill, Angel wishes this wasn't her life. She's been taking medicine to control her powers since she was a child. She wants to stop.

"If you don't want to take it, then don't," Ethan says, watching her study the bottle.

"I wish it was that simple, but if I don't, I won't be of any use to anyone," Angel opens the bottle to take her pill.

Ethan gently grabs her hand to stop her. "Have you ever thought maybe it's the medicine that has your visions acting up?" He tosses the pill in the trash. "I think you can handle yourself," he says, smiling down at her, giving her comfort.

Angel leaves the pill bottle in a locker; she's starting over.

"We're about to drop. ETA three minutes," Donovan speaks over an intercom in the cockpit. The rest of the team comes together around the HoloTable on the main level of the jet.

"Does everyone remember their assignments?" Jordan asks. Everyone agrees, although some nod nervously. "This mission is delicate; we can't go in this being sloppy. Everything must be done right or we will fail. This is not a virtual world; this is real life. If you mess this up, you will die," Jordan continues to give her own version of encouraging words. "Clay and his team will not take it easy on us, but I know we can stop him, so let's do what we do best."

As the Tempest lands, everyone understands their assignments. Donovan drops the team off in a forest preserve 30 miles away from the Office of the National Intelligence Agency. Jordan and David make their way to a private SUV as Angel, Ashton, Daniella, Blair, Natalie and Ethan make their way on to an all-white florist van with *Sunshine Florists* advertised on the side.

"So, they get to ride in looking like VIPs and we get to ride in the rusty van that smells like old fertilizer," Daniella says.

"It's meant for them to be seen. We're the ones going undercover," Natalie says, sliding the van doors open to reveal more tech; it's her lab on wheels. They all pile in and Natalie hands them all their designated equipment. "We will communicate with these," Natalie hands them a small listening device that sits inside their ear and only visible when taken out.

"They're so small," Blair says.

"Yes, but don't underestimate them. The receiver has a 3,000-mile radius, and with my specifications you can also see whatever your communicator is seeing," Natalie continues.

"Really?!" Ethan is fascinated. "And how does that work?"

"From here," Natalie spins around in her office chair and shows them the computer system. "I can control everything here, from what you're viewing to what you're hearing."

"Interesting," Ethan says.

"Life of an agent always is," Natalie replies. Natalie begins pressing buttons near her computer system.

"Am I patched in?" a voice on the screen asks.

"Yes, Lieutenant," Natalie says, bringing up a videocall of Jordan.

"Are you guys ready?" Jordan asks everyone in the van.

"Always," Ashton says, sitting back relaxed.

"Great. Remember: stay focused and confident. You got this," Jordan encourages.

"I may be wrong here, but this is the headquarters for all secret intelligence agencies in the Unites States, right?" Angel asks.

"Correct," Jordan answers.

"How are we supposed to sneak our way past their security? I see the future. I'm not invisible," Angel asks

"Oh, I'm not expecting you to. Nat." Jordan signals Natalie to surprise them with a large bouquet of flowers, "Those will do it for you. Blair, how quickly can you conjure up flowers?"

"Pretty quick. That was the first thing I could make," Blair says, excited about her role.

"Perfect. Take the uniform and Natalie will give you further instructions once inside."

Natalie gives Blair and Angel all-tan jumpsuits with matching hats and the company name, Sunshine Florists, advertised.

"How are a bunch of flowers supposed to get us past the most advanced security system in the country?!" Ethan says with disbelief.

"Well one, the NIA wishes their security system was as advanced as mine, and two, let's just say Director Warren is expecting them," Jordan replies. "Remember you guys will be on your own. I can't help you," Jordan explains to them once again.

"Excuse me. I hate to interrupt these encouraging words, but I can't help but to hear the lack of confidence spilling out of your mouth," Ashton comments.

"Ashton, you're an 18-year-old and have been a government agent for all of twelve hours, so you're going to have to excuse me if I'm a little tense."

"I guess that makes sense," Ashton irreverently agrees.

"I'll see you guys soon," Jordan leaves.

"We're here," one of the drivers say over a speaker in the back of the van.

"Blair and Angel, you will take the front entrance while Ethan, you'll wait on my signal from Angel. Then you can enter this side entrance," Natalie shows them a layout of the NIA building, exterior and interior. "Wait for Angel and Blair and then you can proceed to retrieving Dr. Edwards." Angel, Blair and Ethan leave the van.

"And what do we do?" Daniella asks.

"We wait," Natalie replies, turning on overhead screens inside the van, displaying surveillance of the perimeter of the NIA building.

Chapter 35

Jordan and David walk with their heads held high as they move through the busy hallways of the NIA. It's hard to distinguish who are the agents and who everyone else is unless there's a badge attached to them. The men walk around dressed in high-end black suits and the women wear top-notch pants suits or expensive dresses.

"What is the game plan?" David asks, entering the exclusive elevator only used by high-level agents and directors. He places his badge on a scanner and scans his thumb print.

"As far as they know, we're only here on director business," Jordan says. "Once Natalie gives us the signal they have Martin, we're out of here." They exit the elevator to an unauthorized floor, where only confidential information is discussed.

"I haven't seen him." It's hard for David to mention Clay's name, especially around Jordan.

"Knowing Clay, he would want to make an entrance." Just thinking about being in the same room with him makes her skin crawl. The directors from each intelligence agency in the country are here today. Some have entered the boardroom, and others are waiting in the hallway for the meeting to begin. "I'll meet you inside," Jordan says as she spots Director Crystal Warren by herself away from the boardroom. "Don't you just love these things?" Jordan says, walking towards her, getting her attention as she looks down at her phone.

"What? You mean being in a room full of men with egos bigger than their bank accounts?" Crystal replies. "No."

Jordan takes a moment to confess to her friend, "They're here."

"Savan-," Crystal pauses, almost revealing something she shouldn't. "J, what the hell are you thinking? They're nowhere near ready to be in the field, even if they have superpowers," Crystal expresses.

"Supernatural powers, big difference," Jordan says irreverently.

"Same difference." Crystal pulls Jordan out of sight from the rest of the directors. "Every director in the country is here," she says. "What do you think will happen if they were to get caught by one of them or another agent?" Crystal waits for a reply from Jordan. "It will be over, that's it, nothing left for you or me."

Jordan isn't sure if this is the time to tell her friend her daughters are back in her life. She doesn't want to cause any more problems and add any more pressure. "Right now, Clay has a device in this building that can create a super army. I had no choice," Jordan defends, "especially since you gave me rundown agents to work with in the first place."

"That was my father that assigned them to you. I just hope you know what you're doing."

"Don't I always," Jordan smiles as she walks back into the boardroom. Crystal is not too far behind.

They enter a room filled by an oversize table, so large that one would question how they got it in there. Being only two of three women in the room, Jordan and Crystal sit on opposite sides of the table where their nameplates specify.

The director of the NIA sits at the head of the table. Clay sits at his right hand. "Thank you all for attending this meeting, especially with your busy schedules," the director proceeds with caution as he speaks to a room full of people who don't know why they're there and would rather be somewhere else. The director stands firm, tightening his tie. "As you all should know, our success rates in missions have not increased; we need better outcomes. So, when I was approached with an offer to help with those success rates indefinitely, I considered it." Confusion flows throughout the room. The directors know their success rates have been appropriate. "I'm sure you all are familiar with Silas Clay." Clay proceeds to lean forward to look down at the table full of directors, waving his hand and smiling haughtily. "He has created an initiative; it will advance us."

The room begins to erupt with murmurs. "Sir, with all due respect, why are we here wasting our time with this man who has committed numerous crimes?" Director Davis of the FBI says passionately.

"Those crimes you speak of were mostly accusations, and Agent Clay has served his time…respectively," Director Mills states.

"Ex," Jordan says under her breath but loud enough for the director of the NIA and everyone else in the room to hear.

"Excuse me?" he says, feeling disrespected.

Jordan turns her chair to face Director Mills. "I said 'ex'. He's an ex-agent and everyone in this room knows if he was anyone else, he wouldn't be allowed to step foot at the front door, let alone on the property."

"I have to agree with Lieutenant Knox. We're putting our jobs in jeopardy just by being in the same room," Director Burns of the DEA says.

Director Mills begins to take back control of the meeting, but Clay proudly stands.

Jordan, with red filling her eyes and fire burning in her chest, watches as Clay arrogantly places his hand on the director's shoulder, guiding him back down to his seat while he takes the head of the table. "I understand there are concerns about my presence here. Many of you may feel that I'm presumptuous, frightening, intimidating," Clay slowly makes eye contact with David and Jordan. "But that's going to change. The forces outside this country are more advanced and it's more than clear we're failing," he begins to show schematics on the wall-size projector screen. "This is Project X, a new initiative that will allow agents and soldiers to act as one. With this," he takes the biochip out of his pocket and the directors are bewildered at the object he's holding up, "we can merge one army: the military, navy, air force, and intelligence. One force, under one roof." Clay is superior in his speech. The room is in disbelief. One army – he's crazy.

"You want to combine all our militia forces into one? That's impossible! Sir?! Are we really entertaining this?" Director Clark of the NSA questions.

"Director Clark," Clay calls out, "there is no such thing as the impossible because only with determination can you move heaven and earth.".

"Well Clay, how do you specifically plan to merge all of our forces?" Director Warren asks, ready for this meeting to be over.

"Why, supernatural forces, of course," Clays says so naturally.

The room is quiet for a moment. Jordan holds her head down in shame. She can't believe she let it get this far.

"Supernatural forces? So, you plan on giving our military superpowers?" Director Warren asks, trying her best to covertly persuade the other directors to vote against him. "Now that's impossible and too big of a risk to take."

"It's unfortunate that you feel that way. I can't fault you for your ignorance and disbelief, but I can assure you this project has been proven successful by one of the most knowledgeable men in the world and for sure the most brilliant scientist in our intelligence agency division," Clay begins taunting Jordan. "And I'm sure Lieutenant Knox can attest to his credibility."

All eyes are on Jordan. She isn't fazed; she knows exactly what Clay is doing. "I'm not sure I know what you're talking about."

"Oh, come on!" he dramatically shouts and then proceeds to taunt her. "You of all people should know Dr. Hawthorne. He worked with us at Phantom," he turns his attention on to David. "You remember, don't you, Captain? He created this exact experiment in your lab." Clay smiles, waiting for an idiotic response to come out of his mouth.

"I don't recall any experiments done in my agency," David says, trying his best not to leap across the table and choke Clay.

"Well, it doesn't matter now. What matters now is that I can show you what the biochip can do."

"I think we should vote first. It will save us all a lot of time and energy," Director Warren says.

Director Mills takes back control of the room, Clay still standing beside him. "We've heard an abundance of information today and it's best we consider all the possibilities. I believe this initiative would put us ahead of any country. We'll be ahead of our time. I encourage you all to take that into consideration."

Everyone begins to vote, the outcome fifteen to three by raised hands. "You all have made your decisions. Project X has been denied," Director Mills announces.

Clay is oddly calm and Jordan notices. She signals Natalie through a silent beeper within the sleeve of her shirt, tapping it three times to proceed as planned and find Dr. Edwards immediately. The meeting ends, and Clay exits without a word to anyone. He's oddly content with the outcome. Jordan and David quickly follow behind.

Chapter 36

B lair? Blair? Blair?!" Natalie calls out for a response through Blair's earpiece.

"Oh! yes, I hear you now. I'm still trying to figure this thing out." Blair rubs her ear.

"All you have to do is talk. It's simple," Natalie explains.

"Got it. Talk and button."

"Do you remember what to do?" Natalie asks.

"Yes, while I sweet talk security, Angel unlocks the doors and then we meet up with Ethan."

"Great, see you soon," Natalie says, exiting the connection.

"Are you ready?" Angel asks.

"No readier than you," Blair says as she sees how uneasy Angel appears. They dust off their floral uniforms and walk through the front doors of the NIA. Blair carries in the large bouquet. "We are walking into a building filled with government agents and if we're caught, I'm pretty sure they will have no problem throwing us in jail," Blair whispers to Angel.

"Then we better use every bit of training we learned in the last month," Angel says.

They approach the front desk, which is more like a room, before they're officially inside the building. The secretary continues to work, not paying any attention to Blair or Angel.

"Sign the delivery sheet," he says.

As Angel signs the tablet, she notices they want a thumb print scan. Angel and Blair are concerned.

Angel covertly rubs her ear to get Natalie's attention. "We just place our thumb here?" Angel asks the secretary, hoping Natalie can help her.

"Not a problem guys, place your thumb on the scanner and give me two seconds and… a thumb print has been scanned," Natalie says working her magic at her computers.

Blair stares at the secretary, anxious to speak. Angel taps her foot to speak up. "We have a special delivery for Director Crystal Warren. It's from her husband," Blair says.

"That's fine," the unexpressive secretary says. "Someone will give them to her. You can go." He motions them to exit.

"B-but Mr. Warren required that these be delivered specifically to her. I mean we have a song and a dance," Blair is telling the secretary anything she can. "Do you really want to tell the director of the CIA why she couldn't get her song and dance?!"

"Leave or take the flowers; it's up to you," the secretary says, not giving in to Blair's antics.

"Fine," Blair hands him the large bouquet. "There's more." As Blair was trying to talk to the secretary, she was conjuring up small bouquets on the floor. Blair and Angel bend down to pick up the flowers and they sit them on the desk, obstructing the view of the secretary. Angel bends down one last time and she braces herself to enter astral mode. As her astral self, Angel quickly walks behind the desk and uses the USB drive Natalie gave her to override any computer. Inserting the device, she overrides the side door and the door leading to the floor where Dr. Edwards is being stored. She returns to her physical body, kneeling on the floor as if she's tying her shoe. "And here's this and then this one, oh and you can't forget this one, they're lilies," Blair continues to give the secretary flowers.

"And that's all. Please make sure Director Warren receives them," Angel says, signaling Blair for them to leave.

Leaving the building, Angel tries to contact Ethan. "Ethan, we're on our way. Ethan?"

"Maybe you're doing it wrong," Blair suggests.

Blair presses the button on her earpiece. "Hey, Ethan? Say something, anything."

In the van, Natalie looks on her overhead screens to see what has happened to Ethan. "He's standing by the door. Maybe his connection went bad."

Angel and Blair quickly make their way around to the side of the building with Natalie as their guide.

"Stop. Two agents coming up," Natalie directs them to take cover. "Clear."

Angel and Blair proceed. They meet Ethan by the side door.

"Hey, we were trying to reach you. What happened?" Angel asks.

"I kept hearing static, so I took it out for a minute. Why? What happened?" he asks, concerned.

"We gave them the flowers, but I don't think we have that much time before they figure out the director's husband isn't that romantic," Angel says.

Angel and Blair quickly take off their florist uniforms, only having on their specialty designed suits. They enter the building and make their way down the stairs.

"We are aware there may be guards everywhere down here, right?" Blair reminds them.

"Then let's have some fun," Ethan smirks, readying his weapon as he pushes open the NIA lab doors. They covertly make their way across the balcony of the lab.

"The silence in here is very disturbing," Angel says, the balcony creaking as they walk along.

Looking below, the NIA lab is no bigger than a baseball field and the lab rooms are surrounded by glass walls. The lab is filled with technology only used by the most well-renowned scientists in the world.

"Maybe the scientists went on break," Blair says.

"All of them? At the same time?" Angel asks, knowing that's not possible.

"Well, they clearly went somewhere," Ethan says, pointing down to four men dressed in all black with guns in their hands and on other parts of their bodies where a gun can fit. The men are surrounding Dr. Edwards, who is working erratically.

"Ok, this should be easy. It's only four of them," Angel says.

"Don't forget why we're here. They may already be injected with the biochip," Blair warns. Angel looks below and studies Dr. Edwards' area.

"Follow my lead," Angel says, moving forward. They continue to covertly make their way through the labs until they reach the outside room where four of Clay's men are guarding the outside room where Dr. Edwards is being kept. "Blair, think you can come up with a distraction?" Angel asks as they take cover on the side of room.

"No problem," Blair says.

They split up. Angel and Ethan wait for an opening as Blair takes a moment to embrace her powers and approaches two guards blocking the door.

"Hello," Blair surprises them. They aim their weapons, ready to shoot. Unfortunately, they're not quick enough. Blair conjures vines to wrap around their feet and quickly move up to wrap around their wrists. Their guns fall to the ground. "Cool, isn't it?" Blair asks as they struggle to set themselves free.

Angel and Ethan come from opposite sides of the room and hit the guards with the butt of their weapons, knocking them out cold.

"Nice," Angel compliments Blair's powers.

"Thanks," she says.

Ethan slowly opens the door, noticing the guards aren't paying attention. Ethan, Angel and Blair rush in, attacking the remaining two guards. The guards start to fire their weapons. Blair takes cover near Dr. Edwards, who strangely is continuing to work. Angel, knowing they don't have much time, uses the reflection from a metal canister on the lab counter and aims her weapon from cover to shoot one of the guards in the knee. He falls over and she comes from out of cover to shoot him once more. Unknown to Angel, the final guard hasn't been taken down yet. He aims his weapon and fires at Angel. He misses and falls over. He's been shot by Ethan.

Angel turns around, relieved. "Thanks."

"Told you I had your back," Ethan smiles at her.

"Can you guys flirt another time?" Blair says, coming out from behind the lab table where Dr. Edwards is working.

Dr. Edwards continues to work, mixing chemicals and messing with wires. "Got to see it through, no Leviathan, no Leviathan," he whispers repeatedly to himself.

They know something isn't right. They approach Dr. Edwards cautiously. "Hi, Dr. Edwards. We're with Exodus," Blair calmly says. He ignores her and continues to work. "Great – a mad scientist," Blair says.

Angel contacts Natalie through her earpiece. "Natalie, we got him. Be there soon."

"You might want to hurry. The meeting is over and you'll be expecting company soon," Natalie warns.

"Guys, we got to move," Angel says.

"Tell him that," Ethan says as Dr. Edwards moves from one end of the lab table to the other, continuing to create multiple biochips.

"Dr. Edwards, we have to go now. Your life is in danger," Angel leans towards him across the table, trying to look him in his eyes.

"No, no, no, no, no, no, no, got to see it through, no Leviathan," he spills out.

"What's a Leviathan?" Blair asks.

"Dr. Edwards, what do you have to see through? How can we help?" Angel places her hands on his hands, and he snatches away. Back to work he goes.

"We don't have time for this." Ethan approaches Dr. Edwards and lands a right hook to his face.

"Ethan! What are you doing?!" Angel shouts.

"Do you want to risk getting caught? In and out, remember?" Ethan says, lifting Dr. Edwards around his shoulders.

"Works for me," Blair says, leading the way out of the labs and back up the staircase.

Natalie, Daniella and Ashton wait patiently inside the florist's van parked near the courtyard of the NIA building for Clay's men to arrive.

"Why do I feel like I'm on a stakeout?" Ashton says, sitting in the back of the van, feet up, eating a bag of gummy bears.

"How did you manage to grab candy before we left?" Daniella asks.

"If you thought I was going to sit in this rust bucket with no food, you were clearly mistaken," Ashton replies.

"Point taken," Daniella says, snatching Ashton's gummy bears and grabbing a few for herself.

"Everyone should be here in approximately ten minutes," Natalie says. "And Clay should be exiting in five."

"Is this what you do all day?" Ashton asks.

"What do you mean?" Natalie replies.

"Like sit in a van and hack stuff," Ashton says.

"Ummm…no, I do other things," Natalie continues to work on her computer. "I make weapons, devices, the armor you're wearing and -"

"No, have you ever been in the field?" Ashton continues.

"Jordan doesn't think I'm ready for that," Natalie says.

"What? With your abilities you can take down anyone," Daniella says.

"Exactly. I can hurt anyone," Natalie says with sadness.

"You just have to embrace your abilities, which I have been teaching you how to do," Ashton says with confidence.

"And I'm grateful," Natalie smiles.

"So, what do you want for your birthday," Daniella says, remembering it's Natalie's birthday today.

"I actually haven't thought about it. Birthdays were never a big deal to me," Natalie says.

"Are you serious?! It's the one day where it's all about you and no one can say or do anything about it," Ashton tries to get Natalie excited.

"It's also the day that reminds you of when you were born." A gloomy and dreary mood comes over Natalie and she goes back to working on her computer.

"Isn't that the point?" Ashton asks before thinking.

Daniella kicks Ashton, wanting her to think before opening her big mouth. She tilts her head towards Natalie, and Ashton realizes she put her foot in her mouth.

"I still think you need to celebrate; it's your sixteenth birthday," Ashton says, trying to recover.

"If you don't do something, we're doing something for you," Daniella encourages her.

Natalie looks back and smiles. "I'll think about it."

Ashton, Daniella and Natalie continue to wait in the van for Clay, or anyone, to appear. "How long does it take one man to leave a building?" Daniella says, watching the front entrance of the NIA building on one of the overhead screens.

"I wouldn't be surprised if the lieutenant or the captain stopped him," Natalie says.

"Of course they did," Daniella says.

"Hey, so I may not know much about tech or whatever, but isn't the point of surveillance meant to have the camera pointing away from us?" Ashton says, standing to look at the overhead cameras.

"What? The cameras are pointing away from us," Natalie looks at the same screen and is confused as to how her surveillance footage became disrupted. "This can't be right." She checks her connection at her workspace, and she notices someone hacked her. "How?! No! This can't happen!" Natalie becomes anxious. She's never been hacked.

Ashton watches the surveillance footage of the courtyard; she notices a black van circling the driveway. Watching it closely, something about it doesn't feel right. The black van stops, facing the side of their van. "This has to be Clay. Maybe he has someone working inside and they know we're here," Natalie says, quickly trying to fix her cameras and add more security.

"I think we have a bigger problem," Daniella says, pointing to the screen showing Clay exiting a side door with two guards. "Where's his army?" Daniella asks.

"Hey." Ashton tries to get their attention.

"Something's not right. I'll contact Jordan," Natalie says.

"Guys!?" Ashton shouts again. "We need to move."

"Why?" Daniella asks.

The black van revs their engine and begins speeding towards their van.

"Move!" Ashton shouts, pushing them away from the side of the van that's about to get plowed. Ashton jumps out from the back of their van and rushes to face the black van head on. Daniella and Natalie watch as Ashton risks her life. Ashton stretches her hands out and with her telekinetic abilities slows down the van. The tires screech as the driver tries to fight Ashton's powers, but he's no match. The tires explode and the engine bursts, sending the van into smoke.

"Ashton!" Daniella warns Ashton to prepare for a fight. Clay's men come by the dozens from multiple areas around the NIA building. They don't waste any time and fire their weapons at the florist van. Ashton runs to take cover inside the van with Daniella and Natalie. "How did they know we were here?!" Daniella shouts over the bullets ricocheting off the van and the screams of NIA workers.

"We can figure that out later. Where is everybody else?!" Ashton yells.

Natalie takes cover on the floor and grabs her receiver to contact Jordan, "Lieutenant?! We're being ambushed. Clay must have known we were here!"

Jordan stops following Clay once she hears Natalie and the chaos through her earpiece. "Do you have Dr. Edwards?!"

"No! They haven't arrived yet," Natalie says, trying to stay in as much cover as she can.

"Okay, just hold tight. I'm on my way," Jordan says calmly. She and David rush back to the entrance. "Donovan, get to the courtyard now," Jordan demands over her earpiece.

"Nat, contact Angel and tell them to get here now! I'm not just going to sit here," Ashton says, getting up and loading her weapons. "Are you with me?" she asks Daniella.

"I got your back," Daniella says.

Ashton and Daniella leave the van. Slowly and covertly, they make their way to Clay's men. They take cover behind a nearby concrete wall. Ashton, with the flick of her wrist, launches one of the men into the black van and she begins to fire her weapon from out of cover. Daniella aims her gun and quickly begins to fire at anyone that looks like they're with Clay. She stands from out of cover and stretches her hands towards a group of Clay's men and lets out a small blast, destroying their weapons and making them fall back, unconscious.

"We need to get out of here! Where are they?!" Daniella shouts for Angel, Blair and Ethan to get here as soon as possible.

Blair, Angel and Ethan, with Dr. Edwards laying across his shoulders, run from the side of the building to meet the rest of the team in the parking lot.

"We're almost there," Blair encourages, excited they've made it this far until she hears the gunshots and blasts from the parking lot near the courtyard where they're supposed to meet everyone.

"What was that?!" Angel asks, hearing the noise as well.

"It's coming from the lot, we need to go…now," Blair says as they sprint towards the parking lot.

Unfortunately, they've been cut off by someone on a black and white Kawasaki 300 Ninja motorcycle. That someone takes off their white and black tinted helmet, shaking their long crimson hair. It's Alexandria.

"And where are you going?" she asks.

"Look, I don't know who you are, but you need to move now!" Angel says, worrying about the rest of her team.

"Yeah, that's not going to happen," Alexandria taunts. She steps off her bike and moves closer to Blair and Angel; they're now face to face. "Until you give me the doctor." They realize she's on Clay's team.

"That's not happening," Angel says. She looks over to Blair who can't help but to stare at her. Angel nudges her.

"Right, you're not touching him," Blair shakes off the feeling she gets from staring into Alexandria's heterochromia eyes.

Alexandria pulls out a gun from her leather jacket and aims it at Blair. "Either you drop the doctor or I'm putting a bullet in this beauty."

Angel gets ready to lunge for the woman, but she stops. "Oh no, watch it," Alexandria says pulling down the hammer of the gun ready to fire.

"All right!" Ethan shouts, carefully placing an unconscious Dr. Edwards on the ground.

"That's a good boy," Alexandria taunts them. She moves the gun away from Blair and two men come from behind Ethan to take Dr. Edwards away.

"Hmm…You're not as dumb as you look," she says to Angel as she walks away.

Angel refuses to fail. She sprints towards Alexandria, ready to punch her with all her strength, but Alexandria quickly turns towards her. She deeply stares into Angel's eyes, and they begin to turn grey like smoke from a flame.

"Angel!" Ethan calls out.

Angel immediately stops. She turns to face Blair.

"Angel? What's wrong?" Blair can see Angel is not herself. She looks at Alexandria and can see the similarity in her eyes as well; Alexandria is controlling Angel.

Angel faces Blair and tightens her fist. "Angel, this is not you," Blair says. "She's controlling you…in a very weird way, but it's not you." Blair is trying her best to stop Angel from turning her face black and blue.

Alexandria gets back on her bike. "Don't worry, it won't last long," she smiles, her eyes still smoke grey.

Angel punches Blair in the nose, causing Blair to fall back, nose beginning to leak with blood. "I'm not going to fight you…even though you're making it really hard," Blair says.

Angel leaps on top of her, ready to punch her once more, until the control is stopped. Ethan has snuck his way behind Clay's men and attacks them. This startles Alexandria, breaking her manipulation with Angel. Ethan continues to fight off both men as Angel tries to gain back control over herself. Alexandria lets her men handle Ethan; she takes her gun out once more. Angel and Blair are unaware of Alexandria behind them. She aims and pulls the trigger. Angel and Blair are still on the ground. They duck and cover their heads, believing they've been shot.

"Are you okay?!" Angel asks Blair.

"Aside from getting punched in the face, yeah, I'm good," Blair pats herself down.

They quickly stand to see Donovan fighting Alexandria. He's blocking her hits as he lands a couple of his own in her face and abdomen.

"Get the doctor and go!" Donovan shouts as Alexandria jumps and spins her right leg, kicking him in the jaw.

As Ethan and Donovan fight with Alexandria and her back-up, Angel and Blair quickly make their way to Dr. Edwards sitting sluggish in the back seat of a BMW. Blair wraps one of Dr. Edwards' arms around her shoulder and Angel takes the other. They rush towards the courtyard where bullets are still flying.

"Ang! Blair!" Ashton shouts seeing them from a distance.

Angel and Blair attempt to make their way to the van, but there's too many of Clay's men in their way. They're trapped. Ashton can see they need help. She stands firm, lifts her hands in the air and lets out a huge blast. Most of Clay's men were in the radius of the blast. They flew sky high and some of the windows of the NIA building took a hit too. Angel and Blair see their opportunity to make a run for it; they're almost to the van.

"What happened to you guys?!" Daniella asks, struggling to help them bring Dr. Edwards to the van.

"Yeah, because me and Daniella are out here risking our lives while you guys go sight-seeing," Ashton says as she helps carry Dr. Edwards in the van.

"Really not the time Ash," Angel says.

"Lieutenant, we have Dr. Edwards," Natalie says over her earpiece.

"Get to the Tempest. We're bringing an extra passenger," Jordan replies.

Jordan and David were able to catch up with Donovan and Ethan. Ethan taken down two guards on his own and Donovan has detained Alexandria. Jordan helps to handcuff Alexandria and they put her in the truck with them.

"He played us again!" David says, speeding out of the NIA parking lot.

"I hate it just as much as you do, but we've got him on this one. It's going to take him awhile to have his army without director approval," Jordan reassures.

Alexandria lets out a small chuckle that escalates to full-blown laughter.

"Somebody shut her up!" David commands.

"I'm sorry, but the fact that you think you've got the upper hand in this is hilarious," Alexandria continues to laugh.

"And I'm sure you're going to tell us why," Jordan says, annoyed, as she keeps busy on her phone.

"Oh no, you're going to find that out all on your own," Alexandria says, smiling at Ethan as he places tape over her mouth.

Jordan and David realize there may be more coming their way now that they've stopped the plans of Clay and his militia.

Chapter 37

Angel, Blair, Ashton, Daniella and Natalie fight their way away from what's left of Clay's men. "Is he secured?!" Angel shouts to the van where Natalie and Blair are strapping in an unstable Dr. Edwards. Angel helps Ashton and Daniella shoot the rest of Clay's henchmen.

"We're good, lets-" Blair is interrupted by a shot heard from inside the van that's startles her and Natalie.

"What was that?!" Ashton shouts.

Blair checks the front of the van to see their drivers, agents at Exodus, shot. "Ummm…we have a problem," Blair calls out to them. They rush to the front of the van. Blair shows them the bullet holes in the chests of the drivers.

"What do we do? Jordan is expecting us to be at the jet right now and these guys keep popping up!" Daniella asks.

Ashton runs around to the driver's side. "Blair, help me get these guys out of here." Ashton tosses out the driver and gets in his place.

"What are you doing?!" Natalie panics as they don't follow the plan.

"If you want to stay here, that's on you. I didn't sign up to die today," Ashton puts the car in drive and takes off.

"Ash, you need to drive a little faster," Angel says.

"I'm driving as fast as I can. I don't think Jordan is going to care about how late we are," Ashton replies.

"No, Ashton you really need to speed it up," Daniella says, distressed, looking out the rear windows with Angel. Clay's men have caught up with them.

Ashton looks in her side mirror and starts to drive faster. "Let's have some fun, boys," Ashton says with an arrogant grin as she speeds and weaves through traffic.

"Be careful! There's sensitive equipment back here!" Natalie shouts to Ashton as she tries to keep her balance through Ashton's speeding.

"Are you really protecting your computer over your life right now?" Ashton asks. In an all-black suburban, Clay's men speed on the side of the van. "Ang, on your left," Ashton says, able to see them on her side as they pull out their guns to fire at them. Angel opens the back side windows of the van and begins to shoot on sight. They shoot back at her and the bullets fly inside the van. "It would be nice if we could keep the bullets outside," Ashton says, quickly lowering her head as the bullets ricochet around her.

"How about you worry about driving," Daniella says, helping Angel.

The black suburban drives closer to them and hits them on the driver's side. Angel and Daniella fall back away from the back side window.

"Seriously?!" Blair says from the passenger seat.

"I've got this," Ashton says. Ashton speeds up, but suddenly hits her brakes, allowing the black suburban to speed past her. Ashton takes a hard left and rams the black suburban near its right taillight. Angel quickly gets up and shoots out the right tire. The suburban spins uncontrollably out of the lane and into oncoming traffic, causing a multi-vehicle crash. "Whoooo!" Ashton shouts with joy. "I still got it!"

"The director is going to kill us, and that's if Jordan doesn't get to us first," Natalie expresses.

"Nat, chill. We're good. How's our mad scientist?" Ashton asks irreverently.

Dr. Edwards is fully awake, but he's not facing reality. "As good as any brainwashed doctor could be," Angel replies.

"Great, now let's get out of here," Ashton says.

"Guys!" Blair shouts, looking at the passenger side mirror. "We have bigger problems!"

"Are they multiplying!?" Ashton shouts, once again speeding.

They're not far from the extraction point. Unfortunately, these men are driving at a speed not even Ashton can beat in this rusty van.

Blair leans out of the window, ready to take a shot. The men begin to move at the same speed as Ashton, riding alongside her. Ashton and Blair gaze over at the men in the black sports car, unaware that it's Will. He gives them a brash smile and speeds passed them, then moves closer as if they're going to ram the van. Ashton notices the back left passenger window go down and one of the men jumps out, stretching their hands to grab Blair. He grabs her arm and yanks her through the window.

"Help!" Blair shouts, fighting her way back into the van. Ashton grabs on to the back of her suit, holding her inside while driving at the same time.

"A little help here!" Ashton calls out to Angel, Daniella and Natalie in the back. Daniella rushes to the front of the van, helping to pull Blair inside as Ashton continues to maneuver her way around traffic. "Ang, I need you to do something now!" Ashton says, referring to Angel's powers.

"I'm trying!" Angel snaps back. She sits near Dr. Edwards, trying to enter astral mode and she gets nothing but a headache brewing.

"Angel!" Ashton shouts, running into a car on her left side.

The men pull Blair out of the van and into their car.

"I-I can't get anything," Angel can't conjure up her powers. "I didn't take them."

"You didn't take your pills!? What were you thinking!?" Ashton chastises her.

"I don't know, all right? But we have to do something. I'm not letting them take her!" Angel shouts, running to the window with an automatic weapon and beginning to fire at the car.

Ashton speeds as fast as she can in the van, trying to keep up with Will and the sports car.

"I have something!" Natalie shouts, remembering an emergency device equipped within the van for situations like this. "Just get really close and I can get us out of here."

"Make it quick, Nat," Ashton says, doing as she says.

Natalie types on her computer and loads schematics of the van. She touches the screen showing the right side of the van and presses a nearby button. A slot on the van opens and an automatic machine gun comes out.

"Now, that's awesome," Daniella is astonished.

"Wait, we have to get Blair out of there," Angel says.

In the sports car, Blair is fighting her way out against two men: one in the passenger seat and one in the backseat. Looking behind the man in the backset, she sees the van's machine gun. Blair kicks and punches the man repeatedly, but her strength is no match. She's grabbed by her neck from the guy in the passenger seat with a syringe in his hand, ready to press into her neck. Blair places her scalding hot hand firmly on his face, moving it away from her neck. He screams in agony as smokes comes from his right cheek. She kicks the man in the backseat with all her strength and manages to escape. Rushing to the left backseat window, Blair leaps out of the window.

"Grab my hand!" Daniella stretches out, Angel holds onto Daniella. Blair stretches out and grabs her arm.

"Now, Natalie," Angel says.

Natalie presses the button, and the machine gun locks on its target and fires at the sports car. Daniella and Angel pull Blair inside the van.

"Oh my gosh, thank you so much," Blair says as the adrenaline pumps through her body.

Will and his remaining passenger take cover, swerving away from traffic.

"Yes!" The girls shout and cheer. They're free.

"We did it," Daniella says, amazed at her abilities and her team, her friends.

"Now, can someone call Jordan before she has a heart attack?" Ashton says, making her way to the extraction point.

"I got it," Angel says, calling Jordan on her phone.

As Natalie is picking up her equipment, she notices blood spilling from Dr. Edwards' chest.

"Yes, we're on the way," Angel says. She notices the wound as well and quickly hangs up the phone. "Is he going to be, okay?" she asks.

"I can't tell. It looks like a flesh wound, but I don't have the proper equipment to confirm. Seth will know more about it," Natalie says, examining Dr. Edwards.

Angel holds pressure on the wound. "Dr. Edwards, everything is going to be okay," she reassures him as he attempts to open his eyes.

Jordan and Seth wait by the jet's entrance as Ashton pulls into the forest preserve.

"Somebody care to tell me what happened?" Jordan asks, as the girls get out of the bullet hole filled van.

"We ran into some trouble with Clay's guys on our way here," Ashton says.

"And my agents?" Jordan mentions the drivers.

"Oh, they got it back at the NIA," Daniella replies. "Ashton got us out of there." Daniella gives Ashton her credit and Ashton appreciates it.

Seth, with a team from his lab, takes Dr. Edwards and rushes him onto the Tempest.

"And what happened to him?!" Jordan panics.

"Vitals are stable and there's an exit wound. I'm taking him in for surgery now," Seth says, reading information on his tablet.

Jordan wants to chastise them for getting Dr. Edwards shot, but she can't; there's too much holding her back. They did exactly what was asked of them. They did what she would have done. "You guys did good, I couldn't have asked for better," she smiles proudly at them.

"Awww…I'm touched, LT," Ashton says sarcastically, placing her hands across her heart.

"You're welcome, Ash," Jordan and the girls laugh as they walk onto the jet.

Walking on to the Tempest, Ethan waits for Angel. "Hey, are you okay? I saw her controlling you and I didn't know what to do and then you left, and I couldn't find you," he cradles her face in his hands and she does the same.

"I'm fine, okay? I'm fine," Angel wraps her arms around his waist and holds him tight.

Ashton watches the exchange from a distance and realizes Angel is slowly slipping away from her.

"You know that's not going to last, right?" Daniella comes from behind.

"I wish that was true, but when Angel cares, she cares hard," Ashton says.

Daniella sees how much Ashton is missing her sister and right now she needs a friend even if she won't admit it. "Do you want to help me plan Natalie's party tonight?"

Ashton attempts to grow a friendship. "Sure. I think we all could use a break."

"Lieutenant, our prisoner is locked down and I have a team on standby ready to take her into lockup back at the agency," Donovan reports in as he gets ready to take off.

"Thank you, Agent James," Jordan says. "Blair? What happened to your nose?" she asks concerned, as Blair's nose drips with blood again.

"Really?! It's bleeding again," Blair grabs a napkin from the bar and holds her head high to stop the bleeding. "Angel kind of punched me when she was under the witch's spell."

"I'll take her down to Seth," Natalie says, guiding Blair down the stairs of the jet.

"And we're off," Donovan speaks over the intercoms.

"You know we're going to hear an earful from the director," David says, sitting with her in the lobby of the Tempest.

"We had a shoot-out and left multiple casualties around his building, and they possibly saw the girls, so I'm expecting nothing less than an earful from him," Jordan says. "I'm just glad they made it out of there in one piece."

"Speaking of, I want to apologize. You were right, they did great out there. They'll be a great addition to the team." He understands now why Jordan had to keep information from him. Jordan never expected him to accept the girls, but she's glad he did, and they can move on. Unfortunately, there's so much more he doesn't know about her and her past life, including her daughters. She doesn't know how he will react if she were to tell him the truth, but what she does know is that it won't be good – for anyone.

Chapter 38

The team has safely made their way back to Exodus. Seth's team meets him at the entrance of the agency to take Dr. Edwards to the medical wing for further testing. They exit The Tempest, heads held high, joyous they've successfully completed their first mission together. Donovan stops to instruct the garage crew to do repairs on the mission vehicles and to inspect The Tempest.

"Seth, I want a full report in half an hour," Jordan calls out. "And I want you to handle lock-up protocols. I want to speak with her in a few," she instructs Donovan.

Ashton, Daniella, and Blair walk past Jordan, giddy as only teenage girls can be, "Hey, LT!" Ashton shouts spinning around. "Penthouse. Party. In 1300 hours." Ashton stops and salutes.

Jordan lifts her wrist, checking her watch. "Ash, 1300 hours was four hours ago."

"Oh, well then in two hours, seven o'clock." Ashton jogs to catch up with the other girls. Strangely, Ashton always finds a way to make Jordan forget about her problems. Something Jordan doesn't want to lose if she were to tell Angel and Ashton the truth.

Jordan enters her agency with numerous officers and agents approaching her with business to handle. She answers everyone's questions and handles all the business brought to her. She looks up and David stands along the hallway wall on the phone, his face revealing something is wrong.

She leaves the crowd. "What's wrong?" she asks.

"The director saw the security footage from the courtyard with the girls and Clay's team and they also captured traffic footage of the damage on the highway," he pauses. "He's scheduled a meeting."

Jordan slumps on the wall and exhales her problems. "I knew this day would come and now I have to explain why I have four psychic teenagers," she says. Jordan leaves, taking on another heavy load she has to carry. "I'll deal with it after I go check on Martin and our other guest." David watches as she tacks on yet another problem.

Jordan steps out of the elevator, entering the medical wing. Scientists and doctors move in and out of areas developing new experiments. Seth and his associates are working over a lethargic Dr. Edwards in a secluded section with equipment only used by Seth and those he allows. They check his temperature, draw blood and take notes on his vitals.

"Lieutenant, I'm happy you're here," Seth rushes to her, handing her his tablet with all the information he has discovered on Dr. Edwards.

"How's he doing?"

"He coded a couple of times," he says like it's a normal occurrence. "But we were able to bring him back."

"And the gunshot wound? Did it do any more damage?" Jordan steps closer to Martin, hoping he wakes fully and remembers her.

"Oh that. I fixed it on the Tempest. He'll make a full recovery," Seth comes near her, and swipes left on the tablet. "But you see here, all of his vitals are stable, I checked everything and found nothing. But then I decided to look deeper at the 3D MRI test." Seth takes his tablet and places it on a HoloTable like the one on The Tempest. He pulls a literal image from the table showing the fully constructed brain of Dr. Edwards. "I found these specs in his frontal lobe near the optic nerve," he moves the holographic brain around. "Then I remembered Blair and Natalie telling me about the woman that controlled Angel and I'm not one-hundred percent sure, more like 90 percent, that years of mind control caused this."

"What do you need to be 100 percent sure?" Jordan asks.

Seth opens a nearby drawer and gives Jordan a lancet device. "I need blood. If you can get close enough to prick her finger with this, it will store the amount of blood I need to compare."

Jordan takes the device. That's one item checked off her long list of tasks. "I'm on my way down to see her, so I'll be able to get it to you tonight."

Seth becomes worried the stress and worry of the agency are taking a toll on Jordan. "Lieutenant?" he asks.

"Yes?" Jordan responds.

Seth is careful with his next choice of words; he approaches gently. "Is everything okay? You seem…not yourself, like something is bothering you."

Jordan wants to tell Seth everything, not because he deserves to know, but because she wants to release it to anyone that would listen.

"I'm fine. Seth. We've just had a lot going on the last couple of weeks," Jordan says. Seth erases the feelings of worry for Jordan. She's strong; he's never seen a day where she's folded under the pressures of work.

"Well, I'm sure you'll feel better at Natalie's party tonight," Seth says, excited.

"Hopefully." Jordan leaves the lab, making her way on to the agency elevator, ready to tackle on another issue: Alexandria.

Taking the elevator down, Jordan enters the hallway of the garage. In this same darkened hallway surrounded by cold, concrete walls is a carbon steel door. Jordan enters a code, gives a finger and retina scan at the same time to enter. This is lockup, where the hardest, toughest, and most mentally unstable criminals are stored until Exodus sends them to a prison where the government takes them over. There isn't much activity in this area. There are only a handful of agents guarding the three holding cells, but the technology holding these prisoners is state of the art. The designs are like any ordinary holding cell with steel bars, but those ordinary cells don't have a protection shield and sensors that disable the prisoners from becoming too aggressive. A sedative chemical is sprayed like rain mist into the cell to calm the prisoners.

The agents guarding these cells are fooling around until Jordan enters and they stand at attention, going back to work. Donovan stands in front of the two-way mirror showing Alexandria's holding cell. He studies her; there's something different about her. He's seen a lot of prisoners come in and out of this agency and all have either fought or wouldn't shut up during their duration there, but she's too calm.

"How's our guest?" Jordan joins him.

"Pretty calm. She hasn't said a word since we brought her down."

"Okay, can you empty the room? I want to talk to her alone."

"Got it, Lieutenant."

Alexandria sits on a metal bench, at peace. She has no worries about what might come her way. She sits, legs stretched out and crossed over one another, hands locked together, and head held high resting on the wall. Alexandria stops resting and smirks as Jordan steps in front of her cage. "The infamous Lieutenant Jordan Knox. I was wondering when you would make an appearance."

"Sorry to keep you waiting. I had to go check on my agents. You know how mind control can take a lot out of you," Jordan gives back the sarcasm.

"They'll be fine. That was child's play compared to what I could've done," Alexandria sits up from her relaxed position.

"You mean manipulation? Inducement?"

Alexandria continues to smile through Jordan's questioning. "It's clear you've done your research so, Lieutenant, why don't we get to the real reason you're down here?" If this is the way she wants to handle this, then let's do it, Jordan thought.

"Okay… Alexandria, why did your father have you at the NIA office today?" Jordan asks.

"To stop you and your minions."

"Even though you had no idea my team would be there."

"Well, Lieutenant, as much as you would hate to admit it, you're very predictable." Alexandria tries her best to get under Jordan's skin, but it's clear she has no clue who she's dealing with.

"I guess I am, but your father…now he's hard to read. He doesn't seem like the fatherly type." Jordan takes her time finding out what makes Alexandria tick. She tries to not let the comment bother her. Her father is a difficult topic to discuss.

"Looks can be deceiving."

"But you're the only one in your family with these abilities. You sure he isn't using you for his army or as leverage?"

"I use them because I want to."

"But he needs blood from a supernatural in order to complete the serum for the biochip, correct?" Jordan waits for a reply from her.

"You know, it must be hard having a parent that uses you for their gain." Jordan keeps pressing Alexandria for information. "You're adopted, right? Or do they call it something else? I guess Clay figured what better way to get what he wanted than having a supernatural right there in his living room."

Alexandria hops from her seat and aggressively approaches Jordan, trying her best to fight the feeling of reaching through these bars and strangling her. As the protection shield shocks her, Jordan grabs Alexandria's hand and pricks her finger. Alexandria takes a couple steps back, wincing in pain. "What the hell was that?!"

"Just a little insurance, in case your father decides to try anything. But don't worry, he won't be coming for you anytime soon."

"You don't know what the hell you're talking about! My father may be a lot of things, but he does love me," Alexandria says, convincing herself of the goodness that's in Clay.

Jordan has her where she wants, ready to jump off the ledge. Jordan feels empathy for Alexandria because she knows who she truly is, Alexandria Hawthorne.

Jordan has tried on several occasions to get her back, but Clay was always one step ahead. "Then tell me, Alexandria, what is your father planning?" This time Jordan speaks with sincerity.

A part of Alexandria wants to give Jordan information; it would teach Clay a lesson for the next time he decides to take her for granted. Instead, Alexandria walks away and sits calmly back on her bench. "You'll find out soon enough."

Jordan isn't getting anywhere with Alexandria, and she doesn't have the time or the energy to go back and forth with her about Clay. If she wants to find out information, she'll do it on her own, the way she's always done things. Jordan leaves Alexandria to sulk for the next few hours. Before she exits the room, Alexandria stops her. Jordan doesn't turn to face her.

"Lieutenant? Just a bit of advice. You should keep an eye on those new agents of yours. They're very popular."

Chapter 39

The walls tremble as the music blasts the latest songs of the year. The team is scattered throughout the girls' penthouse. Everyone is here – Donovan, Angel, Ethan, Blair, Daniella, Seth, Natalie, David and even Charlie. Ashton and Daniella were able to put together a party for Natalie quickly. This is the first time in a month they have come together, and they are enjoying themselves.

Blair, with a drink in her hand and a bandage over her nose, sits with Donovan and Seth. "The guy has his hand around my neck, and I look out the window. There's the machine gun sticking out the side of the van and I'm like 'are they really going to fire that while I'm in here' so I'm freaking out and knew then it was time to get out of there because this can't be how I die." The three of them begin to laugh, sharing similar experiences about missions with Exodus.

"Happy birthday, Agent Hawthorne." David comes up from behind Natalie with a gift and a smile.

"Oh, thank you, Captain." David steps in as if he should give her a hug, but instead Natalie awkwardly stretches her hand out for a shake instead.

"And it's okay if you call me Natalie."

"Sorry, I'll try to remember that." David and Natalie have always had an awkward and delicate relationship. Not many know of David and Jordan's relationship, but Natalie has seen the relationship rollercoaster firsthand. Jordan has raised Natalie most of her life;

she's her mother, in a way. Natalie opens her gift and it's a jewelry box.

"A bracelet…nice," she says, not too fond of the gift.

"It's not just any bracelet. I had our techs put in a communicator. You can make contact through video or phone."

Natalie puts the feelings she has against David aside. "It's great. Thank you," she says.

Leaving him, Natalie joins Ashton and Daniella in the kitchen. She sits with Daniella at the kitchen bar and watches as Ashton makes a mess with the fattiest foods she could fine.

"I hope you aren't mad at us for throwing this party," Daniella says, concerned.

Natalie may be upset after she deliberately told them she didn't want a party. "Not at all, I'm actually having a good time," Natalie says.

"Of course, you are! Especially after you eat this," Ashton gives Natalie a plate with a giant burger. "I call it the 'murder burger'. It's a half-pound burger with crisp onions, bacon, shredded chicken and pulled pork, five different cheeses, barbeque sauce on a toasted brioche bun. You need two hands to eat it and that's not even the hard part. The struggle to get it in your mouth requires some maneuvering."

"Wow, thanks Ashton." Natalie has no idea how she's going to eat a burger that's the size of her face.

"It's my specialty. I always make it for me and Angel's birthday – well, when we finally got a place with a kitchen."

Natalie grins. Ashton has grown fond of Natalie. Natalie loves the way she's sharing a tradition normally shared between her and Angel. "Thanks, Ash."

"I'm going to take half because you're clearly not going to eat all of this, plus I've been sitting here for the longest listening to her talk about how good it is," Daniella grins.

Natalie cuts the burger in thirds. Each of them takes a piece and cheers as if they're toasting with drinks.

"Yeah, this is amazing." Daniella speaks with a mouth full.

"The best." Natalie wipes the grease running down her chin.

"I told you," Ashton says.

Jordan finally joins the festivities, taking a break from the overwhelming problems coming her way.

"LT!" Ashton strangely is happy to see Jordan come to the party.

Jordan waves to the other partygoers and joins them in the kitchen. "Hey guys. Happy birthday, Nat."

"Are you hungry? I can make you a murder burger," Ashton asks Jordan.

"I think I'm good. I try to stay away from things that are going to kill me."

Daniella and Natalie chuckle.

"It's a turkey burger!" Ashton shouts.

Jordan joins the rest of the team.

Angel and Ethan have been sitting on the balcony of the penthouse, legs dangling and watching the team interact with one another. They've enjoyed their time together, sharing personal stories and similar experiences. It's been her and Ashton for so long, she's never had a real emotional connection with someone like Ethan. He could be the one, but only time would tell.

"Okay, favorite place to travel?" Angel asks.

"Hmm…The Maldives." Angel is shocked.

"What? You just go there casually?"

"My grandfather has a beach house out there."

"You surprise me every day." They laugh.

"Okay, Ms. Judgmental, where's your place?"

"Orlando." Angel is confident in her answer, but Ethan believes it's a joke.

"Orlando, Florida? You're kidding, right?"

"What?! Shut up!" Angel doesn't take offense to his laughter.

"What could you possibly love about Florida?"

"When me and Ash where nine, weeks just before my dad passed, he promised that for our tenth birthday he would take us to Disney World, so now every year on our birthday we pack up, get in the car and drive to Disney to watch the fireworks. We didn't have the money to actually go inside the parks." Ethan deeply listens to Angel as she shares yet another personal story from her life. He can't understand how she can trust him within the little time they've known each other. Maybe she sees something more in him than he does himself. "We kept it up for a while, but work got in the way, and we haven't been back since. We finally have the money and we can't go." Angel wanted a life.

"Well, I guess we have somewhere to go next year." Ethan takes her hand and smiles.

"Thanks, but I've talked too much. You've never told me about your parents."

Ethan becomes slightly uncomfortable; his parents are a sensitive topic. They aren't the best people in the world. "There isn't much to tell. My dad loves his work more than his children and my mother plots and schemes."

"They had to do something right. I mean, you're an agent for the CIA."

"My parents demand perfection. It's the only way I could even become an agent."

In a way, they have their similarities when it comes to problems with their parents. Angel realizes the conversation struck something in Ethan; he slips into a trance. Staring off into space, he's losing his sense of reality. Angel touches his shoulder lightly, bringing him back to reality.

"But I'm away from them now, so I'm good."

"I think you're doing great."

Ethan smiles, leans in and kisses her on the cheek. "Thank you, but I think I'm going to go."

"Why?" Angel asks, concerned. They both stand from the balcony.

"It's getting late, and I have a training session in the a.m." He gives her a simple hug, like he was hugging his grandmother, and made his way down the stairs, passing Ashton along the way. He makes his way past the rest of the team and out the door.

"Trouble in paradise?" Ashton comes to check on her sister.

"Haha, very funny. You know he's not my boyfriend."

"True. I give it a week." Ashton gives her a plate of leftover murder burger and from her back-pocket hands Angel her pill bottle. "Take them, please." There aren't many moments where Ashton is the mature one between them. Angel knows she made a mistake when she decided not to take her medicine. Angel takes the pills and instantly feels refreshed. "Now let's go make this party lit!" Ashton shouts.

Ashton and Angel join the team in the living room as Blair turns up the music on the intercom connected to the speakers throughout the penthouse. Everyone dances around together enjoying the time with one another. Each of them don't have to worry about anything right now. They're just here, taking in the moment.

The night continues to go on with each of them socializing and playing games. Donovan, Ashton, Blair and Seth are in the penthouse training room playing their version of darts. A large wooden bullseye hangs on the wall as they stand six feet away from it.

Ashton and Donovan stand on the line, each holding three steak knives. "Are you sure you're ready to take this loss? I don't want you to mess up your cashmere sweater," Ashton teases.

Donovan doesn't talk. He lets his skills speak for themselves. He motions Ashton to the line like she's a princess being presented at a ball. Ashton gets into a stance and positions herself accordingly. With the flick of her wrist, she launches the steak knives into the wooden bullseye. Two of her knives hit the bull and one knife hits the bullseye. Blair and Seth applaud behind them. Ashton steps back arrogantly, knowing Donovan wouldn't come close to her score.

"That was pretty good. I'm nervous now." Donovan pulls up his sleeves, steps on the line and positions himself to get the right aim. "Bear with me. I'm a little rusty." He pulls his arm back and with the flick of his wrist launches all three of his knives straight into the bullseye. If they blinked, they for sure were going to miss it. Blair and Seth have no words, just mouths wide open in amazement. Ashton stands unexpressive but feeling like Seth and Blair internally. She's never seen someone handle knives the way he did.

"How do you know how to do that?" Ashton asks.

He rolls down his sleeves. "Bit of advice. Never judge a book by its cover and less talking is essential, too." He pats Ashton on the shoulder. "Not bad for a guy on Wall Street, huh?"

"I have to give it to you. That was very impressive." Ashton gives credit where credit is due. Donovan isn't so bad after all. Maybe for now she can let go of the vengeful feeling when she sees his face.

"It's easy. I can teach you if you want," Donovan suggests.

"All right."

Donovan extends an olive branch to her. He no longer wants to judge them; they've proven their loyalty time and time again.

"Cake time!" Jordan shouts from the kitchen. The team gathers around the circular dining table. Jordan, David, Donovan, Daniella, Seth, Blair, Angel, Ashton and Natalie are coming together for a common goal: celebrating Natalie. They sing 'Happy Birthday' in unison – well, almost.

"Now make a wish," Seth encourages.

Natalie takes her time on making the perfect wish. This is serious; making the wrong wish could cause damage. Natalie may need to loosen up a little. She exhales, closes her eyes and blows out her candles on her favorite cake – chocolate dream buttercream. The team cheers for Natalie.

"What did you wish for?" Blair asks.

"She can't tell you. That'll defeat the whole purpose," Daniella replies.

"It's okay. I want to." Natalie raises her plastic cup to make a toast, and everyone follows along. "I wished we would stay a team. No matter how hard it gets, we stay together, fight for one another, because all we have is each other."

"I think that is a perfect wish, Nat," Jordan smiles. Jordan had forgotten with all the worries surrounding the discovery of her daughters that Natalie is just as much a daughter to her and she is so proud of the young woman she has become.

"Yes, great wish. Now cut the cake. It's calling my name," Ashton interrupts as her mouth waters watching the chocolate drip on the side of the cake. Natalie cuts everyone a slice and they socialize a little while longer until it gets late.

"I haven't been to a party this fun in a long time," Donovan slowly gets up from slouching on the couch. "But I can barely stand, so I'm going to get out here so I can pass out on my own couch."

"See ya, Wall Street!" Ashton shouts. Normally she would insult him with such a name, but this time it's her own fun little nickname for him and he doesn't mind it.

"I'm going to head out, too," David says to Jordan, caressing the back of her forearm. "Bye, girls."

"Bye, Captain," Natalie, Daniella and Angel say in unison.

"I think it's time for us all to go to sleep," Angel says, sitting next to Jordan as they glance at Blair and Ashton asleep on the couch, one at one end and one at the other. They chuckle at their snoring.

"Did you have a good time?" Angel asks her.

"Actually, I did. I have to commend you guys for throwing this party for Natalie. She really needed it."

"Thanks, but the credit should go to Daniella and Ash. Speaking of, I want to thank you."

"For what?"

"She'll kill me if I told you this, but Ashton really is trying to change and she would never tell you, but I know it's because of you. You've taken the time to train her and get to know her and no one has done that since our dad." Jordan is uncomfortable; the room begins spinning. She can't lie to them anymore. Her heart is telling her to tell them the truth, but her mind is telling her now is not the time. This is too much.

"Ummm…you know what? It…it is getting pretty late. I-I'm going to go home."

Angel notices how flushed Jordan just became. "Okay. I guess we'll see you tomorrow."

"Yes. Tomorrow." Jordan hastily exits the penthouse.

Making her way through the hallway, she slowly feels the walls around her caving in. It's lie after lie. When will it stop, she thought. She needs to get home now. A few more minutes in this agency and she's sure to lose her mind. The exterior hallway of the penthouse is silent, so silent one can hear the squeaks of the tile floors.

The elevator approaches the penthouse level. As Jordan gets on the elevator, she hears the squeaks of the floor become louder. She steps out to check and finds nothing. Walking back to the elevator, it quickly closes on her. Calling for the elevator once more, Jordan isn't paying attention to her surroundings. She's attacked from behind. A muscular arm, covered in a thermal long-sleeve shirt, wraps an arm around Jordan's neck and then a black leather glove around her mouth, preventing her from screaming. It's obvious that whoever this is doesn't know what they're getting themselves into.

Chapter 40

Jordan struggles, trying to release herself from this person. They're trying to knock her out, but Jordan doesn't go down without a battle. Reaching her hands behind her to feel for this person's height, she rubs her hands across a hard, cold material. They have on a helmet and they're tall, possibly six foot three, she thought. They squeeze harder on Jordan's neck. Realizing she isn't going down easily, they take out a syringe and try to stick it into the side of her neck. They don't move fast enough. They may have her neck and her mouth, but they've idiotically left her arms and legs free. With all her strength, Jordan elbows them in their side and kicks them in their knee, sending their knees and themselves falling back. The grip on her neck is free. She quickly takes their arm, twists and flips them over. Who is this person? Why are they dressed in full armor? How did they get in my agency?!, she thought.

As they quickly stand, Jordan immediately knows this is a man, but how he got in her building is another mystery. He rushes towards her like he's a defensive tight end ready to take down the quarterback. He slams her into the wall, knocking the wind out of her. She continues to fight; she refuses to let someone best her in her own agency. His arms are wrapped around her waist, and she elbows him repeatedly in his back. It's not doing any damage. He rams his shoulder into her stomach repeatedly. Jordan waits for an opening. As he moves back for another ram, she leaps and jumps on his back. He rams his head into the wall and loses balance for a moment. She leaps up from the floor, a little sore and trying to catch her breath.

"Okay, let's do this." Jordan shakes off the soreness and lunges towards him, throwing quick combinations: jab, left hook to the body, left hook, rear hook, uppercut and spinning hook kick.

She hits him with these combinations and he blocks and dodges each one. It's almost like he knows her moves before she makes them. Jordan goes for one last combination move; she does a spinning kick. He stands tall, grabs her ankle like a branch flew across his face and slams her to the ground. Hitting her head on the floor, she becomes unsteady. She struggles to stand, putting all her weight on her right arm. Gaining her balance and becoming steady again, she sees the syringe. She conceals the syringe in her sleeve. He stands over her, wraps both of his hands around her neck and picks her up like a rag doll. He's covered in armor from head to toe and her eyes are protruding out of her face.

She needs to find an opening to stick the syringe in, and she does. His helmet isn't connected to his armor. When he moves, the helmet reveals sweat dripping onto his caramel skin. Jordan slips the syringe out of her sleeve. He presses harder onto her neck. Passing out is not an option and she's fighting. Pressing on his helmet, she forces his head to the side to reveal his neck. She stabs him right in the neck and he hollers. It's the most he's said this entire time. He releases Jordan, and he falls to the ground unconscious. Jordan lays on the ground with a hacking cough.

"Jordan! Are you all right?!" Angel along with the rest of the girls come rushing towards her aid.

Jordan lays on the floor regaining her strength. "I-I'll be f-fine. Get him," Jordan says. Blair, Daniella and Ashton drag him into the penthouse.

"I am beyond amazed you survived that," Ashton says.

"Ash!" Angel shouts at her. She and Natalie help Jordan to her feet.

"What?! This guy is huge!" Ashton explains.

"She has a point," Blair agrees, struggling to drag him into the penthouse.

"Okay, I'm not doing this," Ashton says as she drops him and lifts her hands. He begins to float in the air and into the penthouse.

"You couldn't have done that sooner." Daniella watches as she concentrates to place him on the couch.

"I don't like to show off," Ashton replies.

"Natalie, call Seth and tell him to get down here now, and I need you to try and get that helmet off." Jordan sits at the dining table drinking water, gaining her strength back.

"LT, what happened?" Ashton asks.

"I was on my way to the elevator, and he attacked me from behind."

"How did he get down here?" Daniella asks. "There's only one way out."

"That's what I'm trying to figure out, but I think we have a mole."

"A mole? What's that?" Blair isn't as aware of the secret agent language as everyone else.

"Someone who we think is on our side, but they're just taking information and giving it back to their team," Angel explains.

"Exactly, and I think they gave whoever this is intel on where we are and where they could hide down here," Jordan explains.

"And the party was their distraction," Angel says, giving Jordan a bag of ice to place on her wounds.

"Then let's see who this guy is," Ashton rushes over to the couch and tries to take off the man's helmet, but it's not giving. "Is it sewed on?!" Ashton says, frustrated.

"The technology is too advanced. I knew it the moment I saw it. But it looks like an easy hack that I should be able to get into once Seth comes with my tools," Natalie says.

Jordan wonders who could have technology this advanced.

Seth rushes into the penthouse with a metal suitcase by his side. "Lieutenant, I came as quickly as I could. Is everyone okay?" he asks, looking over at the man.

"We're fine. I need you to tell me what this is," Jordan gives Seth the syringe that was meant for her.

"I'll get right on it," he says. He opened his briefcase on the coffee table. He and Natalie do what they do best: solve problems.

"Do you have any idea who could have sent him?" Angel asks.

"Everything in me wants it to be Clay, but I can't go around assuming," Jordan replies.

"It would make sense. He could be getting back at us for ruining his meeting," Daniella says.

"But that still doesn't explain how he got in here. How would Clay even know where to find us if there wasn't a mole?" Ashton rationalizes.

"Ash is right. There's someone in this agency I can't trust, and I'm not going to sit around and wait for them to get me again," Jordan pulls her phone out and calls Donovan. "Hey, we just had a breach and it's someone from the inside. I need you to come back down and gather all the agents and officers so Lucy can screen them."

"What do you want us to do?" Daniella asks.

"For now, I just need you to stand by. We may be facing Clay again sooner than we expected," Jordan prepares herself to go interrogate her agents, but not until she finds out who attacked her. "How far are we on the helmet, Nat?"

"I almost have it," Natalie says, using a specialized screwdriver and moving wires around to release the helmet. "And…there. Got it." Natalie lifts the helmet to reveal a man who has been roughed up.

Bruises cover the right side of his face, and his pepper beard is full. He isn't awake, but his presence brings silence into the room. Jordan stares down at him. She can't move. Her balance is no longer steady, and she falls into the chair, covering her mouth and trying to hold back the tears and screams. She starts to cry profusely and uncontrollably.

"Wh-what's wrong? What's happening?" Natalie asks.

She looks up to see Angel and Ashton frozen, their whole world has just come crashing down within seconds.

"D-Dad," Angel approaches him with caution. Maybe it's a dream, she thought. Moving closer, Angel takes off his glove and holds his hand and instantly feels the connection. It's her father, Aaron Cross. She falls to her knees and places her head onto his arm and cries out.

Ashton isn't sure where she is. This must be a dream, it just has to be, it needs to be, she thought. She wants to move, but her feet won't allow her. Somebody help me, she thought. She gains enough strength to slowly approach her father. Ashton notices the bruises and she for sure knows it's her father. "No, no, no, no, no, no, no, no, no," she says, holding her big hair in her hands as if she's going to pull it out. She tries to catch her breath, but instead breathes harder until she begins hyperventilating, on the verge of throwing up.

Seth rushes towards her and sits her down in a seat. "Ashton, look straight at me. Focus on my eyes and breathe." Seth inhales and exhales slowly for Ashton, but she's not calming down. "Okay, here," he cups her hands together and puts them on her mouth. "Breathe, just breathe."

Ashton slowly regains control. She has to make sense of this, and she needs answers now. Ashton walks to Angel, who is still laying on her father, and pulls her up. "Ang, come on, get up," Ashton says. Angel turns to Ashton, her eyes puffy and red from the strain. She hugs Ashton tightly, wrapping her arms around her neck and cries. Ashton comforts her.

Daniella, Blair, and Seth watch the exchange and are overwhelmed with emotions. "I hate to ask this right now, but I thought you guys said your dad died," Blair asks.

"He did…or so we thought," Ashton says releasing Angel. "We saw him get taken away, but that was almost ten years ago. We knew he was dead; he had to be," Ashton says, sure of herself.

Jordan sits bouncing her leg up and down rapidly. Her past has caught up with her and now she has no choice but to deal with it. She's numb. Her body is in the room, but her soul has left. There are too many emotions coming over her at once.

"Lieutenant? Did you know him?" Natalie asks cautiously.

She's never seen Jordan in this state before. She has always been strong and able to handle anything that comes her way, even when it seemed like she was going to lose. They hadn't paid attention because they too were overwhelmed with their own emotions, but Angel and Ashton see a numb Jordan and wonder why she's just as emotional, maybe more.

"No. The lieutenant doesn't know my father because we've talked about it together and she didn't say anything," Angel says, waiting for Jordan to say no, but Jordan sits there, unresponsive.

After a moment of silence, Ashton wants answers. "LT? How do you know our father?" There still isn't a response. "Jordan!" Ashton shouts her name, wanting her to snap out of it.

Jordan sits up in the chair and faces her daughters; it's time. She looks up at the ceiling and inhales and then releases her fears. She walks towards them as they stand side by side next to their father. She gently wipes away their tears and places her hands on their shoulders. "I know your father because…," she struggles, "he's my husband."

Everyone stands in disbelief at what they just heard, especially Angel and Ashton. Ashton snatches her shoulder away from Jordan. She's fuming. She only sees rage when looking at Jordan.

Natalie is unsure of what she is hearing. Could the women that raised and trained her be a fraud? Who truly is this woman that she's been so close to her entire life?

"I hate to jump in and state the obvious but how could you be around your daughters for weeks and not know who they are?" Blair asks proceeding with caution.

Jordan looks to Angel and Ashton waiting for them to give her the approval that she can further explain. Unfortunately, they are still trying to come to terms with this unbelievable revelation. "My…my memory is still pretty foggy from that night but what I do remember is that I had to do anything to protect you," she looks at Angel and Ashton, "from my enemies and my mistakes."

"It sounds like you did everything to protect yourself rather than your kids." Daniella says to another liar in her life.

Seth being the only sane person in the room, needs to take control and ease the tension. "I think we should give them a moment," Seth says to Blair, Natalie and Daniella. They give the Cross family some time to work out all of the confusion. "Lieutenant, he should be waking up soon," Seth says after fully analyzing the components within the syringe.

The Cross family are alone, trying to make sense of everything in their lives. "I promise I never meant for you to find out this way," Jordan says.

"Are you serious?" Ashton steps back because if she steps closer it could get bloody.

"None of this can be true because I told you who our father was and I told you our last name and you said nothing," Angel is trying to be the rational one like she always is, but this, this is too much. "You said nothing!"

"Are you serious?!?!" Ashton has to walk away; her fists are balled up at her side and she can't see straight.

"I-I didn't know what to say, I wasn't sure," Jordan pleads to them.

"You're lying!" Ashton turns to face her.

"Ash…" Jordan knows how much Ashton was beginning to trust her and how she just destroyed their thriving relationship.

"Don't call me that!" Ashton steps to her ready to fight and Angel pulls her back. "You knew! How long?!" Ashton shouts.

Jordan knows what to say but can't summon up the words.

"HOW LONG?!" Ashton screams so loud her voice cracks and the glass dining table bursts into pieces.

"Hey, we are not doing this. Take it easy," Angel says, watching as rage grows in Ashton, causing her to release unwanted energy from her powers. Angel knows from experience you don't want to be near Ashton when she gets so angry she can't see straight.

"Get off me, Angel!" Ashton pushes her sister away. "Are you going to stand here and defend this woman?"

"I'm not defending her, but we can't get any answers if you can't control yourself."

"I don't give a damn! I don't need any answers from her because as far as I'm concerned, my parents are dead! They died in Boston!"

Jordan hates herself tremendously for what she's done to everyone – Angel, Ashton, Daniella, Blair, Natalie, Seth, Donovan and David. She's lied to all of them and now she must face them with the truth. Before pleading to them once more, they hear movement on the couch.

Aaron begins to wake up. He moans and groans through the pain and he has no idea where he is. He opens his eyes enough to make out his girls standing straight ahead. "Hey, Bunny. Hey, Princess," he smiles at Ashton and Angel. "I told you I'd be back." He smiles at them as if ten years hadn't gone by. Maybe he's dreaming, but who cares? He looks up and by his side is Jordan. "Hey, you," he gently grabs her hands with the little amount of strength he can summon up and Jordan breaks down crying with a smile on her face. She holds his hand tightly, happy he's alive. "Hey, you." She replies.

"I-I-I can't do this," Ashton says. She's no longer filled with rage, but heartache, and quickly exits the penthouse.

"Ashton!? Ashton!" Aaron calls out, but it physically only hurts him more.

"Be careful," Jordan bends down to aid him, wiping his forehead with a cold towel.

Angel stands, watching the exchange between her father and Jordan. She wants answers but where does she start, she thought.

"Angel, I am so sorry," Jordan pleads to her once more.

"You've said that already. I want to know the truth. Did you know when I told you my last name?"

"Yes, but a part of me wasn't sure, so I looked up your father and it was an exact match."

"So, you knew all this time!?"

"What could I say, Angel?! That I left you because I was afraid and didn't have the courage to come find you? That I birthed you and didn't even have the courage to look at you because of my guilt?"

"Yes! Say something! Anything!" Angel pleads to her.

"Angie, it's not her fault," Aaron struggles to say. "She couldn't have known this would happen."

"Says the man that sent his daughters away and never came to find them," Angel cuts her father. He has no right to insert his opinion here, she thought. The damage is done. Angel and Ashton are adults now and there's nothing Jordan or Aaron can do to fix it.

"You know that's not fair; you know why I sent you away."

"To protect us. Yeah, I've been saying that line for years, it's kind of hard to believe now." Angel abruptly leaves the penthouse.

"Angel, where are you going?" Jordan asks.

Jordan can understand Ashton leaving, but she thought if she couldn't reason with anyone she could at least reason with Angel. "Oh, so now you care?!" She leaves, slamming the door behind her. Aaron tries to stand and run after her, but he doesn't have the energy or strength.

"Hey, don't force it. We'll talk to them," Jordan eases him back down.

Aaron forces himself to sit up. He pats the couch cushion, wanting Jordan to sit next to him. "Remind you of someone?" he refers to his daughters' personalities, as they are like hers.

"Unfortunately," she says. They sit for a moment, not knowing what to say or do. Jordan hopes he understands why she didn't tell them about their relation. "Aaron, I promise you I didn't know. I only found out about two weeks ago and even then, I couldn't tell them. I would have uprooted their entire world."

"I know and I tried to find them, I did," he pleads to her, hoping she wouldn't be upset with him after the promise he made her. "But where I was…who I was trying to escape from, I couldn't."

Jordan grabs his chin and studies his bruises, then helps him to unzip his armor, revealing his once chiseled chest, easily revealing his ribs and showing bruises that made his caramel skin turn black. Jordan begins to shed tears once more, hating herself that she wasn't there to protect him. "Who did this to you?"

"I don't know. Most of my memory is black. I barely even know how I got here. All I remember is a white room and a doctor coming towards me with a syringe. Then next thing I know I'm here."

"Well, at least you're here and alive." They take in the moment of finally being back together again, but Jordan knows this joyous feeling isn't going to last long when David meets Aaron.

"The Crosses are reunited," Aaron says, finally at peace.

Ashton leans against the hood of her car in the garage of Exodus. She continues to wipe away her tears as she types on her phone. It's happening again. Why does this always happen, she thought. Every time she opens herself up, there's always someone that comes in and breaks her trust, her heart. Ashton has cleared the room of any crew members; she wants no one to see her vulnerability.

Daniella knocks on the door, easing her way into the garage. "Hey, are you okay?"

Ashton quickly turns her back to Daniella, not wanting her to see her tears. "I'm fine."

Daniella knows this isn't true. She moves closer to Ashton and stands with her in silence for a moment. As a friend, Daniella just wants to be there; she would want the same in return if she were in this situation. "You know, if you want to talk, we're here."

"Thanks, but I'm good," Ashton opens her passenger door and takes out a black duffle bag.

"Where are you going?"

"I'm leaving."

"Like forever?" Daniella doesn't want her to go. They just started to grow on each other.

"Yep. I can't stand to be in this place any longer and if I stay here, I'm likely to kill someone." Ashton walks around her, treating her like when they first met.

"Leaving isn't going to solve anything," Daniella grabs her arm, stopping her.

Ashton snatches her arm away, "I'm not trying to solve anything because I don't care. I don't care what Angel does and I don't care about this agency or the people in it."

Daniella is taken aback by Ashton's comment after everything they've been through Ashton still refuses to accept her. "Wow, after everything? I thought we-"

"We were what?!" Ashton asks. "Friends? You thought we would complete missions and stop bad guys and then become this one big happy family?! You're just as delusional as my so-called relatives."

After she takes her frustrations out on Daniella, Ashton opens the garages bay's doors leading outside to an empty field. "You're really going to leave? What about your car?" Daniella asks.

Ashton twirls the keys in her hand and then tosses them to Daniella. "It was my father's. He's alive, so go give it to him." Ashton walks out of the garage, up the ramp, never to be seen again.

Angel moves through the agency not knowing where she's going but anywhere is better than here. She takes the elevator up to the boutique and it's strangely quiet. Charlotte is usually at the register, perky and chipper, ready to greet anyone that comes or goes, but she's nowhere to be found. Come to think of it, Jamie wasn't on the administrative floor either. Maybe they went to get some dinner or something, Angel thought. She goes outside, only to find Ethan leaning against the building, back facing the brick walls. "Ethan?" Ethan is in another world. He doesn't hear Angel. "Ethan," she taps him. He snaps out of his trance. "Are you okay?" she asks.

"Yeah, I'm fine, what are you doing out here? Are you guys still celebrating?"

"No, it's over…it's been over."

Ethan notices the puffiness in her eyes and the dry tear stains on her face. "What's wrong?"

"I just found out my entire life has been a lie."

"What do you mean?"

Angel doesn't know if she should tell Ethan her problems. She doesn't want to scare him away. "It's a long story."

"I have nothing but time," he smiles at her, sparking his charm.

"My father's alive."

"What?!"

"And apparently Jordan knows him because she's his wife and my mother." Ethan can't believe what he's hearing. "She gave us up when we were born. It's crazy because I feel like I've been reborn in a way. I feel like I'm meeting my parents for the first time." Ethan pulls her close to him and holds her tightly. "What is this for?" she asks him.

"It's needed," Ethan says. They embrace for a moment, letting go of their problems. Ethan gently holds her face in his hands and brushes her hair behind her ear and brings his lips close to hers. "No matter what happens, I will never stop caring for you," Ethan says.

Angel looks into his eyes and wonders what he means. "What are you-" Angel abruptly stops speaking, her eyes still fixated on Ethan, lingering in them. The once-charming guy has now turned his face cold-blooded. He pulls out a syringe from behind Angel's neck, a similar syringe that was supposed to be used for Jordan.

"I'm sorry, I was really beginning to fall for you," he says to Angel as she becomes limp in his arms. Her eyes closed, Ethan tosses her over his shoulder and waits as a black truck pulls up in front of him.

"Took you long enough," Alexandria says in the passenger seat. Ethan ignores her and gets in the backseat along with Angel.

"Oh, come on, baby brother, you couldn't have liked her that much."

"Not right now, Lex," Ethan dismisses her.

"I'm sorry, man, I had to tell her. You were getting whipped," Mark Parker says, giving a smug grin from the driver's seat. Ethan ignores them, focusing on his plan. They leave Exodus and make their way to their father's compound – Silas Clay's Compound – where a new beginning happens for everyone.

Daniella stands in the silence of the garage contemplating the decision she made to come here to Exodus. Was it the right choice? Did she get herself involved with even more dangerous people? She tosses Ashton's keys in her hand thinking that maybe she should leave too. She is free and her record is wiped cleaned; she could start an entire new life. But this team – Jordan, Blair, Ashton, Angel, Seth and Natalie have grown on her. If she were to leave all she would feel is regret. Daniella puts Ashton's keys in her pocket hoping she would come back. As Daniella leaves the garage, she notices the steel door to the cells is cracked open. She approaches cautiously, not knowing what to expect from a door that has extensive security measures to enter. Entering the room, she sees two guards with stab wounds laid out on the floor and a missing Alexandria. "What the hell is going on in this place?"

Chapter 41

I just find it really hard to believe that she didn't know who her daughters were, I mean they look just alike, right?" Blair says to Seth and Natalie as she attempts to assist him with monitoring Dr. Martin Edwards vitals in the med bay of the medical wing.

"Well, now that we know they are related. I can see some resemblance." Seth replies. "Ashton and the Lieutenant are basically one in the same."

"Exactly! She can hunt down a rogue agent and a militia group but she doesn't know her own kids. Either she's lying or-"

"Would you shut up!" Natalie shouts slamming a tablet on the lab table. She tried to divert her attention elsewhere rather than thinking of the woman she considered a mentor and a mother figure.

Blair and Seth are surprised by Natalie's outburst. Seth rushes over to comfort her. "Nat, I'm sorry. I forgot how much all of this affects you, too," Seth says gently rubbing her back.

"I'm sorry, too, Natalie. I didn't realize how much Jordan means to you."

"It's fine," Natalie says sniffing and rubbing her eyes. "If I can't trust her then who can I trust," Natalie says to herself, but Seth and Blair hear her clearly.

Seth looks over and sees Blair bracelet sporadically blinking. "Why is your bracelet blinking?" Seth points.

Blair looks down perplexed. "I don't know. It's never done that before; my dad gave it to me as a gift before I left."

Natalie takes Blair's hand and studies the bracelet. "May I?"

Blair takes off the bracelet and gives it to Natalie. Natalie takes out her cell phone and begins to scan the bracelet.

"You're not going to like this Blair but there is a tracker in here," Natalie explains.

"What?!" Blair says shocked her father really hasn't changed.

"That must have been how Angel and Ashton's dad got here," Seth says not too sure of his findings.

"So, you're saying my dad could be working for Clay?!" Blair asks.

"It could be a possibility but to be safe we have to destroy it." Natalie says.

Blair without hesitation takes a hammer from a nearby lab table and destroys the bracelet in small pieces. Remembering the frustrations, anger and heartache her father has caused.

In the bathroom of the penthouse, Jordan helps to clean up Aaron's bruises. Either wants to speak but what is there to say? It's been 18 years since they've been in the same room. Jordan runs a wet towel along the planes of his weakened chest. "I think I can properly tend to the bruises I made," Jordan says not making eye contact with Aaron but taking ointment and rubbing it on the bruises on his forearm.

He winces in pain. "Yeah, you'd think I would have got used to your punches," he chuckles in a deep, hoarse voice.

Jordan awkwardly smiles. They sit in the silence for a while until Aaron breaks the tension.

"What's wrong, Van?"

"What do you mean? Nothing's wrong," she says, focusing on the bruises around his neck rather than the topic at hand.

"You're chewing on your bottom lip. You always do that when you're stressed or out of your element. I know this because I know you. It's not something you forget because when is the 'Great Savannah Taylor-Cross' ever out of her element," Aaron expresses.

Jordan stops tending to his wounds and releases the breath she's been holding. "After all these years you still know what to say to me." She says sitting next to him on the ottoman, "And I still hate it."

They laugh together as if 18 years haven't passed between them. "Before…all of this we were inseparable that doesn't just go away," Aaron reassures her that even though they've been apart, they're bond is much stronger.

"They'll never forgive me, will they?" Jordan asks biting her lip and fiddling with her fingers.

"I wish I knew. They probably hate me even more. I sent them away."

Jordan and Aaron take in the rare quietness. She gently rest her head on his shoulder. "Thank you."

"For what?"

"For raising our girls. They're so strong and fearless. I couldn't have asked for better parents in you and Elise."

"You may not have been there to see them grow up, but they have you written all over them."

Jordan smiles. She glances up at him and the emotions from their time being apart and being reunited, flood into the room. He glances down at her, lingering on her eyes and then down to her smooth, full lips. Jordan moves in closer, her nose brushing his and she softly places her hand on his neck. Aaron leans in closer, his lips centimeters away from hers but Jordan pulls back.

"I'm – I'm sorry. It's been a difficult night."

"It's okay, we'll get through this…together," Aaron comforts her, realizing they aren't the same people they once were years ago.

Jordan grabs his hands and helps him up from the ottoman. As he stands, he stumbles and Jordan braces his fall by wrapping her arms around his waist. He places his arm around her neck to steady himself. Just then David Lawrence comes barging in, gun in hand. He shoves Jordan away from Aaron and tackles him on to the bathroom floor. "Jordan. Go!" David shouts as Jordan falls near the bathtub.

"David! What the hell are you doing?!" Jordan watches as the two men in her life wrestle on the floor. David has the upper hand as he punches a weakened and bruised Aaron in his ribs. Jordan rushes into the fight and aggressively pushes David off Aaron with all her strength. "Get off of him!"

"What!? I come in here to save you from the man that breached our agency and you're attacking me!"

"Okay one, I don't need saving. Never have, never will, and if I needed your help I would have called you! I had it under control!"

David stands winded. "You call this controlled!?" David references the bloody towels on the floor, the broken glass table in the living room and an injured Aaron on the floor.

As David and Jordan continue to argue, Aaron groans on the bathroom floor, holding tightly to his stomach. He attempts to roll over and stand but he's instantly attacked by a high pitch noise inside his head. "ARGHHHHHH!" Aaron cries out holding his head in his hands, trying to stop the murderous noise.

Jordan immediately rushes over and kneels in front of him. "Aaron! Aaron! What's wrong?!" She asks frantically and he can't respond. He only screams.

David watches as Jordan comforts and cares for this man, "Do you know him?!"

Jordan doesn't respond. Her focus is on Aaron, she can't lose him again.

"Jordan! Who is he?" David asks once again.

"He's my husband!" Jordan shouts at him, hoping it would shut him up. She had no intentions on telling David like this but when would have been a right time.

David feels his world stop.

"He's my…husband and I will explain everything but I need you to help me get him to Seth. Please. He's innocent in all of this, I swear." Jordan pleads to David as she struggles to pull Aaron up to stand. David isn't sure what to do. Unable to move after hearing Jordan's shocking revelation. Who is this person he has been working side by side with for all these years? He detaches his Exodus badge from his hip and lays it on the bathroom sink, never to see it or Exodus again. Although Jordan has hurt him time and time again, she still has a hold on him.

David helps Jordan. He picks up a limp and fragile Aaron and throws him over his shoulders, taking him to medical for Seth to examine.

"Seth!" Jordan shouts as she brings Aaron into medical, still laid across David's shoulders. David quickly lays Aaron on a nearby examination table.

"What happened? He was supposed to be awake an hour ago." Seth asks Jordan.

"He was. I helped clean some of his wounds and then he starts screaming and holding his head, then he passed out." Jordan explains frantically as Seth begins to quickly examine Aaron.

"His blood pressure is going up fast. Someone bring me a shot of Trimethaphan! Now!" Seth calls out to his assistants. He immediately shoots Aaron with the Trimethaphan and his pressure immediately increases.

"What's happening?!" Jordan panics.

"Something else is wrong," Seth says calmly. He begins examining Aaron's head remembering what Jordan said. He uses a highly designed portable x-ray and moves it around Aaron's head. He stops at the back of his neck and does a double take at his screen. He immediately puts down the x-ray device and grabs a scalpel nearby. Seth makes a small incision and takes small forceps to feel around.

"What is it?" Jordan asks.

Seth eyes grow big and he's unable to summon up the words. "It's a biochip. A self-destructing one."

Jordan turns around to let David know what Seth has found but he's gone. He must have left during the chaos. She's sad that he's gone but has no time to dwell on the matter.

"Okay, Seth. Listen to me, I want you to slowly place the biochip on to the counter while I go get Natalie." Jordan instructs him as calmly as she can seeing the fear pour from his body.

He slowly nods.

Jordan steadily backs out of the med bay makes her way to Natalie in the room with Blair and Dr. Martin Edwards. "Nat, I need you."

Natalie refuses to acknowledge her presence and Blair watches the uncomfortable exchange.

"I understand you're upset with me and just like I've been telling everyone else – 'I will tell you the truth as soon as I can' – but there is a literal bomb in the next room with Seth so unless you want to die before you hear the truth then I suggest you come do what you do best."

Natalie doesn't hesitate. She immediately follows Jordan to the med bay with a nervous Seth and an unconscious Aaron. Blair watches from outside the room. Natalie studies the device, its time reading a minute and 30 seconds.

"Whoever created this wanted it to blow quickly but they were messy," Natalie says using her tools to carefully stop the time on the device. Jordan and Seth don't move an inch as Natalie moves wires around the device. "Done." Natalie cuts the wire and stops the clock at 20 seconds.

Jordan and Seth breathe a sigh of relief. "Thanks, Nat," Seth says as he goes to sew Aaron's neck closed.

"Thank you, Natalie," Jordan says.

"I didn't do it for you," Natalie says in a resentful tone.

"I-" Jordan is immediately interrupted by Daniella bursting through the med bay doors out of breath.

"Lieutenant! Someone broke in the cells!" Daniella exclaims.

"What? Daniella, calm down. What exactly happened?" Jordan asks.

Daniella breathes in and exhales slowly. "Someone broke into the cells. Both guards are dead. Someone stab them. I think it was the girl we took because she's gone too."

Before Jordan can take in the news Daniella gave her, Donovan comes into the medical wing with an injured Charlotte.

"Boss, they found us," Charlotte says. Her arm draped around Donovan's shoulders as she limps into the room.

"I found her unconscious behind the counter in the boutique," Donovan explains helping Charlotte to a chair.

Jordan feels her world crumbling around her. It's been a revolving door of bad news all night. "Who found us, Charlotte? What happened?"

"Agent Carmichael. He's with Clay. I was doing inventory and he knocked me out, it was blurry but I saw him before I went down," Charlotte reveals.

"Okay. Okay." Jordan tries to summon the words to restore order. "Blair, Daniella I need you two to go get Angel and Ashton and meet us in Ops."

Daniella is puzzled. Does Jordan not know Ashton is gone? "Ashton left."

"What?!" Jordan is shocked. This set of news might send her over the edge. "Where did she go?!" Jordan asks concerned.

"I don't know. She left a while ago. Gave me her car keys," Daniella hands Jordan Ashton's prize possession.

Jordan holds the keys tight in hand. "And where is Angel?"

Everyone looks around the room and they're quiet. No one knows.

"I'm on it," Natalie says opening her laptop and swiftly types. As Natalie pulls up multiple video surveillances around and inside the agency, she's reluctant to show Jordan.

"What is it, Natalie?" Jordan asks.

Natalie brings the images up on a TV screen inside the medical wing lab. The video is captured from a distance facing the boutique across the street. It shows Angel and Ethan in close conversation and then Angel goes limp and is taken away with Ethan inside a black SUV.

Jordan braces herself near a lab table. She's barely able to hold herself together, she holds her head down in shame and wants to break down right here but she can't. Weakness is not an option. Her team needs her. Her family needs her. The world needs her.

"I know this is a bad time to mention this but…I may be the reason we were breached," Blair cautiously reveals.

"What do you mean?" Donovan asks.

"My dad gifted me a bracelet before I came here and I swear I didn't know. It had a tracker in it."

"I can concur. There was no way she could have known," Natalie steps in.

They all look for some type of response from Jordan, but nothing. Until, "We can't stay here," Jordan says in an eerie tone.

Donovan, Blair, Daniella, Natalie, Seth and Charlotte are baffled.

"Lieutenant, what do you mean?" Donovan asks as now second-in-command.

"Everyone grab what you need that is essential and meet in the garage in 10 minutes. Seth, I want you to make sure Aaron and Dr. Edwards are as stable as possible to move. Natalie, deactivate every system and protocol. Remove everyone that's in this room from every system known to man. We're going dark." Jordan gives out instructions as she exits the medical wing leaving everyone to ponder what just took place.

"Are we really leaving?" Blair asks breaking the silence.

"Yes. Everyone, go grab what you need." Donovan instructs them. They all go their separate ways, packing the items that are most important to them.

Jordan, driving Ashton's car with Aaron laid sound asleep in the backseat, leads her team deeper into the city of Chicago until they reach an abandoned building. The exterior is an ordinary, bland building with no signage. The interior is closed, rundown to the normal eye but to Jordan it's so much more. Jordan parks near a curb as well as the two vans holding the rest of the team.

"Where are we?" Seth asks.

"This is it. This is how I die isn't it?" Blair says dramatically.

Jordan ignores them all and proceeds to lead them deeper into the abandoned building until they reach the back door. The only one who is relaxed and knows what Jordan is up to is Charlotte.

Jordan flips up a cover to reveal a high-tech keypad where she enters in a lengthy code and then gives a retinal scan. A familiar voice appears on the scanner.

"Passkey," LIS says.

"The Adder," Jordan says with confidence. A nickname given to her during her early years of fighting her enemies.

Everyone enters the building and walks down a set of dusty, rust filled stairs covered with cobwebs. They approach another set of doors and Jordan takes out a chain holding an ouroboros ring like that of Angel's and scans it on the door. The doors open and they've entered an underground subway but it's been transformed into an underground elite operation that only the CIA wish they had access to.

"The Exodus that you once knew is no more. This is my Exodus. I built this team of misfits to help those who couldn't help themselves." Jordan leads them further underground passing by different tunnels that hold different rooms – armories, tech labs, medical labs, training rooms and bed quarters. She stops in front of two double doors. "I know I have not told you all the truth about who I am so here it is. My name is Savannah Taylor-Cross. I'm an assassin – well, I haven't been one for a while. Since the day I decided to leave the most dangerous criminal organization – Leviathan – I have been on the run. Until they decided to come after my own family. I thought I was doing what was best for them by giving them up and protecting them from my own enemies but apparently I was only thinking of myself. My family is danger. The people I care about – you – you're in danger and I am not one to ask for help but I'm asking now because I've realized I can't do it on my own. I need you."

Everyone nods their head in agreement.

"We got your back, Lieutenant." Seth says.

"Unfortunately, you all have grown on me," Daniella says.

"You're pretty cool," Blair smiles at her.

"I think I speak for everyone when I say we're here for you," Donovan says.

Jordan gives a relieved smiled and opens the double doors to reveal a control room. "Let's find my girls."

TO BE CONTINUED....

Acknowledgement

The more that I write the more I'm grateful for the gift God has given me and I can't thank him enough. I love creating stories. I love immersing myself in new worlds and characters. Not only am I thankful for this gift, but I'm also thankful for those in my life who have supported me and made this novel a dream come true.

To my Parents, thank you for all the sacrifices you've made that have allowed me to become the successful woman I am today. Thank you for allowing me to express myself even as a young girl writing simple poems. To my brother Trey, thank you for listening to me go on and on continuously about these stories.

To Books and Things Publishing, thank you for taking a chance on me. You were that 'Yes' in a sea of No's.

To all the Black and Brown young women, thank you for being unapologetically you. Thank you for setting the standard. Thank you for not allowing the pressures of society change you. Continue to dream, continue to create and if it can happen for me it can happen for you.

And finally, Thank YOU; the reader. Thank you for embarking on this journey with me, Jordan, Angel, Ashton, Blair and Daniella. We'll see you soon!

www.ingramcontent.com/pod-product-compliance
Lightning Source LLC
Chambersburg PA
CBHW010603310726
48969CB00010B/2546